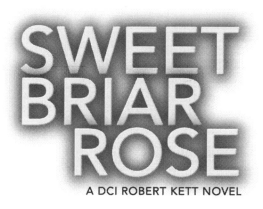

A DCI ROBERT KETT NOVEL

ALEX SMITH

RELENTLESS
M E D I A

ALSO BY ALEX SMITH

The DCI Robert Kett Thrillers

Paper Girls

Bad Dog

Three Little Pigs

Whip Crack

Run Rabbit Run

Stone Cold Dead

Every Mother's Son

Sweet Briar Rose

Cry Baby: A Novella

The Softley Softley Thrillers

The Harder They Fall

Hard Luck House (Coming Soon)

Other Books

Six Days, Six Hours, Six Minutes

For Jacqueline

PROLOGUE

Friday

As far as Kevin Dufrane was concerned, Friday nights were made for fishing.

Not fishing for fish, obviously. Fishing for *women*.

The problem was that he was about as good at catching women as he was at catching fish—and he was a lousy fisherman.

Kevin sighed, shifting his considerable weight on the uncomfortable barstool. Thanks to some hipster nonsense it was made from a bicycle seat and it felt as if it had wedged itself halfway up his backside. But he didn't want to move because the pub was crammed and he felt self-conscious enough as it was.

Self-conscious *and* worried, because the other problem Kevin had was that people seemed to be quite good at fishing for him.

*Cat*fishing, that was.

He'd never even heard of the word catfish until the day it had plopped out of his mother's ugly, flapping mouth. He'd accidentally left his laptop open and the nosy cow had gone through his messages like he was thirteen years old, not twenty-eight. Facebook, Instagram, Messenger, the whole damn lot of them. When he'd got home, stinking of fish from the supermarket, everything aching, she'd actually laughed in his face.

"You do realise that girl you're talking to probably *in't* even a girl," she'd said. "It'll be some hairy-arsed biker tryin' to catfish you."

He'd had to look it up on Google, and even then he was none the wiser. And the really shitty thing about it all was that his mum had been right. Melanie, the girl he'd been talking to for three months, who'd sent dozens of photos of her perfect face and perfect smile, who'd balanced her time between teaching orphans how to read and training to be a brain surgeon while also volunteering at animal shelters around the world, who'd seemed far too good to be real...

Well, she hadn't been real at all.

She'd been Dave. A hairy-arsed biker from Hull.

But this time it was different.

Enya was different.

Kevin swirled the last inch of beer in the glass then downed it. It was warm because it had been sitting there for a good hour, but he didn't really have the money for another one, especially if he and Enya were going to go to the cinema or head out for dinner. He'd had to take out his last two-hundred pounds in cash to give her, to help with her emergency fund for getting away from her parents. And he'd already offered to pay for everything, the way a gentleman should.

In Enya's last message, sent that afternoon on Messenger, she'd told him she probably wouldn't have long. Her dad was an RAF pilot on one of his rare visits home, and she found it hard to get away from him. He was an ogre, apparently, who didn't want his daughter to find true love.

It didn't matter how long they had. He was just grateful for the chance to finally meet her after spending so long talking online.

Enya was his soulmate. It had only been two weeks since she'd first messaged him, but he was sure of it. She enjoyed the same things as him, she listened to the same music, she liked video games and trains, and she hated her parents the same way he hated his. He couldn't have asked for a better person to hook up with, to maybe fall in love with, to spend the rest of his life with. And she was fit, too, like proper fit. A model.

It'll be some hairy-arsed biker tryin' to catfish you, he heard his mum say.

"Not this time," he replied, speaking into the empty glass. "Enya's the real deal."

"What's that, mate?" asked the barman. He was annoyingly young and handsome, veins running up and down his arms the way they never had on Kevin's, even though he worked on the Morrison's fish counter every day and ached like a bastard every night. "You ready for another one?"

Kevin shook his head, checking his phone. It was coming up for eight, and that realisation made him feel like he'd just necked a pint of ice water. He actually shivered, the barstool rocking beneath him.

"Can't," he said. "Got a date."

"Right," said the barman, and the way he looked Kevin up and down made Kevin want to leap over the bar and smack him right in the chops. Not that he'd be able to, of course. He'd end up falling on his arse, no doubt about it, then the barman would laugh him out the door.

He held up his phone instead, where a photo of Enya waited for him on the lock screen. It was one of the first pictures she'd sent him, all those months ago: her sitting on a picnic table in a white string vest and short shorts. One hand was pushing the hair back from her eyes, the other was held out, palm up, finger extended as if she was about to beckon him. It made his heart melt every time he saw it. It snatched the air from his lungs.

He thrust the phone at the barman.

"With her," he said.

"Sure," the guy replied, drawing the word out.

Fuck you, Kevin thought as he climbed off the stool, his arse numb. *Fuck you sideways and upside down and back to front then fuck your mother too.*

He gave the man a smug smile then turned and made for the exit. He'd only had one pint and he'd taken an hour to drink it, but it had gone straight to his head. It had been a brutal shift at work and he'd been too nervous to have any dinner, spending an hour in the shower instead to try to shift the smell of dead fish.

It was pitch black outside and he checked his reflection in the window. He looked like the ghost that was supposed to haunt this pub, his plump cheeks sallow, his hair creeping back from his forehead, his eyes dark pits. For a second, the courage fled him. He could literally feel it flowing out like a plug had been pulled.

She already knows what you look like, he told himself. And it was true. Enya had seen dozens of photos of him over the last couple of weeks, although of course he'd only sent the good ones. It wasn't like they'd ever video called each other. It hadn't been possible, because Enya had told him how when she wasn't travelling the world she lived in a mansion in the middle of nowhere and the internet connection was shit.

Kevin opened the door, ducking beneath the low lintel and almost tripping up the steps on the other side. The wind was waiting, battering him with fistfuls of fallen leaves and hurling grit into his eyes. It was November, and after a mild autumn the winter had descended like Thor's frozen hammer. He put one hand to his thinning hair like that might make any difference at all, pushing past the empty outdoor tables into the car park of the Adam and Eve.

It was a short walk to the river, the path practically deserted other than a couple of miserable dog walkers. By the time he reached the water, the rain had started, a fine mist that soaked him to the bone within seconds.

"Great," he muttered, upping his speed. He'd half hoped to take Enya for a walk up to the cathedral, maybe stop for food outside somewhere. But the heavens were determined to take a giant shit on him, as always. "Well fuck you and your mother. Sideways."

The further he got from the pub, the darker it grew. There were streetlights, but not many, and the pools of darkness that separated them were huge. It was like somebody had scratched those parts of the world out of existence completely. Anyone could have been sitting there, *hiding* there, waiting for somebody like him to walk past. Why had they arranged to meet here? It had been Enya's idea, he knew that much. He stuffed his hands into his trouser pockets, feeling his wallet and his phone in one and his keys and his inhaler in the other. If anyone tried to rob him he'd kick the shit out of them.

Yeah, right, came his mum's voice, and he almost answered her back when a figure broke out of the shadows, running right for him. Kevin actually screamed and ducked, his fingers scrabbling in the wet dirt as the man thundered closer, *closer*, then pounded past.

"Sorry!" the guy yelled over his shoulder, his reflective gear blazing as he passed the light.

"I was..." Kevin called back, choking on spit as he stood. "I dropped my... my coins. I was picking them up!"

But the jogger was gone.

"Twat," Kevin said, his heart booming in his ears, the loudest sound in the night.

He pushed on, hollowed out by adrenaline. The river moved with him, the soft noise of it like snoring, as if it was fast asleep. Across the water, an audience of houses watched him with brightly lit eyes and he had to push away the notion that they were laughing. He took a couple of deep breaths, puffing them out through his lips. His fingertips had gone numb and he flapped his hands, trying to remember how far away Cow Tower was, and what it looked like.

And just like that, it peeled its way from the night.

It was huge, much bigger than he remembered it being from the few times he'd passed it. He couldn't see the top, even though there were more lights here. The trees held their branches in front of it like they were doing their best to hide something, and another gust of wind churned a second river of leaves and dirt, driving him back.

He swallowed past the lump in his throat, coughing quietly. Pulling his phone out, he saw that eight o'clock had come and gone three minutes ago. Had he missed her? Had she thought he wasn't coming and already left?

"Fuck," he said, trying to unlock his phone with wet fingers. He didn't have Enya's number because her mum was in the British Intelligence and she couldn't let mobile phones in the house, but he checked Facebook to see that there were no new messages. She would have told him if she was leaving, wouldn't she? Kevin cleared his throat again, approaching the giant tower like a knight about to enter a dragon's castle.

"Enya?" he said, the word torn to shreds by the wind, hurled into the night. "Enya?" he tried again, louder this time.

Footsteps from the path. He squinted into the dark, seeing the river dogleg to the right, heading south. Two men were walking towards him, each holding a beer can.

"Enya!" one of them shouted, and both of them broke into a wheezing chorus of laughter as they passed.

Wankers, Kevin thought, although he kept the word as far from his lips as possible in case they heard it and came after him. He waited until the sound of their footsteps had faded before turning his attention back to the tower. There was only one entrance, and even from where he stood he could see that it was locked with a padlock as big as his hand. The gate was as old as the tower, and darkness leaked out of it, polluting the night. He fumbled with his phone, trying to get the torch to work.

"Come on, you bellend," he said.

It pinged to life, doing little other than illuminating the drizzle. Kevin aimed it at the brick tower as he walked, looking for a way in. There were no other doors, and the windows were too high to reach even if they hadn't been barred. It took less than twenty seconds to circle the tower, and when he beamed the torch into the trees, the bushes, the river, he found no sign of life at all.

"Enya?" he said, feeling the rain creep down the back of his jacket, creep *inside* him—that same cold dread he'd felt when he'd realised the truth about Melanie. "It's me, Kev. Please, Enya, don't be scared."

Please be real.

He walked to the gate, closer this time, his torch doing battle with the shadows and losing. He wondered if there was a curtain on the other side, because surely nothing on earth could be that dark. Then he shifted the phone and the inside of the tower came into view.

The wide, circular interior was deserted—no animals scurrying for cover, no plants growing in the gravel, and certainly no Enya.

It was starting to piss him off, because he didn't deserve to be treated this way—especially not by a woman. He took another step, noticing that the gate wasn't flush with the tower walls. It was set a little way inside, and it wasn't alone. There was a second gate to the right, at a ninety-degree angle to the first, and through the gaps between the bars he saw a stone staircase spiralling upwards. This gate, too, was padlocked.

But the padlock was open, hanging there like a loose tooth.

"Hello?" Kevin said. "Enya? Are you up there?"

Somebody answered him in a whisper and his skin shuddered so much he thought the whole thing might just slide off his bones, leaving him chattering in the wind like a Halloween skeleton. He leaned in, his ear almost against the metal. There was definitely a voice, painfully quiet, as monotonous as a radio newsreader.

Kevin stood back, considering his options. Right now, the best of them seemed to be turning around and getting the hell out of there. He lifted his phone, seeing Enya on the screen, that beautiful smile, that beckoning hand. What if she was in there right now? What if she was hurt? Or what if—and here the warmth rushed back into him with some ferocity—she was waiting for him, ready to move their relationship to the next level?

He shivered, swallowing.

"I'm coming in," he said, pushing the gate, then pulling it when it wouldn't budge. It opened with the squeal of a drunken brass band, shuddering hard. The padlock came loose, thumping to the floor. And still that voice spoke to him in hushed whispers, urging him on.

He ducked through the door and tripped on the first step, collapsing onto the spiral staircase. Something dug into his hand, razor-sharp. He aimed his torch to see a scrap of plant, a bramble or a thorn, the barb root-deep in his palm.

"Fuck," he said, angrier than ever. He used his teeth to pluck the barb from his skin, spitting out the bitterness of it, the copper aftertaste of his own blood.

He called Enya's name again, the tower swallowing his voice. It was swallowing *him*, too, gobbling him up one step at a time as he climbed. The voice grew louder. Not a news reader but something else. A storyteller, maybe. The pitch of it rose and fell, punctuated by ridiculous sound effects. He had to move carefully because there was no handrail, and coils of blackberry tried to trip him. The vegetation was growing thicker, so much of it that the stairs were almost invisible.

The *foot* was almost invisible, too.

Kevin angled the phone and saw it just in time, poking from the brambles. It was bare, apart from the scratches that crisscrossed the sole, and the jagged leaves that had caught between the toes. He stopped walking, actually gasping with the shock of what lay before him. He moved the light up, following the leg, seeing a Space Invader tattoo on the ankle, then a slim calf, a bare thigh. His heart thumped at the promise of nudity before his gut caught up, almost cramping.

He had to take another step to see past the curve in the staircase, careful not to crush those exposed toes, those long legs. The light rose past a blanket of thorns, wet with sap, up past naked shoulders, past a slender neck, up and up and up to where two eyes found him.

It was Enya. It was his girl, the love of his life. The smile broke onto his face and he actually laughed.

You're real, he said to himself. And the next thought hit him just as hard.

You're dead.

Because she was. She was dead, her eyes glassy and crawling with ants.

She was dead.

And still that singsong voice played on, dropping from further up the steps.

"*... and what did the wicked fairy do next? Why, she put the whole castle to sleep! The cats, the dogs, the mice, the frogs.*"

Kevin turned around, the walls too close, the stairs too steep. Brambles wound their way around his ankles like they were living things, pulling tight.

"*The cooks and the cleaners and all those brave knights, all dozing off wherever they were standing!*"

And suddenly he was falling into the yawning darkness of the tower while the lunatic voice broke into laughter behind him.

"*All asleep! All asleep! All asleep!*"

CHAPTER ONE

Saturday

"You're looking good, DCI Kett."

Billie brushed her hands over the shoulders of Robbie Kett's brand new charcoal grey suit, pulling out a loose thread and flicking it onto the kitchen floor. Light flooded through the window, the morning cold but eager, the birds loud. Evie and Moira sat at the table, lost in whatever they were colouring in—Moira using jam instead of crayons. The whole house smelled of toast and tea, the aroma somehow both nostalgic for the past and hopeful for the future.

Billie fiddled with the knot of Kett's sky-blue tie, loosening it a little so that he could breathe.

"Thanks," Kett said. "The suit's going to take some getting used to."

The job too, he thought.

"You're going to be great," she replied, although she didn't meet his eye. It had been nearly six months since

Superintendent Clare had asked Kett to re-join the Force; six months of meetings and hearings and committees before the request had finally been granted. Six months. 174 days. Not nearly long enough for Billie to accept the idea of him being a copper again.

But he knew that she was trying.

She kissed him on the lips, a kiss that tasted of strawberry jam.

"It will work out," she said. "It has to."

She smiled, running her hand down his freshly shaven cheek then ruffling his unruly hair. He shied away with a laugh.

"Easy, Billie, you're not my mum."

"But *I* am," said Mary Kett as she walked into the kitchen. It was almost as if she was a different woman to the one Kett had found in the Whytetail commune, as if she'd cast away the cocoon of her old self and grown anew—taller, stronger, brighter. Shooing Billie out of the way, she tightened his tie again. She licked her thumb and ran it over the corner of his mouth. "You've still got jam on you, Robbie. This won't do at all."

"Come on, Mum," he said, backing away so hard he hit the counter, knocking a teaspoon to the floor. "I'm not a baby."

Evie and Moira laughed.

"You are a baby," said Evie. "*My* baby."

"I just want to make sure you're ready for your big day," Mary said, repositioning her glasses on her nose. "You want to look like you're in charge, not like you've just climbed out of a pig sty."

"A *pig sty*?" Kett said. "This suit is new!"

"Have you brushed your teeth, Daddy?" Evie asked.

"Good question, Evie," said Mary. "Teeth brushed?"

"Yes. Of course."

"Hair brushed?" Evie said.

"Yes, although you wouldn't think it," Billie answered for him.

"Fresh pants?" Evie asked, bursting into a fresh round of laughter.

"Fesh pants?" Moira echoed.

"Fresh pants?" said Mary.

"I have fresh pants every day!" Kett replied, fuming.

"That reminds me," said Mary, taking a seat next to Moira. "Have I told you about Robbie's first day of primary school?"

"Mum, don't."

"Robbie loved Superman. He loved all the superheroes, but especially Superman. And we couldn't afford to buy him a costume so he—"

"Mum," Kett said, a growl now.

"He put on his red underpants *over* his trousers. And he went to school like that."

"Right, pack your bags," Kett said. "You're moving out."

But nobody could hear him over the laughter. He recovered the spoon from the floor and threw it into the sink, glowering at his mother, then at his wife. He waited until he'd walked out of the kitchen before he let the smile reach his face, the memory of that first day of school leaving its heat on his cheeks.

He patted his pockets to make sure his keys were there and grabbed his overcoat from the peg next to the front door. By the time he'd pulled it on, everyone had followed him into the hallway.

"What do we say to Daddy?" asked Billie, holding Moira in her arms.

"Love you," Moira said, grinning.

Evie clung to her mum's leg, her face full of worry.

"I don't want you to go," she said. "I want you to stay and read me stories."

"I will," he said. "As soon as I'm back."

There was a thumping from overhead and Alice appeared at the top of the stairs, Maggie the chinchilla cradled in her arms.

"Dad?" she said. "Don't go."

"Daddy has to go," Billie said.

"No he doesn't," said Evie, frowning.

"Yeah, he's going to die," said Alice, as blunt as always.

"Alice," said Kett, a little too firmly. "Don't say that."

"He is going to be fine," Billie said. "I don't want him to go either. I want to keep him here so that we don't have to share him. But your daddy does something important. He has a job to do. Other people need him, and that's okay because he's going to be careful, isn't he?"

Kett nodded.

"If he finds himself in danger he's going to think about us, about all of us. He's going to do the right thing for his family, isn't he?"

"I am. I promise."

Kett put his hand on the door but there he hesitated, looking at the people he loved most in the world. A sudden wave of anxiety washed over him and he wondered if he should call Clare and tell him he'd changed his mind, tell him that he'd made the wrong decision.

But Billie was right. He had a job to do.

"We're proud of you," Billie said. "I mean it. *I'm* proud of you."

"Thanks," Kett said. "Be good while I'm gone, okay kids?"

"No chance," said Billie. "But we'll be fine. I mean it, though. Be careful. Be safe."

Kett opened the door, greeted with a cold, damp hug from outside.

"I will," he said.

No chance.

IT WAS like he'd never left.

Kett walked through the doors of the Norfolk Constabulary HQ and took a big breath of warm air. The place looked the same, sounded the same, smelled the same too, and as he walked past the reception desk he wondered if he really had been away for all that time, or if he'd dreamed it. None of it felt real, even the pain from Keefe's bullet had dulled—still there behind his ribs but so familiar now he sometimes went hours without thinking about it. The scars of the last year were hidden beneath his new suit. Right now, they didn't matter.

Nobody looked at him as he followed the corridors to the Major Investigation Team's offices, not so much as a double-take from the Uniforms and Detectives he passed. The Whytetail case had been on the news for a week or so after they'd uncovered the trafficking ring, with updates every time the police dismantled another part of the operation, but Kett had stayed well out of it. Porter and Savage had taken the credit—rightly so—alongside Superintendent Colin Clare. The whole country had celebrated them.

He walked into the bullpen, seeing half a dozen people sitting at their desks. It wasn't even eight yet and the smell of coffee hung heavy in the air. He made for Clare's office only to hear a familiar wheezing voice.

"The prodigal son returns!"

DI Keith Dunst was strolling out of the corridor leading to the toilet, still zipping up his fly. He looked almost yellow in the harsh light, and he broke into a coughing fit before he could get another word out.

"How are you still going, Keith?" Kett asked as the other man limped over. "You look like the walking dead."

"Just need another cigarette, sir," Dunst said, gorging a particularly phlegmy cough into his right hand before offering it to Kett.

"Um... no," Kett said, patting the old DI on the shoulder. "But it's good to see you. Where is everyone?"

"Incident Room," Dunst said, smearing his palm down his trousers. "They're waiting for you."

Kett nodded his thanks and made his way to the other side of the bullpen, pushing through the door. Superintendent Clare was perched on the desk at the front of the large room, the end of his pencil so far up his hairy nose it looked like he was trying to lobotomise himself. Sitting at the back of the room and whispering to each other like a couple of naughty children were DI Peter Porter and DC Kate Savage. PC Aaron Duke sat on a chair at the front, a blank notepad open in front of him and an expression of deep concentration on his heavily bearded face.

The only other person present was Richard Johnson, the irritating psychologist who Kett had spoken to after the Paper Girls case, and who had led the campaign against him coming back to work.

As one, they all turned to look at him.

"Morning," he said, raising a hand in welcome.

"Kett," barked Clare, the pencil still up his nose. "I was about to send out a search party."

"You won't find me up there, sir," he said, closing the door behind him.

Clare pulled the pencil free and slid it into his pocket, then he pushed himself off the desk and started pacing. He was wearing an ordinary suit jacket with a pair of trousers that seemed two sizes too big for him, but Kett didn't want to ask if it was anything to do with the now legendary trouser incident at Whytetail.

"Take a seat, DCI Kett," Clare said. "Let's get this party started. Everyone, you know why you're here."

Kett walked to the row of desks in front of Porter and Savage, nodding to them.

"Good to see you, sir," Savage whispered as he sat down.

"Things are going to shit out there," Clare continued, his brash voice echoing off the walls. "People are getting worse. Crime is getting worse. We've seen it ourselves, with Stillwater and Percival and Figg and those newspaper girls. With the Bad Dog case, with Kett and his pig-faced bogeyman. With those poor young men sacrificed on the stones. And with the trafficking ring you all broke open earlier this year. These are cases we might have seen once a decade, but this has all been in the space of a year and change. I don't know what's going on but I do know that we are the thin blue line that stands between monsters like that and the good, decent people of this county and this country."

"I wonder how many times he rehearsed this," Porter muttered.

"I debated for a long time about whether to set up a unit like this," the Superintendent went on. "A unit with the power and the authority to go after the very worst of humankind. But I know now that we have no choice. I said it to you before, that sometimes in order to catch a monster, you have to send a monster."

Clare looked at Kett.

"I don't think you're a monster, Robbie. Far from it. You're a good man, but you're also a man who won't stop, a man who isn't afraid of doing monstrous *things*. As much as I hate it, I know that sometimes that's what it takes."

At this, Richard Johnson raised a hand and opened his mouth. Clare shut him up with a look.

"You'll get your turn, *Dick*," he said.

Another hand shot up, this one belonging to Duke. He was scribbling something in his notebook.

"Can you slow down a bit?" the PC said. "What came after the bit about the worst of humankind?"

"You don't have to take notes, Constable," Clare said, although Duke showed no sign of stopping.

"I really think now is the time to go over some ground rules," said Johnson, turning to the room, one hand stroking his long, downy beard. "This will be a specialist unit within the police, but it doesn't mean that you have free rein to do whatever you like. My job is to go over some basic health and safety requirements that you will all need to follow."

Porter groaned.

"For example, Robbie, if you find yourself in a confrontation with a suspect, what is the correct course of action for you to take?"

"Uh..." said Kett. "What kind of confrontation?"

"Richard, I said you'd get your turn," Clare said, but the other man wasn't listening.

"Say you're both in a room and the suspect grabs hold of your jacket."

"If it's that jacket, I think you should just give it to him," said Porter.

"What do you mean?" Kett said, swivelling in his chair. "This is a new suit."

"New to *you*?" Porter said with a frown. "But handed down from your elderly grandmother?"

"Kett!" said Johnson.

"Richard!" said Clare. "This is my bit. Your health and safety bollocks can wait."

"I don't think things like this can wait," Johnson said, infuriatingly calm. "Anger management is a primary focus of my therapy, and Robbie here is in dire need of it. So, Robbie, what do you do?"

Kett looked at Clare, who was fuming quietly, then at the psychologist.

"You're asking me what I'd do if a suspect grabs me?"

Johnson nodded.

"I guess I'd... arrest him?"

"How?" asked Johnson.

"With some cuffs?"

"And?"

"Uh..." Kett shrugged.

"Your fists?" Johnson said. "Because we all know how much you like punching people."

"I don't *like* punching people," Kett said. "But sometimes—"

"No punching," said Johnson. "Under any circumstances. Is that clear? The first rule of this particular unit is that you are not allowed to punch anyone."

"I'm going to punch *you* in a minute," mumbled Clare, eyeballing the psychologist.

"What?" said Johnson.

"What?" Clare echoed, doing his best to pull an expression of innocence.

"Can somebody tell me what you said after the bit

where Kett said he was wearing his elderly grandmother's suit?" asked Duke, scribbling furiously.

"Enough!" roared Clare, ripping Duke's pen from his hand and lobbing it across the room. It pinged off a wall and Johnson had to duck to avoid being hit by the rebound. "Health and safety can wait. Your notes can wait. Your cheap suit can wait."

"It's not a cheap—"

"Our priority is setting up this tossing unit. We don't even have a name for it yet."

"I *definitely* wouldn't call it the Tossing Unit," said Savage.

"I don't know," said Porter with a grin. "It would probably make the bad guys run off. 'Get out of here, it's the Tossing Unit!'"

Clare threw Porter a look of pure fury.

"Sorry," the DI said. "How about the Bad Crime Task Force?"

"*Bad* crime?" Savage said. "That's ridiculous, sir. All crime is bad. That's the worst name for a task force I've ever heard."

Porter pouted, looking at Kett for backup.

"It's pretty bad," said Kett.

"I don't care about the name!" Clare said, his eyes bulging. "Listen to me. Listen to me very carefully. This is a trial. A probation. Okay? I have been tossed over by every single one of you at some point in the last few months."

As one, the entire room groaned.

"Doesn't mean what you think it means," said Kett.

"So one mistake, one error, one foot out of line, and this entire unit will be disbanded. Is that clear?"

Kett nodded.

"This only survives if we work together. If we work as a

team. The bad guys out there aren't messing around. They are deadly serious, they are prepared, they are ruthless. We cannot beat them unless we are just as serious, and just as prepared."

And just as ruthless, Kett thought.

Clare looked as if he was about to say something else but he was cut off by the sound of his phone vibrating across the desk. He picked it up, speaking quietly. Johnson rushed in to fill the void.

"Let me present you with a different scenario," he said in his unshakably calm voice. "A suspect has taken a car, you are in pursuit in a vehicle, what steps do you take to keep civilians safe?"

"We let Porter drive," Savage said. "It's hard to hurt anyone when you drive everywhere at twelve miles per hour."

Porter almost choked on his outrage.

"I don't think you're paying a sufficient amount of attention to how serious this—"

Clare shouldered his way past the psychologist, pocketing his phone.

"Looks like you're back just in time, Kett," he said. "We've got a body. A young woman. Throat cut, wrapped in brambles, dumped in the city."

The room fell silent, the mood shifting.

"Brambles?" said Porter after a moment. "That's a little extreme."

"Extreme Crime," Savage said. "That's our name, sir."

Kett nodded, pushing himself up from the desk.

"The Extreme Crime Task Force," he said. "You hit the nail on the head, Kate."

"I'll make it official," said Clare, pointing to the door. "Now off you toss."

CHAPTER TWO

Norwich had never looked more medieval than it did now.

The riverside path had been sealed off, lines of police tape snapping like jousting banners in the wind as Kett approached from the south. A dozen uniformed constables stood guard, pushing back curious passers-by. They looked like knights in black, and behind them stood their castle, a circular brick fortification taller than the trees and pock-marked with small windows. Despite the traffic on the road on the other side of the river, and the chatter from the police radios, he felt as though he had fallen through time.

"Where's the body?" he asked as he got within shouting distance of the nearest constable. The young PC aimed her thumb over her shoulder, using her other hand to push the hair out of her face only for the wind to throw it right back.

"In the tower. On the steps. Forensics are there already."

Kett nodded his thanks. Savage walked beside him, Porter and Duke jostling for third place. To the left, the path angled west, following the bend in the river. A crowd had gathered there, some ogling the scene with wide, hungry eyes, others annoyed that their route to work had been barricaded. A couple of Uniforms held them back but they looked like they were struggling.

"Oi, you lot," Kett boomed, loud enough to make one of the constables jump in fright. "Back off, unless you've got something to do with this."

His tone was clear enough and people began to peel away. A couple of men at the front were holding their phones out, he realised. Reporters. A middle-aged guy with a voice like gravel pushed against the tape, his arm out as far as it would go.

"Kett, you're back? Norfolk Constabulary must be desperate, then. Any comment?"

Yeah, Kett thought. *Fuck you.*

But he clamped his mouth around the words, offering a glare instead.

"How do the families of your victims feel about you being back?" the man persisted.

"Ignore him, sir," Savage said. "He's a parasite."

Another PC guarded the tower's only door and he looked at Duke like he'd seen a bear on a bike.

"Morning, guvs," he said. "How on earth did you get in the big boys' club, Duke?"

"His sparkling personality," said Kett, making Duke grunt in protest. "And his stimulating conversational skills. Where are we going?"

He didn't need to ask. The opening in the tower led to two gates. Through the first was the interior of the building, drenched in daylight and completely empty. The second gate was on the right, leading to a narrow, spiral stairwell that ran up the inside of the wall. Cables stretched inside and the passage was lit by harsh portable halogens. Shadows spilled over the walls, distorted by the light and by the rough bricks and looking every bit like monsters from a Disney film. Kett could hear voices inside, hushed whispers.

"It's tight," said the PC. "And treacherous. Watch your feet."

"Thanks," Kett said, ducking beneath the low arch. "Savage, with me. Porter, I don't think you'll fit."

It stank of death, but he was ready for it. What he wasn't ready for was the smell of decomposing vegetation, like he'd pushed his head inside a compost heap. He put the back of his hand to his mouth as he climbed up the first couple of steps, then he stopped, because there was nowhere else to go. A carpet of brambles lay in his way, more of them stretching up the walls, fixed there by what looked like duct tape.

And wrapped up in the middle of them, almost mummi-fied in leaf and thorn, was a body.

"Jesus," said Kett.

"Like Christmas, isn't it?" came a familiar Trinidadian accent from further up the steps.

"Cara?" Kett said.

"And I *hate* Christmas," Cara Hay continued. There was a shuffling sound, then the forensic advisor's hawk-like face appeared, her shaven head reflecting the lights. "I hate when people give you presents because you never know what's inside. Why wrap things up? Why hide it? Just give the present, no?"

"You think that's what we've got here?" Kett asked. "A present?"

He put one hand on the wall to steady himself as he climbed, thorns popping beneath his boots. Beneath its wrap-ping of thorns, the body was obviously female and obviously young. The skin was marked by countless little wounds from the barbs but there wasn't much blood—not until he took another step and saw her throat. It had been sawn from side to side, and in the unnatural light the blood looked artificial.

The young woman's eyes were open, frozen in the unbearable horror of the last thing she ever saw. So was her mouth, her throat a dark hole. It looked as if she was still screaming.

"Maybe," Hay said. "Somebody went to a great deal of trouble to present their victim. The body was wrapped tight in *Rubus fruticosus*. Blackberry, to you and me. You can even see some fruit."

She aimed a gloved finger at the girl's ear and Kett saw a cluster of bulging, overripe berries. For some reason, the sight of them turned his stomach more than the body itself. There were ants everywhere, thousands of them.

"Little late for blackberries, isn't it?" he said. "November?"

"Quite," said Hay. "They're not attached to the stem. They've been added."

"Added?"

"Bought from a supermarket, I guess, and positioned there for effect."

"Oh no," said Savage.

Kett pressed himself against the wall, allowing her to squeeze in next to him. It felt ridiculously claustrophobic in here and he focussed for a moment on drawing deep breaths of stagnant air.

"Her throat was cut?" Savage asked.

"I'll leave that to the pathologist, but it seems like it. There's no evidence of other injuries. The cuts on her skin seem to have been made post-mortem when she was wrapped up in brambles. The killer waited until she was dead."

"Small mercies," said Savage. "Any ID?"

"No clothes, but she has a tattoo on her ankle. There."

Kett tracked the girl's legs, seeing the little Space Invader alien tattooed in black ink right on the bone of her ankle—the size of a fifty pence piece. Ants were crawling off the woman's bare foot onto his boots and he tried to shake them off.

"And there was this," Hay said, vanishing into the curve of the stairwell. When she reappeared she was holding a phone in an evidence bag. It was a Samsung Galaxy in a pink *Hello Kitty* case. "This was located on the step above the victim's head. According to the witness, it was playing some kind of narration, a story. He thought it might have been a fairy tale. It's dead, so it will need to be charged before we find out for sure, and find out if it belonged to her."

"I'll do it," said Kett. He stepped up, reaching over the body and taking the phone from Hay's outstretched hand. "Who found her?"

"The police downstairs have got the details but it was a young man. He was supposed to meet the woman here for a date around eight o'clock but she was dead when he arrived. He tripped and fell, knocked himself out. When he woke up he was out of it, went walkies and fell in the river. Somebody called it in and the paramedics had to fish him out."

"He's alive?" Savage asked. Hay nodded.

"And talking?" said Kett.

"That I don't know. He was out of it most of the night, came around an hour or so ago, which is why we've only just got here. Might be drink, drugs, they're not sure. He gave the girl's name, though. Enya."

"Like the singer?" said Savage. "Unusual."

"That's it?" Kett asked.

"Not quite," said Hay. She sighed, wiping her brow on her forearm. "There's something in the victim's mouth."

"In her mouth?" Kett echoed.

His back was aching from having to stand in such an awkward position against the wall, but with Savage next to him there was no room to move. The stones radiated cold like the building was refrigerated.

"Her throat, really," said Hay. "It's deep, like she swallowed it. I was going to leave it to Franklin but she's been held up."

"You do it," said Kett.

Hay nodded, vanishing again and speaking to somebody further up the stairs before returning with a pair of steel tongs.

"I won't be as good at this as Emily."

She shuffled into a better position, angling the tongs into the corpse's mouth. It helped that the woman's jaws were locked wide open, and after a couple of gentle tugs, the tongs slid free. The smell in the stairwell changed instantly, the acidic stench of stomach acid making a cold sweat break out on Kett's face.

Hay took the object from the tongs and held it up. It was a wrap of red cloth the size and shape of a cigar.

"Another present," Hay said, without any trace of humour. "You want to do it?"

"I don't have gloves," Kett replied.

"Hang on."

Hay laid the object on an evidence bag and retrieved her camera, the stairwell strobing as she took her photos. When she was finished, she used a pair of metal tweezers to pry open the edge of the cloth. It seemed to take forever, but finally she managed to unwrap whatever had been lodged in the victim's throat.

"No," said Savage.

"What?" Kett asked. He couldn't make sense of what he saw there. It looked almost like a slim sausage, or a...

"It's a finger," said Hay, even as Kett worked it out. "Not one of our victim's, either. I'd say female, young adult. Clean cut through the joint."

The walls of the stairwell seemed to shrink in even further, the space constricting. Kett felt like he was standing inside a snake's stomach.

"And there's something else," Hay said, turning her attention to the cloth. "There's paper here. Writing. I think somebody's left you a note."

Kett and Savage waited while Hay turned the fabric around, her face a portrait of concentration. There was a scrap of paper lying on it, the size of an index card.

"*Once upon a time*,'" she read, her voice muffled by the stone walls. "'*A young maiden waited to be saved from a hideous monster*.'"

"That's all?" Kett asked, and the woman shook her head.

"'*But nobody came. Nobody came for her*.'"

Hay looked up, her eyes glassy.

"'*And time after time, she died*.'"

CHAPTER THREE

DI PORTER WAS OFTEN HAPPY TO BE THE SIZE HE WAS— six-foot-four and almost half as wide—but never more so than right now. The gate of Cow Tower's dark, narrow stairwell yawned open and even from here, he could smell death inside. The passage had swallowed Kett and Savage like they were food, like it meant to digest them, and he was grateful there hadn't been room for him.

He sucked in a lungful of chilled November air, shielding his eyes against the sun as it broke through the fast-moving clouds. The river gurgled past, kicked around the sharp bend, oblivious to the horrors that dwelled beside it. PC Duke had wandered over to the water and was staring into its depths like he expected to find another body there. He still had his bloody notepad in his hand.

Porter left him to it, scanning the paths and the neatly trimmed lawns around the tower. The forensic team was hard at it, the scene crawling with people in white overalls and blue gloves. They'd placed a few evidence markers, but not many. Chances were, this wasn't the scene of the crime. He'd put money on it.

He turned his attention to the fringe of the scene, where the crowd had swollen again despite Kett's warning. The reporters were still there, of course, more of them now than ever. And it was easy enough to spot the punters, the ones with rubber necks who were only here for a bit of a thrill. They all had their phones out, snapping photographs through the line of bad-tempered PCs who really didn't have any power to stop them.

Another man stood behind the eager onlookers. He didn't have a phone and his hands were jammed into the pockets of his dirty, oversized jeans. He was in his early fifties, his hair and his beard almost entirely grey and his face weathered. He had a large, red hiker's rucksack over one shoulder. He looked like a vagrant, and when he pulled a hand free to scratch his nose his fingers were filthy.

And green.

Porter walked towards the line, the reporters clamouring for his attention, a barrage of questions that made his head pound. He didn't answer a single one of them, waiting for a PC to lift the police tape before ducking underneath it. The man with the rucksack was already on the move, walking down the path that led towards the cathedral. Walking *fast*.

"Hey," Porter said. "Hey, you."

The man looked over his shoulder, the bag jiggling as he picked up speed.

"Oi, mate!" Porter yelled. "You do *not* want me taking you down. Stop moving."

The man showed no sign of listening, breaking into a jog. The path was narrow, a hedge to the left and the river to the right. There was nowhere for him to go. Porter started to run, catching up in a heartbeat. Before he could touch him, though, the man ducked past a wooden bench, grabbing one of the trees that lined the riverbank and doing his best to hide behind it. Porter stopped beside him, frowning at the back of the man's head and his bright red rucksack.

"Holy shit!" he said with no small amount of sarcasm. "Where has he gone? He's disappeared!"

The man's only reply was a wet, wheezing breath, then a phlegmy cough. He leaned back and looked at Porter.

"Peekaboo," Porter said. "What's your name, mate?"

"My name?"

"Yeah. Your name. I can tell you what it isn't. It's not Harry Potter, because you can't turn invisible. So what is it?"

"Rupert," said the man.

"The bear?"

"No," he replied with a frown. "Holden."

"Mr Holden, can you tell me why you were running away from me?"

"Because you're big," said Holden. "And scary."

"Then can you tell me why you were watching the tower?"

Holden cleared his throat, struggling away from the tree and almost falling into the river. He yelped and Porter grabbed one of his outstretched hands, holding onto it even when the man had steadied himself.

"Green fingers," he said. "You haven't been cutting any brambles recently, have you?"

The man pulled his arm free, almost tumbling backwards again.

"You do realise you're standing in my house," he puffed, his cheeks brighter than ever beneath his grey beard. "I have rights too, you know."

Porter looked at the tree, then at the rucksack. He nodded, pulling out his warrant card.

"DI Peter Porter, Norfolk Constabulary. You're homeless?"

"No," Holden said, studying Porter's ID. "I'm free. I'm like the guy from that film, *Into the Wild*. The one who went to live in the mountains."

"I think he died," Porter said, returning the wallet to his pocket. "I'll ask you again, what were you doing over by the tower?"

"Just looking," said the man. "Not often you hear such a kerfuffle in your own back garden."

"You know what happened?"

"A body," he said. "I heard them police talking. A woman. She's dead?"

"Bodies usually are," said Porter. "Were you here last night, by any chance?"

"Here most nights," Holden said. "Not all, though. Getting colder. I'll be going home for the winter soon."

"Home?"

"My house."

"You've got a house?"

Holden nodded.

"Just over the river there. This is a choice, not a necessity. It's a way to see the world, to see people for who they really are. Like you. You saw me in that crowd and decided I was the one worth chasing. Why is that?"

"Fair enough," Porter said with a shrug. "I don't know. Call it copper's instinct. Murderers often return to the scene of a crime, especially if it means something to them. I was keeping my eye out, and you caught it. Didn't help that you ran."

Holden swallowed, staring past Porter to where the tower could still be seen, hunkered amongst the trees like some mythical giant.

"I was here in the evening," he said after a moment. "But I got tired of the pissing rain. Moved over to Pull's Ferry at about half six, as it was dark. I shelter under the canopy sometimes, until they move me on."

"You didn't see anyone suspicious? Anything out of the ordinary?"

Holden moved to the bench and sat down, letting his rucksack slide off his shoulders between his legs. Porter thought about asking for a look inside then decided against it. Holden wasn't wrong. Just because he lived out here didn't mean he didn't have rights.

"I saw a couple of fellas going at it on the playing fields yonder," he said. "Not much romance there I can tell you. And then a fox took a shit right by my bed."

He pointed at a foul-smelling turd beside the bench that was thick with flies.

"A handful of joggers, a few walkers and dogs, not many boats. But no, nothing suspicious."

"And your fingers?" Porter said, nodding at the man's hands.

"The council's just mowed the grass. It's a nightmare because everything goes green. Doesn't come off."

Porter pulled out his wallet again, retrieving a business card.

"You think of anything else, let me know," he said. "And think hard, okay? Ask around for me."

The man took the card, tucking it into his rucksack.

"Sure, I'll add it to my Filofax when I get to my office, and fax you if I think of anything."

He said it with such seriousness that Porter didn't know whether to believe him or not.

"Right, okay. And a word of advice, Mr Holden. If a copper tells you to stop, just stop."

"Sure. Close the door on the way out, will you?"

The man broke into a breathless laugh as Porter headed back the way he'd come. The river was to his left now and a tourist boat chugged down it, a couple of bored kids sitting on the roof. They waved to him and he waved back, smiling. By the time he'd ducked under the tape again, Kett and Savage were walking out of the tower. Both of them looked a couple of decades older than when they'd entered. Savage bent over, bracing her hands on her knees.

"Bad?" Porter asked.

"Awful," she replied, straightening. "That poor woman. Her throat was cut and she was mummified in brambles. And that's not even the worst of it."

"The killer left a finger in her mouth," said Kett, a bagged phone in his hand. "Somebody *else's* finger."

"Fuck me," said Porter, his stomach lurching in a sudden cramp. "ID?"

"Not yet, sir," said Savage.

"I'll send a PC back to HQ with this," Kett said, looking at the phone. "It should help. Only witness was a man who thought he was supposed to meet her for a date. Claimed her name was Enya."

"Where's the man?" Porter asked.

"Ran off when he saw the body, fell in the river. He's in the hospital."

"Did he say what time he found the body?"

"Eight, give or take," said Kett. "But he didn't wake up until early this morning which is why we're only just here. What do you make of this?"

Kett used his free hand to pull out his phone, squinting as he flicked through the apps.

"You need reading glasses, sir?" Savage said.

"No, I bloody do not," Kett grumbled, holding the

phone at arm's length until he found whatever it was he was looking for. He handed it over and Porter saw a photograph of a note, white paper smeared with blood. It had been written using a typewriter, or on a computer with a similar font. He read it in silence.

Once upon a time, a young maiden waited to be saved from a hideous monster.

But nobody came. Nobody came for her.

And time after time, she died.

First, she called herself Sweet Briar Rose. This noisy girl thought she would live forever, she thought that her beauty would make her eternal. But even the prettiest roses have to die, because monsters hate pretty things. He wrapped her in thorns to mar her beauty, but the princess fell asleep and woke again—just as beautiful, just as arrogant.

Once upon a time... our princess, reborn, dances now with two strong men, but she won't dance for long.

She won't dance past tomorrow's midnight.

"Fuck me," Porter said again, handing the phone back. "Does this mean what I think it means?"

"Yeah," said Kett, looking back at the tower. "Unless we figure out who killed our girl, somebody else is going to die."

CHAPTER FOUR

"It's un-tossing-believable!"

Clare's voice was so loud it was distorting the speakers in Porter's car, and Kett turned the volume down before they all went deaf. The Mondeo was caught in traffic in Norwich's aptly named Tombland because a bus had broken down by the cathedral gates, steam rising from the engine at the back. The air was full of angry honks and Kett was half tempted to climb out of the car and start shouting.

"This is exactly what I was talking about," Clare went on. "A serial killer, right here on our doorstep. This is Norwich, not bloody Juárez."

"We don't know it's a serial killer yet," Kett said. "The letter might be an empty threat. This feels more like a crime of anger, or passion. You don't kill somebody like that without knowing them, without them meaning something to you."

"It was almost ceremonial," said Savage.

"Or sacrificial," Porter added as he pulled the car around the bus. "An offering, or something."

"Or floral," said Duke from the back. Kett turned to look at him, one eyebrow raised.

"Floral?"

"Yeah, you know, like a florist. The brambles…"

Duke trailed off, shrinking into his seat.

"Yeah, it could be *floral*," Kett said, rolling his eyes. "Duke's cracked it. Any hope of an ID?"

"Spalding's going through *misper* reports as we speak, but there's nobody called Enya. It's not exactly a common name. We've got one possible lead, though. A young woman reported missing by her mum this morning. Claims she never came home, and that's unusual. Bears a passing resemblance to our victim."

"Savage will check it out," said Kett, his neck cricking as he turned to the back again. "If that's okay with you?"

"Of course, sir," she said.

"Porter and I will head to the hospital to speak with the man who found her. I think it's weird that he didn't mention it to anyone until this morning."

"Yeah," said Clare. "Very weird. His name's… uh, hang on… Kevin Dufrane. Christ, if there was ever a good name for a serial killer, that's it. He's got no record, though. He's up at the NNUH. I've posted a constable outside the ward just in case Dufrane decides he has better places to be."

"Sir," said Kett.

Clare sighed down the line.

"And be quick about it," the Super said. "Because I've got a bad feeling about this."

Me too, Kett thought as he ended the call. *Me too*.

IT TOOK over an hour to reach the hospital, and that was only partly because they dropped off Savage and Duke on the way. By the time Porter pulled into the drop-off area it was coming up for ten and a fine drizzle was falling. The Mondeo's wipers squeaked like angry rodents as they ground back and forth.

"West wing," Kett said.

"How does it feel?" Porter asked as they climbed out. "Being back."

"It feels..."

Kett hesitated, not quite sure how to answer. Or maybe there were *too many* answers to that question. Because he felt anxious that he'd been thrown right back into the deep end, and worried that he wouldn't have what it took to find the woman's killer. He felt bad for betraying his promise to Billie that they would have a fresh start, and guilty for potentially putting himself in harm's way again when the girls needed him. He felt furious that the world was so messed up he needed to be here in the first place, that there were people who would kill a young woman and wrap her in brambles. But he felt relieved, too, that he was back where he belonged, back where he could do the most good, where he could help.

And above all, he felt excited. There was no denying it. It churned inside his stomach, it drove the adrenaline through his body, it made the world feel crystal clear, as sharp as a blade. It made him feel *alive*.

"...fine," he finished.

They waited for the automatic door to open painfully slowly before making their way to the lifts.

"Well, I for one am glad to have you back," Porter said as they rode up. He clapped a big hand on Kett's shoulder. "It's good to have you here."

"You're not going to break into a song and a dance are you, Pete?"

Porter's laugh was almost deafening in the confined space.

"Only if it's an order, sir."

The doors opened and they followed the signs, spotting an older uniformed constable who was reading the newspaper outside of the ward door. She looked up, nodding to them.

"Either of you any good at crosswords?" she asked. "*Heard about ink? You bait a device for warming eggs.* Nine letters."

"Uh..." said Kett. "No idea, sorry."

"Try incubator," said Porter.

The woman studied the newspaper, then smiled.

"Spot on," she said.

Kett actually felt his jaw drop. The big DI shrugged.

"What? Allie and I do them at the weekend. It's a lost art. *Ink, you, bait.* Answer's right there in the clue."

"Full of surprises, you are," Kett said, looking through the door. There were six beds in the ward but only two were occupied. An older man lay in one by the window, lost in the pattern of the rain on the glass. A younger guy sat up in a bed in the middle, staring at the wall opposite with a hundred-yard stare. Kett knew exactly what he was seeing. He'd probably be seeing it for the rest of his life.

"Dufrane?" he asked the PC, and she nodded at the younger man.

"He's an arsehole, just to warn you," she said. "Does his best to hide it, but even if you bury a shit beneath a fancy carpet you can still smell it."

Kett laughed quietly as he entered the ward. Dufrane heard him coming, snapping his head around, his whole body flinching beneath the thin sheets like he'd been given an electric shock. From this angle, Kett could see the ugly bruise that mottled the side of his head, stretching over the bridge of his nose. His left eye was so bloodshot that it was almost entirely red. It made him look vampiric.

"Kevin Dufrane?" Kett asked when he reached the end of the bed. He pulled out his brand new warrant card, realising that this was the first time he'd flashed it since being back. "DCI Robert Kett, Norfolk Constabulary. This is DI Peter Porter. We'd like a moment to speak with you, if that's okay?"

Dufrane took a sharp breath as if he meant to reply, then held it. He licked his lips as he studied them, his bad eye winking like he was trying to convey a secret message.

"Do I—?" He broke into a hacking cough that was far more dramatic than it needed to be. "Do I need to call my lawyer?"

"Do you have a lawyer?" Kett asked. "Most men your age don't."

"No, of course I..." Dufrane hesitated again. "Look, I don't know why you're here. I told that old woman over there my story already and I'm injured. I was hurt."

"Your story," said Kett. "That's an odd word to use. Do you like stories?"

"Do you like fairy tales?" Porter added. "*Sleeping Beauty*, maybe?"

"I'm a grown man," Dufrane spat back. "Of course I don't like fairy tales. They're for children. And *women*."

The way he spat out that last word spoke volumes. Kett had to bite down on his anger.

"Can you tell me what you told my colleague," he said. "It would really help us out. You were planning on meeting a woman for a date? This was somebody you'd spoken to before? Enya?"

Dufrane nodded, some of the fight leaving him. He stared at his sheets, lost in his memories.

"We've been speaking for a little while, online. Facebook, mainly."

"Days? Weeks?"

"A couple of weeks."

"And you know her name?"

"Enya," he spat back as if it was the stupidest question in the world.

"Surname?"

At this, his mouth flapped.

"She didn't have one. Not on Facebook anyway. Her mother is a British spy, she can't give out all her information."

"I'm sorry, what?" said Porter, a smile on his face. "A *spy?*"

"Look, she's not like all the other women. She doesn't just care about... about muscles and good looks."

Dufrane glared at Porter and Kett saw the hate there, a lifetime of impotent, jealous rage. He'd met men like this before, too many of them. A desperate sense of entitlement that quickly turned to anger—and sometimes violence.

"She liked me, and she was the one who asked to meet."

"She wanted to meet you last night?" Kett asked. "At the tower?"

"She liked history. She said she wanted to show me somewhere magical."

"That's the word she used? Magical?"

"I can't remember," Dufrane said, rubbing his swollen temple. "But she wanted to meet me there. At eight."

"Did she say what for?" Kett asked.

"What do you mean? Have you never been on a date? Talking, kissing, I don't know. The usual stuff."

"And you've never met her in the flesh before?" Porter asked.

"Never. But you just know when it's real. You know when you've met your soulmate, even if you don't actually, you know, see each other. I loved her."

"Did she ask you to bring money?" Kett asked, and Dufrane's mouth hung open.

"Just a little," he said after a moment. "To help her move away from home."

"You ever heard of the word catfish, Kevin?" said Porter, and the look that flashed over the young man's face made it seem like he was about to leap out of the bed and jump on the DI.

"Walk us through what happened," Kett said when Dufrane didn't answer.

He didn't want to answer this question either, his reluctance was worked into every flinch, every uncomfortable movement. But after a moment he started talking.

"I had a pint at the pub. The Adam and Eve. Left just before eight. Maybe ten to eight. Walked along the river, saw a jogger and a couple of people walking. But it was quiet because of the rain. Found the tower, looked inside. The gate to the stairs was open and I could hear her talking."

"Wait, you heard her *talking*?" Kett said.

"Well if you'd let me finish you'd find out. I thought it was her talking, but then I climbed a couple of steps and..." He swallowed like he was trying to work down a double-decker bus. "She was just lying there, naked, and I thought..." His eyes bulged. "But then I saw her face, and the ants, and all those plants that were growing out of her and it wasn't her talking at all. It was her phone. It was playing this story. And I panicked, I turned and then..."

He reached for his head again, as if checking that it was still there.

"I don't remember the rest."

"You tripped down the stairs, banged your noggin, ran outside, fell in the river, and luckily for you somebody fished you out. You were unconscious until about three this morning and incomprehensible for a little while after that."

"I'm pretty sure that's not what happened," Dufrane said sheepishly.

"You didn't see anyone else in the tower, or around it? Anyone or anything at all?"

"There was just her. Enya. The love of my life."

Kett nodded, looking at the bedside cabinet.

"You were talking to Enya on your phone last night, right?"

"Messaging, yeah. But she stopped replying."

"When?"

He shrugged limply.

"Maybe six, half past. I can't remember."

"You happen to know where your phone is? You didn't have it when you reached the hospital."

Dufrane patted his legs beneath the sheets as if he'd only just noticed it was gone.

"I must have dropped it."

"Helpful," said Kett. "You own a computer?"

"Yes, of course I own a..." Dufrane saw where the question was leading, suddenly shaking his head. "I mean, no."

"We're going to need to take a look at it."

"Absolutely not," he blustered. "There's private stuff on there. Messages, and... research. Lots of research. Into intimate... things."

"We're not interested in your browser history," said Kett. "But I need to know who this girl was, and right now our best shot at that is your computer. Do I have your permission?"

Dufrane swallowed again, then nodded.

"But only if you promise me you won't let my mum see it."

"Sure," said Kett. "Anything else you want to tell me?"

He shook his head, lost once again in the memory of the dead girl. The PC was right, the guy was a turd, but he didn't scream killer.

Kett's phone rang, the volume down but the *Mexican Hat Dance* still uncomfortably loud in the quiet ward. When he answered it he heard Savage's voice.

"Sir, I've found our girl. Name's Jenny Eyler."

"You're sure?"

"You tell me. I'll send a photo."

"And an address. We'll be there as soon as we leave the hospital." Kett turned to Dufrane. "Hey, does the name Jenny Eyler mean anything to you?"

The young man shook his head, wincing at the pain.

"Why?"

"No reason," Kett said, walking away. "You think of anything else, be sure to call us."

CHAPTER FIVE

SAVAGE HUNG UP THE PHONE, CLOSING HER EYES FOR A moment and taking the deepest breath she could. She was standing inside a kitchen that had seemed ridiculously small five minutes ago, and which now felt like a coffin. The last of the air had been sucked out the moment she'd seen the photograph of the young woman on the living room wall.

It was almost certainly the same young woman who now lay in a shroud of thorns on the steps of Cow Tower.

"You done?" came a shrill voice from the other side of the door.

"Yes," Savage said. "Sorry."

She found the photo she'd taken and texted it to Kett, then she slid the phone into her pocket. The woman who'd greeted her at the front door a few minutes ago—Shannon Eyler—was a four-foot-ten bundle of barbed wire and dynamite, but then terror did that to you, didn't it? The terror of your child going missing, and the police showing up at your door.

"Best be on your way, then," she said in a voice rubbed raw by cigarettes and sadness.

Savage took another breath to steady herself as she opened the kitchen door. Shannon stood there in the shadows of the hallway, an unlit cigarette in one hand. She was still in her pyjamas, Moana ones that would have been too small for any adult who wasn't as drainpipe thin as she was. Her face gave away her age, crinkled by a lifetime of smoking and caked in a layer of makeup that might have been weeks old. Her hair was long and pulled tight, making her forehead look huge. Perched on the top was a silver hair-band that might have been a child's plastic tiara.

"Do you mind if I take a look at another photograph of Jenny?" Savage asked.

"She's only got the one face," Shannon said. "Same in every fuckin' photo."

That was difficult to argue with, but to Savage's relief the woman huffed out of her way and gestured at the stairs which took up most of the narrow hallway.

"Bedroom's up there. Obviously. Go knock yourself out."

"Thank you," said Savage. She edged past, drowning in the cigarette and perfume smell of the woman. "So, you say it's unusual for Jenny not to be here in the morning?"

"Not without telling me," Shannon said. "She's not always a good girl, but she's always good to me. There are only a few places she ever stops out, and she's not at any of them."

"If you wouldn't mind giving me those details, I can double-check," Savage said. She hadn't mentioned the body yet, of course. She couldn't, not until she was sure. "How old is your daughter?"

"Twenty-one," she said. "Barely. Birthday was last week."

"And she went out last night?"

"For a drink, yeah," said Shannon. "She's always out."

"What time did she leave?"

"I don't know. I was at work. But I got home at six and she was already gone. Took my voddy with her too, a whole bottle."

"You know who she was out with?"

"Her friends," Shannon said.

"I'll need names, if that's okay? Has she always lived with you?"

Savage started up the stairs, and even though Shannon didn't follow, the house was small enough and the walls thin enough for the woman's voice to carry.

"Yeah. She used to stay with her dad more when she was a kid, over in Taverham, but then he remarried and went north. Scotland. They didn't speak much after that, he was busy with his new kids. No great loss for Jenny."

"Is she at college? University?"

"Nah," said Shannon from downstairs. "She never liked school, and they didn't like her either. Was kicked out of more than one."

"Yeah? For anything in particular?"

"Just for being her," Shannon said. The smell of fresh cigarette smoke wafted up the stairs along with her words. "Some kids aren't cut out for the machine, and some kids just attract the wrong kind of attention."

"Like?" Savage prompted, but Shannon didn't answer.

The landing was small and windowless. Four doors led into two bedrooms, a small bathroom and an airing cupboard. The walls were yellow, apart from little white rectangles where pictures had once hung. Savage peeked into the front bedroom, seeing a double bed in the middle of a mountain range of old clothes. Beer cans sat on both bedside tables, as well as a towering ashtray. Judging by the smell, the bedding hadn't been changed and the window hadn't been opened for a long time.

"Anyone else live here?" Savage asked.

"Nope, just me and Jenny."

"Who have you been drinking beer with?"

"Howie," came the reply. "He stays over now and again. It's no biggie."

"Howard what?"

"He's harmless," said Shannon, appearing at the bottom of the stairs. "But his name's Barber if you're desperate to know. Plumber. Always at work, or so he tells me."

Stepping into the smaller bedroom, Savage was greeted immediately by the smell of weed. Sure enough, there was an ashtray on the desk to her left, half a joint perched on the side of it. Above that was a large white mirror, a dozen or so photographs taped around the frame. The room looked more like it belonged to a teenager than a woman in her twenties, complete with a Robbie Williams poster above the bed.

"Is Jenny working?"

"If you can call it working," Shannon replied, her voice more muffled now, as if she'd moved. "Helps out down the pub sometimes. A bit of modelling but she always finds an excuse never to go to auditions. Tried that bike delivery thing, the food one."

"Deliveroo?"

"The other one. Uber. But she was never fast enough. Bad lungs since she was a kid, no idea why."

Savage breathed in stale cigarette smoke as she scanned the photos, her heart sinking a little further with each one.

There was no doubt in her mind now that this was their victim.

"Does she have any piercings or tattoos?" she said.

"One."

Don't say on her ankle, Savage prayed. *Not on her ankle.*

"An alien thing. It's on her leg. Her ankle."

Savage felt something crack inside her chest, an actual sound, as if her heart had broken.

"I told her not to get it but she said it was so small nobody would ever notice. They all got one, her and her friends. Stupid, like they thought they'd be mates forever. Never works that way."

The photographs made it clear that Jenny had been an attractive girl, a big smile and big eyes. *TV good looks*, Savage thought, the kind you always saw in Australian soaps or Netflix dramas. In most of the photos she was standing with the same group of girls, all slim, all young, well dressed, and each striking in her own way. In one they stood in a pub garden, singing into upturned beer bottles, oblivious to the group of lads leering at them from another table. In another they lay in their bikinis and sunglasses on beach loungers, five of them in a neat row, drenched in sunshine. There they were again on a mini-golf course, and in a nightclub, and much younger, playing *MarioKart* in the living room downstairs, goofy grins on their faces.

"People like her," said Shannon from the bedroom door, close enough to startle Savage. She took a puff of her cigarette, breathing out more smoke than seemed possible, enough to make Savage's eyes water. "She's a popular girl. Always has been."

"Good friends?" Savage said.

"Clones, pretty much," Shannon replied, and Savage felt like there were cold fingers crawling over her skin as she remembered the note that had been left inside the young woman's mouth, wrapped around a severed finger.

But nobody came. Nobody came for her.

And time after time, she died.

"Maybe sisters is a better word, I don't know."

"This is who Jenny was out with last night?"

"It's who she *said* she was out with, but who knows with her. Anybody's guess because she don't tell me."

"Do you mind if I take one of these?"

"Just bring it back," Shannon said. "Jenny'll bust a nut if she sees one missing."

Savage gently pried loose the photograph of the five girls in the pub garden, peeling the Blu-Tack from the back and rolling it between her fingers.

"I'll be careful," she said. "When you mentioned that there were a few places Jenny stayed when she wasn't here, did you mean with any of these friends?"

Shannon nodded, doing her best to suck the life out of her cigarette in a single breath.

"She wasn't with them?"

"She'd have told me if she was."

"You've called them?"

Shannon nodded as she exhaled, creating a rippling wave of smoke. The room seemed to swim, like it was underwater.

"No answer."

"None of them answered?" Savage asked, coughing quietly as the smoke pushed its way into her lungs.

"But that's not the point. Jenny would have called or texted. She always does. No matter where she is, no matter how drunk she is, she always lets me know."

"Can you get me their details?" Savage asked, still rolling the little ball of Blu-Tack.

Shannon looked like she was going to refuse, but she nodded again. She lifted the cigarette to her lips with trembling fingers, beckoning for Savage to show her the photo. She used her pinkie, working from left to right.

"Fran Herbert, Fortune Quinn, Jenny in the middle, she was always in the middle, Poppy Butterfield, and there's Batty Goodwin, or Beatrice, at the end. She's the quiet one, wouldn't say boo to a gooseberry."

"They've been friends for a while?"

"Forever," Shannon said. "Or near enough. Met at primary school down the road. They drifted apart a little. Poppy had a kid last year from some loser boyfriend, Fortune was more into sports than drinking. Karate or some shit. Jenny was always close with Fran, though."

"Does Jenny have a boyfriend?"

"Hasn't for a while," said Shannon. "Last one was a proper fucking scrote and I think he put her off men for life. Spunked all his money up his own nose, if you know what I mean."

"Drugs," said Savage. "Jenny uses them too?"

"Never," said Shannon. Then, when Savage pointed at the ashtray. "Oh, you know, a bit of leaf doesn't count. She never does *proper* drugs, she never does coke like that squirrel's nutsack she went out with."

"What was his name?"

"Ryan Snelling."

"I think I know him," Savage said. "Does she ever hang out with a man called Kevin Dufrane?"

Shannon shook her head.

"Never heard of him."

"And does she ever call herself Enya?"

"What kind of stupid name is that? Never."

"Does she have a computer, Shannon?"

Shannon nodded towards the bed and Savage ducked down to see a laptop beneath it, a brand-new Mac Power-Book. She laid it on the desk and opened it up, the machine prompting her for a password.

"Up the butt," Shannon said. "All one word, lower case. It's a private joke."

Savage typed it in, then tried again when it didn't work.

"That little... She isn't supposed to change it."

"Mind if I borrow this?"

"Yeah," Shannon said. "I do."

Savage didn't press her, closing the lid of the laptop.

"Expensive bit of kit, that, for somebody working in a pub. Jenny ever mention any other money?"

Shannon's mouth clamped shut, her lips a white line. She shook her head a little too quickly. Savage looked at the sun-bleached Robbie Williams poster—the singer showing off his bare stomach—and Shannon followed her gaze.

"That's been up there for near enough ten years. She don't even like him anymore. But she's too bloody lazy to change it."

"You mentioned that Jenny might have attracted the wrong kind of attention. What did you mean by that?"

Shannon sighed, something rattling deep in her throat.

"It was nothing. She told me it was nothing. The police said it was nothing. That girl was headed for disaster whether my Jenny was there or not."

"What girl?"

Shannon didn't answer, clucking her tongue at Robbie Williams.

"I don't even remember her name. It doesn't matter. She had an accident and tried to blame my girl. Jenny can tell you all about it when she comes home."

Savage turned to the window so she wouldn't have to look Shannon in the eye.

"Miss Eyler, do you know anyone who might want to hurt your daughter? Anyone who might have had a grudge against her? Ryan, maybe? Or this girl?"

Shannon made a noise like somebody choking, then doubled over as she broke into a gasping cough. Savage moved to help but the woman held up her hand to wave her back until she recovered. When she spoke next, it was more wheeze than words.

"Ryan's in prison. Was dealing for some local gang. Stupid prick. But..."

"But what?" Savage asked when the woman didn't continue.

"But somebody *has* hurt her, haven't they? Why else would you ask that? Somebody's hurt my baby girl. You tell me I'm wrong."

"I..."

Savage hesitated, and Shannon saw the truth in that awful absence of words. The woman covered her face with both hands, the ash from her cigarette wilting.

"Is she dead?" she asked through her fingers. "Just tell me. Just fucking tell me."

"We found the body of a young woman this morning," Savage said, her thrashing heart making her words sound hollow and strange. "I can't be sure that it's Jenny, but she had a tattoo of a Space Invader on her ankle, and her description matches your daughter. I'm so sorry, Miss Eyler."

Shannon wasn't crying, she was *vibrating*, like a broken engine about to explode. The noise coming out of her was almost mechanical, a noise that Savage had never heard before and never wanted to hear again.

"We'll need somebody to come and identify the body," she said.

"So it might not be her?" Shannon answered, still not moving her hands. "It might not be? All her friends had the same tattoo, it could have been one of them?"

"Is there anyone I can call?"

Another low, alien groan from the woman's mouth.

"Or I can stay, if you like?" Savage said. "I can stay with you."

It was the worst feeling ever, watching the little woman fold herself into as small a space as possible. Savage didn't know what to do, she didn't know how to make it better. She took a step towards her but Shannon heard her coming, finally ripping her hands from her face. Her eyes were wild.

"Just go!" she said, almost a scream. "Just leave me alone. Leave us alone."

Savage backed out of the room, almost tripping. She skittered down the steep stairs, looking back to see that Shannon had collapsed in the door of her daughter's bedroom. Savage couldn't tell if she was crying or not because the roar of blood in her skull was too loud. All she could do was open the front door and step into the cool air, into the fine rain.

PC Duke sat on the low wall of the Eyler's overgrown front garden and he stood up when Savage appeared, a look of concern creasing his heavy brow.

"You okay?" he asked.

"Yeah," she said. She closed the door, shaking her head. "Actually no. Not really. I've never had to do that before."

She pinched the bridge of her nose, trying to stop the throbbing pain that was building there from the smoke, the sadness, the stress.

"I never want to do that again."

She thought of Shannon Eyler's wild eyes, she thought again about the note.

But nobody came. Nobody came for her.

And time after time, she died.

And she had an awful feeling that this would be the first of many.

CHAPTER SIX

"THERE SHE IS," PORTER SAID.

Kett followed the DI's finger and thought he'd made a mistake. But it *was* Savage who was perched on the low garden wall of a small, wood-clad semi-detached house, her brow furrowed and her arms wrapped around herself straitjacket-tight. She was toying with the old silver police whistle that hung on a chain around her neck. When she looked up there was something in her dark eyes that made Kett's heart heavy.

He knew what had happened. He knew what she'd had to do.

The hardest thing.

Porter pulled up alongside her and wound his window down.

"You okay?" he asked.

"No, sir," said Savage, standing up but keeping her arms across her chest, like she was trying to hold herself in. She was shivering, Kett saw, although doing her best not to show it. She opened the door and slumped into the Mondeo's back seat, tucking the whistle into her shirt.

"Our dead woman's mother?" Kett asked, and she nodded. "How did she take it?"

"I don't know if she did. She told me to get out, wouldn't accept it. But it's her, sir. Same face, same tattoo. Jenny Eyler is our victim. She's only just had her twenty-first birthday."

Kett could feel the anger coming off the young DC, cold and dangerous.

"I sent Duke in to wait with her until the FLO arrives. Neither of them wanted it but we can't leave her alone. Clare's going to send somebody to take her to the body, as soon as we've moved it."

"Already *en route*," Kett said. "We'll know more when Franklin's taken a look."

Savage nodded, close to hyperventilating.

"Breathe," Kett said, the same advice she'd given him countless times. "Slow down, take a moment."

She heard him, her chest rising and falling more slowly beneath her folded arms. Something inside her seemed to detach and uncoil.

"I got some names," she said after a moment. "There were five of them in their friendship group. Five women. Jenny's mum told me they were more like clones of each other."

"Clones?" said Kett. "Weird expression."

"Yeah. I thought so too. Poppy Butterfield, Fortune Quinn, uh, Beatrice Goodwin and Fran Herbert."

"How do you remember all that without a notepad?" Porter asked.

"Spent my teenage years waitressing at the beach," she said, the smallest of smiles appearing on her lips. "We used to see who could remember the biggest orders. My record was fifty-two things for a birthday party, not a single mistake."

"I wish my memory was better," Porter said.

"Me too," Kett replied. "You might remember how to make a decent cup of tea."

Porter gasped.

"We should follow up on the women," Kett said before the DI could argue.

"Shannon Eyler claims she tried calling them all this morning when she was looking for Jenny. But nobody answered."

"That's not good," Kett said. "Okay, for now, this is priority number one. Find the other women. We've got a severed finger that belongs to somebody, let's make sure it's not one of them."

He pulled out his phone, calling DS Alison Spalding.

"You at your desk?" he asked when she answered.

"No, *sir*," she replied, the second word dragged up like a ball of spit. She'd made it perfectly clear how she felt about Kett getting his old job back. "I'm climbing Mount fucking Kilimanjaro."

"Spalding!" Clare roared somewhere close by. Spalding sighed.

"What do you want?"

"I need you to run some names for me. Poppy Butter-field, um, Fortune Quinn?"

Savage reached over and took the phone, reeling off the names.

"Yeah," she said when she'd finished. "He's behaving. Thanks, ma'am."

She laughed.

"Yeah, me too."

"You what?" Kett asked, craning back. Savage laughed again.

"I'll be sure to tell him."

"Tell me *what*?"

"Yeah, ma'am, he looks very confused."

Savage laughed again, listening for a minute or so.

"Skeleton Road?" She frowned. "Oh, right. *Skelton*. We'll start there. Can you text the others over when you find them? Thanks, ma'am. Do you want to speak to DCI Kett again?"

The answer must have been no, because Savage ended the call and handed the phone back.

"What did she say?" Kett asked.

"You probably don't want to know, sir."

"About the *case*."

"Oh, right. Poppy Butterfield is actually Penelope Butterfield. Poppy's a nickname. She has a house right around the corner from here. Skelton Road. For the record, Shannon told me Poppy had a child last year. DS Spalding is going to find the addresses for the other girls and she'll check them out with Dunst."

Porter gunned the engine, pulling them away from the kerb and earning a honk from the car behind them. He ignored it, scanning the satnav as he accelerated.

"She also says the phone they found in Cow Tower belongs to Jenny Eyler. She'd been talking to Kevin Dufrane under an alias, Enya, and he wasn't the only one she was communicating with. There are a few conversations there that look like catfishing. Spalding thinks she was doing it to make some money. The story that was playing was an audio file from Apple Music, freely available. She'll get back to us when she knows more."

"Did you get anything else from Jenny's mother?" Kett asked.

"There's a boyfriend, drug dealer, but he's in prison. Ryan Snelling. I know the name."

"Snelling?" said Porter. "Yeah, we know him. His brothers, too. There's three of them, they ran point on a county lines thing a couple of years back. Or tried to, anyway. They got absolutely smashed by another gang and Ryan and his older brother got jail. The younger one... I can't remember his name, but he got off with community service. All shitbags."

"Oh, yeah, I remember."

"Capable of something like this?" Kett asked.

"I don't know. The county lines gangs are getting worse but they tend to keep the violence in-house, and they don't really have the imagination for what happened to Jenny. They'd cut a throat, but the fairy tale stuff, I don't think so."

"We'll check them out," Kett said. He opened the notes app on his phone, doing his best to type while Porter steered them around the corner.

"There was something else," Savage said. "I couldn't get much out of her but Shannon Eyler mentioned that Jenny had been thrown out of school a few times, that she attracted the wrong kind of attention. She mentioned that a girl had accused her of something, of maybe trying to hurt her. Might be motive for revenge?"

"No name?"

"No, sorry. I'll dig."

Porter drove into a narrow road lined with brick terraces. Almost all of the gardens here had been dug up and replaced with driveways, and when Savage pointed to one with a faded blue door he pulled up outside it.

"That's it," she said.

They climbed out of the car together, a brittle finger of pain working its way into the bullet wound in Kett's chest— not awful, just a reminder that the fragment of Keefe's bullet was still there.

Just a reminder that it could happen again.

The house was right in the middle of the row, and there was no car in the weed-strewn drive. There was no vehicle in the property to the right, either. Instead, a skip sat there, a toilet perching proudly on top of a mountain of rubble.

"Whose house is this again?" Kett asked as he approached the door.

"Poppy's, sir," Savage said. "Penelope Butterfield."

Kett went to knock, then stood to one side instead.

"You can do it."

Savage made a fist and pounded on the door, loud enough for the hollow sound of it to reverberate inside the skip. Behind them, on the other side of the street, somebody opened their door and peered outside, frowning, and Kett heard another door creaking open further down the road. He laughed quietly.

"One of these days you're going to knock clean through," he said.

Even so, nobody answered. Kett ducked down and pushed open the letterbox, peering into a small, dark hallway. A breath of stale air wafted out, silent and dead.

"I don't think anyone is here," he said.

Nobody living, anyway.

"See if you can get around the back, Pete."

Porter nodded, breaking into a run. Savage knocked again, somehow even louder this time. While they waited, Kett turned his attention to the skip. It was a big one, and he had to push up onto his tiptoes to get a better look at what was inside.

"Kate, what do you make of this?"

Savage walked up beside him, but she was too short. She hopped over a low hedge into the neighbour's garden so that she could peek over the lower end.

"Brambles," she said.

Lots of them, still a vibrant shade of green but already rotting.

"Might be a coincidence," she said. "A clearance, maybe. Brambles are everywhere this time of year. My garden is literally full of them."

"Maybe," said Kett.

He stood back, looking up at the house. There were pictures taped to the windows, little rainbows and hearts that had been drawn by a child. Savage went to knock again but before she could make contact the door swung open. Porter was there, and he flinched at Savage's raised fist. He was wearing blue forensic gloves.

"Easy, *Tyson*," he said, only half-joking. "Back door is open. Nobody home."

He moved to the side and Kett squeezed past, through swirling funnels of dust and muted daylight. The house was definitely empty, he had no doubt about it.

"Upstairs?" he said.

"Nothing. Three bedrooms, though, one belongs to a kid. It's a little messy but no sign of a struggle."

Kett peeked into the living room, seeing a dozen toy cars on the deep-pile carpet and a basket of colourful DVDs. There were some framed prints on the walls and some dried flowers in a tiger-headed vase on the coffee table, but no photographs anywhere. He followed the living room into the kitchen. It was a little brighter in here, the dust more agitated, like it was trying to tell them something. More children's drawings were pinned to the fridge with *Paw Patrol* magnets.

"That's weird," Savage said, pointing to the wall above the table. A frame hung there, full of different-sized holes for a photo collage.

It was empty.

"See if you can find any photos," Kett said.

"Sir," Savage replied, heading for the stairs.

On the table beneath the empty frame was a phone, and the red light in the cradle was blinking. Kett used a knuckle to press *Play* and the digital answering machine came to life.

"You have three new messages and no saved messages."

He walked to the window while he listened, seeing a small, square garden that was mostly lawn. Splintered fences hid the neighbours' properties from view, and the skeletal remains of a couple of sunflowers were the only sign that anyone had tended this place.

"First message, received yesterday at 11:47 pm. Hi Poppy, it's Shannon, Jenny's mum. I think you were supposed to be going out tonight with Jenny but she hasn't texted me and you know I worry. Anyway, tell her to switch her phone on. Have fun, don't do anything I wouldn't."

Nearly midnight. Jenny had already been long dead. There was a key in the lock of the back door and Kett patted his pockets, knowing full well that he didn't have any gloves with him.

"Here," said Porter, handing some over. Kett pulled them on, his fingers refusing to go in properly. Somehow, he ended up with two fingers of his right hand in one hole and the pinkie flapping around, empty.

"Good Dunst impression," said Porter with a laugh that was far too loud. Then he seemed to remember the finger that they'd found inside Jenny Eyler's mouth, because the colour drained right out of him. "Oh, shit. I didn't..."

"Hush," Kett said as the answer machine continued.

"*Next message, received today at 07:17 am.* Oh, hi. You're probably still asleep, Poppy. I just didn't hear from Jenny last night at all and it's not like her. Is she with you? I can't seem to reach Fran either. Could you send me a quick text if so, or ask her to do it? It's Shannon, by the way. Eyler. Jenny's mum. But you know that, right? Sorry. I'll try Beatrice. Hope you had fun!"

The panic was already there, drenching every word. Kett turned the key in the back door but it wouldn't budge, the old lock rusted up. There was no other way of securing it, the house open to anyone who might have wanted to come in. Savage was thumping down the stairs and she burst into the kitchen just as the third message started to play. Kett raised a hand to silence her before she could open her mouth.

"*Next message, received today at 09.58 am.* Poppy, get your bum out of bed, we need to be on the road. Raff's made you some biscuits, he's desperate for you to try some."

A young boy's voice rose up in the background, calling wordlessly. Kett felt the blood drain from his face, the room suddenly icy.

"Your father says they're bogie flavoured but they're not. I made him wash his hands. Anyway, you're probably extremely hungover but remember your father has his appointment at eleven and we can't be late. Love you, darling."

The little boy called out again but the answer machine cut him off with a beep.

"That is not good," said Kett. He plucked the phone from the cradle, cycling through the missed calls then returning to the last one. He glanced at Savage while it rung. "Anything?"

"Yeah," she said. "There's not a single photo of Poppy or her kid or her friends or family in the entire place. But I did find this."

She laid a large, white photo album on the table and opened it. The clear plastic pages fluttered, all of them empty.

All except one.

"Oh shit," said Kett, ending the call before it could be answered.

On a page in the middle of the book was a picture of Snow White, taken from the Disney film. It had been badly cut out from a magazine, the edges ripped. Whoever had left it there had taken more care with the typewritten note that was stuck underneath, the paper pristine. It was clear enough for Kett to make out but Savage read it aloud anyway, her voice quiet even in the silence of the kitchen.

"*Once upon a time, there lived a princess who thought she could outrun death...*"

CHAPTER SEVEN

"AND YOU HAVEN'T SEEN OR HEARD FROM HER SINCE yesterday?"

Kett clung to the strap over the door as Savage drove, the big Mondeo as nimble as a go-kart in her hands. He had his phone to his ear, Poppy Butterfield's father on the end of the line. His voice was heavy with worry.

"No. It's most unlike her, she's always early to pick up Rafferty, if anything."

Savage barely touched the brakes as they thumped onto a roundabout, Kett's stomach rising so fast it was like it was trying to switch places with his lungs. She took the third exit like she was attempting to slingshot her way around the moon.

"And she was supposed to be with you at—"

The car crossed a speed bump and Kett grunted as he hit the ceiling.

"At nine this morning, yes," Mr Butterfield said. "At the latest. She always goes out on a Friday night but she never gets drunk. *Properly* drunk. She hasn't been drunk since she had the boy. We called her quite a few times but she didn't answer."

"Who was she out with last night?" Kett asked, glaring at Savage as she hit another speed bump.

"The usual lot. Batty and the girls."

"Jenny Eyler?"

"Yes. Not that we encourage it."

Savage jerked the wheel and Kett felt like he was on a rollercoaster that was about to spin off the tracks.

"Hang on," he said into the phone, before pressing it to his shirt. "Kate, if you don't slow down I'm going to either vomit or shit myself, and I can promise that neither will be much fun."

Savage laughed and gently pumped the brakes. Kett lifted the phone to his ear.

"You don't like Jenny?" he asked, and Mr Butterfield spat out a laugh.

"Not since she started…" He cleared his throat. "It's not my place to speak ill of other people but she's always been a little wild, that one. Poppy knows how to keep her at arm's length, don't worry."

"They ever been in trouble together?"

"No," said the man, although the word was laden with something that might have been uncertainty. "Nothing serious, anyway. Teenage girl stuff."

Savage slowed down as she pulled into the mortuary car park.

"Look, Poppy's a good girl. A kind soul. She's got her head screwed on right and she's a brilliant mum. But I'm worried about her, because she always checks in, and she's never late to see Rafferty. Never. If she's not here, and she's not at home, then something is wrong. Please find her."

"I will," Kett said. "If you think of anything else, call me back, or call the police station."

By the time the man had muttered a reply and hung up, Savage had parked. She switched off the engine and they climbed out together, the sound of their slamming doors echoing across the car park. Kett led the way towards the mortuary doors, letting Savage in first. They traipsed down the steps in silence to find Superintendent Clare waiting for them at the bottom.

"That was quick," he said.

"I think we averaged about a hundred miles an hour," Kett replied, rubbing his stomach.

"I'm not sure if you know, Shannon Eyler identified the body a short while ago. It's Jenny."

"How was she?" Savage asked Clare. He ignored her.

"Where's Porter?"

"He's checking out Fran Herbert's house," said Kett. "It's just around the corner from Poppy."

"Who?"

"Poppy. Real name Penelope Butterfield. She's missing. She was out with four other women last night, including Jenny, and she never turned up to collect her son this morning. Highly out of character, according to her dad. We found a note at her house that matches the one we found in Jenny's mouth."

"Christ," said Clare. "I thought Jenny was on a date last night?"

"Not according to anyone else we've spoken to. It's looking a little like Jenny was seducing men online to get a bit of cash. I wonder if maybe she was supposed to meet Kevin Dufrane last night to pick up the money he'd brought her, then go and meet her friends afterwards. But that's a very loose theory."

"You think Dufrane found out? Killed her?"

"Maybe," said Kett. "I'm not ruling it out."

Clare patted the pocket of his suit, as if looking for his cigarettes. When he reached inside, though, it was a Bounty that appeared. He opened it up and devoured half of it in one go, spraying coconut and chocolate as he spoke.

"What do you make of the parents?"

"The parents?" Kett replied, brushing soggy crumbs from his chest.

"It's weird," Savage said. "Both Jenny's mum and Poppy's parents seemed worried that they were on a night out. I mean, *really* worried."

"So?" Clare said, upending the wrapper and letting the second chunk of Bounty fall into his open mouth. He said something else that was so full of food it didn't make any sense, then he swallowed noisily and tried again. "I still get terrified anytime one of mine goes out, it's natural."

"Yours aren't adults," Savage said. "Well, not all of them. Jenny and Poppy were both twenty-one, it seems strange that the parents would worry so much. As soon as I turned eighteen my mum didn't check up on me once, even if I didn't come home. I think..."

She stopped, frowning.

"I think something might have happened before, maybe? Something bad. Something that made the parents worry so much."

"No idea," spat Clare. "But file it away for later."

He was already on the move, pushing through the doors into Franklin's domain. The young pathologist was waiting for them and she looked even angrier than she usually did. She offered an abrupt nod of welcome as she pulled on a rubber glove, then led the way around a partition to where the dead waited.

Jenny Eyler lay on the forensic table, stripped of her robe of leaves and thorns. She looked unbearably exposed, Kett thought. He'd seen more of the dead than he could remember, but each victim seemed somehow worse than the last, as if their effect on him was cumulative. It was in a way, because he carried them all on his back, the men, the women, the children who had died under his watch. He carried them all, and the weight of them was becoming more than he could bear.

He rubbed his chest as the pain from Keefe's bullet began to sing.

"Jennifer Eyler," said Franklin, her voice too loud for the small room. "Twenty-one years of age. Same age as me. And yes, because it's going to come out sooner or later, I knew her."

"You *knew* her?" echoed Clare. "Tossing hell, Franklin, you should have said something."

"I just did. I didn't know her well. We attended the same summer camp when we were eleven, and we stayed friends for a couple of years."

"I had no idea," said Savage.

"Why would you? Norwich is a small city. It's a village, really. It was bound to happen."

"I'll call in somebody else," Clare said. "You shouldn't have to—"

"You will not," Franklin shot back. "And I *should* be the one to do this. Too many people end up here surrounded by strangers, I don't think a familiar face will do her any harm."

She winced as she swallowed, obviously struggling. Then she picked up a metal ruler and held it like she was a teacher.

"Dead less than twenty-four hours. I'd say with some certainty that it happened somewhere between five and eight pm. Forensics have the brambles. I'm sure Cara gave you the Latin bollocks, but to me and you, they're blackberries. Whoever killed her wrapped her good and tight in them after she was dead, so at least she didn't suffer that particular cruelty. See the marks on her skin?"

Franklin pointed to one of hundreds—possibly thousands—of tiny scratches that crisscrossed the woman's body, all the way from her toes to her forehead.

"There's not enough blood for it to have happened when she was alive. Most are slight abrasions but there are some more severe puncture wounds caused by particularly nasty thorns. The ones on her back are the worst, obviously. She was lying there for some time and I'm pretty sure she was dragged for quite a way."

She paused, pursing her lips and studying the dead woman.

"You'll understand that I haven't had an opportunity yet for proper analysis. But my preliminary examination revealed no sign of sexual assault, and no other secondary injuries. There are no defensive wounds, no sign of matter beneath her nails, no ligature marks on her wrists or ankles. She doesn't appear to have been touched in any other way. There's just this."

All eyes followed Franklin's outstretched ruler to Jenny Eyler's throat. Now that it had been cleaned it didn't look anywhere near as brutal an injury as it had back in the tower. If anything, it looked almost clinical—a scalpel-sharp red line which curved from a little way beneath her left ear and around the cord of her windpipe.

"It's a perfect surgical cut," Franklin said. "I couldn't have made it any neater myself. It's deep enough to sever both the external and internal carotids, plus the trachea, with no sawing. That takes a long, razor-sharp blade and a lot of strength. The good news is that it would have been quick. Dead within a minute. The better news, depending on your definition of better, is that I don't think Jenny was conscious when it happened."

"She was sedated?" Kett asked.

"I'll have to wait for the Tox Screen to come back, but yes, I think she was out cold. There's no sign of any injury that would have rendered her unconscious, and if she'd been asleep then she would have woken, panicked, and spent her last few seconds fighting hell for leather. Some kind of sedative makes sense."

For a few seconds, nobody spoke. It brought Kett little relief that the young woman had died in her sleep. She hadn't even had a chance to fight back.

"You mentioned there was a note?" Franklin said to Clare. The Super waved his hand in Kett's direction.

"Yeah," Kett said, digging out his phone and finding the photo he'd taken of the note. "'*Once upon a time, a young maiden waited to be saved from a hideous monster. But nobody came. Nobody came for her. And time after time, she died. First, she called herself Sweet Briar Rose. This noisy girl thought she would live forever, she thought that her beauty would make her eternal. But even the prettiest roses have to die, because monsters hate pretty things. He wrapped her in thorns to mar her beauty, but the princess fell asleep and woke again—just as beautiful, just as arrogant. Once upon a time, our princess, reborn, dances now with two strong men, but she won't dance for long. She won't dance past midnight.*'"

He switched to the next photo.

"We found another one at Poppy's house. Same font, same kind of paper. '*Once upon a time, there lived a princess who thought she could outrun death. She boasted all day long that death couldn't catch her because she was too beautiful. And she should have known better, because death had killed her three times before already, the monster had ended her life three times and he was going to do it again. But he made a pact with her, saying that although he would end her life, he would let the world look upon her forever, a butterfly in a glass cage whose beauty would never fade.'"*

"What do you make of it?" Clare asked, and Franklin shrugged.

"It's atrocious, as far as fairy tales go. But... I don't know. The whole fairy tale thing? Why would anyone do it? Why would anyone go to the trouble of killing someone, wrapping them in brambles and dragging them into a tower? It doesn't fit what I'm seeing on the table."

"No," said Savage. "I was thinking the same thing. The note seems to be saying that the murder was personal, that there's a message to be found here. But that wound to her throat is clinical. There's no sign of hesitation or thought. I don't know what I'm getting at, really, but if you kill somebody like that, that *easily*, then their death doesn't seem to mean anything at all. Does that make sense?"

"Yeah," said Franklin. "You said it better than I could. The wound is saying one thing, the note is saying another. And, of course, there's the small matter of the finger."

"Any idea where it might have come from?" Clare asked.

"I'm guessing a hand," Franklin replied impatiently.

She walked to the stainless-steel fridge, returning a moment later with a metal tray. The finger sat there, small and crooked. The long nail was covered with pearl-white varnish and stick-on gems that caught the light, giving the weird impression that the digit was moving.

"It's the index finger from a right hand, severed right

above the metacarpal. This is a surgical job too, see how neat it is? They knew where the metacarpal meets the proximal phalanx, which saved them the effort of trying to cut through bone. A quick cut through the connective tissue and job done."

"Can you tell if they were alive or dead when the finger was cut?" Kett asked.

"Not really. But see the way the common digital arteries have retracted?"

"Um, no," said Kett.

"Well, there's a chance our victim is still alive."

"We came up blank with the prints," Clare said. "Whoever this belonged to, they've never been in trouble with us."

"But that nail varnish is professional," said Savage. "Those are gels. If we put a photo out we might find whoever did them."

"Good thinking," said Clare. "Get on it."

"Now?" asked Savage, and the Super nodded.

Savage pulled out her phone, leaning in to take a photograph of the nail.

"Don't get any of the blood or gross bits," Clare said. "Just the nail."

Savage took a couple of photographs, checked them, then returned her phone to her pocket.

"It may belong to our second missing woman," Kett said. "But it might not be Poppy's. You heard the second note, he spoke about the princess already dying *three* times. I'm not sure this killer is going to stop at two victims. Did you know Jenny well enough to guess why somebody might have done this to her? Why she was targeted like this?"

Franklin shrugged again.

"She was a regular kid. Not really enough there to

remember her by. I did hear that she went off the rails a little, though. I don't know anything else about it."

"You ever hang out with Poppy Butterfield, Fortune Quinn, Batty Goodwin or Fran Herbert?"

"No," said Franklin. "But if those are our missing women then I get the feeling I'll be hanging out with them soon enough."

Kett shook his head, studying the corpse one more time before making for the door.

"Not if I can help it."

CHAPTER EIGHT

Porter hated walking. There was absolutely no bloody need for it. Exercise, yes. That's why he spent so much of his spare time in the gym. He loved the weights, he liked the pool, he tolerated the treadmill. But walking was the most pointless task imaginable, because there was no need for it anymore. That's why cars had been invented, right?

Not that he had a car right now, because Kett and Savage had bloody stolen it.

He pulled up the collar of his jacket against the relentless drizzle, pushing into the shitty November wind. The trees had already given up, their branches naked and their leaves turning to stinking mush in the gutters. They whipped back and forth in a demented frenzy as he passed, like they were ridiculing him.

He hated bloody trees as well.

He saw a handful of people as he walked, most of them miserable-arse dog owners with their miserable-arse dogs, but the streets were largely empty. Kett had told him that Fran Herbert's house was just around the corner, two streets away. But what he *hadn't* mentioned was that both of those streets were about a mile long. He'd already been walking for a good thirty minutes and he still wasn't there. He'd half thought about calling for an IRV but he knew he'd never hear the end of it if he did.

A bus splashed past, pissing puddle water all over his Cleverleys.

He hated bloody buses.

He wasn't sure why he was in such a foul mood. It was partly the dead woman, yes. Cases like this always got to him, the horrific violence. He hadn't even seen the body and still he couldn't think about anything other than poor Jenny Eyler being murdered then wrapped in thorns. *Sweet Briar Rose*. He knew that's what the press would call her, as soon as the news broke. They'd fictionalise her, turn her into a character in their own twisted version of the story.

No, it was more than that. He didn't want to admit that part of him was still back at Whytetail, back in that moment before they'd found out the truth about the place, before they'd found Mihaela and baby Luca, back when he'd thought for a moment that he might have found an answer to his troubles.

That he might have found a way to be a dad.

"Stupid," he said to himself. Why would anyone even want a child, when at any moment somebody could cut their throat, wrap them in weeds and hide them in a medieval tower? What was the point?

He and Allie had an appointment next month to talk about IVF but he couldn't get excited about it. He'd resigned himself to the fact that the reason he had it so good in life—his health, his job, his wife—was because he was losing out on *this*. The universe had compensated him for something he'd never even known he could lose.

Another bus squealed to a halt in front of him, the doors opening. He crossed the street in front of it to avoid being trampled, holding up a hand as a Fiesta pumped its brakes. The driver looked annoyed but he kept his hand off the horn. In his overcoat and his black gloves Porter knew he looked like a nightclub bouncer—complete with the "don't give me any shit" stare.

He hopped onto the kerb and checked the nearest road sign to see that he was finally here. Well, almost, because the Herbert house ended up being right at the far end of the quiet little cul-de-sac. He double-checked the address that Kett had sent him then stepped over the low gate and knocked on the door. The drizzle was as thin as gauze but it had soaked him through to the bone on the walk over, and he scrubbed the rainwater from his face as he waited.

It didn't take long, the door opening a crack and the security chain snapping tight. A woman's face peered through the gap beneath a nest of crazy white hair, frowning through the wire-rim glasses she wore on the end of her long nose.

"Yes?" she said. "I'm not buying, renovating, or looking for Jesus, if that saves you the effort of starting."

Porter smiled, pulling out his warrant card. She studied it for a moment, the frown deepening.

"Is this about Fran?" she asked. "Or Peter?"

"Hopefully neither," said Porter, pocketing his wallet. "Are you Mrs Herbert?"

She nodded.

"Have you heard from Fran today?"

"I haven't heard from Fran—"

She fell silent as somebody else appeared behind her, whispering.

"I'm obviously going to do that, Geoff," she said. She turned to Porter again. "One minute."

The door closed and Porter heard the sound of the chain being pulled free. When it opened again he saw a man standing next to the woman, his hair as wild and grey as a mad scientist's. He wore the exact same glasses as his wife, and when Porter studied their clothing he realised they were dressed in almost identical plaid suits. They might have been twins, but they both wore wedding rings. If they noticed him looking, neither of them mentioned it.

"Come in," said the man in a mild American accent, ushering Porter over the threshold. "Eileen would have you freezing your bananas off out there."

"My *bananas*?" Porter said. "It's fine, it's not cold. Just wet. Thank you."

The hallway was dark and narrow, and there was a smell he couldn't put his finger on. Something that might once have been fish. He tried not to let it show.

"I can take your coat?" said Eileen.

"I'm not staying long. My name is DI Peter Porter, Norfolk Police. I'm not here directly because of Fran, don't worry. I'm here because of a friend of hers. Jenny Eyler. Do you know her?"

Geoff and Eileen shared a look that was impossible to miss and equally impossible to read. When Eileen spoke, her voice was cold.

"Yes, of course we know Jenny. What has she done now?"

"We, uh, we think she might have been murdered."

"Good," spat Geoff, the word like a gunshot in the small hallway. Porter actually laughed with shock, Eileen giving the man a hefty backhand.

"Geoffrey!" she said, looking at Porter. "I'm so sorry."

"You think it's good that a young woman has been killed?" Porter asked, leaning into the man. Instead of shrinking back, Geoff doubled down.

"Nobody will miss her. She was a menace, that girl. She almost took everything from our Fran."

"Fran made her own choices, Geoffrey," said Eileen, close to tears. "Nobody forced her to do anything. Could you ever make her do something she didn't want to? No, me neither. Nobody could. And what an awful thing to say about Jenny. She didn't deserve this, she didn't deserve to die. How? What happened to her?"

"It's an ongoing case, I'm afraid," said Porter. "I can't go into details. But we think Jenny might be one of a number of people who have been targeted. I'm doing my best to make sure that Fran isn't one of them. Have you spoken to her today? Is she here?"

That look between them again, nervous.

"We haven't spoken to her in weeks," Geoff said. "Not since that godawful thing in the summer. And barely even then."

"Geoffrey!" Eileen said again. She'd balled up the cuffs of her shirt in her hands, squeezing them tight.

"They probably already know!" he shot back. "It's the police, Leeny, they're not stupid."

Porter held up a gloved hand.

"Slow down," he said. "What do we already know?"

"The *incident*," Geoff said, sounding out each syllable. "With Martha Hansen-Andrews."

Porter recognised the name but he couldn't place it.

"Don't talk about her," Eileen said, stamping a foot like she was three years old. "I don't want to hear that name in my house. Not one more time."

"Then leave," Geoffrey said, stamping his own foot so

hard that his glasses slipped off his nose and clattered to the floor. "Oh, gosh darn it!"

Porter picked them up for him, handing them back. The smell seemed to be getting worse, the unmistakable aroma of shit lingering beneath the fishy top notes.

"Maybe we could sit for a moment and take a breath," he said, while trying not to take too deep a breath of his own. "Mrs Herbert, if this is something you don't want to talk about then I'm sure your..." He looked at their matching glasses and clothes—and at faces that seemed frighteningly similar now that he'd had a chance to study them—chancing it. "Husband?"

She nodded.

"I'm sure that he can answer any questions I might have."

"I'm fine," she replied, taking a deep breath, still tugging on her shirt sleeves. "I just thought that it might be over, that the whole *fucking* thing might be behind us."

She stamped her foot again, without any real strength, then walked through the closest door into a living room. There was no sofa here and no TV, just a massive wooden contraption that looked almost like a catapult. It was only when Porter clocked the spinning wheel beside it that he realised it was a loom.

A handful of uncomfortable wooden chairs were dotted around the room and Eileen collapsed into the closest, Geoff taking up a position behind her, one hand on her shoulder like Porter was a photographer, not a policeman. Even their shoes matched, he saw. Shiny brown brogues that Superintendent Clare might have coveted if he was here.

"Right," said Porter, perching on the chair closest to the window. Drab net curtains cut out what little light was squeezed from the day, and even though it wasn't even midday it felt like evening had already taken this little house prisoner. He pulled a notepad and pen from his suit pocket. "Let's start with the basics. Fran is your daughter, yes?"

They both nodded in time with each other.

"Fran or Francesca?"

"Frances," said Geoff. "We named her after my mother. Frances Clementine Herbert."

"Her middle name is Clementine?"

"No, my mother's is. Fran doesn't have a middle name."

"Right," said Porter, scribbling out the note he'd just made. "She's twenty? Twenty—"

He hesitated as a monstrous cry floated into the room, the sound of a distressed baby. Geoff and Eileen didn't seem in the least bit concerned.

"Did you hear...?" he asked as the noise came again, like something from a horror film.

"That's just Beck," said Eileen. "The cat."

"A *cat* is making that noise?" Porter said.

"She's old. She turns twenty-one in a couple of weeks," said Eileen.

"The cat?"

"No, Fran. I had already resigned myself to not seeing her on her birthday."

"You said you haven't seen her for a few weeks?"

"We haven't seen her since New Year," said Geoff. "Properly, that is."

"No, it was Christmas," Eileen countered. "She stormed out because of the..."

She stopped, chewing on whatever word had been about to come out of her mouth.

"The..." Porter prompted.

"Drugs, Eileen," Geoff said, pronouncing it like he was on stage. "You can't lie to the police, they know everything."

"Not quite everything, we're not nuns," Porter said. "What drugs?"

"They weren't hers," said Eileen. "They belonged to Jenny. We think that horrid girl was selling them but we couldn't prove it. She had this boyfriend, this horrible little oik called Ryan. He's the one who introduced Fran to her boyfriend."

"Who is also a horrible little oik," said Geoff. "Small-time drug dealer, but she claims she loves him. Enough to make you sick. I wish somebody would murder him too."

"Geoffrey!" wailed Eileen.

"We had an argument at New Year, about the drugs and the boys. Peter wouldn't let it go, he was winding her up something wicked."

"Christmas," said Eileen.

"Peter's her brother?" said Porter, his head reeling.

More synchronised nodding. The wailing meow came again and something walked through the door. Porter was hesitant to use the word cat, because this thing didn't look anything like one. It was bald, its skin hanging off it in saggy wrinkles, its face like some kind of dribbling gremlin.

"Dear god," he said.

"Beck's just old," said Eileen again. "Older than our children, if you can believe it. She's a sweet girl, aren't you? Come on."

She clapped her lap, but to Porter's horror the cat approached *him* and began to nuzzle his trousers with its horrible face. Its purr filled the room like a B-24 Liberator.

"She likes you!" Geoff said, obviously delighted.

Porter tried to nudge the animal away without looking

like he was nudging it away, but it only seemed to make it purr harder.

"So, Christmas, Peter was teasing his sister?" he said, trying to keep the conversation flowing.

"He's a kid," said Geoff. "He didn't mean anything by it."

"But it must have been bad, if you haven't seen her since?"

"We saw her briefly in September, the whole Martha thing," said Geoff. "But she didn't want our help."

"It was the culmination of everything that had come before," said Eileen. "The camel on the straw's back."

"Straw on camel," said Geoff.

"That's what I said, you moron. Fran can be atrociously infuriating, like her father."

Eileen paused for a moment, looking like the conversation had finally caught up to her.

"Wait, is Fran okay? Have you spoken to her?"

"No," said Porter. "I mean no I haven't spoken to her. We're having trouble getting in touch with any of Jenny's close friends. Poppy, Beatrice, Fran and..."

He blinked at the ceiling, his mind suddenly blank.

"Fortune," said Geoff, nodding. "Odd name, but a lovely girl."

"That's the one. We're just checking boxes, trying to make sure everyone is safe. Can I ask—"

Porter almost screamed as the cat stood on its back legs, dug its claws into his thighs and proceeded to haul itself onto his lap like a mountain climber. The pain was unbearable, but the smell was worse. It was like somebody had eaten a bucketful of old trout and had explosive diarrhoea. He actually gagged.

"Do you mind?" Eileen said as the cat proceeded to tread.

"No," croaked Porter. "Can one of you tell me—*quickly* —what happened in September? With Martha Hansen-Andrews. I know the name but can't think from where. She was a friend of the other women? With Jenny and Fran?"

Eileen sighed, studying her hands, which were clenched in her lap. Geoff sniffed, staring past Porter at the net curtains and the miserable day beyond. It was a good thirty seconds before he started to speak.

"She used to be their friend," he said. "When they were at school. Fran met Jenny and the others at Bluebell, then they all moved over to CNS together. Martha was part of their friend-ship group from the start. We had her here for sleepovers countless times. She was the nicest of them all, if you ask me."

"Geoff!" spat Eileen. He ignored her.

"A sweet, sweet girl who didn't deserve what happened to her. What they did."

"What she did to *herself*," said Eileen. She gave Porter a pleading look. "Nobody blamed Fran for the incident. Everyone said it was an accident. There was an investiga-tion, you must know about it."

Beck the cat arched its back, seemed to vibrate, then proceeded to sneeze from *both ends*. The smell was like nothing else on earth.

"What happened?" Porter asked, urgently.

"Boys," said Geoff. "It all went wrong when they started dating. You know what girls are like when they're young, always fighting over squeezes and crushes."

"Squeezes and crushes?" said Eileen. "How old are you?"

"He knows what I mean. In high school, Jenny was the

queen of the pack. The top dog. Where she led, Fran and the others followed, including Martha. Jenny was always so charismatic when she was younger. Full of pep and vim and vigour."

Eileen put her fingers to her mouth and made a silent gagging motion that her husband missed.

"For a long time, she was dating a boy. I can't remember his name. Louie something. They had quite a romance, if the stories are to be believed."

Porter wheeled a hand through the air to encourage him to get to the point. The cat had collapsed onto its side now and it was anybody's guess whether it was still alive.

"Then at some point, I'm guessing the last year of school, Louie ended his relationship with Jenny and started dating Martha. She'd fledged those ugly duckling feathers by then and she was quite the pretty little thing."

Another gagging noise from Eileen.

"Well, that put a spanner in the friendship group for sure," he said. "It was never the same after that, not even when Martha and Louie parted ways. Jenny could have let it go, of course, but she never would. She wasn't a nice girl. Nice on the surface, maybe, and nice to look at, but deep down she was rotten. Like her mother. Unkind. She was a bully. And whatever my wife tells you, she did coerce Fran into quite a few things that she would never otherwise have done, including the drugs."

For the first time, Eileen conceded the point.

"And the incident you mentioned?" Porter asked. "The one in September?"

"I don't know everything about it," Geoff said. "All I know is that Martha moved away to go to university, but she didn't stick it out. She came back to Norwich in the Summer and tried to reclaim her old friendship group."

"They *were* friends," said Eileen. "I saw them all together, and Fran told us how nice it was to have her home. Jenny wasn't a monster, she was just a young woman. All was forgiven."

"Don't listen to my wife, she doesn't know what she's talking about. Always a rose-tinted view of the world, lives in a realm of pure fantasy."

"Which would explain why I've stayed married to you for so long," she said, with genuine anger. She looked at the cat on Porter's lap.

"Beck likes her tummy tickled."

"I'm not touching it," Porter said. "Sorry."

"Probably for the best," said Geoff. "She leaks a bit."

"*Leaks*?"

"It was a ruse," Geoff went on, his hand still on his wife's shoulder. "Jenny was playing nice because she was planning something. A few weeks ago, beginning of September, she invited Martha to a party or a gathering of some kind, with her and the girls one evening. Fran was there too. While they were out, something happened. Martha was badly injured."

"I remember," Porter said, the name finally clicking. "She got hit by a car, right?"

"Right. In the city. Nobody knows how but the driver of the vehicle says she ran right out in front of her. Dark clothes, a dark night, she didn't stand a chance of stopping in time. Martha wasn't killed but the head injuries she sustained that night put her in hospital for weeks. She still can't walk, can't talk."

"Jesus," said Porter. Eileen had put her face in her hands, although she seemed to be hiding rather than crying. "And what happened to Jenny and Fran and the others?"

"Nothing," said Geoff. "They had their story and they

stuck to it. Martha and Jenny had an argument, Martha bolted, she ran into the road. The driver didn't see anyone else nearby, it wasn't like the girl was pushed. But—"

"But nothing," said Eileen, slapping her hands into her lap again. "Why does everything have to be a conspiracy with you? Martha ran into the road, that's the end of it. Fran didn't do anything wrong, and neither did Jenny."

"Did Martha's family see it that way?" Porter asked.

"Would you?" Geoff replied. "I know Joffre Andrews, Martha's father, he did some work for me back in the day. He was furious with Jenny, always blamed her. He tried to have Jenny arrested, and when the police wouldn't touch her he tried to take her to civil court. He never got anywhere because she was nowhere near the crash—CCTV showed that—and all of the girls backed Jenny's version of events."

"Because it was the truth," said Eileen. "It's boring and tragic, but it's the truth. Not everything has to be a story."

"But he harassed them all for a little while. Sat outside their houses in his truck, posted letters through the door. I think he got in trouble for it."

"Did he ever hurt them, or threaten to?"

"Not as far as I know, although hurt doesn't have to be a physical thing, does it? Joffre's a big man, and he's quite intimidating when he wants to be."

Porter wrote a few notes then tucked the pad and pen back into his jacket. Beck the cat was fast asleep, its claws still deep in Porter's leg and dribble oozing from its mouth. He tried to stand up but the cat wouldn't budge.

"Thanks for your time," he said, jiggling his leg. "Can you let me know where Fran is living? I'll go check on her."

"She's been staying with her boyfriend," said Eileen. "Scumbag that he is. I'll find the address for their flat."

Porter was almost upright now and the cat was still

clinging on. He thrust his hips and it finally dropped, landing with a fart that was so loud it might have come from a person. He raced Eileen out of the room before the smell could reach him, opening the front door. The woman rummaged in the sideboard and pulled out a scrap of paper, handing it to him.

"We have another copy, you can have this one."

"I'll try hailing her by phone," said Geoff as he joined them. "But she won't answer if she knows it's us."

He sighed, and in the half-light of the hallway he looked genuinely heartbroken.

"I often wonder what Fran would be like now if she had never crossed paths with Jenny," he said. "I wonder what we would be like, too."

"I'll let you know as soon as we hear anything," Porter said, handing them a card. "And if there's anything else you think of, let me know. Try not to worry."

He stepped outside, sucking in fresh air like he'd been underwater.

"Oh," he said, turning back. "One more thing. Do you know where I can find Martha's dad? Joffre Andrews?"

CHAPTER NINE

"Shit," said Kett.

He ended the call but held onto the phone, closing his eyes for a minute while he collected his thoughts. Savage was driving, the wipers going full steam now that the rain had picked up.

"Bad news, sir?"

"That was Clare. Spalding says there's nobody at Fortune's student let. She lives with a housemate who's away at the moment. Camera from down the street shows her leaving yesterday late afternoon, just after five-thirty, dressed in jeans and a jumper. Nobody has seen her since. Beatrice Goodwin is unaccounted for too. She lives at home but she never came back last night. Dunst is on his way to speak to her folks. Porter's *en route* to Fran Herbert's flat now, she doesn't live at home anymore. Her parents haven't heard from her in a while."

He paused, chewing his lip for a second.

"I think we're looking at a mass abduction."

"Just hopefully not a mass murder," Savage replied.

Yeah, Kett thought. *But it's only a matter of time.*

"Where to now?" Savage asked.

They were approaching a junction, the DC's hand hovering next to the indicator. Kett checked his watch to see that midday had come and gone. He knew how time worked on cases like these, as if it had been greased. It was going to be midnight before they knew it.

"We need to work on the assumption that Jenny's killer is telling the truth," he said. "He has one or maybe more of the women, and if we don't get to them in time then he's going to kill them too."

"You know what this reminds me of?" Savage said. "Elsham, those teenagers."

"Yeah," said Kett. "I thought the same. But we've got one dead body already, I don't think this is a hoax."

"No, but it might be one of the girls doing this to the others?"

"It might," Kett said.

He lifted his phone again, navigating to his photos and opening the one of the note they'd found in Jenny Eyler's mouth. He read the last part aloud.

"'*Once upon a time, our princess, reborn, dances now with two strong men, but she won't dance for long. She won't dance past midnight.*' A princess reborn. Each one might be one of our missing women, and the dancing part feels like he's leaving us a clue. Any ideas?"

Savage shook her head, pulling to a halt at the end of the road. There was nothing coming but she didn't make the turn.

"Two strong men," Kett said. "Boyfriends? A father or brother?"

"Maybe there's more than one kidnapper?" said Savage. "We've seen it before, right? Figg and Percival and Still-water were working together to kidnap the newspaper girls.

Dancing with two strong men might be a reference to the two men who have her."

"I hope not," Kett said, wincing at the memory of Figg's knife sliding into his shoulder, slicing across his chest. "But it's good thinking."

He tried to fit the ideas together, to find a pattern. But these weren't jigsaw pieces, they were moving parts. There was a honk from behind them as a car waited to turn.

"Go left," Kett said. "Let's meet up with Porter at Fran Herbert's flat, try and get ahead of this thing."

Savage made the turn, accelerating fast. It was a long drive to Heartsease but the traffic was light and they made good time. They spotted Porter walking up Fran's street, drenched from head to toe, and when Savage beeped the horn he almost leapt straight up. She drove past close enough to spray puddle water onto his shoes, and when she pulled up fifty yards further down the road she was laughing.

"That was a little mean," said Kett.

"He looked like he could do with a wash."

She laughed again as she got out, slamming the door. By the time Kett had joined her Porter had reached them, and he didn't look happy.

"You should get yourself a car, sir," Savage said, laughing so hard this time that she snorted. She put a hand to her mouth. "Sorry."

"Remind me not to lend you my Mondeo again."

"At least you *have* a car," Kett said, giving Porter a look. "My Volvo still has holes in it."

Porter's face fell, and Kett opened his mouth to tell him it was a joke but stopped when a disgusting reek pushed its way into the back of his nose.

"What is that?" he said.

"What?" said Porter.

"That smell? It's like... I can't even think of any words that would do it justice. Like somebody's taken a dump in a barrel of fish."

"No idea," said Porter, blushing.

"Told you he needed a wash," muttered Savage.

The big DI wiped his hands down his trousers, glowering at her, before turning his attention to the block of flats which sat by the road.

"Fran's place is in there, number six on the right, top floor. Her folks say they haven't spoken to her much this year but she's been living here with a boyfriend. No answer on the phone."

"I'll take it," Kett said. "You head around the back, make sure nobody clears out. Savage, wait here and watch the door."

"Sir," they said together.

Porter stepped over the railing and cut across the lawn, disappearing down the side of the three-storey building. Kett made his way along the cracked concrete path to the communal doors. There was no buzzer but he didn't need one, the doors were open—one almost ripped clean off its hinges. He could smell the piss from inside before he entered, strong enough to make his eyes water. A single, severed bike wheel was chained to a cast iron radiator, but other than that the stairwell was empty.

Kett made his way up the stairs, doubling back on the landing past broken pots and split bags of rubbish, their contents strewn over the floor. The second floor was in better shape, plants doing their best to sun themselves on the balcony and a couple of deck chairs set up on a rug. The door to the left had no number and the one on the right said it was number nine until he swung the brass digit upside down to its original place. He knocked, then immediately tried the handle to find that it was locked.

"Fran?" he called out. "Fran Herbert, my name is DCI Robert Kett. If you have a moment, I'd like to talk with you."

He held his breath, leaning in, but there was no sound inside the flat.

"You're not in any trouble," he said, his voice echoing back to him. "It will only take a second."

Nothing, and his heart was sinking fast. He knocked again, standing back when he heard a crashing noise—not from Fran's flat but from the one behind him, Number Five. He walked to the opposite door. It was in bad shape, the wood warped and splintered. When he thumped on it, it sounded like it was about to fall out of the frame.

"Police," he said. "Open up, I need a word."

Heavy footsteps on wood, walking slowly, getting closer. There was somebody on the other side of the door, Kett was sure of it. He looked at the viewing hole, wondering who was staring back.

"My name is DCI Kett," he said, pulling out his warrant card and holding it up. "Nobody is in trouble, I just need to know if you've seen your neighbour today. Fran Herbert. She's the young woman who lives in Number Six."

There was movement behind the tiny circle of glass, just a flash, but whoever it was they were walking away, the sound of their feet receding. Kett frowned, trying the handle. The door creaked open, chunks of wood falling from the frame. It wasn't rotten, Kett saw, it had been forced open with a crowbar or a chisel. Recently.

"Hello?" he said. "Police. Make yourself known."

The flat's narrow hallway was almost entirely bare apart from a pair of battered trainers that got caught beneath the door before it could fully open. Kett leaned through the gap, catching a whiff of weed.

"Tell you what, if you come and talk to me I'll ignore the drugs."

There was a scuffling sound from the other end of the flat. Kett walked past a small bedroom and a smaller kitchen, no sign of life. His heart was already pounding from climbing the stairs and the adrenaline made each beat a hammer blow of pain in his wounded chest.

"I really can't be arsed with this," he shouted as he pushed through the final door to see a large living room. A set of glass doors had been opened onto a patio that was laden with dead potted plants, but there was no sign of anyone here. It was as he was walking across the room he realised why.

"Oi, mate, don't be stupid."

It was Porter's voice, and it was coming from outside. Kett stepped onto the patio and peered over the rusted railing to see the big DI in the communal back garden. Halfway between them, hanging from the railing of the flat underneath, was a man. He was in his late twenties, dressed in nothing but a dressing gown. His legs flailed as he tried to find purchase, his lips puffing in exertion. He met Kett's eye and made a noise that might have been a word.

"Hi," said Kett, smiling. "Having fun down there?"

"Not as much fun as I am," said Porter, grimacing. "He's bloody naked under that dressing gown."

"Yeesh," said Kett. "You've got a view of the whole moon?"

"And a couple of planets, too," Porter said. "What's the smallest one again? Mercury?"

"Pluto," said Savage as she appeared from the passage. "It will always be a planet in my eyes."

She walked to Porter's side, looking up.

"I'm not sure that even qualifies as Pluto, to be honest. A space pebble, maybe."

"Space dust?" Porter offered.

The man grunted again, sweat rolling off him as he tried to pull himself back up.

"I'll see if I can find a ladder," Porter said.

"I'll get the fire service," Savage added, her phone already to her ear.

"You need a hand?" Kett asked.

"Fuck off," said the man. He spat at Kett, the gob of milky saliva arcing up and landing on his own forehead. His dressing gown was almost entirely undone, which wasn't great news for anyone looking out of the windows of the flats below.

"You got a name?"

"Fuck off!" he roared.

"Mr Fuck Off, do you want to tell me what on Earth you think you're doing?"

"Yeah," he said. "I'll fucking tell you—"

He pointed an angry finger at Kett and lost his grip on the railing, squawking as he spun earthwards. It was a good fifteen feet to the garden below, but fortunately for him there was a bush to break his fall. He hit it face first, his dressing gown spread out beside him like a pair of faulty wings, and loosed a scream of pure agony.

"He alright?" Kett said.

"It's holly," Savage shouted back.

Kett winced.

"I'll be right down. Stick some cuffs on him, will you?"

"Sure, sir, but I honestly don't think he's going anywhere."

Kett made his way back inside the flat, taking a second

to check the living room. There was nothing in here apart from a handful of folding tables, some plastic tubing and a lot of tin foil. The weed smell was stronger, though, fresher and sharper too. There was a massive circular hole in the ceiling by the far window, big enough for an extraction fan, which told Kett everything he needed to know.

There was nothing of note in any of the other rooms so he cantered down the steps and out through the front doors. By the time he'd reached the garden, Savage had managed to pull the young man out of the holly bush and cuff him. It probably wasn't necessary, because he was curled up in a ball and mewling like a kitten.

"Right," Kett said as he ducked down beside him. "Name."

"Phil," the man said. "Spenser."

"Your *real* name," Kett said.

"It is. It's the same as the fella from the telly, but with an *s* not a *c*. Can you call an ambulance for me? My cock feels like it's been shredded. I'm too scared to look."

Kett nodded to Savage, who walked away to make the call. Behind her, Porter was climbing over the low fence from a neighbour's property with a ladder over his shoulder.

"You're too late," Kett said, and the DI wheeled around to take it back. Kett turned his attention back to Spenser. "Let me see your face."

The man's head pushed free of his dressing gown like a tortoise emerging from its shell. He screwed his eyes shut against the miserable light, his mouth a perfect inverted smile. Most of the hair on his head had gone, and his face was red from a recent shave. With his thin neck and his skinny body, he didn't actually look a million miles away from the TV presenter he shared a name with.

"You got ID, Phil?"

"Yeah, sure, it's right here up my fucking arse," he spat back. "What do you think?"

"What I think is that you were running some kind of hydroponics lab up there. Marijuana. That's why you thought perforating your balls in a holly bush would be better than opening the door. But you've recently cleared everything out. Did you know we were coming? Did you have a hunch that there would be coppers here today? Anything to do with Fran, perhaps?"

"Fran?" Spenser said. "Fuck's that?"

"The young woman who lives opposite you, with her boyfriend."

"Womack's bit of fanny? Don't speak to her. What's she done?"

"I don't know," Kett said. "I was about to try to find out, but I got distracted. Have you seen her today?"

Spenser shook his head, managing to roll himself into a sitting position, his hands secured behind his back. His stomach was slick with blood from the holly bush, the scratches red-raw and angry. It made Kett think about Jenny Eyler, torn apart by brambles.

"You're not here for me, then?"

"Should I be?" Kett said, and Spenser shook his head.

"Not doing anything wrong. Flat's empty."

"Then let me ask you again, have you seen Fran today?"

"No."

"Have you seen her at all, recently?"

"Like, yesterday I think," he said.

"You think? What time?"

There was the bleep of a siren from the other side of the flats, although Kett couldn't see who it was.

"Morning," Spenser said. "Right after I got up. About half one."

"In the morning?"

"Yeah. Well, no, I guess that's the afternoon, but morning for me. She was just going out her door. I was looking through the hole-thing. She didn't see me."

"Was she with anyone?"

Spenser shrugged.

"Not that I saw."

"Not her boyfriend? Womack?"

"Like I said, no."

"What was she wearing?"

"Fucking *clothes*," he said with a shrug. "Dress, jacket, shoes."

"For a night out?"

"Yeah, I guess."

Shouts echoed between the buildings as a handful of firefighters appeared. Kett stood up, his knees cracking.

"Sorry lads, gravity did your job for you."

"No worries," said the man at the front. "Your guy just told us he'd taken a cheese grater to the cock or something, had to see it for ourselves."

"Holly bush," Kett said, and the men all pulled faces.

"Next time use the stairs, yeah?" said the firefighter. "Need us for anything else?"

"Actually, while you're here, can you get the door of Number Six open for me? Save me using my boot."

"Sure thing," said the man, heading back the way he'd come.

Kett looked down at Spenser, who was close to tears.

"I guess that just leaves the one question," he said. "Why were you running?"

"You promise you won't care if I tell the truth?"

"I couldn't care less about you," Kett said.

"I thought you were them, coming back."

"Them?"

"Blokes who done me over last time. Came and took everything a couple of days ago. All me gear, all me plants. Smashed in the door and robbed me blind and threatened to kill me if I told."

"This was here?" Kett said. "In the flat?"

Spenser nodded.

"Who were they?"

"Some stupid fucking local crew," he said, leaning forward and speaking quietly. "Simon Womack, slimy fucker across the way, he used to work with me but I think he fuckin' shafted me. Think he started rolling with the Beggars."

"Beggars?"

"You know, Beggar Boys. Fucking pricks. He must have told them about the... about the things I had in the flat, because they done me over. Thought they were going to do it again."

Savage was wandering back over, one ear on the conversation.

"Ambulance *en route*," she said. "Why did you think they were coming back? The crew who robbed you the first time."

"Heard them, didn't I?" Spenser said. "Least I thought I did. Shouting and yelling and stuff. Thought they were coming back to finish me off. But it wasn't them, it was coming from over the way."

"Over the way as in Simon and Fran's flat?" said Kett.

"Yeah. Whole ruckus. No idea what it was about."

"When was this?" Savage asked. "Exactly."

"Just now," he said, taking a forlorn peek down the front of his dressing gown. "About twenty minutes before you lot showed up."

CHAPTER TEN

"It's empty."

Kett turned around at the sound of Porter's voice. The DI was walking down the hallway from the living room inside Fran's flat, peeling off his latex gloves. He stuffed them inside his trouser pockct, shrugging.

"No sign of Fran or her boyfriend, Womack."

"He's known to us," said Savage from inside the kitchen.

"Yeah," said Kett. "Drugs, right? The fella next door said they used to work together before Womack jumped ship."

"We picked him up on a handful of drugs charges, possession but not intent. Arrested once, never charged. Things must have got a little more serious if he started working with the Beggar Boys."

"They're big league?" Kett asked. Savage shook her head.

"Hardly, but they don't mess around."

"Whatever else Womack is doing, he's got a job," said Porter. "If his payslips are right then he works in the Lidl down the road. Drives a gold 306."

"Find him," Kett said.

Savage nodded, squeezing past. Kett heard her clattering down the steps and the sound of her voice as she called somebody on the phone. He took another look around the flat but there wasn't much here. Either Fran and her boyfriend had been the messiest people ever or the place had been turned over. Kett suspected it was the former, because the sink was clogged with old toast crusts and the bin was overflowing. Somebody had left a turd in the toilet that was as big as a battleship.

"You think this is our man?" Porter asked, and it took Kett a moment to work out that he wasn't referring to the turd.

"Womack? Maybe. But whoever it is, they showed up here in the middle of the day making a lot of noise." Kett shook his head. "I don't know. That seems sloppy, careless."

He walked to the stairs, peering down the gap between the flights.

"But we know he's bold. We know he doesn't mind taking risks. He dumped Jenny's body in a public place. Anyone could have seen him."

"Maybe he doesn't care if he gets caught," Porter said. "Maybe he *wants* us to find him."

"I don't know."

Kett sighed, rubbing his chest. The pain from Keefe's bullet was growing worse and he didn't know why. It was probably his body telling him to slow down. It was probably his body telling him that he'd made a mistake coming back to the job.

"You mentioned another girl, the one who was injured. Martha somebody?"

"Yeah," said Porter. "Martha Hansen-Andrews. Hit by a car a couple of months ago, in September, while on a night out with Jenny and her friends. Suffered massive head trauma. The dad always blamed Jenny."

"That's motive," said Kett, thinking about his own girls, thinking about what he'd do to somebody who hurt them.

What he *had* done.

"Something like that would make you a desperate man, wouldn't it?" Kett asked.

"I think something like that would make you capable of anything."

"Then he's our next stop. What's his name?"

"Joffre Andrews."

"You got anyone on him?"

"Clare has," said Porter.

"Sir?" came Savage's voice from the next flight down. She poked her head over the railing, looking up. "Simon Womack's Peugeot isn't on the street, and he hasn't shown up at work today. But somebody's just called in a car on fire across town. A gold 306. That's some coincidence."

"Or not," said Kett. "Let's check it out."

THEY SAW the smoke from a mile away, towering over the trees and the buildings of the busy Ipswich Road. By the time they'd reached the Holiday Inn just outside of town the street had been completely closed off, a sea of flashing blue lights blocking the way and a frazzled PC trying to direct people through the hotel's crammed car park.

"Down there," the constable shouted to Kett when he leaned out of the window. She pointed to a track opposite the hotel, almost lost between the trees that grew there, and Porter steered the Mondeo around a tight corner into the woods. That was as far as he could go, though, as the rear end of a fire engine sat in their way.

As soon as Kett got out of the car he could smell the smoke. He skirted around the fire engine, almost slipping on the muddy bank. The firefighters had managed to put the fire out but it was far too late for the little car. It was a blackened shell with only smudges of dirty gold still visible, the tyres burned away, the windows shattered and the interior melted beyond recognition. The air reeked of burnt plastic, Kett's eyes watering uncontrollably as he stumbled across the car park.

"You stalking us?" yelled one of the firefighters. He pulled off his mask and Kett saw that it was the same man he'd spoken to just half an hour ago at the block of flats. Kett smiled and lifted and hand in welcome.

"Safe?" he asked, and the man nodded.

"It's out. We got lucky, there was barely any fuel in the tank."

"Arson?"

The firefighter nodded sadly. He stood to one side, gesturing at the Peugeot's driver's seat, and Kett actually felt like he'd been kicked in the stomach when he made out the shape there, charred and twisted but undeniably human.

"Murder," said Kett.

"We won't know for sure until we get our forensic team out here," said the man. "But from experience, I'd say this was a lazy job. Somebody cracked open the window, doused the interior with petrol or lighter fluid, and tossed in a match. You'd be surprised how easy it is. The inside of your car is a bloody tinderbox. Carpets, seat foam, windscreen wiper fluid."

"Is the body a woman?" asked Savage.

"I don't know. It's impossible to tell, and it's still too hot to get inside."

"Can you see if they were tied up?" Savage said.

"Nope."

"She'd have to be, right? Otherwise, she'd have got out when the fire started."

"Unless she was already dead," said Kett. He sighed, taking in the rest of the car park. There were three other cars, filthy with soot and smoke.

"Was anyone else here when you arrived?"

"Just the woman who called it in," said the firefighter, nodding up a wooded hill. "I told her to move back but she said she'd wait. She's up there."

"Thanks," Kett said. He coughed, his lungs aching from the poisonous air. "Kate, Pete, take a look and see if you can find a note, like the one we found with Jenny and the one in Poppy's house. If this is our killer he'll have left us one, I'm certain of it."

"Sure thing, sir," Savage said.

"Then go speak to Joffre Andrews, Martha's dad. And take a couple of Uniforms, just in case. He's a good fit for this, I think. I'll meet you back at HQ. We need to start getting some of this on the wall."

He watched them go, the mechanism of his mind stuttering and stalling. There were already too many moving pieces in this case, an engine of suspects and clues that was too complex for him to see clearly. One missing person was bad enough. A murder was worse. But this was something else. Four missing people meant an exponentially larger number of suspects to rule out. They simply didn't have the time—not if the note was right, and midnight was their deadline. He looked at the hill that walled off the back of the car park, littered with sickly trees.

"Up there?" he asked, and the fireman answered with a nod.

It was surprisingly hard work, the slope steep and the terrain treacherous. It wasn't just the tree roots, it was the dog shit—the floor was caked in it, some in bags, the rest quietly rotting. The smell was overpowering, making it hard to see as he grabbed at branches to pull himself up. By the time he got to the top he was sweating, his shirt sticking to his skin.

The woods here were just as dense and it took him a moment to spot the grey-haired woman who sat on the trunk of a felled tree thirty yards away. At her feet sat a Dalmatian, its dark eyes already on Kett. He could hear it growling from where he was. The woman heard it too, suddenly alert as she squinted through the trees.

"Hello?" she said.

"Hi," Kett replied, still breathless. "Sorry, it's a bit of a climb."

"You should try the path," the woman said, pointing to the side. "Right there. Much easier."

"Thank you. That is definitely some information I could have done with five minutes ago."

"That hill's a bit of a toilet," the woman said, hopping down. "It's where all the dogs go when they jump out of the car."

"Noted," said Kett, pulling out his warrant card. "DCI Kett, Norfolk Constabulary."

"Matilda Faire," the woman said. "Dog walker."

She laughed quietly at her own joke, pushing a strand of hair away from her face with a hand that was visibly trembling. Her hair was a striking shade of silver, but it must have been dyed that way because she was only in her thirties. She caught him looking and rolled her eyes up as if to study her own head.

"My mother's fault," she said. "She went grey at twenty-one. I made it to twenty-four. I used to hate it, but now I kinda like it."

The Dalmatian had stopped growling and was sniffing Kett's shoe, its tail thumping. He reached down and let it sniff his hand before scratching its ear.

"Sorry to keep you," Kett said. "And sorry you had to see..."

He looked back for a second, the column of smoke still rising.

"Sorry you had to see that. It can't have been easy."

The woman laughed again, an edge of panic to it.

"I'd ask if they were okay," she said. "But I don't think there's any way."

Kett shook his head.

"Can you tell me what you saw?"

She lifted the same hand, but this time it was to bite her thumbnail.

"I was just walking back to my car when that one pulled in. I was on the path, so not a clear view or anything, but I noticed it because my first boyfriend had a gold car. A Punto. You don't see them so much. Merryweather here was about to roll in some fox shit."

She stopped, her eyes widening with worry.

"Sorry, *poo*. Fox poo. So I was distracted. But I heard shouting."

"Shouting? From the car?"

"Yeah. I wasn't worried, though. You hear it all the time here. *'Peppa, get back in the car!' 'Waldo, let go of that squirrel!'*"

She laughed quietly again, through gritted teeth. Her eyes scrolled the trees, seeing something else.

"But then I heard a scream and the car was on fire. It happened so quickly, in a second. You wouldn't believe it."

She put a hand to her mouth. Sensing her distress the dog nuzzled her leg, whining. It looked at Kett as if he was responsible.

"Did you happen to see who was in the car?" he asked. "Who was driving? Was it a young woman?"

He was reaching for his phone to find a photo of Fran Herbert, but he stopped when Matilda shook her head.

"It wasn't a young woman," she said. "Definitely not. It was a man."

"The person in the driver's seat was a man?"

"I'm sure of it," she said. "One hundred percent. He was young, I think. Dark hair, black hoody. He had a tattoo on his neck, a face or something. Then..."

She swallowed hard and Kett let her find the words.

"Then he was gone, just like that. He was looking at me. He was looking at me when he was burning and I wanted to do something but I... I froze."

The Dalmatian barked, loud enough to make every muscle in Kett's body suddenly contract. Matilda ducked onto her haunches and wrapped the dog in a hug, pushing her face into its flank.

"There was nothing you could do," said Kett. "Nothing anyone could do. This isn't on you, Ms Faire."

He knew his words were meaningless, though. The guilt would follow her for the rest of her days.

"Did you see anyone else?"

"Yeah," she said without hesitation. "Another man. He was running from the car but I saw his back."

"You remember what he looked like? Clothes, hair colour, age?"

"Big guy, I think," she said. "I'm not sure. He moved like a bear."

"How so?"

She shrugged.

"Like, lumbering. I don't know. He wasn't athletic, he was struggling. Not like an injury or anything, just like he wasn't very fit. Or did he have a limp? I'm sorry, I can't think. He was in black, I think. I don't know. A long coat. Or a cloak, maybe?"

"A cloak?"

"Yeah, and a hood. It looked like a monk's robe or something. Like a fancy dress outfit."

"Did you see his face?"

"No," she said. "He never looked back, and I didn't really pay him much attention because of the... because of the other man. I thought he was just running from the fire. But I think his hood came away from his head at one point. I saw grey hair, like mine. I *think*. Sorry, that's not much help."

"It's extremely helpful," Kett said. "Thank you. Did the police take your details?"

She nodded, and Kett pulled out a card, handing it to her.

"If you think of anything else, please let me know."

She sniffed, nodding again.

"I'll get one of the PCs to take you home. If that was your car down there, I'm afraid it won't be going anywhere for a while."

"Oh dear," she said. "Thank you."

"And it might not be a bad thing to have somebody meet

you at home," Kett said, tapping his head. "Something like this can get worse before it gets better."

"Merryweather will look after me," she said. "She always does."

The Dalmatian barked again, softer this time. Kett left them to it, pulling out his phone as he walked away. He aimed for the path this time, finding it a little way to his right and following its gentle arc down until the car park came into view. By the time the stench of smoke had entered his nose again, Clare had answered.

"It's going to be bad news," the Superintendent said. "You don't even have to tell me, my arsehole is tingling the way it always does when there's bad news."

"Your *what*, sir?"

"It's like it's psychic. Like the Oracle of Ancient Greece. Itchy arse? Definitely bad news."

"Sure it's not piles, sir? You do eat a lot of Bounties."

"No, Kett. It's my psychic arsehole. The story's in the news, did you hear? Hit the local broadcast a few minutes ago, they're already calling Jenny *Sweet Briar Rose*. I have no tossing idea how they found out about that. It'll be head-lining on the Nationals this evening. Which is why I can't take any more bad news."

"Well, it could be worse," Kett said. "There's a body in the car, but it's not Fran. It's not any of our women. Chances are it's Fran's boyfriend, Simon Womack. By all accounts a drug-dealing lowlife. A witness saw a man flee the scene, big guy, lumbering gait. Was wearing a cloak and a hood, but he may have had grey hair. Put the word out, he might not have gone far."

"Will do," said Clare. "That's surprisingly good news. You think it's our killer?

"I don't know why he'd be going after Simon Womack if

he's got the women," said Kett. "It doesn't feel like him. It might be drug-related, there's some heat between Simon and his Beggar Boys crew and some other gangs in the city."

"Anything else?"

"Nothing concrete, sir, but we're working on it."

"Work faster," Clare said. "For the sake of my tingly arsehole."

Kett shuddered as he hung up. He'd reached the car park, where the shell of the burnt-out car waited for him, the driver's blackened face pulled back into a Halloween grin. It was a terrible way to go, there was no doubt about it.

But there were worse ways, too.

Kett just hoped that Fran and the other women weren't about to discover that for themselves.

CHAPTER ELEVEN

SAVAGE SHUT THE CAR DOOR AND STRETCHED, FEELING something crick in her back. She waited for Porter to walk to her side, both of them staring at the brick block of flats in front of them while they gathered their thoughts.

It was quiet here, a few cars rattling over speed bumps behind them and pigeons warbling from the rooftops, but little else in the way of noise. A couple of kids played in the garden of the next block over, their faces and hands caked in dirt, their faces frozen. The girl waved and pulled a face before screaming with laughter as she ran back inside, her little brother toddling after her.

"They live there," said Porter, pointing to the ground floor flat that was home to the Hansen-Andrews family. He took the lead but Savage didn't follow straightaway. Porter glanced back at her. "You okay?"

Savage tried to smile but her face felt stiff, almost brittle. It felt like a mask that might snap at any time.

"Yes, sir," she said, and the lie floated between them for a handful of seconds before the wind caught it, pulling it up the street. She balled her hands into fists and Porter saw it.

"It's been a rough morning," he said, one eyebrow cocked. "You can sit this one out, if you want?"

Sit in the car with nothing but dead women and burned men in her head. It was bad company, and she waved him away.

"You remember anything about this?" she asked. "About the accident?"

"Yeah," Porter said quietly. "I mean, not much, because it was nothing to do with us. Martha was drunk, she fell into the road and got hit by a car. It was on the news for a couple of days, but only barely. Accidents happen, right?"

"Right," said Savage, uncertain.

She made her way down the path, trying to make sense of the shapes she saw behind the dark windows. Like the flats they'd visited earlier, this block had three stories. Unlike that one, though, these flats all had their own entrance. Number twenty-eight's was a PVC door that was more yellow than white, the frosted glass window cracked. There had been a cat flap here once but it had been removed, the hole covered with plywood. An old Hoover sat next to the door like a vagrant.

"You'd better knock, sir," Savage said, trying again for a smile. "I think I'd take the door out."

Porter did as he was told, rapping gently on the glass. He was answered by the sound of birds from inside, a chorus that seemed totally at odds with the run-down building. It was so loud that Savage thought it might be artificial until she took a step back and saw a finch sitting on the windowsill beside her. It tapped at the glass with its beak before darting away.

"Weird," she said.

She heard footsteps over the commotion, then the sound of a key turning in the lock. The door swung halfway then stuck, somebody tugging on it from the other side until it wobbled open. For a moment, Savage thought that the woman who stood in the darkness of the corridor was a bird too. She was dressed in a loose-fitting gown that caught in the wind, fluttering like wings. In her fifties, her face was sharp, her nose long and thin, and she angled her head forwards, tilting it slightly as she took in the two police officers at the door.

Then she stepped into the light and there was nothing bird-like there at all, just a woman who looked like she carried the weight of the world on her bony shoulders. She looked at Savage, then at Porter, and turned back to Savage.

"You're police," she said.

"DI Peter Porter," said Porter as they both held out their warrant cards. "This is DC Kate Savage. Are you Mrs Hansen-Andrews?"

"No," said the woman. "Just Hansen. Sue. Other half is Andrews."

"Is this a good time to talk?" asked Savage.

"Good as any," the woman replied, pulling her dressing gown around herself as she stepped back. "I'm amazed you remember who we are."

Savage didn't know how to reply to that, so she stayed quiet as she entered the house.

"Just keep your shoes on," said Sue. "Bird shit everywhere, sorry. Don't open any doors until I've got this one closed or the little buggers'll get out."

She pushed the stubborn front door closed with some force, shouldering it for good measure.

"Nothing in this shithole actually works," she said as she edged past them. "But you didn't exactly leave us with much, did you?"

There was anger in her voice, quiet but unmissable. Savage glanced at Porter and he shrugged.

"Brace yourself," Sue said. "They won't hurt you."

She opened the closest door and a handful of birds immediately flew out. One landed on Porter's head and he screamed, ducking like he was under attack. Another perched weightlessly on the front of Savage's suit jacket, studying her for a second with dark, intelligent eyes before flying off again. The noise they were making was unreal, surely too loud to come from such delicate creatures. Savage gently waved one away from her hair as she followed Sue into a large room.

There, all thoughts of the birds left her head.

It was a living room, but only just. In the centre of the space sat a hospital bed, so out of place here that Savage felt a rush of vertigo, like she'd just realised she was in a dream. The young woman in the bed seemed dead. That was Savage's first thought. Surely somebody so pale, so still, so quiet, couldn't still be alive. She felt another immense jolt of panic at the thought, before her logical mind caught up.

The woman wasn't dead, of course. She was sleeping.

Like Sweet Briar Rose, Savage thought, picturing Jenny in her shroud of thorns.

A blanket had been pulled up to the top of the woman's chest but it wasn't enough to conceal how thin she was, how much of her had been eaten away. Birds alighted on her face, sitting there like she was a stone statue. There were streaks of bird droppings in her hair, matting it.

Savage put a hand to her mouth before she could stop herself, and Sue saw it.

"You didn't know?" the woman said as she moved to the sleeping woman's side. She chased the birds away. "What are you doing here, then?"

"I'm sorry," said Savage. "This is Martha?"

The woman nodded, brushing the hair away from the girl's face. Savage saw the scar that ran from the top of her skull down to her left ear, a ridge of mangled skin.

"My Martha, yes. My sleeping beauty."

Savage met Porter's eyes again.

"Sleeping beauty? Why did you call her that?"

"Why do you think? Pretty obvious, isn't it? She's always been beautiful, till they did this to her. But you lot made it pretty clear you don't give a shit about all that. Which leads me to the question, why are you here?"

Savage opened her mouth to answer, but Porter beat her to it.

"Do you know Jenny Eyler?"

Sue actually spat, the spittle catching the light as it arced to the floor. A bird landed on her shoulder, pecking gently, but if she noticed it there she made no sign of it.

"You really are ignorant, aren't you?" she said. "After everything we've been through, everything we've lost. You took it all from us. Our daughter, our family, our life. And you have the temerity to show up here completely oblivious to our pain."

"I'm sorry," Savage said. "It must be incredibly hard for you. We're here as part of another investigation, we weren't involved with your daughter's case."

She took a step towards the woman and the bird took flight, escaping with a flurry of wingbeats. Savage felt the thrum of it as it passed her face, surprisingly powerful.

"I'm not sure what happened when you dealt with the police before, but I can promise you, we're here to help."

"Of course you are," said Sue with no small amount of bitterness. "That's all you do, promise to help. Then you disappear, every last one of you. You do nothing."

Martha stirred, her body writhing beneath the blanket. Sue tutted, turning her attention to her daughter, running a hand down her cheek and attempting to hush her.

"She's still Martha in there," she said, quieter now. "The doctors tell me otherwise, but I know it. She's still there, and you're upsetting her. She talks sometimes, you know that? She speaks to me. It's her, it's my little girl."

"We just need to ask a couple of questions, then we'll go," said Porter. "Jenny Eyler? You thought she was to blame for what happened to Martha?"

"I don't think it, I *know* it," she said. "She did this to Martha and she got those other girls to lie about it. She hurt her then covered it up. But nobody believes me, everyone believes that wicked girl and her lies."

"Could you give us your version of what happened?" Savage asked.

"What's the point? You must have thousands of pages of my testimony, for all the good it did. They pushed her in front of that car. I know it, *she* knows it."

The birds had broken into a chorus again from elsewhere in the flat. Sue looked up, licking her lips.

"Is your husband here?" Savage asked. "Joffre Andrews?"

"No," she said. "He hasn't been here for days. He's given up on us."

"Do you know where we could get hold of him?" Porter asked.

She licked her lips again, her brow creasing for a moment before she shook her head. Nothing else followed, she just gently stroked her daughter's face.

"Could you maybe tell us what you think happened to Martha?" Savage prompted.

Sue looked like she was going to object, then she sighed.

Savage could see the anger that burned inside her, the words that boiled towards the surface. She knew Sue was holding back but only because she'd trained herself to. Only because it hurt too much to let go.

"She'd only just come back from uni," she said, slow and controlled. "It was too much for her. She missed it here, our old house, her so-called friends. She held it together for the first year but she didn't want to go back. Maths. It's so hard. I told her it didn't matter. I told her she could quit, that she could stay here for as long as she wanted."

She balled her fist into a hammer, striking the air in front of her.

"I should have sent her back. None of this would have happened if I'd sent her back."

"The accident—sorry, *incident*—happened in September?" Savage asked.

"Yeah. September Fourth. It was a Friday. Martha had connected with Jenny again over the summer. I always hated that girl. She'd run hot when she wanted something from somebody then ditch them when it would do the most damage. A narcissist, a sociopath. That's why I didn't mind Martha going all that way for university, because she'd get away from *her*. But Martha always clung onto some hope that they'd be friends. She was so excited that Jenny wanted her to go out with them over the summer, so happy to be back in Norwich."

She rubbed her face with her free hand, everything shaking.

"On... on *that night* they were supposed to go to the Waterfront for some Nineties event, at least that's what Jenny told her. But they never made it."

"What happened?" Savage asked.

"It's all on camera. The police checked it. They went

for a drink at the Bell first, then another at the Garnet by the market. Martha texted me from there, the last I ever heard from her. Just after eleven. Said she loved me, that she was happy, that they were just about to go to the club. But they didn't go that way, because an hour later she was lying on the street halfway across the city, good as dead."

"She ran in front of a car?" Porter said.

"She was *pushed*," Sue replied without missing a beat. "Right at the bottom of those steps. One of those girls pushed her, I know it."

"Steps?" Savage asked.

"By St Lawrence's, the church."

"That's definitely the wrong side of town for the Waterfront. What were they doing over there?"

Sue scoffed, as if Savage was a child.

"Funny how you're so interested in that question now, when you didn't give a shit when I asked it two months ago. The girls all said they were heading to the club, they all gave the same answer and not one person asked why they were all the way over there."

Savage found that hard to believe, but she bit back on her comment.

"I'm sorry," she said again. "I'll take a look at the case, see what I can find out."

Even though she wasn't looking at Porter, she didn't miss the expression on his face.

"The investigation didn't find any evidence that Martha was pushed in front of the car, Mrs Hansen," he said. "And there was no indication that Jenny and the other women caused her accident. The CCTV footage *cleared* them, in fact."

"That's more like it," Sue said. "That's the Norfolk

Police I've come to know and love. Full of compassion, this one."

"Can I ask," Savage said, trying to diffuse the growing tension, "did you see Jenny much after the incident?"

"Enough," said Sue. "Enough to know that this was her. She came here once, do you know that? She actually turned up at the door and asked to come in."

"You let her?"

She seemed shocked by the question, then angry.

"I didn't know what else to do, so yes, I let her in. Because Martha knew she was here. She *reacted* to her."

Savage frowned, and Sue scoffed.

"No, nobody believes me, but she did. Like I said, Martha's still in there. She's still *her*. The second she saw Jenny she started to make noises, words."

"What did she say?"

"I wasn't close enough to hear. But I'll tell you what *Jenny* said. She said she was sorry. She apologised. That's what guilty people do, isn't it? They apologise because they've done something wrong."

She put a hand to her mouth like it might be the only thing to stop her unwinding. Savage took a breath.

"Sue, we're here because Jenny Eyler was found dead this morning. Murdered."

Sue's reaction was slight, but it was unmistakable. This was news to her. She looked from Savage to Porter before closing her eyes.

"You're sure it's her?" she said.

"We are," Porter replied.

"Thank God," Sue whispered, clasping her hands together. "Thank you."

"You're happy she's dead?" Savage asked.

"I'm delighted," Sue replied, glaring at them. "And I hope it hurt like hell. I hope it hurt like hell."

"Can I ask you where you were yesterday, between four and eight pm?" asked Porter.

"Right here," Sue said. She was smiling, but her eyes were bloodshot with tears. "I never leave her side."

"What about your husband?" said Savage.

She didn't answer, she just turned to the bed.

"Did you hear that, Martha? She's gone. Jenny's gone. You don't have to worry about her anymore. Not ever."

"Mrs Hansen?" Savage prompted. "Your husband?"

There was a tiny drumbeat of wings as the birds chased each other into the room, darting back and forth so fast it was a wonder they didn't hit the walls. Two of them landed on the sleeping girl, fighting on her chest as it rose and fell. Another landed on the shape of her arm beneath the sheet, then hopped onto Sue's shoulder. The sound of them was almost deafening.

"Please," Savage said. "It's not just Jenny. They're all missing. Fran, Beatrice, Poppy and Fortune. We think somebody has taken them. If there's even a small chance that Martha's father has something to do with this, you can help us. You can help save them."

"Like they helped my girl?" Sue said, that strange smile still carved into her face. "Like they helped save her, like they helped tell the police the truth about what happened to her? No. I don't think I have anything to say."

"Then maybe we should bring you in," Porter said, taking a step towards the woman. "You can come with me right now and we can ask you the same questions down the station."

It was harsh, but it worked.

"Threaten the grieving mother," she said. "Why not, eh?

I wouldn't expect anything else from you lot. You ever wonder if that's why somebody killed that foul girl? Because Jenny deserved to die and you didn't have the guts to do it?"

"That isn't what we do, Mrs Hansen," said Savage.

"Well somebody did it. I hope you never catch him. And if it was Joff who did it, good for him. I hope he kills them all."

"Where is he?" Porter asked, no patience there anymore.

"The only place he ever is these days," Sue replied. "Up his allotment. No end of shit to clear. Those brambles run wild this time of year."

And in the soft light of the room, beneath a storm of whirling finches, the smile on her face seemed to grow.

CHAPTER TWELVE

KETT CLIMBED OUT OF THE IRV INTO THE COLD, DAMP afternoon, the pain needling between his ribs like a toothpick. He hesitated for a second before gingerly closing the door, enough time for Porter to jog over.

"Give me a second, sir," the big DI said. "I'll have one of the constables grab you a Zimmer Frame and a hot water bottle."

"Piss off," Kett growled. "Where is it?"

Porter nodded up the street to where two more IRVs waited, their lights off. Savage stood with a civilian woman who was pointing past a row of houses. They were right at the top of the city here, Norwich rolled out beneath them and the spire of the cathedral puncturing the unsettled sky.

"That's Joffre Andrews' allotment right there," said Porter. "Martha's mother, Sue Hansen, gave us the address. We've got another unit coming up from the south in case he makes a break for it."

"Armed?"

"No, but Clare's working on it."

"You got a photo of this guy?"

Porter pulled out his phone, swiping through a couple of pictures before holding it up. On the screen was a wide, blunt-faced man who looked like he was posing for his mug shot. His hair was cropped short, and although it was black it was shot through with a lot of grey. He looked a little like a bear.

"Matches the man our witness described," Kett said. "The guy who incinerated Simon Womack inside his car. Anyone gone in yet?"

"We were waiting for you."

Kett started walking, ignoring the people who stood in open doorways or watched with blank faces through their windows. A couple of cars honked at the IRVs that blocked the road, a PC doing her best to turn them away. Even with the lights and sirens off they weren't exactly being subtle. If Joffre Andrews was here, he'd had plenty of warning.

And plenty of time to get away.

"You know which plot is his?" Kett asked as they walked past the final house in the row. The grid of allotments stretched down the hill, pockmarked with sheds of all shapes and sizes. A handful of people looked back at them, spades in their hands. The only other building in sight was a squat little scout hut with a tin roof.

"No," Porter said. "But it's in there somewhere."

"Helpful," Kett said. "Savage, anything?"

"Apparently his pitch is halfway down," she said.

"Little less," said the woman Savage had been talking to, brushing dirt from her hands. "I think it's that one with the flag."

Kett squinted, seeing a dog-eared Union Jack hanging limply from a metal pole. There wasn't much more life in the potting shed that sat beside it, or in the allotment pitch itself, which looked barren.

Like it had just been cleared.

"I thought he was here all the time," Kett said.

"That's what Martha's mum told us," Porter replied with a shrug. "Maybe he's just a shit gardener."

"Or maybe he needed those brambles for something else," added Savage.

Kett cut past a parked car onto a dirt track, walking quickly. Porter whistled and the PCs jogged with them, hands on their batons.

"If Andrews is our man then he's extremely dangerous," Kett shouted back. "Do not engage him, just contain him. Is that clear?"

A murmur of replies. There was a gate in the chain link fence and Kett pushed it open so hard that the elderly man in the nearest allotment almost fell into his runner beans in surprise. Kett broke into a jog, weaving through the narrow paths and leaping the low fences.

"Police!" he roared as he approached Andrews' shed. "Stay where you are!"

He grabbed the handle to find it locked, then stepped back and used his boot. The flimsy shack didn't stand a chance, the wooden frame squealing in outrage as the door collapsed inwards. There was so much dust that it took Kett a second or two to work out that the building was empty.

"Bollocks," he said, coughing hard as he backed away. "Porter, check it out, bag anything that looks suspicious."

Porter groaned. Kett scanned the hill, searching the faces who looked back at him. None of them matched the photograph of Andrews.

"Savage, I need you to check out as many of these sheds as you can," he said. "Andrews may have been using an empty lot. Or he may have help. Start at the top and work down. I'll go the other way."

"Sir," she said, bounding off with a PC in tow.

"Keep your eyes peeled," Kett shouted as he walked down the hill. Two more Uniforms followed him and he directed one to either side.

"Check doors and windows. All of them. If he saw us coming he could be hiding."

The allotment was huge, expanding outwards in every direction. As he walked, more people appeared, elderly couples and young families.

"Joffre Andrews?" Kett asked them, but he was met with blank stares and shaking heads.

Pretty much every plot had a shed and he dutifully checked the doors as he went, peering through windows that were thick with grime. Towards the bottom of the hill the plots grew messier, the outbuildings barely standing. Old sofas and broken TVs littered the land like mutant crops, herring gulls scratching at the dirt in search of morsels, their cries painfully loud.

Kett checked another shed to find it empty, and he was closing the door behind him when he heard a cry from up the hill.

It was one of the PCs, a young man who was staggering back like he'd been pushed. He tripped, falling on his arse to reveal another man behind him. This one was bolting, looking like he was doing up his belt as he went. He was a hundred yards away so it was impossible to ID him, but his short, greying hair was enough to tell Kett that this was their guy. Joffre Andrews vaulted a bush, almost tripping, before barrelling down the hill in a lumbering, ungainly run.

"Oi!" Porter shouted. "Stop!"

Andrews ran through another allotment, sending a woman flying as he leapt a low fence. Porter was chasing him, Savage too, overtaking the big DI in a heartbeat. But for all his size, Andrews was fast, and he was fit.

And Kett was the only one standing in his way.

"For fuck's sake," he muttered. He stepped away from the shed, taking a breath. "Oi, Joffre, stop running!"

The man's eyes bulged when he saw Kett, but if anything he was speeding up—thirty yards now and closing fast. He put his head down, his breaths like cannon shots in the quiet air.

"Stop!" Kett said.

He wasn't going to. He was coming at Kett head-on, grunting hard. Twenty yards. His fists were bunched, his eyes still looking like they were being squeezed out of his skull.

"Last chance," Kett said, more to himself than to the other man.

Ten yards, then it was too late to do anything but brace. Kett stepped back as Andrews charged, his heel catching on something and pulling him off balance. He lifted his arms in defence, the knuckles of his left hand cracking into the man's nose.

Andrews let out a wet cry, then his shoulder crunched into Kett and the world flipped head over heels. Kett hit the wall of the shed and fell right through it.

He lay there for a moment, listening to the thunder of footsteps fade away, then rise up again as Porter and Savage and half a dozen PCs galloped past. One poked her head through the demolished wall of the shed.

"Need a hand, sir?"

"I'll be okay," Kett groaned, waiting for her to vanish before trying to sit up. "I think."

He grumbled his way to his feet, shaking the pain from the hand that had connected with Joffre Andrews' face. Stepping out of the ruined shed, he looked down the hill to see the man still running, dragging a tail of coppers behind him.

There wasn't much he could do to help so he started up the hill again, trying to remember which building Andrews had run from. They all looked the same, but it had been one on the far side of the green. Kett searched and found it, the shed's neat red door still open.

There was somebody else inside it.

A woman.

"Hey," Kett called out. "Police."

Was it one of the missing women? He couldn't be sure, he was too far away and the face was drenched in shadow. He wasn't even certain it was real until the head tilted upwards at the sound of his voice, dark eyes blinking.

"Wait there," Kett said, breaking into a jog. "Nobody is going to hurt you."

The woman vanished inside the shed, then reappeared. As soon as she was out in the daylight Kett realised she wasn't one of Jenny's friends. She was in her forties with dark, curly hair almost down to her waist. She was dressed in a velour tracksuit and trainers, a dozen different silver chains hanging from her neck. She held a terracotta flowerpot, and when she lifted it above her head Kett realised she was planning to use it as a weapon.

"Wait," he said. "You're not in any trouble."

"Says the man who's trespassing," she said. "Says the man who's chasing down my boyfriend. What do you want us for, eh? We haven't done anything wrong."

"Nobody is saying you have," Kett said, approaching carefully. "We just want to talk."

"Gonna be hard to talk when I smash your fucking face in," she said, brandishing the flowerpot.

"You really don't want to do that."

Kett pulled out his warrant card, holding it up until she reluctantly glanced at it. She made no attempt to back down, though, her knuckles white, her arm trembling with the weight of the pot.

"DCI Robert Kett, Norfolk Constabulary."

"You're him off the telly," she said, her teeth bared. "The one who killed that man."

Kett sighed, shaking his head.

"I—"

"Stay away," she said. "You ain't gonna put a hammer through *my* head."

She looked up the hill to where a crowd of spectators had gathered, most of them holding their phones up so they could capture the events happening below.

"Help!" she called out. "Help, he's threatening me!"

Kett puffed out a breath, trying to control his anger.

"He's going to hurt me," the woman yelled, her voice cracking. "Somebody help!"

"I'm not going to—"

Kett took a step towards her and she panicked, lobbing the pot at him with some force. He ducked, feeling it whisper past the top of his head, almost scalping him, before exploding on the ground.

"Fuck this," he said, lunging at her. The woman retreated, tripping with a squawk and landing on her backside.

"Help!" she screamed, Kett's ears ringing with the force of it as he moved in. "Help me! Somebody help me!"

"Somebody help *me!*" he said, gently flipping her onto her stomach and pinning her hands behind her back. "I think you've perforated my bloody eardrums."

"I'll perforate more than that, you fucking arsehole," the woman said. "Get off me."

"No chance."

Kett craned back, looking down the hill to see that Andrews was *still* running like a headless chicken, tying the police in knots as he sprinted back and forth. Up the hill, their audience was whooping and jeering, thoroughly entertained.

"What's your name?" Kett asked.

The woman squirmed in the dirt.

"If you want my name, get me a lawyer," she said. "I'm going to have your fucking balls."

"I have no idea what you'd want them for," Kett said.

"We ain't done nothing wrong. Nothing. Love isn't a crime. No matter what anyone says. Love isn't a crime!"

"No," Kett said. "But I'm pretty sure throwing a flowerpot at a police officer is."

He leant in.

"Not to mention kidnap and murder."

And at this, the woman finally stopped shouting.

CHAPTER THIRTEEN

"In all my years in the police, of all the tossing horror shows I've been a witness to, of all the empty-headed pisspots I've ever had the displeasure of working with, this takes the absolute biscuit."

Superintendent Colin Clare paced back and forth at the front of the Incident Room like he was trying to dig a trench with his brogues. His cheeks were glowing, the heat coming off him almost visible.

Kett sat in the second row of chairs, wincing at every word. His ears were still ringing, his head pounding after the incident at the allotment a couple of hours ago. The room was heated but he was soaked through from the rain, the cold nesting in his bones and making it painful to move.

In front of him sat Savage, while Porter had quite wisely taken a chair at the very back of the room. The rest of the space was filled with Uniforms and Detectives, all united in their desire not to be the one taking a bollocking from the boss.

Only Richard Johnson, the psychologist, looked happy.

He stood in the corner in his yellow shirt and *Bugs Bunny* tie with a smug smile on his face.

Clare stopped pacing in front of the TV screen mounted on the wall, where a YouTube video had been paused. Kett had no idea what was on it, but the view down the hill into the allotments made it pretty obvious it had been filmed during the arrest of Joffre Andrews.

"I've actually never seen anything like it," the Super said, spit flying from his lips. "Never. Not once. Not even in my worst nightmares."

He picked up a remote control from the desk in front of him and pressed play. Immediately the room was full of unkind laughter from whoever had been filming—teenage lads, by the sound of it. On-screen, Kett watched Joffre Andrews burst from the shed with the red door while still hoicking up his trousers, pushing over the policeman who had been knocking. He bolted down the hill, Porter and Savage giving chase. Kett saw himself in the distance, thankfully too blurry to make out in any detail. Andrews crunched into him, sending him flying into the shed and causing a phantom memory of pain in his chest.

"How many coppers does it take to catch one suspect with his pants around his ankles?" Clare said, aghast.

"It's not that bad," Porter replied. "You can hardly see anything."

"Is that so?" Clare said. "How about this one?"

He clicked out of the first video and loaded the next. One of the people standing on their allotment must have filmed this because it was much closer to the action. Kett saw Andrews running from right to left, followed by Porter and Savage and then by half a dozen other coppers. They disappeared off-screen then immediately came back again, running the other way.

In the row of chairs behind him, Kett heard Dunst wheezing with laughter.

"Does this look *not that bad*, Porter?" Clare said as the camera panned around.

Andrews was climbing onto a shed roof, yelling obscenities. One of the PCs ran after him but tripped, vanishing into a patch of lettuce. Then Porter was there, grabbing the man's leg and only succeeding in pulling his trousers back down. Beneath them, he was stark bollock naked. Andrews hurled himself off the shed like a wrestler, Porter diving out of his way with a squeak.

"He was naked," the DI grumbled. "No way I was going to catch him."

On the TV, Savage threw herself onto Andrews' back. But he was like a bull, kicking his trousers off completely and bounding away, Savage clinging on for a handful of seconds before sliding free. Then they were all off again, a line of police chasing Andrews and his flapping genitalia back up the hill. Dunst was now roaring with laughter, it was a wonder he could get a breath in.

"It's like something from a *Benny Hill* sketch," Clare said, finally ending the video. "It's only a matter of time before somebody adds the music."

"You haven't got to the bit where we actually catch him," said Savage.

"Because whoever posted this chopped that bit off," Clare said. "I don't have to tell you what this does for our public image. It's a joke. It shouldn't be this hard to catch one man."

"But we *did* catch him," Kett said, and Clare glowered at him.

"I haven't even got to you yet, *Bill or Ben*," he said.

"Huh?"

"The Flower Pot Men," Clare said. "The woman you apprehended seemed pretty convinced that you were going to try to put a hammer through her head."

"I wasn't—"

"It's making me have serious doubts about this whole thing."

Richard Johnson saw his opportunity, stepping out from the corner.

"I think this is a good moment to address the violence," he said in that insufferably quiet voice. "I thought I made it very clear that nobody was to be punched."

"Nobody *was* punched," Kett said.

"I beg to differ. If you could return us to the first video, Superintendent Clare, you'll see quite clearly that DCI Kett's fist connects with Joffre Andrews' face."

"His *face* connected with my *fist*," Kett said, lifting his hands in innocence. "I was trying to get out of the way."

"Unlikely," Johnson said. "Faces aren't magnetically attracted to fists."

"My fist is going to be magnetically attracted to your arse in a minute!" Clare said, causing a groan of disgust to ripple across the room. The boss looked like he was close to exploding, and even Johnson slunk back to his corner. Clare leaned on the desk. "If you lot fuck up one more time I'm going to ensure that you are all tossed off."

"Doesn't mean what you think it means," Kett muttered.

"The *Force*, Kett," Clare shot back. "Tossed off the Force! You'll be out. *Again!*"

Clare closed his eyes, everyone waiting in silence—except for Dunst, who was literally crying with quiet laughter.

"Right," Clare said, opening his eyes. "The good news is that we have Andrews. He's the closest thing to a lead so let's milk it. Kett, I want you and Savage in on the interview. Porter, question the woman he was with. If Joffre Andrews is our killer then God willing we can get those girls home before the end of the day."

KETT CLOSED the door behind him, turning to look at the interview room. It seemed smaller than he remembered, the illusion not helped by the man who sat on the other side of the table.

Joffre Andrews was big, his broad shoulders making it difficult for the reedy solicitor to sit comfortably beside him. His head was wide and weirdly flat beneath his salt and pepper hair, like somebody had chiselled him from a concrete block. His features seemed to be clustered in the middle and a nasty bruise had formed over the bridge of his nose. When he looked up there didn't seem to be any emotion at all in his eyes, as if they had been painted on his face. It gave Kett the creeps.

Savage took the seat closest to the recorder, firing it up and giving their names and the date.

"You ready?" Kett asked Andrews when she'd finished. "You declined to make a statement when we arrested you, how do you feel about that now?"

Andrews scoffed.

"I remember making plenty of statements," he said, his voice as dull as his eyes. "You've got a short memory."

"Can you tell us where you were yesterday, between say four and nine pm?"

Andrews shrugged, shifting his weight in the chair. He folded his hands over his barrel chest, sniffing.

"You're saying you don't remember?" Kett said. "Or you don't want us to know?"

"My client is choosing to—"

"You know Cow Tower?" Kett pressed, riding over the solicitor.

Another shrug, Andrews doing his best to look bored.

"How about Jenny Eyler?"

That caught his attention. He shifted his weight again, leaning forward.

"I haven't been anywhere near her," he said. "I don't give a shit what she's saying, I never touched her. Wouldn't waste my fucking energy on that evil little cunt."

"I never asked you if you touched her," said Kett. "Why would you assume that was what I was going to ask?"

Andrews swallowed, glancing at the wiry solicitor. Then he sat back with such force that his chair scraped across the floor.

"I think we need to clarify why Mr Andrews is here," said the solicitor. "Why was he arrested?"

"He was arrested for assaulting a police officer," said Kett. "But he's here because of Jenny. She was found dead this morning."

Kett watched the man's face for a reaction and found it. Andrews' mouth opened, just a fraction, his eyes widening. He looked at his solicitor again, moving his weight on the chair, restless.

"Now wait a minute," Andrews said. "I told you, I didn't touch her."

"When was the last time you saw Jenny?"

"Uh..." he wiped the back of his hand over his nose, wincing. "Not for a while."

"That doesn't help us, Joffre. Be more specific."

"Maybe three weeks." He sighed, shaking his head. "No, less than that. It was this month."

"Were you parked outside her house?" Kett asked, remembering the information that Porter had collected from Fran Herbert's parents. "Posting something through her door? Intimidating her?"

"No," he said through gritted teeth. "It was a coincidence. She was at the market, same as me. She didn't see me. We didn't talk."

"And before that?"

"I haven't been near Jenny. I've not been near any of them. It's too..."

The man's stone exterior broke, his face sagging. He wiped his hand over his nose again, his eyes wet.

"You do what you can for them, don't you? You fucking try. That bitch deserved to be in prison for what she did to Martha. And I know she did it. I fucking know it. She pushed my girl in front of that car. But she's a devil. She's a silver-tongued devil and she talked her way out of it. I did what I could for Martha, I tried to get her justice. But there isn't any, is there? There's no justice for girls like her, for people like us. I don't know what you think I'm guilty of, but I'm not. The only thing I'm fucking guilty of is giving up on Martha. I let them win."

"Jenny didn't win," Savage said. "She's dead. Murdered. How do you feel about that?"

Andrews' mouth opened, but nothing came out. The tears were rolling freely now, even though he scrubbed them away shamefully. He didn't seem like a giant anymore, he seemed like a broken thing, crumpled in his chair, his elbows on the table.

"I didn't do that," he said, sniffing hard. "I wouldn't. I hated her. I wanted the world to know what she'd done.

And yeah, I scared her a few times when the police gave up on us. But I wanted her to suffer, not to die."

"What about the others?" Savage said. "Fran, Beatrice, Fortune and Poppy? Did you scare them, too?"

"I..." His eyes wandered back and forth over the table. "Maybe Fran, because she was as bad as Jenny. But only once, on her street when I was in my car. I wasn't going to hurt her. And I was angry with them all for not telling the truth about my Martha. I hated them for that. But I never went near them, just Jenny. She was always the worst."

"Joffre, can you tell me what you think happened on the night that Martha was injured?" Kett said.

"She wasn't injured, she was *killed*," he spat back. "Her heart's still beating but there's nothing there. She's gone."

He slammed a fist on the table and everyone jumped.

"They killed my girl," he sobbed. "How are you supposed to deal with that? How can you keep going?"

Savage blew out a loud breath.

"Can we go back to our first question?" she said. "Where were you yesterday afternoon?"

"Round at Linda's. I live there now, pretty much."

"Linda is the woman we picked up today?" Kett asked. "The one who lobbed a flowerpot at my head?"

"You're lucky that's all she threw. Hell of a temper. Her pitch is just down the hill from mine, on the allotment. Well, you saw it. That's how we met. We've been friends for a long time and when everything happened with Martha she... I don't know. You've been to see Sue?"

Both Kett and Savage nodded.

"Those fucking birds. We used to have one but when Martha came home from the hospital, all empty, Sue got the rest. Thought they'd wake her up, somehow, the songs. But all they do is crawl over her, shit on her. You see that? She's always got shit on her. How is that good? I said it was them or me and Sue picked them, so I fucked off. I couldn't do it no more."

He used both meaty fists to rub away a fresh round of tears.

"Linda's not like that, she's not crazy like that. She talked me out..."

He paused, coughing wetly.

"Talked you out of what?" Savage said.

"Talked me out of doing something I would regret, talked me out of getting my own justice."

"Out of hurting Jenny?" said Kett, and he nodded.

"Yeah. Because it's there, right? It's there in anyone. Somebody hurts your child then all you want to do is hurt them. I'm not ashamed to say it, because I didn't do anything. Linda made me see how awful that would be, not just for me but for Martha too. Martha never would have wanted that, even after what they did to her."

He shook his head, struggling.

"I was there most of yesterday, round Linda's house, you can ask her. She's got kids, two lads, and they'll say the same. I play FIFA with the older one. They're good kids, you know? Made me think that maybe I might get a second shot at all this. I don't want to fuck that up. I'll never forgive Jenny, but I'd never kill her."

He turned his attention back to the table, studying it for some secret message. Then he looked at Kett.

"How did she die?"

"Horribly," Kett replied. "Do you know anyone else who might have wanted to hurt her?"

He shook his head, but he answered anyway.

"She was a bitch. And she hung out with some shitty people. Some fella, I can't remember his name. Dealer.

Everyone said she'd fallen down the toilet, hanging out with druggies. You could try him. Fran was just as bad so you can ask her."

"What about Sue?" Savage added. "Your wife. Would she have tried to hurt Jenny?"

Andrews paused, his eyes still scrolling back and forth.

"No," he said, bluntly.

"You don't seem sure about that," Savage went on.

He didn't answer. He didn't even look at them.

"Just a couple more questions," said Kett. "Do you grow much on your allotment? It looks pretty bare to me."

"Everything's been harvested," he said. "Just getting it ready for next year."

"What about brambles? Blackberries?"

"What about them? Bloody things are everywhere. Everyone helps clear them but they just come back. Why are you asking about blackberries?"

"No reason," Kett said. "Last thing. You might be able to help us with something. Savage, have you got the note?"

Savage pulled out her phone, taking a moment to find what she needed.

"'*She dances now with two strong men, but she won't dance for long. She won't dance past midnight.*' Does that mean anything to you?"

His look of utter puzzlement would have been hard to fake.

"No idea, sorry."

"It's already hit the news, so I'm going to tell you," said Kett. "Jenny's friends are all missing. Poppy, Fran, Beatrice and Fortune. We think the person who killed Jenny may have taken them too. What you just heard was the only clue we were given. Think, because it might make the difference between life and death. Between another parent hugging their child goodnight or saying goodbye forever. Dancing with two strong men."

Andrews took a big, shuddering breath, leaning back and staring at the ceiling.

"This world is fucked," he said. "I wish the whole planet would just fucking burn."

"Joffre," warned the solicitor, but Andrews waved him away.

"Dancing with two strong men. Only thing I can think of is that place in the city, in Tombland. Did some work there a few years back and I can't remember the name of it. Got two statues by the door, couple of old people from the legends."

"The Samson and Hercules," said Savage, suddenly brightening. "The old dance hall. I completely forgot about it."

She pushed herself out of her chair, Kett right behind her.

"Interview terminated at 14:51," she said, clicking off the recorder. "Come on."

"What about me?" Andrews called out after them. Kett paused by the door.

"You can make yourself comfortable, mate. You're not off the hook yet."

CHAPTER FOURTEEN

"I'M SUCH AN IDIOT."

Savage slapped a hand to her forehead as they walked back into the bullpen.

"The Samson and Hercules. It's so obvious. You remember it?"

Kett shook his head, although the name did ring a bell. He made his way towards Clare's office as Savage carried on.

"It's been there forever, but it was a dance hall for a while. A ballroom, I think. It fits with our killer, right? Samson and Hercules are from stories."

"I don't know," said Kett. "It's a bit of a stretch. Greek myths and Bible legends aren't exactly fairy tales."

He raised a hand to knock on the door but Clare must have been waiting for them because it was ripped open, the boss' angry face appearing.

"I was watching on the monitor," he said, spraying shrapnel from the Bounty bar he was devouring. "I don't think it's Andrews. What about you?"

"Gut tells me the same," said Kett. "Hard to fake those

reactions. But I'm not convinced yet so don't let him go. Any word on his alibi?"

"Porter's talking to Linda Rosetti now, she's singing from the same hymn sheet. Backs up his alibi and so do her kids. I heard you talking about the nightclub, the Samson and what-not."

"Hercules, sir," said Savage. "Old building. I don't think it's being used at the moment."

"Weird that Andrews did some work there, though, don't you think?" said Kett. "Didn't Porter say that Andrews did some work for Fran's dad once, too? Something's not sitting right with his story and I can't figure it out. Don't let him go."

"You said that already," said Clare. "He's not going anywhere, don't worry. I need you both to check out the Samson and Hercules."

"If this is our place, sir, then the killer will be expecting us," said Kett. "He might not be there himself, but it could be dangerous."

"So be careful," said Clare, looking at Kett like he'd made the stupidest statement in history. "I'll drum up a tactical unit. Just find our missing women."

"I'm going too," said Porter as he strode towards them. "Linda's a bust, she's got one of those Nest cams on her front door and Andrews is all over it. Pops out for a fag a dozen times between two in the afternoon and the time Jenny's body was found."

"That's most of our timeframe," said Clare. "But it's not impossible that he snuck the body inside Cow Tower earlier, or had somebody else do it for him."

"Don't let him go," said Porter.

"Why do people keep saying that?" Clare barked back.

"I'm not a sieve. I don't just let people drip right out of my tosshole."

"So wrong," said Savage. Clare ignored her.

"Right, the three of you, then. Take Duke too, if you can find him. I'll have a tactical team meet you around the back of the building, but this is right in the middle of the city and the last thing we want is another debacle."

Clare checked his watch.

"We're a long way from midnight. With any luck, we'll get ahead of this. Now toss off, all of you."

Kett retreated across the bullpen, only for Clare's voice to chase him.

"And I mean it, be careful."

TOMBLAND WAS EVEN BUSIER NOW than it had been when they'd driven through it a few hours ago. The broken-down bus had been moved but cars clogged both sides of the road and even when Duke flicked on the IRV's lights and blipped the siren people seemed reluctant to move. It took a good five minutes of horn blasting and foul language before the PC pulled up in front of the ancient cathedral gates.

"You can't miss it, can you?" he said, looking across the street. Kett followed his line of sight to see a three-storey Tudor-style building directly opposite where they were parked. It wouldn't have been noticeable at all if it wasn't for the two statues that stood on either side of the main door, each as big as a person and painted white. The sign beside them advertised a lobster restaurant but it was long gone. The windows were boarded tight, a metal panel over the door. Duke cut the engine. "Good place to hide a body."

"We don't know she's dead," Kett said sharply. "And we don't know if this is the right place."

We don't even know who she *is*, he thought as he opened the car door. The air was wet and heavy, so much moisture in it that he couldn't tell if it was raining or not. He wiped a hand over his mouth, feeling the scratch of his stubble and missing the warmth of his beard.

"Any luck with the keys?" he asked as he crossed the wide road, holding out a hand to stop the slow-moving traffic.

"Nothing," said Savage. "Owner's not picking up and the estate agent has no idea where they are. Abroad, somewhere. The building's just been sold, they're trying to turn it into flats."

"No surprise there," said Porter.

They reached the far side of the street and Kett spotted an alleyway to his right. He heard chatter, and when he rounded the corner he came face to face with a tactical unit. They were wearing visors, but he recognised the lead officer by her copper-coloured hair.

"Sergeant Gorski," he said with a nod. "You were quick."

"We were primed," she replied. "Nasty case, this one. But you've seen worse, right?"

"Yeah," said Kett, looking at her rifle. "Hopefully we won't need *that* this time around."

Not like before, he thought, seeing Keefe lifting his weapon, hearing the crack of the world ending, feeling that impossible, endless darkness. According to Clare, it had been Julia Gorski who had taken Keefe out after he'd shot Kett, and even though he hadn't spoken to her much—other than to thank her—he knew it had taken its toll on her.

"How're you doing?" she asked, just as the same words were about to spill from his lips. "Good to be back?"

Kett laughed, although there wasn't much joy there.

"Let me answer that in half an hour or so. You okay to breach?"

"Well I wasn't going to ask you to do it," she replied. "On me."

She set off at a pace, cutting across an empty courtyard towards the back of the Samson and Hercules. It was an enormous building, sprawling down the far side of the courtyard. Every single window was boarded up but the wooden panel over the back door had been pried loose and hurled to the ground. The door itself looked like it had been here since the building was first built—panelled and low.

"We got here early," said Savage. "If this is where the kidnapper is holding his next victim, we may still have time. But..."

She didn't need to finish, because Kett was thinking the same thing.

"It feels too easy."

"Yeah," she said. "It does."

Kett didn't answer, following the tactical team to the door and hanging back. Gorski tried the handle and shook her head, standing to one side as another officer ran forward with a bright red enforcer ram. It hit the door once, a cannon-shot echoing around the courtyard. He tried again and this time the lock gave way, the old door crunching open.

Gorski ran in, her weapon up and her torch blazing. The other officers flowed neatly through the door behind her like an oil-black river.

"Armed police!" Gorski yelled. "Make your presence known."

Kett checked his watch, impatient. From inside he heard "Clear!" yelled over and over, each one fainter than the last. When he moved towards the door, though, Savage grabbed the sleeve of his overcoat.

"Uh-uh, sir," she said.

"Who made you the boss?" he replied. But she was right, and he held his ground until Gorski reappeared a few minutes later.

"Empty," she said, pulling off her visor. "Sorry."

"Not your fault," Kett said, doing his best to crush the cold current of disappointment in his gut. "Safe to go in?"

"There's no bad guys, but the floor's shot to shit. Watch your step."

Kett ducked beneath the low lintel pushing the broken door all the way open with his knuckles. With the windows boarded it was pitch black inside, and when he pulled out his phone and fired up the torch it barely made any difference.

"Here," said Porter, pulling a proper torch from his pocket and clicking it on.

Kett let him take the lead into a short stretch of corridor. Gorski hadn't been lying, the floor was in tatters—the boards so plagued by rising damp that Kett's boots actually sank into them. The smell was like something from an old cemetery, soil and stone and something unspeakably foul. It wasn't a *dead* smell, though. Not like in the tower they'd visited this morning.

"Somebody has definitely been here," said Savage, using her own torch to illuminate a cigarette butt on the floor. She peeked through the first door and Kett saw more of them there, a little pile in one corner. "Bottles too, and there's a mattress under all that stuff. Squatters."

"Or our killer," said Porter, moving deeper into the building.

They checked the next room to find it empty. Past that was a small kitchen that had been cleared out, the walls pulled apart and the pipework gone. At the far end of the corridor was the gated front door, a little puddle of leaflets sitting beneath it. Kett followed the corridor around and doubled back to where the bulk of the building should have been. All he found was a wall of empty wooden bookcases.

"Odd," he said.

"Sir?" asked Savage.

"It's smaller than I thought."

He stumbled over the detritus on the floor, taking hold of the first case and giving it a shake. It was heavy, but it wobbled.

"Pete, Kate, give me a hand, would you?"

Together, they heaved the bookcase over, jumping back as it fell to the ground like a tree. Past the dust, Kett could see one side of a low door.

"This one," he said, hooking his fingers behind the next bookcase and pulling. Porter joined in and it gave up easily, crashing beside the first.

The door there was as old as the one they'd come in through, crude carvings on the sturdy panels. Kett tried the handle but it was locked, and he doubted even his size elevens could get through it.

"Gorski?" he yelled. "We need the ram."

He heard the sound of the order being relayed through the building, and seconds later an officer appeared holding the ram. He went to work, the thick door releasing only after four attempts, snapping against the wall so hard it was like it had been sprung. Kett heard what sounded like a boat's anchor dropping, then a hollow boom that seemed to vibrate through the asphalt and up into the soles of his boots.

"You hear that?" Savage said.

"Feels like the whole building is coming down," Porter said, looking at the ceiling.

Kett walked through, finding himself in a huge, open room.

"This must be the old dance hall," said Savage, something ghostly about the way her words echoed back from the far wall.

They swept their torches, the three beams angling over the room like searchlights. The space was empty. No furniture, no piles of rubbish. Nothing. It reminded Kett of the Hackney gym where he'd found his wife. Only there were no lights, no music, no sign that anyone had been here for years. It was impossibly quiet, too. You couldn't even hear the sound of traffic from outside.

"I really thought this was it," said Savage. "'*She dances with two strong men.*' I was so sure."

"Call forensics and get them out here anyway," Kett said. "And let's split up, there must be plenty of rooms on this side of the building."

He aimed the torch at the high ceiling, something up there taking flight with a chorus of clapping wings. Pigeons, he realised, when the rush of adrenaline had passed, three of them, watching with dark-eyed curiosity.

"Must have got trapped in here," said Savage. "Poor things."

"If only they could talk," said Kett.

There was a flash of silver in the light and he directed the torch at the wall to see a length of thick chain fixed there, running through steel mounts all the way from the door they'd just come through to the far side of the room.

"What's that?" he asked.

"Some kind of pulley?" said Savage. "I don't know. Never seen one before. Maybe they're using it to haul in building materials?"

"Maybe," he said.

Savage crossed the room, the wooden floor squeaking beneath her. Porter went the other way, his footsteps hollow. Kett turned his attention back to the chain. It had been fastened to the door with an enormous steel plate, and whatever was on the other end of it was heavy enough to stop the door from closing again. Whoever had done it had gone to some trouble, because it snaked through a dozen or more metal rungs before dropping into the floor.

"What did this place used to be?" he asked, his voice batting back and forth like another trapped bird.

"Restaurant," said Porter as he opened a door. "Lobster, I think. Never came."

"Before that."

"Dance hall," Savage shouted back. "That's why I thought it fit. Two strong men on the door, and plenty of dancing."

There was something nagging at the back of Kett's head, something about the building that he couldn't put his finger on. He thought back to London, to the underground lair where the Pig Man had kept Billie. He'd moved her to another basement, too, and told her that if she wanted her daughters to live she had to kill her own husband if he came to find her. Savage had found a secret room in their last case too, hidden beneath the wooden church at Whytetail.

"Is there a cellar here?" he asked.

"Yeah," came a voice from behind him as Gorski entered the room. "Empty."

"Shit," he said again. "I think we were wrong."

He turned to go, hesitating again, looking at the chain.

"Can you make any sense of that, Gorski?" he asked. The firearms officer frowned as she tracked the wall.

"Pulley system," she said. "But it wouldn't work because anything you were pulling would get stuck in the mounts."

"Chain's taut," Kett said. "Something heavy on the other end."

"Maybe it's just decoration?" Savage said as she made her way back. "Lobster restaurant. An old fishing chain or something?"

"*Fishing chain?*" said Porter as he closed the last door. "How many times have you been fishing?"

"Zero," said Savage.

"You're sure there's nothing in the basement?" Kett asked.

"It's a vaulted cellar and it's empty," Gorski replied. "Brick walls and floor. There's nowhere to hide anything down there. But it's under the other part of the building, not under here."

"Keep looking," he said.

He switched off the torch on his phone, calling Clare. The Super must have been waiting for the call because he answered before the first ring had faded.

"Tell me good news."

"There's nothing here, sir. Place is deserted."

"Tossing hell. You're sure?"

"I'm..."

He hesitated, holding the phone away from his ear. For a second he thought he'd heard something, the faintest of noises. Overhead, the pigeons flew between the rafters, their wings clapping like castanets.

"Hang on, sir," he said. "I'll call you back."

There was something wrong with the building, something in the sound of it. He'd always prided himself on his ability to work out if a house was empty or not just by the feel of it, by the currents of air, that intangible stillness. This place was a lot larger than a house but the rules were the same. It wasn't still here.

It wasn't empty.

He walked to the wall where the chain dropped into the wooden boards. A hole had been cut for it, the size of his palm—too small to see anything but darkness.

"Sir?" asked Savage.

"You all heard that noise when we opened the door, right?" he said.

"The boom," Savage replied, nodding. By the light of the torches her face was as ghostly as her voice.

"I thought it sounded like an anchor," he said. "The noise it makes when it drops."

He crouched by the hole, tugging on the chain. It didn't budge.

"What the hell is it?"

"Maybe it's to do with the founda—"

Porter shut his mouth as a gentle rumble trembled through the boards. Kett leant closer, holding his breath.

Thump.

The chain vibrated, the sound almost too faint to hear.

"Wait a minute," said Savage. "I might be wrong but I think they used to have a swimming pool here. I thought they'd filled it in, but..."

Another thump, and the chain moved as if somebody was tugging on it.

"I think they just built the ballroom floor over it," Savage said.

"Shit," Kett replied. "Somebody's down there."

CHAPTER FIFTEEN

SOMEBODY'S DOWN THERE.

But there was no way to get to them.

"Nothing here!" Savage yelled.

She scrabbled by the wall where the chain dropped into the floor, prying at the wooden boards and searching for a weak point. Her lucky silver whistle swung wildly on its own little silver chain as she moved.

Porter was on the other side of the hole, using his boot to try to stamp through the floor.

"Rock solid," the DI shouted. "There must be another way down."

Kett swept his phone across the room, looking for anything that might help. Hundreds of pieces of graffiti had been scored into the old floor, but despite the rot the boards had been laid well and there were no obvious places where they had been cut open.

"We're running out of time," Kett said.

There had been two more thumps from below, and one final rattle of the chain a minute or so ago, but if there was anyone down there they'd fallen silent.

It wasn't a good sign.

"Gorsky!" Kett yelled into the corridor. "Hurry up!"

The firearms officer had gone to get a motorised saw but she was taking her sweet time about it. Kett reached the wall and turned around, heading back, still searching.

"Our killer likes fairy tales, right?" he shouted. "Sweet Briar Rose wrapped in thorns, sleeping in her castle. What are we dealing with here?"

"The note mentioned beauty and dancing," Savage said. "Beauty and the Beast, right?"

"Right," said Kett. "That's what I thought too. What do you think of when you think about Beauty and the Beast?"

"Teapots?" Savage replied.

"Porter?"

"Uh, I've never seen it, sir. Sorry."

"Wolves," Savage went on. "Uh, mirrors, fancy furniture."

The sound of footsteps rose and Gorsky entered the room, followed by a couple of officers. Her visor was off and her face was damp with sweat. In her hands, she held a breaching saw.

"Where?" she barked.

"Start by the chain," Kett said. "But be careful. We don't know what's down there."

She ran towards Savage, ripping the cord. Instantly, the room was filled with the roar of the motor. Gorsky ducked down onto one knee, the blade sliding into the wooden floor with an eruption of sparks.

"Shit," she shouted. "Steel."

Kett turned away, sweeping his torch over the floor, still searching. It took him a moment to hear Savage over the saw.

"Huh?" he said.

"Flowers," she yelled back. "Roses. It's what Belle asks her father for, I think."

Roses.

He'd already seen one, he was sure of it.

He moved towards the centre of the room, the torchlight making every scratch and carving in the wood seem to dance. Just when he thought he'd never find it again he caught sight of a carved Tudor rose, the size of a dinner plate. It was crude, made with some force.

And it had been done *recently*.

"Sweet Briar Rose," he said, kicking himself for not making the connection. "Hey, Gorski, here."

She couldn't hear him over the sound of the saw so Savage tapped her on the shoulder. Gorski looked back, then carried the saw over, its motor revving.

"Here," Kett said again, using his boot to tap the wood to the side of the flower. "Take it slow."

She did as she was asked, the floor seeming to scream as the blade cut through it—no sparks this time. Kett stood back to escape the fumes, the smell of burning wood making his head pound. Gorski cut out a metre-wide circle then stood back, shutting the saw down. Another of the firearms officers filled the space she'd just vacated, prying up the stubborn boards with a crowbar.

Below yawned an ocean of darkness, a bottomless void.

Kett got down on his knees and shone his torch into the hole, chasing the darkness away to reveal the tiled floor of a swimming pool. He dropped onto his belly, ignoring the pain in his chest as he ducked his head through the gap. He was over the shallow end here, the floor maybe five feet beneath him. His light wasn't powerful enough to see much, but there was definitely something at the deep end of the pool, right where the chain dropped down from the ball-room wall.

Something squat and black.

Something coffin-like.

"Shit," he said, scrabbling onto his backside then sliding through the gap. The rough wood scraped the skin from his back, far more painful than it had any right to be. But he'd gauged the distance right because his feet hit the bottom of the empty pool before his hands left the floor above.

"Sir, be careful," said Savage. "We have no idea what's down there."

He ignored her, aiming the light towards the deep end. The pool was wide but it was as claustrophobic as hell in here, even as the floor started to dip down. He heard a grunt as Porter landed behind him, then the slap of Savage's feet as she dropped in.

It was a short run to the end of the pool, and with every step he took he realised his first guess had been right.

A coffin sat there, as black as pitch. From the top of it jutted the end of the chain, a glimmer of light pushing through from the hole above. The scaffold that held up the floor at the deep end was steel, it would have been impossible to get through even with Gorski's saw.

"Come on," Kett said, already breathless.

He skidded to a halt, his boots sliding on the smooth tiles. The coffin was solid mahogany, expensive and brand new. The only mark on it was a hole right in the centre of the lid through which the chain passed. Kett dropped to his knees and checked the clasps to find they were already open. He took hold of the rim instead, trying to get his fingers into the gap. Savage was there in a heartbeat, helping him, while Porter kept his light up. Gorski was running over, the saw still in her hand.

"What the hell?" she said.

"Get it open," roared Kett.

He grabbed the lid and tried to pull it up, but it wouldn't budge.

"Crowbar," he yelled, and Gorski dropped the saw, doubling back. "Is it nailed? I can't see any?"

"No," said Savage, getting her fingers under the rim. "Try again. Pete, give us a hand."

The pool grew dark as Porter dropped his torch, getting his big hands beneath the lid.

"Now," he said, and the three of them grunted together as they tried to open the coffin.

This time it moved—just an inch or two before slamming back down.

Long enough for Kett to see the body inside.

"Here!" Gorski yelled, sliding the crowbar over the floor. Porter grabbed it, jamming it into the gap then putting all his weight on it.

The lid lifted and Kett hooked his fingers in the gap, pulling hard.

"Do not fucking drop it," he said.

Gorski pushed in next to Savage, the tendons in her neck like steel wires as she fought to get the lid open.

"Why the hell is it so heavy?" said Savage.

More of the firearms officers were dropping through the floor and Kett made way for them. The top of the coffin lifted, almost vertical now, the chain going limp. There was something fixed to the underside of the lid, a massive grey block that looked like stone or concrete.

Beneath it, barely visible in the dark, was a young woman.

"Now!" Gorski yelled, and everyone cried out in unison as they flipped the lid all the way open.

"Wait," Kett shouted, but it was too late.

Gravity took hold of the concrete block and the coffin flipped onto its side, the body rolling out. The whole thing would have snapped shut around her if Porter hadn't clung on, groaning with the effort. Kett grabbed the woman by her feet, dragging her clear. Then Porter fell back and the coffin rolled onto its lid, snapping shut like a bear trap.

"Everyone alright?" Kett shouted over the ringing in his ears.

"I think I might have shit myself," said Porter.

Kett dropped to his knees, his fingers on the woman's neck, searching for a pulse. There wasn't one, and blood ran freely from her nose and mouth.

"She's still warm," he said. "Savage, ambulance, now."

She already had her phone out.

"No signal," she said as she sprinted back to the hole. "That's Frances Herbert, sir."

Kett ripped open Fran's shirt, linking his fingers and pushing down on her chest.

Thump. Thump. Thump.

It felt wrong in there, her ribs like shattered glass inside a binbag.

"Come on," he said.

Thump. Thump. Thump.

Gorski dropped down beside him, giving the young woman the kiss of life. Kett kept pushing, never letting up.

"Don't you fucking die," he growled.

Thump. Thump. Thump.

"Savage? Ambulance!"

"On its way, sir," she shouted from overhead.

Gorski breathed more life into the woman, one hand on her cheek, stroking gently.

"Come on, Fran," Kett said. "You do not want to leave us."

Thump. Thump. Thump.

The woman's body jolted like she'd been electrocuted, her head snapping up from the floor so hard that it cracked into Gorski's jaw, knocking her back. Fran rolled onto her side, heaving, drawing her legs to her chest before kicking them out again. She made a choking noise, drew a breath, then screamed weakly, blood erupting from between her pale lips. Her hands grasped at her chest as she tried to get air in, everything spasming.

"Hey," Kett said, falling back to avoid her flailing legs. "Hey, you're okay. You're safe."

Something was wrong with her, she couldn't breathe. Her eyes were open now, rolling in their sockets like loose marbles. She found Kett then lost him again, then seemed to lose herself in another explosive fit. Her fists drummed the ground, her feet kicking.

She was missing a finger, Kett saw. The index finger of her right hand.

He wrapped his arms around hers and pulled her close, doing his best to absorb some of the violence. Gorski moved to the woman's other side, sandwiching her.

"You're safe, Fran," he said.

And she must have heard him because her movements softened, her arms dropping to her sides, her breathless screams becoming sobs, and then hoarse whispers.

"Can't breathe. Can't breathe."

But she did, one heaving breath at a time, each one longer and deeper until, at last, her head lolled back onto Kett's chest and she dropped into unconsciousness.

CHAPTER SIXTEEN

KETT COULDN'T REMEMBER A TIME HE'D EVER BEEN more desperate for fresh air.

He leaned against the cold wall of the empty swimming pool, rubbing his eyes so hard that splashes of colour exploded against the darkness. For a moment he just listened as the forensic team went about their work, thinking he might keep his eyes closed forever and try to forget about all this. Forget about Jenny Eyler wrapped in thorns, forget about poor Fran Herbert trapped inside a coffin.

"Sir?"

Maybe if he refused to look then it would all go away.

"Sir?"

If only.

He opened his eyes to see Savage there. She had her hands planted on her knees like it was the only thing keeping her from toppling over, and even though her eyes were hard and full of anger, tears pooled there.

Behind her, Cara Hay was crouched beside the upside-down coffin, her toolkit open. The paramedics had managed to get Fran's unconscious body up through the hole that Gorski had cut half an hour ago—although they'd needed the firearms team's help and a stepladder to do it—and she was on her way to the hospital. Porter was with her, just in case she started to talk.

And just in case whoever had done this to her came back to finish the job.

"Sorry, Kate," he said. "What?"

"Cara was asking if she could open the coffin," Savage said.

"Oh, right, sure. Of course."

He waved to Hay and she nodded back, her face carved from stone. Kett pushed himself from the wall and walked down the slope of the pool. It seemed much colder at the bottom, the smell of damp making him feel like he was descending into a tomb.

The coffin didn't help, of course.

"Anything?" he asked.

"There are prints, but I get the feeling they belong to you lot," Hay replied. "They're all around the lid."

"Didn't have time to put gloves on, sorry."

"No matter. I don't think our suspect would make things so easy for us. Coffin is new, manufacturing date on it is this year. It's expensive. Quartz. We're talking a few thousand here."

"Custom?" Kett asked.

"No. You can order these online. But we'll be able to figure out where and when. Can we get it open?"

"We can try," said Kett. "Gorski? A hand?"

The firearms team had congregated at the shallow end, sitting on the slope and watching quietly. Gorski stood and the others followed, two of them cracking their helmets on the low ceiling.

"It might be better to get it on its side," Kett said. "There's a weight in the lid and it'll just flip over again. Be careful, though, it's heavy."

"Yeah, I remember," said Gorski. She took hold of the head end and her team spread out.

"Now," said Kett, grunting as he fought to get the coffin moving. It resisted, but it must have known it was beaten because the base rolled onto its side after a second or two and stayed there, the lid lying flat. The chain was coiled beside it like a snake.

"What is this?" Hay said, the barest tremor in her voice.

The coffin was lined with purple satin, plush and embroidered and spattered with blood. A concrete block had been fixed to the lid with a dozen or so bolts, two foot wide, five foot long and maybe ten inches thick. It wasn't flat, it was covered with bumps and ridges, some as big as Kett's fist. This, too, was decorated with a spray of blood, as dark as ink. A metal anchor plate sat in the block, the chain connected to the other side of it.

"It was designed to crush her," Kett said, his arms erupting into goosebumps. "When the lid snapped shut. Christ, no wonder she couldn't breathe."

"How long was she in there?" Hay asked.

"Long enough," Kett said, checking his watch. "It took us five minutes to find her, same again to get her out."

"Long enough to do some damage," Hay said. "But not long enough to kill her."

"It *did* kill her," Kett said. "She wasn't breathing when we found her. We brought her back."

"You did good. Whoever did this to her wanted her to die, there's absolutely no question there at all. What's the chain for? Was it locked?"

"No," said Kett. He followed the chain along the floor

and up the wall where it disappeared through the hole in the ceiling. It went all the way to the ballroom door, he knew, running through its mountings. "The killer fixed one end of the chain to the coffin, holding the lid up. The other end was connected to the door we came in through."

He remembered the sound of an anchor being dropped, the boom of something heavy. They'd thought it might be the building falling down, but it had been so much worse.

"As soon as we entered the dance hall the full weight of the lid would have fallen, crushing her. *We* did this to her."

"You can't think about it like that, sir," said Savage.

"Indeed you can't," Hay confirmed. "This person is clever, cunning, and cruel too."

She frowned, looking into the body of the coffin.

"It begs the question, though, if the lid was open before you breached the door then why didn't our victim escape? What was stopping her from climbing out? Or simply *calling* out when she heard you?"

"Maybe it was only partially open," Kett said. "Enough to keep the block off her but not enough for her to crawl out. It took a lot of us to open it, Fran wouldn't have stood a chance by herself. We wouldn't have heard her through the walls if she was shouting, and by the time the door was open it would have been too late."

"She could have been drugged," Savage added. "Have we had the Tox Screen back from Jenny yet?"

"Find out," said Kett. "We'll reset the coffin, work out how long the chain was. That will give us an idea of how much space she had inside."

"Let me finish first," Hay said as they watched Savage climb the ladder out of the pool. "This bastard must have left something for us, although he's not stupid."

"He?" Kett said.

"Can you see a woman doing this? Dragging a coffin here, and a body, rigging this up?" She shook her head. "From my experience, when a woman wants something she pursues it in a direct and honest way. Only a man could be this convoluted and egotistical. But this is why I'm a scientist and not a detective. It is not my job to guess. It's yours."

"I try not to do too much guessing," Kett said. "But this must be somebody strong. He'd need to move all of this by himself, get the coffin into the pool, line it with concrete, rig up the pulley. It's a big ask for one person."

"So maybe it's not just one person," said Hay. "In my experience, something like this needs either lots of people, or lots of time."

"He'd need time, for sure," said Kett. "He fixed the floorboards back in after he'd finished. He wasn't in any hurry."

Savage's head appeared through the hole.

"Tox positive on Jenny," she shouted. "Benzos. Boss wants you back."

"Right," Kett said.

He grimaced as he walked the length of the pool, but he wasn't upset to be leaving. The walls had been closing in on him since he'd arrived, and the panic was a black mass growing heavier in his chest. He craved sunlight with a force that was overwhelming.

"Need a hand, sir?" Savage asked as he reached the ladder.

"I'm not an old man, Kate," he snapped back, a little too sharply.

But he was wheezing like an accordion by the time he'd made it to the floor above. Savage looked at him with what might have been pity and he scowled at her.

"I'm not an old man!" he said again, and she held up her hands in surrender.

He made his way towards the door, muttering to himself.

"But I do need a cup of tea."

IT WAS twilight by the time he stepped out of the Samson and Hercules, something magical about the rolling half-dark, about the gently waking lights of the city.

Kett took a deep breath of damp air, nodding to the two PCs who stood guard before cutting across the car park. Now that Fran had been found, all efforts at discretion had been abandoned. The alleyway they'd walked down less than an hour ago was rammed with police vehicles and more were parked on the street outside, traffic once again backed up both ways. The reporters were already gathered there, drawn to the scene like piranhas to a drowning horse.

"Kett! Over here!" said one. "Another dead woman? Is this related to Sweet Briar Rose? Who've we got now? Red Riding Hood?"

Kett pictured himself slapping the man as he walked past, his hand twitching. Another constable lifted the police tape and Kett walked through, giving the reporters a wide berth as he made for Duke's IRV on the other side of the street. He was halfway there when he had another thought, scanning the surrounding buildings and trying to get his bearings. A VW honked at him and he jogged back, cutting down an alleyway on the other side of the Samson and Hercules and walking through an old churchyard that was full of skeletal lavender plants.

He followed the cobbled streets past old churches and grand buildings, past the places he had visited with his mum and dad when he was a kid, past the little cinema where he'd seen his first movie—*E.T.*—and the hall where he'd been dragged to watch a classical concert as part of a school trip.

The memories came faster and harder than he expected, a tide of them which, at times, literally stopped him in his tracks. When he'd moved to London he'd forgotten so much of what had happened here, but those memories had never left him, they'd just been waiting, and they bounced back into his head without hesitation or mercy—and one more than any other, one that hit him so hard he felt like he'd been punched.

It was a restaurant, a Pizza Express that he walked past five minutes after leaving the old ballroom. They'd come here all the time, him and his mum and his dad. Every Tuesday, he remembered, right after school. They'd parked in town outside the old library and walked here and ordered the exact same thing every week—a margarita for him, of course, because kids don't eat anything but cheese, a Fiorentina for his dad and a pepperoni for his mum, even though she'd always picked the meat off and left it on the side of her plate.

Kett put his hand to the glass, his scalp shrinking so much that it was painful, the street seeming to twist and fold as if he was actually being pulled back in time. And for a moment he thought he saw them there, a nervous young woman, a kind, sad man, a little boy with his crayons and his colouring book, his tongue pinched between his lips as he concentrated.

Then a van drove past, its reflection filling the glass, and there was nobody there.

He stood back, a lump in his throat that felt big enough to choke him.

He coughed it away, pushing past two more restaurants

and stopping at the top of a steep set of stone stairs. To his right was the side wall of a comic shop, and to his left was an impressive church—presumably called St Lawrence's, because the steps bore the same name. An old man was struggling up them, hauling a trolley behind him.

"Need a hand?" Kett said.

The man stopped, evidently highly irritated as he pulled back his sleeve and squinted at his watch.

"Four-fifteen," he said in a voice made from dust. "And time you bought a watch of your own."

He kept climbing, scowling at Kett as he reached the top.

"Maybe that way you can offer to help a fellow rather than demand something from him."

"I *did* offer," Kett protested, but the old guy wasn't listening.

"Ignore him," said a girl who was standing in the open door of the comic shop. "Miserable git's always going up and down those stairs. Five or six times a day."

"Yeah?" said Kett.

The girl stepped onto the threshold. She was in her late teens, early twenties maybe. The same age as the missing women, Kett thought. Her hair had been dyed a shade of bubble-gum pink that was so bright it made his eyes hurt to look at it. She was chewing gum, too, the fruity smell of it overpowering.

"I know you," she said.

"I doubt it," Kett replied. "Police."

"Are you going to arrest me?" she asked, holding up her hands. He laughed.

"Not planning to. Just looking for something to drink. Haven't had a cup of tea all day."

The girl pointed a long finger down the steps.

"Try Bert's place. Can't speak for his tea but the coffee's good."

"Thanks," said Kett.

He made his way carefully down the first set of steps. They were solid stone, but they had been cratered by time and a million passing feet, and the rain had made them treacherous. Halfway down was a flat stretch of path before the next flight of stairs. To his left was the enormous retaining wall for the church and its grounds, but there were doors on the right. The first had been bricked up and covered with posters and fliers. The next was barred, but through the window, Kett saw the basement of the shop above.

Past that was a café. Stencilled on the window was the word FONTAINE'S in a pink that was almost as bright as the hair of the girl he'd just spoken to. The door was open, and through it wafted the smell of coffee. Kett was practically floating as he entered.

It had to have been the smallest café he'd ever seen, just a short bar on the far side that took up over half of the available space, and a couple of tables positioned in front of the large front window. At one of these tables sat two young women—students, by the look of it—leaning into each other conspiratorially as they spoke and not giving him so much as a glance. At the other was a man in his thirties who was too engrossed in his crossword to look up. He was wearing a huge black parka with a bristling fake fur hood and there were two woolly hats on his head, but he still looked half-frozen.

Kett walked to the bar, seeing another door beside the enormous coffee machine. He rapped his knuckles gently on the wood.

"Hello?"

No answer, but he was happy to wait. He scanned the little collection of cakes and pastries on the counter, wondering whether to pick up some croissants for the girls. But he still carried the smell of the old pool on his hands and on his clothes and he didn't want it anywhere near them.

"Hello?" he said, knocking the wood again. "Anyone here?"

"Bert," said one of the girls, and Kett turned to her. She was talking to the man who was hunched over his crossword, and he seemed to stir at the sound of his name. He glanced at her, then at Kett.

"Oh, shoot," he said, his head almost scraping the low ceiling as he stood up. "Sorry, miles away."

Bert skirted apologetically around Kett to get to the bar, ducking self-consciously the way tall men often did. Beneath the coat he looked every part the barista in his cheque shirt and his suspenders, his beard neatly trimmed.

"I've been stuck on a clue all morning, and *they're* no help," he said, nodding to the women. "You any good?"

"At crosswords?" Kett replied, shaking his head. "No. But I know a man who is. What's the clue?"

"Continue a poem willy-nilly," Bert said, shrugging his bony shoulders. He was shivering, his teeth chattering like castanets. "Cold," he said, somewhat unnecessarily. "Heating's bust and I can't afford to fix it. Hence the coat."

"And the hats," said Kett. "Two of them."

"*Four*," he said. "My head feels like it's in a nutcracker."

"You realise you could close the door?"

"That's broken too," he said, somewhat forlornly. "Takes about ten minutes to shunt it open in the morning and the same again to close it. Customers think we're closed unless I leave it like that."

"You doing tea?" said Kett.

"I can," said the man, pulling a face. "But I'm better at coffee. I never really got the appeal of tea. It's like puddle water."

Kett bristled, but he managed to bite his tongue.

"I can do you a great flat white?"

"Isn't that a shark?" Kett said. "Tea is fine. Milk, no sugar."

The man sighed as he turned to work.

"You been here long?" Kett asked him.

"The café? No, six months or so. To be honest it's not going great. These two come in most days and order a coffee to share—last of the big spenders, right?—and half of the coffees and cakes I make are for the old folks' homes, and I don't even charge for them. I don't get as much passing trade here as I thought I would. People don't like the steps."

"I can see why," said Kett, looking through the window. "I nearly went arse over tit myself."

"Worse in the winter. I've had to help a couple of people who've fallen, both ended up in ambulances."

"That's actually why I'm here," Kett said. The man looked back, the kettle frozen over Kett's mug. "There was an incident here a couple of months ago. First week of September, Friday night or early Saturday morning. A woman was hit by a car at the bottom of the steps."

Bert put the kettle back down, the mug empty.

"You're police?" he asked, and Kett nodded. "I've already spoken to a few police people. I didn't see the... I didn't see it happen. It was at night, long after we close. But it was really horrible. That poor girl. Is she still, you know...?"

He shrugged again.

"She's still alive," said Kett.

"Thank God," he said.

"I'm just following up some leads on another case, but I wanted to come and have a look. Do you have any idea what might have happened?"

Bert shrugged.

"Any of you?" Kett asked, turning to the two women at the table. They sat back in their chairs, terrified.

"No," said one. "I wasn't at uni back then, I lived in Hull."

The other woman shook her head, her mouth clamped shut. Kett turned to the bar again.

"But..." he said, trying to coax out whatever the man was holding back.

"It was an accident, wasn't it?" said Bert. "News said she was out with some friends, that she ran out in front of a car on Westwick Street, down the bottom of the steps."

Kett nodded.

"Easily done," he went on. "I see kids running down these steps all the time, hell for leather. If you miss your footing then you either fall over or you just snowball."

"Snowball?"

"Like, you know, have you ever run down a hill? Sometimes you can't stop. If she'd been drinking and she was running hard she might not have been able to stop herself."

He remembered the kettle, pouring water into the mug. The air was instantly full of the fragrant smell of tea, strong enough that Kett felt drunk on it.

"I only really know about it because her dad comes in here. I can't remember his name."

"Joffre Andrews?" said Kett.

"That's it. He used to come in all the time, asking the same questions like he thought I might be lying to him. I know what he wanted me to say, like."

"Yeah?"

"Yeah, he kept going on about the other women his daughter was out with. He kept trying to plant it in my head that they'd pushed her or something."

"He said that to you?" Kett asked.

"Multiple times. But I told him what I'm telling you, I wasn't there and I didn't see anything. I can't lie about it, can I? It's like the news said, she'd had one too many and she fell over at the bottom of the steps. The woman in the car was driving too fast, it was dark." Bert shrugged. "It's awful, but it happens. That's what I kept telling him."

"Does he still come in?"

"No," said Bert. "Haven't seen him for a few weeks now."

"He's a scary guy," said one of the women. "Massive. Had Bert by the throat once and we were going to call the police."

"You didn't?"

"No," said Bert, blushing. "It was nothing. Wasn't my throat, it was my collar. And I didn't blame him because who wouldn't feel like that? I wish I'd been able to tell him something."

"You have any idea what Martha might have been running from that night?" Kett asked.

Bert licked his lips, something unspoken right there.

"Bert?" Kett said. "If there's anything you want to tell me, now's your chance."

"Just tell him, Bert," said the same woman. "They're full of shit anyway."

Kett waited, watching Bert's brow furrow, watching him lick his lips.

"Fine," the young man said. He leaned over the bar, beckoning for Kett to do the same. When he continued, it was in a whisper. "There are a lot of drugs around here. A lot of deals. We have junkies come in all the time asking for a toilet because they want to shoot up, but we don't have one, thankfully. Just a storeroom. Most of the time they go up the old graveyard."

He nodded through the window to the flint retaining wall of the church.

"And that's where a lot of the deals happen too. We see it all the time. And most of the dealers are harmless, to us anyway. But..." He hesitated, wrestling with something. "But recently there's been these new guys, and they've started asking us for money."

"Money," Kett said, and Bert motioned for him to keep his voice down.

"Like, extortion or whatever. I have to fork out two hundred quid every Sunday, and they tell me that will protect me."

"From who?"

"*Whom,*" said Bert. "From them, I'm guessing."

"How long has this been going on?"

"A few months. It wouldn't be so bad, but I barely make enough for the rent anyway. Ask around. We're a close community here on the Lanes and they make us all pay. It's not worth the hassle of standing up to them."

"I can look into it," Kett said. "What they're doing isn't right."

"Don't," Bert replied. "Please. If it keeps the peace then I'm happy to do it. That's not why I mentioned it. It's just these guys look the part, if you know what I mean. They're scary. I've seen them in the churchyard when I lock up sometimes, they hang out there causing all sorts of shit. I'm just thinking that maybe the girl saw them too, the one who ran in front of the car. They might have said something or come after her, and that would have been enough to set her off. I don't know."

"None of the other girls who were out that night mentioned seeing anyone there," Kett said.

"Yeah, but they wouldn't, would they? Same reason I never mentioned it when your colleagues asked me, or when that woman's dad asked me. Fear, right? Better to stay quiet, stick to your lane, do what you're told."

"You know any names?"

"No," Bert said. "Sorry. They just show up. They're not the sort to hand out business cards. I heard somebody call them the Bugger Boys or something." He frowned. "Wait, no, that doesn't sound right."

"Beggar Boys?" Kett said, and Bert nodded. "You did the right thing, telling me. I'll keep it between us, but we'll check it out."

Bert started to protest but Kett cut him off.

"Discreetly. It will never come back to you."

"Thanks," he said. "Oh, crap, I forgot about your tea."

He spun around to the mug, prodding the teabag forlornly with a spoon.

"It may still be drinkable?"

"What's this place called again?" Kett said with a sigh. "*Pete Porter's Teashop?*"

Bert stared back at him blankly.

"I'll pass. Thanks for the help."

He rapped his wedding ring gently on the counter again then made for the door, pulling out his phone when he heard it ring. It was Clare.

"You get lost?" yelled the Super's angry voice. "I need you back here *now*. We've found the next part of our story."

CHAPTER SEVENTEEN

IT WAS WELL AFTER FIVE BY THE TIME KETT MADE IT back to the Major Investigation Team's bullpen, and he was so knackered he wasn't even sure he'd get through the doors. HQ was a hive of activity, plenty of strangers amongst the sea of familiar faces. Some smiled at Kett as he pushed through the crowd, but only a few. The rest were either indifferent or indignant, with more than a few scowls thrown his way. He kept his head down as he approached the Incident Room, knocking once before opening the door.

Superintendent Colin Clare was mid-flow, and even though he shot Kett a look of profound annoyance he didn't offer any words of welcome, sarcastic or otherwise. Kett pushed between the occupied tables, conducting a chorus of scraping chairs and quiet mutterings until he reached the other side of the room where Savage and Duke sat at adjacent desks. Porter crouched next to Savage, his face gaunt. They all nodded to Kett as he took an empty spot against the wall between two PCs.

"So," said Clare, pointing an unopened Bounty at the mosaic of photographs, blueprints and handwritten notes behind him. "For the benefit of those tardy-arsed toss monkeys who came in late, our puzzle continues. The good news is that Frances Herbert is alive, but only just. Franklin's over at the hospital right now and she tells me that—"

"I can tell them, sir," came a voice from the desk in front of the Superintendent. Clare's phone sat there, Franklin on speaker.

"I don't want you to, because you'll take all tossing day. Frances suffered—"

"What's known as compression asphyxia," Franklin continued.

Clare flapped his arms in disgust then collapsed into his chair, the force of his landing propelling it around in a slow circle. He ripped open the Bounty as he spun, growling at the chocolate inside like he'd come face to face with his mortal enemy.

"You've probably heard of Pressing, right?" Franklin continued, her voice fading into static for a second. "They used to use it as a form of torture, centuries ago. Usually with religious martyrs. A weight was placed on the victim's chest, anywhere up to four hundred kilograms of stone. It's not as bad as it sounds, because your diaphragm can still work even under immense pressure."

Clare held up the packet and let both halves of his Bounty drop into his mouth at the same time. He looked almost possessed as he chewed.

"Is he okay?" Kett whispered.

"That's his fourth one," Savage replied.

"I've done the calculations and the concrete blocks inside the coffin weighed just over a hundred kilograms. The weight of a man, give or take. With the coffin lid closed it would have compressed Fran's chest enough to make it very, very difficult for her to draw breath. But it wouldn't have killed her."

"Right," Clare said, slamming a fist into his chest as he choked on coconut. "So—"

"Except our killer was relying on something else," Franklin went on. "He was counting on the fact that the lid would slam down with enough force to break Fran's ribs. Not just one, but several. Did you notice that the concrete slab wasn't flat, it was shaped with several outwardly curved segments? Those were designed to come into contact with Fran's ribs, putting enough pressure on them to generate multiple fractures."

There was an audible collective intake of breath across the room. Kett remembered the way the young woman's ribs had felt as he'd brought her back, wondering if his compressions made it worse.

"This causes what we refer to as flail chest. It's nasty. Snap enough adjacent ribs in enough places and a section of the rib cage will break free and move independently of the chest wall. The entire mechanics of breathing are altered, because suddenly the floating section of soft tissue is moving in the opposite direction to the rest of the rib cage. When that happens, your diaphragm stops working, even if the weight is removed. In medical terms, you're fucked."

"And that's—" Clare started.

"Luckily for us, Fran's ribs held out," Franklin interrupted. "The surgeons tell me four ribs were broken, and three of those were snapped in more than one place. Several had hairline fractures but they didn't break. Fran's obviously a milk drinker, strong bones. The weight was a few kilograms short of being enough to finish her off—or, looking at it another way, if Fran had been any larger in the chest, she'd be dead. But make no mistake, this was attempted murder. And the killer wanted it to be bad for Fran, and for whoever found her."

"How so?" said Porter. "Hi Emily, it's Pete, by the way."

"I know it is," she replied. "Only you could ask such a stupid question. Go on, Porter, tell us why it would have been so bad."

"Uh," Porter said, looking to Kett for help. "Because... uh..."

"Because we wouldn't have been able to save her," said Savage.

"Oh Kate, you're wasted over there," Franklin said. "Leave them, come and work with me. We'd have such fun."

Savage smiled, hiding it behind her hand.

"DC Savage is right," Franklin went on. "The moment you entered the room the coffin slammed shut, snapping Fran's ribs. If it had worked the way the killer wanted it to, she'd have started to asphyxiate straightaway. But he made no attempt to hide the chain, which makes me think that he *wanted* you to find the pool and discover Fran. He wanted you to get her out of the coffin alive. Because it wouldn't have made any difference. Even with the weight off of her chest, it would have been too late to save her. She'd have died right there in your arms."

"Christ," Kett said, trying to imagine the horror of it, of lying there with your bones broken and your lungs empty, pleading with the people who had come to save you only to die anyway.

"As it was, the weight wasn't too much, it didn't snap as many ribs as intended but it did stop her heart. Like I say, Fran won this one. Her ribs are being surgically stabilised as we speak. The bad news for her is that breathing is going to hurt like a bitch for a long, long time."

"What about the finger?" Kett asked.

"Ah, DCI Kett, welcome back to the fold," Franklin said. "Punched anyone yet?"

"Uh, no," he replied. "Not *really*."

"Good to hear. Which finger are you talking about?"

"There's more than one?" he asked.

"There is. The finger we found in Jenny Eyler's mouth belongs to Fran Herbert, no question whatsoever. The amputation wounds match perfectly and she's wearing the same nail varnish. The finger we found in Fran Herbert's hair, though, is unaccounted for."

"Hang on, *what?*" said Kett.

"This is why I wanted you here half an hour ago," barked Clare. "Instead of tossing off in town."

"I wasn't *tossing off*, sir," Kett started, but Franklin rode over him.

"There was a finger tied in Fran's hair. Tied *with* her hair. It was wrapped up in a piece of paper and then a section of cloth, just like before. It's an index finger from a right hand, almost certainly a woman's, cut with some precision at the exact same joint as Fran's. Clare has photos."

"I do," Clare said, getting out of his seat. "I'm glad you didn't forget about me when, as predicted, you took all tossing day."

"I didn't take—" Franklin started, but Clare prodded the phone with his finger. He picked up a sheet of paper.

"That's enough of that," he said. "This is the note—"

"I'm still here," Franklin said. "Were you trying to hang up?"

This time Clare thumped a fist onto the phone hard enough to propel it from the table onto the floor. He cleared his throat and continued.

"It's the same—"

"I'm still on," came Franklin's voice from beneath a desk. "I'm confused as to what's happening."

"Dunst," growled Clare, and DI Dunst scooped up the phone, ending the call. Clare took a breath, his eyes bulging like they were being inflated by a bicycle pump.

"It's the same typewritten font as last time, no doubt at all. Listen to this. *'When the princess woke from the endless slumber of her first death she found that everyone in the castle had gone. For days she walked through the forest in search of shelter until she stumbled upon a fortress. Two strong men danced here, but a third dwelled in the shadows. He was a beast, and his ferocity left her breathless. When she could no longer dance, she paid the price for her beauty. Her time ran out, the last rose petal fell, and she died while all the court looked on.'*"

Clare paused for a moment, clearing his throat.

"*'And so our princess reawakened once again, her third life, blessed with fair looks and fairer hair. This one's good enough to keep, so said the witch who held her in the Northman's Turret as the water snapped in the shadow of the wall, but this time there will be time to hang around. Another day, but when midnight falls, so will she.'*"

The room was silent, as if they had plunged into an ocean. Kett flexed his jaw, swallowing until his ears popped.

"Any thoughts?" Clare asked.

"It's Rapunzel, I think," said Kett. "A tower, a witch, and the princess' hair. I read it to my girls all the time."

"Definitely," said Savage. "Water could mean the river? What's with the *first death, third life* stuff? It's like the killer is talking about the same woman, not different ones. Maybe the identity of the victims isn't personal, maybe it doesn't matter. Maybe they stand for something else in the killer's mind."

"That's good," said Kett.

"Also, there's a witch," said Duke, quietly.

"Huh?" said Clare.

"A witch," Duke said, staring at the open notepad in front of him. "I mean, maybe it's a—"

"Duke, if you're about to say a 'real witch' then I'm going to make you empty your locker and hand in your notice," said Clare, with deadly seriousness.

Duke slumped into his chair, disappointed.

"But Duke's onto something," Savage said, throwing the PC a bone. "Because it's weird that the story mentions a woman here, not a man,"

Clare considered it, then nodded.

"We already know we may be dealing with more than one suspect," he said. "It would be exceedingly hard for somebody to engineer these murders alone, unless they had unlimited time and resources."

"It could be gang related," Porter said. "Lots of people, lots of time."

"We'll come back to the gangs in a minute," Clare said.

"There's something else that's weird, too," said Kett. "We found a note with Jenny and a note with Fran, but we found Poppy's note inside her house, with no sign of *her*."

"You're right," the Superintendent said. "I'll send somebody back to search the house again, just to make sure. In the meantime, tear this note apart. Find every hidden meaning, catalogue every place, every person, every reference. The last piece of the story told us to look for the two strong men outside the Samson and Hercules, so I'm expecting this note to tell us something too. What's the Northman's Turret? I need to know where we look next."

"I'll make a list of all the towers and turrets in Norwich,

sir," Savage said. "Historical and otherwise. I'll start by the river."

"Good," Clare said. "I need somebody to cross-reference our missing women with the places we found them, see if there's a link."

"On it, Guv," said Porter.

"We're pretty close to a timeline of yesterday evening," Clare went on. "One of Jenny Eyler's neighbours tells us she left the house just before six, already drinking from a bottle of vodka. We know Jenny planned to meet Kevin Dufrane at eight, at Cow Tower, but she never made it there alive. Poppy dropped her son with her parents at half five then got a taxi into the city. Fran's movements are unknown, but Dunst, you spoke with the families of the other women."

"I did," said Dunst, clearing a throat that sounded full of tar. "Fortune Quinn lives in a student let near the bus station. Her flatmate is away but cameras show her leaving the flat at a quarter to six, dressed to the nines. Nobody I spoke to knew anything about her plans. Mum's up north, dad passed. The only people who really knew her were the other missing women. Beatrice Goodwin, or Batty, still lives at home. Her mother told me she left the house at lunchtime and she was planning to meet up with Jenny later on. We've found her on a few cameras and we're still tracking her movements."

He stopped talking to hack out a couple of unpleasant coughs.

"Picked up all five women on a camera outside of Frank's Bar on Bedford Street at six-twenty. They meet there, but they don't go in. They move up Bedford Street heading towards St Andrews. We hit a blind spot there and we haven't found them yet."

"I've checked in with most of the pubs and bars down

there," Clare said. "Nobody remembers seeing them. But we'll pick up their movements eventually. What else have we got?"

"Body we found in the car in the woods is definitely Fran's boyfriend, Simon Womack," said DCI Kate Pearson from the back of the room. "Dental records confirmed it. We've got CCTV of the car heading across town from Fran's flat. Womack is driving but there's somebody in the back. Might be wearing a hood, we can't see their face. We've had no luck with footage of the killer after he set fire to the car and legged it. He just vanished."

"It might be unrelated to our killer," said Savage. "We know Simon Womack was working drugs for a local gang, the Beggar Boys. What if he was killed because of that?"

"Hell of a coincidence," said Clare. "Unless the gangs are responsible for the missing women."

"Which is a growing possibility," Kett said. "I went to the place where Martha Hansen-Andrews was hit by a car back in September, the night she was out with Jenny and the others. There's a lot of gang-related crime there too and one of the local shop owners mentioned the Beggar Boys by name. They deal in the churchyard and charge protection fees to the local businesses. It might be worth chasing to see if they have anything to do with this."

"Spalding's already working that angle," Clare said, walking to the door. He opened it and bellowed Spalding's name into the bullpen. A few seconds later the DS rushed in, clutching papers to her chest.

"Sorry, sorry," she said. "Lost track of time."

"Gangs," said Clare.

Spalding dropped her papers onto the nearest desk, sorting through them.

"It's all here," she said. "Lists of active gang members

and all of Simon Womack's affiliates. He used to be part of the same organisation as Phil Spenser, the guy who shagged the holly bush. The word organisation is a little too good for them. Half of them have been busted, the others wouldn't know how to make a cuppa in a tea factory."

She looked at Porter, and so did the rest of the room.

"Huh?" said Porter.

"But word on the street is that Womack had jumped ship, he was working for another gang, the Beggar Boy Crew. County lines, they're mixed up with some outfits in London and they're active all over the city. Quite a stranglehold on the cocaine and meth market, but they don't stray. It's unlikely that they're connected to our dead women. *Woman*, sorry."

"Any other possibles?" Clare said.

"Just two, sir."

She rummaged in the pile of documents again, pulling out a photograph. Everyone craned in but it was too small to really make out.

"Jonah Boner," she said, and Dunst broke into a peal of wheezing laughter.

"Something funny, Detective?" said Clare, and the old DI managed to control himself.

"Jonah Boner, a children's author who was picked up last year after he broke a prostitute's nose."

"Hang on," said Kett. "He's called Jonah Boner, he sleeps with prostitutes, and he's a children's author?"

"Wait for it," said Spalding, throwing Kett an impatient look. "The prostitute thing was an accident, apparently, he opened the door in her face. Bullshit, if you ask me, but she didn't press charges and there wasn't enough evidence to go after him. Thanks to the joys of social media he lost his publisher, his kids and his wife, and now spends most of his time ranting on the internet about how much he hates women. A real winner by all accounts."

"Reminds me of the man who was supposed to meet Jenny for a date," said Savage. "Kevin Dufrane."

"Did Boner write fairy tales, by any chance?" Clare asked, pulling another Bounty from his jacket pocket and tapping it on the palm of his other hand like it was a pack of cigarettes.

"No, action stuff. Fantasy. I've got some Uniforms bringing him in." She turned to Savage. "Speaking of Kevin, we've accessed his laptop, and Jenny Eyler's, too. They were definitely talking. I've printed out the relevant pages but the gist of it is pretty basic. Jenny was talking to a bunch of men and milking them for money. She wasn't doing anything dirty, no naked photos or anything, just a lot of bullshitting about her terrible life, about how she wanted to get away from home, start fresh. She was making a lot of money. We're looking into the men she was speaking with but most were in America and sending her money through PayPal. The others are in the UK and have decent alibis. According to the chats we found on her phone, Jenny met with her friends at six-twenty pm and was planning to meet Kevin at eight. Once she'd taken the money from him she was going to make up an excuse to leave and meet up with the others again."

"Good to know," said Clare. "What else?"

"The other potential suspect is, hang on..."

She flicked through more papers, then swore.

"I've left him in the printer. Rupert Holden."

Porter sat up straight, suddenly alert.

"He got sent down a few years ago for attacking his wife. You want to know what he attacked her with?"

Everyone waited.

"A book of fairy tales. A *big* book. After he knocked her unconscious he tore out a dozen pages and tried to choke her with them. Pushed them into her mouth like he was stuffing a turkey. She only survived because their teenage son walked in and intervened, broke his dad's arm pulling him off her. Holden got eight years, which isn't anywhere near enough if you ask me. Want to know when he got out?"

The room stayed silent, everyone holding their breath.

"Three months ago," Spalding said. "And there's more. Holden used to own a book shop over on St Benedict's, second-hand stuff and a few antiques, including the one he tried to murder his wife with."

"Holy shit," Kett said. "Where is he now?"

"We don't know," Spalding said. "No fixed address but we're looking for him."

"His name's Rupert Holden?" Porter said. "You've got a photo?"

"Yeah," Spalding said, darting out of the room. When she came back she was holding a print-out—much clearer and larger than the last. Porter clamped his hands in his hair.

"Fuck."

"What?" Kett asked.

"Holden. I saw him outside Cow Tower this morning. I *spoke* to him."

"You *what?*" said Clare, the words erupting from his mouth like he'd vomited them. His fist tightened around the Bounty so hard the wrapper split, a chunk of chocolate dropping to the floor.

"I spoke to him," Porter said again. "I stopped him because he looked suspicious. He had..."

He moved his hands from his hair to his face, hiding there.

"He had green fingers, like he'd just been gardening."

"Jesus Fucking Christ, Porter!" Clare roared. "Where was this? Exactly?"

"He said he was homeless, that he lived on the riverside. But he said... hang on, let me remember. He said he had a house, too, I'm sure of it. He just didn't like staying there. He was... I mean he didn't..."

Porter gave up. Clare lifted a gangly leg and booted his empty chair, sending it careening into the wall, then into the legs of a young PC. He pointed his limp Bounty across the room.

"Find him, you dolt, and if you let him go again then I'll shove this so far up your toss hole you'll be tasting coconut for a week."

Everyone winced. Clare sucked in a breath.

"Fucking *go*!"

CHAPTER EIGHTEEN

PLEASE BE HERE, PLEASE BE HERE, PLEASE BE HERE.

Porter stopped by the wooden bench that sat beside the river, bracing his hands on his knees as he fought for breath. He'd sprinted the hundred yards or so from the road, praying with every step, with every frantic beat of his heart, that Rupert Holden would be sitting where he had been that morning, his red rucksack at his feet.

But the man was long gone.

"Fuck," he said, turning to the crowd of uniformed police that had followed him. They were hard to make out in the dark, the sun long gone and the lights doing little to beat back the night. He hated it when the clocks went back because the days gave up far too easily. The river moved past lazily, utterly oblivious. "Search the riverbank, the hedges. Check the cathedral grounds, too, and those cricket pitches. Find him."

The coppers split up, the sound of their feet like thunder as they went on the hunt. Savage walked up in their wake, Kett halfway down the road behind her. Both of them were on their phones.

"I'm going to check the tower," he told them, breaking into a run again until Cow Tower came into view. It was taped off, and two constables stood on either side of the door, shivering their arses off in their yellow jackets. They stood to attention when they saw Porter coming.

"Hey, you seen a man here, fifties, greying hair, red bag, green hands, kind of homeless-looking?"

"Somebody tried to take a piss on the back of the tower a few minutes ago," said the woman. "We chased him off. He was definitely homeless, he's the chap who's always outside the library, though. Much younger. Haven't seen anyone else, you?"

The guy didn't answer, he just shook his head. He was seriously pissed off, by the look of it, but Porter couldn't care less.

"If he shows up, call control immediately, yeah?" he said as he walked away. "And sling some cuffs on the fucker."

"Really?" the first PC shouted after him. "Arrest anyone with grey hair and a bag? Sir? *Sir*?"

Porter started running, breaking right at the dogleg turn in the river and heading south. People moved out of his way with some urgency, less to do with the speed he was moving, he knew, and more to do with the look of desperation on his face. He'd fucked up, and he'd fucked up *big*. It was pretty much the first thing they told you when you started the job—not the teachers and trainers, not the course books, but the *coppers*—trust your gut. Always trust your gut.

He'd known there was something weird about Holden, he'd felt it strongly enough to pick him out of a crowd and follow him, to ask him where he'd been the day before. The man hadn't given a good answer, either, and Porter had just left him to it.

"Idiot," he said, resisting the urge to punch himself in the face. "You're a fucking idiot, Pete."

If Holden was their man, if they'd missed their chance to find him and save the lives of the missing women, Porter would never forgive himself.

They'd be dead because of him.

Come on, he said, skidding through a gate into the garden of an old house. He grabbed the flint wall to steady himself, walking down the side of the building, past students and families and tourists who had absolutely no inkling of what went on in the city after dark, of the horrors that dwelled here.

The monsters who lived amongst them.

He ducked through another gate and saw the wide archway of Pull's Ferry, the water drifting past on the other side of it. There was nobody here. He walked beneath the arch anyway, just to be sure, turning his head to the dark sky and loosing a curse that travelled across the water, turning heads on the other side of the river.

Pulling out his phone, he called Kett.

"Where'd you go?" said the DCI.

"I'm up by Pull's Ferry, sir. No sign of him here. I'll come back."

He hung up before Kett could reply, sliding his phone into his pocket. Kett would never have made a mistake like this. Kett lived on gut instinct, he'd built a career on it. Kett's gut was a finely tuned instrument, and even on the rare occasion when it wasn't, he always erred on the side of caution. Better to be safe than sorry.

"You're a fucking idiot," he told himself again, feeling a creeping sense of shame that made his skin cold, that made his scalp shrivel.

But it wasn't too late. It didn't have to be too late.

He returned to the front of the building, pounding on the door so hard his hand went instantly numb.

"Police!" he shouted. "Open up!"

He heard the door being unlocked and stood back as it opened. A young woman peeked out at Porter from the dark interior.

"Can I help you?" she said.

"You live here?"

"Work," she said. "Norfolk Heritage. Why?"

"I'm police," Porter said, fumbling his warrant card and almost dropping it. "I'm looking for a man who sometimes sleeps under the arch. Early fifties, greying hair, carries a red bag. Have you seen him?"

"Rupert?" she said, letting the door open a little more. "If it's him you mean then yeah, I've seen him. He's always trying to get in here, and he's creepy, you know? Like, a nice guy, but I always catch him staring at me when he thinks I'm not looking. He says some weird stuff too. Inappropriate. I've reported him a few times."

"Have you seen him today?"

"No," she said. "But I wasn't looking. He was here last night for a bit, until the rain got too heavy. I didn't see him but my boss did. He's called Rupert too, Little Rupert. What are the chances? Little Rupert and Creepy Rupert. But Little Rupert is okay. He tells them to move on, if he sees them under the arch. It's dangerous, with the river and everything, and half these guys are off their faces on wine and beer, sometimes drugs."

"Do you know anything about Rupert?" Porter said. "*Creepy* Rupert. Anywhere else he likes to hang out."

"I sometimes see him up by the river when I'm walking home," the woman said. "Past the tower. He sits on a bench and, you know, ogles the women when they walk past. Everyone says it's harmless but..."

She seemed to think of something, shaking her head.

"Wait, this isn't anything to do with that woman they found, is it? In the tower? They're calling her Sweet Briar Rose. My mum called to tell me."

"Anywhere else," Porter said, ignoring her question. "Please, *think*."

She nodded, leaning out of the door to point towards the river.

"He's been moved on a few times, by police. The last couple of times they've taken him over there. Apparently, he's got a house, so I have no idea why he chooses to sleep out here. It's not his house, it belongs to another man, from what I remember."

"You know the address?" Porter asked, leaning in.

"No, but you can see it from here. It's the pink one."

He squinted into the dark, seeing a bright pink house bleached almost white by the street lights.

"Yellow door?" Porter said, and the woman nodded. "Thanks."

He bolted, trying to remember the best way to cross the river. He called Kett as he ran north.

"He's got a house on Riverside Road," he said before Kett could get a word out. "Pink one almost directly opposite the ferry. I'm going there now."

"Don't go in by yourself," Kett said, sounding like he was running. "I'll meet you there and I'll get Clare to send Gorski and her team."

Porter hung up, practically leaping up a set of stairs in one go and finding himself beside a pub. A stone bridge crossed the river here and Porter made his way over, doubling back on the other side. His phone was ringing—

Kett—but he ignored it, scattering pedestrians as he jogged down the narrow pavement.

Holden's place was right in the middle of a long line of brick terraces on the other side of the road, a bus stop right outside it and a bus idling there as a couple of people climbed off. Porter waited for a break in the traffic before crossing, looking up at the building. It was severely neglected, the pink paint peeling and the single upstairs window covered with a sheet of plywood. The garden hadn't been touched for years, dozens of carrier bags and other litter caught in the overgrown bushes.

It looked empty.

Porter's phone was ringing again, and this time it was Clare.

"Boss," Porter said as he answered.

"Do *not* Kett this up, Porter. Where are you?"

"Right outside," he said.

"Then stay there, you hear? That's a tossing order. Kett's on his way, and you will wait for him."

"What about a firearms team?"

"They're *en route* but it's going to take a while. Secure the house. If he's in there, he won't go anywhere."

"What if one of our women is in there with him?" Porter asked, and he heard Clare sigh.

"That's your call, Detective," he said. "But you *will* wait for the rest of your team."

He hung up. Porter stared down the street just as Kett and Savage reached the bridge, a line of Uniforms behind them. Two IRVs were blazing down the road from the other direction, their lights rolling.

The bus hissed, grunted then pulled away, filling the air with fumes.

"You better be in there," Porter said to the house.

"Anything?" Kett shouted as he crossed the street.

"This is his place. I haven't let him know we're here."

"If he's in there, he'll know," Kett said as the IRVs pulled up. "Savage, watch the back, and take a couple of PCs with you."

Savage nodded, peeling off towards the end of the row.

"Gorski's running late," Kett said. "But I don't think we should wait. If this is our man, he could have hostages."

Porter smiled.

"I said the same thing to Clare."

"Then we go in, but we do it carefully."

"Didn't think that word was in your vocabulary, sir," Porter said.

Kett hissed a laugh through his nose, rubbing his chest.

"You do the honours," the DCI said. "Catch this arsehole, make it right."

Porter opened the stiff gate and walked up the steps, thick brambles catching on his suit, clawing at his hands and face. The air here was pungent with the smell of rotting vegetation, piles of what looked like mown grass turning to mulch in the dirt. A little row of beer cans sat on the inside of the living room window, thick with cobwebs.

"You sure this is the place?" Kett said as he followed. "Looks deserted."

"We'll find out."

Porter balled a fist and thumped on the door hard enough to rain flakes of paint from the lintel.

"Police," he bellowed. "Open up."

He looked down the steps to see three PCs waiting, their batons out. More were climbing from the IRVs, including Duke, who pulled a breaching ram from the boot.

"Police," Porter shouted as he knocked again. "Rupert

Holden, if you're in there then this is your last chance to open the door."

Nothing. Duke was climbing the steps with the ram and Porter held out his hands, clicking his fingers.

"Give it," he said.

"Really?" Duke replied, pouting through his beard. "I love this bit."

Porter grabbed the heavy steel ram from him and swung it hard into the Yale. The door opened with a storm of splinters and dust, the corridor beyond thick with darkness.

"Police!" yelled Duke, flicking out his baton as he bundled inside. "Do not move!"

Two more Uniforms rushed in after him, all of them shouting. Then Porter's patience ran out and he pushed through the door. The house stank of rot, the walls black with damp and strips of wallpaper hanging like loose skin. He followed one constable into the living room to find an old sofa covered with blankets, and a TV that had been knocked to the floor, the screen smashed. More beer cars had been stacked against the far wall, hundreds of them.

"Police!" yelled Duke from the kitchen. "Don't move."

"Fuck you!" came a reply.

Porter ran down the corridor, through a narrow dining room into an even smaller kitchen. It was pitch black in here, the window boarded tight, but one of the PCs had her torch out while Duke snapped handcuffs on a man who had been practically folded in two over the table.

"Get out of my house!" the man yelled wetly, craning his head around to look at Porter.

"It's not him," Porter said, seeing his long hair, his moustache. "Rupert Holden, where is he?"

"I don't know," the guy said.

Porter backed out of the room, squeezing past another

PC and heading for the stairs. He ran his hand down the damp wall, searching for a switch but not finding one. He took the stairs two at a time, pulling his torch from his pocket and clicking it on to reveal a small landing with four doors. One was open, leading into a bathroom. The other three were all closed and sealed with heavy-duty locks.

"Get the ram up here," he shouted, leaning over the banister.

He walked to the nearest door, the master bedroom at the front of the house, and tried the lock to see that it wasn't engaged. Even so, the door refused to budge, and he had to put a shoulder to it to drive it open bit by bit. There was something heavy in front of it, he realised.

Heavy enough to be a body.

He rammed his shoulder into the door again, then again, until the gap was wide enough to squeeze through. The room beyond was rammed with clutter. On the floor was a binbag, maybe more than one, and the smell coming from them was enough to make the gorge rise in his throat.

"What have you got?" Duke asked as he came up the stairs, the ram in his hand.

"Not sure yet," Porter replied. "Get those other doors open."

"Yes, sir," Duke replied.

Porter entered the bedroom, the heavy bags trying to close the door behind him. He swept the torch from left to right but it was impossible to see anything past piles of old newspapers and stacks of boxes.

"Police," he said. "Rupert, if you're in here, make yourself known."

He was answered by the crunch of the battering ram as it took out the next door along.

"Police!" Duke roared.

Porter took another step into the room, searching the mess. The binbags slid into each other, snapping the door shut as they avalanched to the floor. He crouched, gagging again at the unspeakable butcher-shop stench of them. There were gloves in his pocket and he held the torch between his teeth as he fumbled them on. Then he pulled the nearest bag open to see a glistening mound of rotting meat.

It was too much and he gagged again, putting his arm over his mouth in an attempt to stop himself from being sick. Somehow, he swallowed it down, but his eyes were watering so much he could barely see. He stood up, groaning.

"Hey," said a quiet voice right behind him.

Porter spun, carving out a Catherine wheel of light before finding a face.

Then something struck the torch from his hand and the room went dark.

"Fuck," Porter said, backing away.

"Am I invisible enough for you now?" Holden said, laughing.

And all Porter felt was the cold kiss of steel as it punched into his flesh.

CHAPTER NINETEEN

KETT WAS CLIMBING THE STAIRS WHEN HE HEARD Porter cry out.

Not a shout of anger, not a bellowed command, but a gargled scream of pain—instantly and unbearably recognisable.

He grabbed the bannister and hauled himself to the top just as Porter called out again. It was coming from the room to the left, the front bedroom. The door was shut. Duke appeared from the room across the landing, the battering ram in his hand.

"Who was that?" the PC asked.

There was a splintering crunch from the bedroom, an angry roar from somebody else. Kett heard the sound of something heavy fall to the floor and he took his chance, running into the door like he was tackling it. A heavy weight was blocking it from the other side but he managed to open it enough to see that it was pitch black in there. More noises spilled out, the sound of two people fighting. He opened the torch on his phone, trying to make sense of what was blocking the way.

"Move!" Duke said, and Kett didn't hesitate as the giant PC hurled himself into the door with every ounce of his bodyweight. The top hinge ripped free and the door tilted open, Duke falling through the gap onto a pile of binbags.

Kett stepped over him, the light from his phone revealing two men on the floor in the middle of the room. The one on the top was Porter, his face a mask of agony and rage as he tried to pin the other guy.

"Knife," Porter grunted, and Kett saw it in the man's hand.

He crossed the room in a heartbeat and kicked the man hard in his hand, the knife sliding into a pile of boxes. Duke was beside him, his hands wrapped tight around the man's other arm.

"Used my cuffs already," he said.

"Here," said a voice from the door as Savage appeared. She hurled a pair of handcuffs and Duke caught them, snapping them shut around the man's wrist. The guy was struggling so much he looked like he was having a fit, a geyser of foam spraying from his lips and the whites of his eyes the brightest things in the room.

"Fuck you!" he spat. "Fuck you fuck you fuck you."

Porter climbed off him, and between him, Duke, and Kett they rolled the man onto his stomach, securing his other arm.

"Rupert Holden," Porter said. "You are under arrest for..."

The words dried up in his throat and he keeled over, his head cracking off the floor.

"Jesus, Pete!" Kett yelled. "Fuck, Savage, get an ambulance!"

"Stuck you good, didn't I!" Holden said, laughing.

"Get him out of here," Kett said. "And get some fucking light in here!"

It was too dark, but when he ran his hands down Porter's body he felt the blood on his sleeve, hot and sticky.

"Hang on, Pete," he said. "Savage, now!"

"It's coming," she said as she ran back into the room, almost tripping on the binbags. She dropped to her knees beside Porter, her torch lighting up his face. "How bad?"

"Bad enough," said Holden as Duke hauled him through the door. He laughed again, the sound cut off suddenly and replaced by the thump of something big falling down the stairs.

"Whoops," said Duke.

"Pete," said Savage, gently touching Porter's face with her free hand. "Pete, can you hear me?"

Kett ripped off Porter's jacket, blood pattering onto the floor. The DI's entire left side was drenched, his shirt crimson.

"Come on," said Kett.

He tore the shirt open, running a hand up Porter's ribs, under his arm.

"Can you see the wound?" he said.

"No," said Savage, leaning in, the torch making the blood so bright it didn't look real. "Wait, there."

She was pointing to Porter's tree trunk arm, and the two-inch gash in the side of his bicep. Blood sluiced out of it, but it wasn't gushing. Savage undid her belt and pulled it free, and Kett held Porter's arm up while she fixed the improvised tourniquet. By the time she'd finished, the big DI was stirring.

"Pete," said Kett. "You're okay, mate, you're safe. Take it slow."

Porter's eyes opened and he blinked up at them both, spit leaking from his lips.

"Is it okay?" he asked, still groggy.

"Your arm? Yeah, it's not a bad cut."

"No," said Porter. "The suit. It's a Tom Ford."

Despite everything, Kett laughed.

"You pratt," he said.

"Don't do that," Savage added, bunching up Porter's jacket and pressing it against the wound. "You bloody scared me, sir."

There was the bleep of a siren outside, somebody yelling up the stairs.

"Ambulance is here!"

Kett slid onto his backside, taking a deep, painful breath.

"Ketted that one up, didn't you," he said.

Porter laughed, then winced.

"We got him, though," he said, resting his head on the floor. "We got that fucker."

"Yeah you got him," Kett said. "Let's just hope he's our man."

IT WAS ALMOST two hours later that Kett walked out of the front door of Holden's house into the cold embrace of the night, and the rain. He took the steps carefully, partly because the wet stone was like ice, and partly because he was exhausted. He didn't trust his limbs to work properly.

He checked his watch to see that it was almost seven, then stood to the side to let a member of the forensic crew out, another binbag in his gloved hands. There hadn't been any bodies in there, just a butcher's shop's worth of meat—

leftovers, mainly, crawling with maggots and thick with mould.

They'd already sifted through two of the three bedrooms upstairs but there was so much crap they still a long way to go. Whatever else he was, Holden was undoubtedly a hoarder.

Kett pulled out his phone to see three missed calls from Billie, and another one from the landline at home—probably his mum. He was in the process of calling his wife back when a text arrived from Savage.

Porter fine. It wasn't a stab wound, it was a slice, not deep. No idea why he fainted.

Kett took a deep breath of relief. For a second there—an awful, terrifying second—he'd thought that Pete Porter was a dead man.

He opened up the call list again but this time it was a shout from across the road that stopped him. Clare was lumbering towards him like a horror film zombie, cars braking hard to avoid hitting him. He tripped up the kerb, then stopped to give the kerb a murderous stare, like he meant to arrest it. Eventually, he made it to Kett.

"How is it that on the first day you're back, somebody gets hurt?" he said.

Kett didn't have an answer, and even if he did he wasn't sure he'd have had the strength to get it out. Clare sighed, patting his jacket pocket but not finding anything. He looked at the house and at the forensics team who were visible through the open front door.

"Tell me good news," he said.

"It's too early to say," Kett replied. "Holden attacked Porter, there's no doubt about it. And it wasn't some self-defence thing. He knew we were police, and he made a comment to Porter relating to something they'd spoken about this morning. He knew exactly who he was attacking."

"Porter's fine, I don't know if you've heard," said Clare, rainwater dripping off the end of his nose, hanging in the hairs there. "Just a scratch. He's a big, soft baby."

"There was a lot of blood, to be fair."

"A baby," Clare said again. "But Holden's finished, you don't attack a copper like that. What we need to know is whether this is the same man who killed Jenny Eyler. So find me something, Kett. Now."

"It's hard finding anything in there, sir," Kett said, shivering as the rain crept down the back of his shirt. "I don't think Holden has thrown a single thing away in his life. His room was the one at the front, where Porter was attacked. There's barely space to move. He didn't even throw his leftovers away. Bags full of rotting food. We counted seven of them piled by the door. Christ, the *stench*."

He could still smell it on himself. He thought he might smell it there for the rest of his life.

"He had piles of books, too," he went on. "Some of them look like antiques but there's nothing related to fairy tales. Not yet, anyway. Nothing on our missing women. No grab and go stuff, ropes or duct tape, anything like that. No drugs, no benzos. No plans, no blueprints, no outlines. For these kinds of crimes we expect research, right? It's hard work, it needs to be planned out. If Holden's behind it then he's using another building as his workspace. He has to be, because there's nothing here that paints him as a serial killer."

Clare pulled a gurning face of disappointment.

"Savage mentioned another man?"

"Flatmate," Kett said. "Uh, Benjamin Gooch, I think his

name was. We've detained him in the kitchen, for now. There are seven men living here."

"Seven?"

"Yeah. I've got their names and we're rounding them up. The rooms are dirt cheap because the house is a shithole. Three men were sharing one room, I think they're Lithuanian. There's an older lad who lives in the front room downstairs, shits in a bucket. I can see why Holden preferred to spend his time outside. But we've checked, and he's been living here on and off since he was released. Gooch said he's a bit weird but a pretty normal guy. The neighbours didn't pick up on anything unusual, although they've made plenty of complaints about the garden and the smell."

"It's not him, is it?" Clare said. "I've got this pain in my arsehole and it's telling me this isn't our man. What's *your* arsehole telling you, Kett?"

"Um, I have no idea, sir," he said. "It's not somewhere I tend to look for inspiration."

He brushed a hand through his wet hair, hearing his phone ring in his pocket and ignoring it.

"Holden doesn't feel right," he said after a few seconds. "I read the arrest report for when he attacked his wife. He thought she was having an affair because he found some messages on her phone. He was in his home office and he literally grabbed the first thing he could reach, which happened to be a book. Not fairy tales but some kind of fantasy book for adults. He didn't even do much damage with it, he just knocked her over. It was the pages he stuffed into her mouth that got him the attempted murder charge, because she almost choked to death. I don't think the book meant anything to him. But this..."

Another forensic scientist walked down the steps

carrying a binbag. She nodded at Clare as she carried it to a waiting van.

"This whole thing with the missing women feels different. This isn't a crime of passion, at least not like Holden's was. This isn't a fit of rage. Hay said it best, I think. This is clever and cunning and cruel. It's *cold*. This is a different kind of statement altogether. So no, I don't think Holden fits."

"I hate you," Clare muttered.

"What?" said Kett.

"I said I hate *this*," the Super continued. "We need to get him into the interview room as soon as possible, but he's currently in hospital with a broken wrist. Know anything about that?"

Kett remembered the sound of Holden falling down the stairs, and Duke's *"Whoops."*

"Probably happened when he attacked Porter," he said, looking down the street. "Want me to go talk to him?"

"No," said Clare. "You've done enough. I'll do it."

Kett's phone was ringing again and he took it out of his pocket, seeing Billie's name.

"I should probably answer this," he said.

"Don't bother," Clare shot back. "You're on your way home anyway."

"I can stay," Kett started, but Clare waved him down.

"You smell like a rubbish tip. You look like a rubbish tip. And you're covered in Porter's blood. We're in front of this, Robbie. Even if it's not Holden, we're running ahead of our killer's game. He gave us until midnight tonight to find Fran and we got her. We saved her. He's given us until midnight tomorrow to find his next victim. The best thing you can do is go home, get a few hours' sleep, then come back fresh tomorrow."

"And hope our killer sticks to his word," Kett said. "Speaking of which, I don't think we should make it public that Fran survived. I want him to think he's winning, because he's more likely to play by his own rules."

"Agreed," said Clare. "Fran's under guard at the hospital and they're keeping her isolated. Her mum and dad are there, but other than us, nobody else knows."

Kett nodded, a bout of vertigo making the street swing in wild circles. Clare was still speaking but his voice sounded tinny.

"We've got eyes on the ballroom where we found her, discreetly, just in case he comes back. But I can't see it happening. I've put cars outside all of our missing women's houses, too, as well as Sue Hansen's house. We might get lucky. We've pulled in help from a couple of other Forces to work through the night, so go home."

"Okay, sir," Kett said. "You win."

He walked away, calling Billie as he went, hearing Clare shout out behind him.

"You picked a hell of a day to come back to work, DCI Kett."

CHAPTER TWENTY

KETT CLOSED THE FRONT DOOR BEHIND HIM, LEANING on it for a moment to let the warmth of the house sink into his bones. Outside, the night was throwing a tantrum, the rain lashing down with some fury and the wind shaking the trees, stripping them bare.

He'd hitched a ride back in an IRV, doing his best to avoid an awkward conversation with the PC who drove him —awkward mainly because the man had wound all the windows down to try to get rid of the smell. It was well past eight now and he felt like an inflatable that had been punctured. It was all he could do not to slide down the door and fall asleep on the mat.

The house was quiet, unnervingly so. All the lights and lamps were on—Billie still insisted on that the moment the sun began to set—and so was the TV, the volume muted. It made everything seem too bright and too artificial. Kett was gripped by the sudden belief that this wasn't his house at all, that he'd stumbled onto the set of some kind of production, and a wash of panic climbed up from his stomach, sitting at the back of his throat.

Somebody has made this look like your house, he thought. *But it isn't. It isn't real.*

And he suddenly pictured his family as little wind-up toys waddling down the corridor, all smiles and dead eyes while more of Hollenbeck's ghosts waited in the shadows.

"Stop it," he said, his arms breaking into goosebumps.

He took off his overcoat, trying to avoid touching the blood that had soaked right through into his suit. His shirt and his vest were just as bad and he tugged off his tie before pulling the entire ensemble over his head. He checked the living room to find it empty and walked to the kitchen to see that it was deserted too. He ran some hot water into the basin and shoved his suit jacket in there to soak, throwing the shirt in the bin. It was well past saving.

He was actually salivating as he filled the kettle, feeling like Pavlov's Dog as he dropped teabags into three mugs. He'd not managed a cup since he left the house that morning—a million years ago, it felt like.

He'd started up the stairs before he heard the sound of his family, and the relief of it made him feel warmer than the central heating had. He stopped for a moment, listening to Moira's goofy belly laugh and laughing softly himself. For a moment he didn't move, because he was gripped by a sensation that he hadn't felt for so long, not since he'd left the Force all those months ago.

The sensation that he didn't belong here. That he wasn't part of this world anymore.

He felt like a spectator, somebody watching a show.

No, it was more than that. He felt almost like a spirit, as if when he walked to the top of the stairs and into the girls' room they simply wouldn't see him there. And he knew why, of course. Because he'd picked the job over his children, over his wife, over his family. He'd picked the fucking job, and it was going to consume him.

He started up the steps again, heading for the master bedroom but stopping when he heard Alice call out.

"Dad?"

She poked her head from the door of the middle bedroom, her smile the biggest thing in the world.

"Dad!"

He barely had time to brace before she thumped into him, her bony arms locking themselves constrictor-tight around his ribs. He grunted, then laughed again, wrapping her in a hug that she instantly wormed her way out of.

"Hey, kiddo," he said.

"Daddy!" came the cries of his youngest two daughters, both of them exploding from the bedroom like cannonballs. Evie hit his legs, Moira toddling past with all the grace of a drunken sailor. Kett had to reach out to stop her from tumbling down the stairs.

"I missed you, Daddy!" said Evie, frowning up at him. "Why are you naked? Did you go to work naked?"

"I'm not naked," he said. "I just put my jacket in—"

"Why do you smell like a bin?" she asked, stepping back and grabbing her nose.

"Bin!" said Moira, imitating her sister. "Gross!"

"You do actually smell like a bin," said Alice.

"You didn't put clean pants on, did you?" said Evie, evidently disgusted. "I told you to. I told you to put clean pants on for your new job."

"I did, Evie."

"Those are very smelly old pants," she insisted.

"Old pants!" Moira added.

"Dad," said Alice, genuinely disappointed. "That's so embarrassing."

"It's not my pants!" Kett protested.

Billie appeared in the door, and she looked as tired as Kett felt. When she smiled at him it was full of love, but full of something else, too. Pity, maybe, or grief. He smiled back as best he could.

"Let Daddy clean himself up," she said. "We were so close to finally being asleep. So close."

"Sorry," he said.

"Maybe he could read you a quick story to settle you down," she said. "If you're not too tired?"

"I'm never too tired for a story," he said. "But only if you get back into bed right now."

The girls cheered as they ran past Billie, and Kett heard the squeal of springs as they leapt into the two beds that waited for them. Ever since his mum had moved in, the girls had been in one room, two beds on opposite walls and Alice on a spare mattress between them. It had started out fine, but it was getting to be a strain—especially for Alice, who really needed her own space.

"Five minutes," he said. "Where's Mum?"

"You've just missed her. She's helping out at the church tonight. She asked me to give you a big kiss when you got back."

Billie stepped up to him and immediately reeled back, her voice hoarse.

"Oh god, Robbie. That's so bad. Why do you smell like a bin?"

"I..." he started, then he caught a whiff of himself. "I really do. Sorry. Maybe make it ten minutes."

He showered as quickly as he could, using half a bottle of Radox body wash before he felt like he'd scrubbed away the last trace of Rupert Holden's mouldering binbags. He'd forgotten to bring a change of clothes so he threw on Billie's oversized dressing gown, walking back to the girls' room to see the three of them sitting in Moira's bed fighting over a picture book—one of the pages already torn.

"Hey, hey! That's enough, I'm here."

"My book," said Moira with a face like thunder.

"It's mine," said Alice. "I got it for Christmas and she's broke it."

"Didn't, butthead."

"Do you want me to read it or not?" Kett asked, clambering over Alice's mattress and sitting on the edge of the bed. He held out a hand. "Gimme."

Alice snatched the book from Moira and passed it over. Kett took it, feeling the warmth of the house drain out of him when he saw the title.

"*Classic Fairy Tales*," he said. "You're sure this is what you want?"

They all nodded, Moira yawning.

"Cinderella," said Alice.

"No, the silly little man one," Evie said. "We always have Cinderella."

"Sleeping one!" said Moira, and Kett had to close his eyes for a second as he saw Jenny Eyler in her casket of thorns.

"Silly little man?" he said, flicking through the book. "What's that one?"

"Flumpywartkins," said Evie.

"Huh?"

"Spankysnortleshorts," said Alice with a laugh.

"No," said Evie, sagely. "Rumplystiltshins."

"Rumpelstiltskin?" Kett said. They all nodded and he found the story in the middle of the book. An illustration of a strange little dancing man giggled up at him, as sinister as all of these pictures always seemed to be. The girls snuggled down, pulling the duvet up to their chins as he started to read. "Once upon a time..."

And he stopped, because something seemed to scratch across the back of his mind, the first tickle of a thought.

"Earth to Dad," said Alice. "Hello?"

It vanished, and he started reading again. He'd only made it through the first couple of pages when Billie reappeared, a mug of tea in each hand.

"Then they all lived happily ever after," he said, snapping the book shut. "The end."

"What?" said Evie. "That's not what happens. That isn't the end!"

"It is tonight," Kett said. "It's late, and Daddy loves you very much but if he doesn't drink a cup of tea in the next few minutes then he's going to dry up into a great big prune. Come on, it's ridiculously late."

Evie held out her arms and he lifted her into her own bed, while Alice rolled dramatically onto her nest of bedding. Moira grumped, but her eyes were already half closed and she was teetering on the edge of sleep. He tucked Evie in and kissed her gently on the forehead.

"Do they always live happily ever after?" she asked through a yawn that spread to him.

Kett thought of Jenny again, of Fran with her broken ribs. He wondered where the other women were now, Beatrice and Poppy and Fortune. He wondered whether they'd be able to find them in time.

Or if it was already too late.

"Yeah," he lied. "They do. Goodnight, girls."

He blew them kisses then met Billie by the door.

"Nice bathrobe," she said. "It's a bit short, but the frilly bits suit you."

Kett laughed, taking the tea when she offered it. It was

far too hot but he didn't care, the first molten mouthful still heavenly.

"You have no idea how much I needed that."

"Bad day?"

"It was fine," he said.

Billie gave him a look that was all too clear.

"Sorry," he said.

He shook his head, leading her into their bedroom and pushing the door halfway shut. When he'd agreed to go back to the job, Billie had made him promise two things: the first was that every time he needed to make a dangerous decision, he would think about his girls. The second was that no matter how bad it got, he wouldn't keep anything from her.

"This is my life too," she said as she climbed into bed, the same thing she'd always told him during those long, difficult conversations they'd had since Whytetail. "It's my life, my pain, my heart. Don't forget, I've been there too."

Of course she had, trapped in a basement for weeks on end with a pig-headed devil. He could never forget it. The scars may have grown faint and familiar, but they were still there.

"You can't do this alone, Robbie. Share it."

He climbed into bed next to her, and when she held out her arms to him he let her cradle his head, her fingers kneading his hair.

"Share it," she said again. "Every last thing."

And he did.

CHAPTER TWENTY-ONE

Sunday

SAVAGE WAS RUNNING ON RAGE.

It wasn't even six yet, the night pushing down on the city like it was trying to suffocate it. It had been raining for hours and the downpour wasn't showing any sign of letting up, the gutters roaring and the drains gargling.

What little sleep Savage had got after she'd left Porter at the hospital hadn't been good sleep. It had been fitful and full of bad dreams. In one, she'd lain on a stone bed while a faceless man wrapped her in thorns, the phantom pain shaking her awake with such urgency that Colin the dog had scampered off the bed and out of the bedroom door, her tail between her legs.

She couldn't even bring herself to think about the other dream, where she'd woken up inside a coffin. It was terrifying, and after that one, she'd given up all hope of getting back to sleep. For her, it had been a nightmare, sluiced from her waking brain in a handful of minutes.

For those women, though—for Jenny, for Fran—it had been real.

Who would do that? Who *could* do that? It was unimaginably cruel. Savage had dealt with more than her fair share of killers on the job, but there was something infinitely worse about this one. This was a man—and Savage was certain that it *was* a man, even though her training told her not to make too many assumptions—who looked at women and saw meat to be butchered. Or was it worse than that? He looked at women and saw cogs in some twisted machine, just a mechanism through which he could share his story with the world.

She crossed the road, her trainers splashing through the puddles. Colin ran ahead, the dog's legs drumming the street, her tongue hanging out. The little Staffy loved these morning runs, although she sometimes struggled. Savage would loop back by the house in a little while and drop her off before finishing the last couple of miles alone.

"Good girl," she called to her.

And even though she tried to smile, she couldn't. Nothing to do with the cold, everything to do with the anger that coursed through her. It *burned*. Only a monster could kill somebody in such a brutal way and then parade their body like a trophy. But even monsters needed a reason to murder, didn't they?

Why now? Why these five women? Why turn them into the pages of a story? Was this personal? A revenge tale? Something to do with what had happened to Martha Hansen-Andrews back in September, perhaps? Or was it just chance and bad luck that had led Jenny and her friends down this dark path?

Savage reached a junction, running on the spot for a moment as a delivery van rumbled past, the arsehole driver on his phone. Colin waited patiently, her big eyes looking up as she waited for the next command.

"Come on," Savage said, and they both started running again.

She hadn't planned a route but she was in the middle of town, the streets of the city almost dead except for the poor souls wrapped in sleeping bags in department store doorways and the packs of drunken students who hadn't yet managed to find their way home from the clubs. How many of them knew about Sweet Briar Rose? How many of them would be happy to stagger around in the dark if they knew a killer lurked in the shadows?

Cutting down an alley, she ran in front of the market—too early even for the deliveries of vegetables and cut flowers. The path here was all cobbles and more than once she caught the toe of her trainer, almost stumbling. From here it was a short run down the hill to St Benedict's Street where the shops were dark and the restaurants were dead.

She slowed her pace as she approached the church that Kett had spoken about, St Lawrence's, then stopped at the top of the stone stairs that dropped all the way to Westwick Street, bending over to catch her breath. Colin jumped up, her breath hot against Savage's frozen skin.

"You're alright, girl," Savage said, scratching her behind the ear. "Not much longer, I promise."

Colin barked, the loudest sound in the night.

The *only* sound, Savage thought.

The church was enormous, one of the biggest in Norwich—and that was saying something in a city that was famous for its churches. The yard was deserted, although a congregation of fat pigeons sat in the leafless trees readying themselves for dawn. It wasn't exactly a surprise that nobody was here, she didn't know many drug dealers who got out of bed before midday. Even so, she'd been hoping to find *something* to kick-start the engine of her thoughts, a clue that might point her in the right direction.

There was a tall metal railing along the front of the church, but the side was guarded by a low wall and she vaulted it easily. Colin tried and failed to follow, yapping her head off until Savage leaned over and scooped her up. She held onto the wet, squirming mass of her, not wanting to let her run willy-nilly around the churchyard—even though she was pretty sure the place had been deconsecrated. It was still dark, but by the glow of the streetlights Savage saw there were no tombstones here. The church was surrounded by a neat, sloping lawn. It took her less than a minute to do a full circuit, and by the time she got back to the steps she was angrier than ever.

"This bloody case," she said. "This bloody *job*."

She clambered back over the wall, turning instead to the words of the story that the killer had left them. Clare was right, he had given a pretty enormous clue in the last part of the story. *Two strong men.* But what had he left them this time?

Not two strong men, but a 'Northman'.

Colin barked from the other side of the wall, running in tight, panicked circles.

"Hang on," Savage said. "I'm just thinking."

Scottish, maybe? Or Viking? Savage tried to remember any buildings in the city that had been occupied by the Vikings. She half-remembered a blue plaque around the back of the mall that had mentioned them, but what about the turret bit? Maybe the killer was just referring to a tower in the north of the city? It was too vague, there wasn't enough to get her teeth into. It could—

"Alright, love?"

The voice was so loud and so close that Savage's entire body contracted with the shock of hearing it—the sensation like being punched. She whirled around, the dark street pulsing with every thrashing beat of her heart, to see three men walking down the other side of the road. They were all in their thirties, smart jeans and shiny shoes and black short-sleeved shirts plastered to their torsos by the rain. Two of them wore their tattoos like tribal markings, all the way up to their necks. Even from here, she could tell they were drunk.

And even from here, she could tell they were dangerous.

"You lost?" said the man at the head of the pack, wiping his neatly bearded face with his hand. "Want some help getting home?"

The other men laughed, and there wasn't a scrap of kindness there.

"No," said Savage.

On the other side of the wall, Colin barked, but if the men noticed they didn't pay any attention. They were crossing over towards her now, their smart shoes beating like drums on the road.

"Don't be like that," said the same guy. "Gorgeous girl like you. We're only being friendly."

"Yeah, cheer up," said another of the men. "Try smiling, it'll make you look a lot prettier."

The stench of their aftershave rolled in front of them and Savage took a step back, almost tumbling down the steps. It was the wrong move, their smiles growing.

"Had a little too much to drink?" said the first guy, beckoning with his hand. "Come on, we'll get you inside. Warm you up a little."

He stepped closer, reaching for her arm, and the fury that had been boiling in Savage's blood seemed to scream. She didn't retreat, she advanced, meeting the first man's eyes and refusing to look away. She was a foot or so shorter than all of them and they were taking full advantage of it, the first man looming over her, the other two fanning out, boxing her in.

"You know you're the problem here, right?" she said. "Men like you. You're the entire problem."

"Calm your tits, love," the man at the back said. "We're only being friendly."

"Yeah?" said Savage. "Knights in shining armour, are you? Here to escort me back to my house. Or yours? And then what?"

The first man smiled.

"Give you the time of your life," he said.

He reached for her again, and she reacted before she even knew it—her hand slapping his away. The sound it made was a pistol crack, echoing down the street. Pain flashed across the guy's face, but only for a microsecond before it gave way to anger. Colin was barking, louder now, and this time they heard her.

Savage moved closer to the first man, her anger driving her, making her feel like she could crush all three of them beneath the heel of her shoe.

"I'm going to count to three," she said. "If I can still see your faces after that then you're going to be in a lot of pain. That is a promise."

The first man scoffed, but he wasn't sure. He licked his lips, breaking eye contact to look up the street.

"One," said Savage. Colin's barks were louder, and there was an unmistakable growl rising up from behind the wall.

"Come on," said the man at the back. "She's not worth it."

"Last chance," said the first man. "Bitch like you doesn't know she's got lucky."

"Two," Savage said, her heartbeat accelerating, the sound of it seeming to fill her entire skull.

"Fuck her," the man said. "Frigid cow. Come on."

He looked her up and down with such insolence that she could have knocked him out on the spot. Then, thank God, he backed away, all three of them sauntering down the kerb.

They weren't going fast enough.

Savage remembered to breathe, sucking in wet air as she reached over the wall and grabbed Colin under the front legs. She hauled her over and set her down, the dog barking her head off, spitting foam.

"Three," she called out.

The men looked back, seeing the dog. Colin was small, but even in the soft light of the street the Staffy's scars were visible, the lifetime of violence she'd suffered before Kett had rescued her and Savage had given her a home.

The *anger*.

Colin barked again and the three men scattered, the first guy slipping off the kerb and falling hard. His two friends didn't wait for him, the sound of their feet machine-gunning into the night. The first man managed to stand, limping after the others until all three of them had disappeared down a side street.

It would have been funny, if she wasn't so angry.

"Arseholes," she said, crouching to give Colin some love.

The dog licked her face, her breath rancid. "Thanks for having my back."

Colin barked loud enough to make Savage's ear break into a tuning fork whine.

"Ow," she said, straightening up.

The adrenaline had sapped her strength, making the run home feel impossible. But Colin was happy to lead the way, her tail wagging as she trotted down the road. Savage followed, feeling the cramps flutter in her calves, in her abdominals, feeling the wash of fear run through her. She'd been lucky, she knew, because she was confident in her own strength, because she was police.

Because she hadn't been drunk off her face.

But what if it had been somebody else? Somebody too drunk to question it, somebody too drunk to know any better? Those three men wouldn't have thought twice about taking a drunk woman home. Because that's how men like them thought, that dangerous sense of entitlement. She'd seen it before, so many times.

This woman belongs to me. I own her. I can lock her in my castle and do whatever the hell I want to her.

She pulled out her phone and called control, giving her details when the operator answered.

"There's three men prowling the city," she said. "Jeans, black shoes, short-sleeved shirt. One with a beard, dark hair. He's limping. Two of them have tattoos all the way from their wrists to their neck. I think they're looking for drunk girls coming out of the clubs. They thought I was one."

"Won't be making that mistake again," said the operator.

"Too right. They ran up Ten Bells Lane, heading back into the city. Can we send a car, maybe help them get home?"

"Home to the dungeons?" said the operator with a laugh. "Sure. Be safe."

"Always."

Savage hung up, trying to recover the thoughts that had scattered when the men had appeared, trying to remember the ones she'd had as she watched them leave. Something was niggling her.

I can lock her in my castle and do whatever the hell I want to her.

Something else, too, something about the note.

A Northman's Turret as the water snapped in the shadow of the wall.

She used her toe to nudge Colin away from a puddle of fresh, bright orange vomit, thinking about the castle in the centre of the city. She hadn't been there since that awful day with Kett when Hollenbeck had tried to frame him for murder, but she'd visited enough times to know that it didn't have any towers or turrets. It was a box on the hill, as typically Norman as you could get.

Norman.

She stopped walking, fishing for whatever had caught her attention, something she'd read about years ago. Whatever it was eluded her, so she pulled out her phone and opened Google. Colin had returned to the puddle of puke but Savage left her to it, scanning the list of results as they loaded.

"Oh shit," she said.

She called Clare, wiping the endless rain from her face as she waited for him to answer. When he didn't, she called Kett instead.

"Hey," he said after three rings.

"Sorry it's early, sir. Did I wake you?"

"Kate, I was woken at a quarter past five with a chinchilla literally taking a shit on my face. An actual shit. Since then, I've made three breakfasts, cleaned up one broken mug, dragged a naked child in from the garden to stop her freezing to death, been called a farty butt cheese no less than seven times and wiped four arses."

"*Four?*" Savage said.

"Three of them were Evie's. What's up?"

"Northman, sir. It was in the story. A Northman's Turret. Remember?"

"Yeah," he said. "What about it?"

She hesitated, the doubt creeping in. She was reaching, she knew.

"Kate?"

"I was thinking about the word Norman. The castle on the hill is Norman. You know what that means, right? The name Norman?"

"Norman?" Kett said. "If you're talking about Norman Balls then I'm guessing it means short, fat and a massive pain in the arse."

"It means Northman," she said. "It's Norse, by way of the French. I just Googled it."

Kett was silent. In the background Savage could hear the girls fighting over something.

"The castle doesn't have any towers," Savage went on. "But there's another tower in Norwich with the same name."

"Normandie Tower," Kett said. "You're right. It's by the river, too."

"And the city wall," said Savage. "I think this is the place."

"I think so too," Kett said. "Let's move."

CHAPTER TWENTY-TWO

THE SUN HAD RELUCTANTLY HAULED ITSELF OVER THE horizon by the time Porter pulled the Mondeo up to the kerb and cut the engine. Kett sat in the passenger seat, watching the big DI massage his injured arm, the bandage visible beneath a suit that looked fresh from Savile Row.

"How is it?" he asked.

"Still attached, sir," Porter said. "Just."

"Don't make a habit of it, Pete. You'll start to look like me."

"Except infinitely more handsome, and much less grey."

"Hey," Kett said as Porter stepped out. "I barely have any grey hairs!"

Kett opened his door and groaned his way into the drizzle, everything aching. His overcoat had still been covered in Porter's blood from yesterday and he hadn't been able to find his raincoat anywhere, so his spare suit was wet through in an instant. He shivered as he jogged to Clare's Mercedes, parked twenty yards down the hill. When he rapped on the wet window, Clare gurned up at him from inside like the world's angriest goldfish. After a few seconds, it wound down an inch or so.

"Savage here yet, sir?" Kett asked.

"Up ahead, scouting the tower. Gorski's there too but they're staying quiet for now, we don't want to give ourselves away. We've got the fire service standing by too with its rescue cushion, just in case. You're sure about this?"

Kett sniffed, shaking his head.

"Savage guessed it, and it's the best we've got. Northman, Norman. Turret, tower. We've got the river down there and we've got the old city wall up the hill. It feels right."

"It feels too easy," said Clare. "The killer's given us over twenty-four hours to crack this clue. Either he thinks we're all idiots, or..."

"Or he wants us here," Kett said. "I thought the same."

"So the tactical team goes first," said Clare. "There are nearly a hundred flats in the building, over sixteen floors. This is a nightmare."

The Super huffed, everything about him suggesting he was having second thoughts.

"We've really got nothing else?"

"Nothing as good as this," said Kett.

"What a tossing nightmare."

"We can end it, sir. If he's in there, we can end it."

"Go end it, then," Clare said.

"You're not coming?"

"I'll be there in a minute. It's cold."

Kett made his way along the street with Porter, keeping close to the embankment that shielded the side of the road. As soon as he turned the corner he saw Savage and Gorski ahead, standing next to a large van that Kett knew held the tactical unit. They both turned at the sound of footsteps,

Savage offering a nod of welcome. She looked like she hadn't slept in a week.

By the time he'd reached them the block of flats had come into view, a monolith against the lightening sky. It was enormous, four times as high as the medieval tower where they'd found Jenny's body. A couple of windows were lit up but other than that the building was dark, and utterly silent.

"How's the arm, sir?" Savage asked Porter.

"He's fine," Kett said before the DI could answer. "Anything useful?"

"Spalding is trying to get a list of tenants and owners," Savage said, shivering. "But it's going to be impossible to check every single one. I think we work on the assumption that the killer is using an empty flat. There are fourteen at the moment, and five of them are on the top three floors. I don't know what he's got planned but if this part of the story is based on Rapunzel then it makes sense that he's high up. Right?"

"Good work," said Kett. "Gorski, you okay to work from the top down?"

"Makes sense to me," she said. "I'll start on the roof and position officers on the stairwells and the fire exits just in case. But when the shouting starts you're gonna get a lot of people breaking loose so I'd have some of your guys there to calm the residents down."

Kett nodded, checking his watch.

"Okay. Let's do this."

Savage lifted her radio.

"Sir, is it a green light?"

A hiss of static, then Clare's voice.

"Yes. Go go go."

Gorski nodded, pulling down her visor and slapping her

hand on the side of the van. It opened immediately, the tactical team funnelling out and following her almost silently down the street. Kett jogged after them, Porter and Savage right behind. They ran onto the wide, empty plaza around the tower together, approaching the main door. A young man stood there, smoking, and when he saw the armed police the cigarette exploded from his mouth, arcing perfectly into a puddle.

"Police!" Gorski said. "Open the door."

The man didn't hesitate. Gorski entered first, barking quiet orders to two of her team. Three of them jogged towards the stairwell, another moved to the corner of the atrium, his gun raised but his finger off the trigger. Kett approached the man who'd been smoking.

"What's your name?"

"Fields, sir," he squeaked. "Craig, sir."

"You live here?"

He nodded.

"What floor?"

"Third," said the man. "Wife doesn't let me smoke inside so I come out here."

"Seen anything unusual in the last day or two, Craig? Anyone you didn't recognise? Anything to set the alarm bells ringing?"

"Yeah," he said, like it was the stupidest question in the world. "But it's the Normandie. Nice place, but every day's a surprise."

"Wait here, and don't move," Kett said, motioning for a PC to stand with the man.

He walked inside to see Gorski and a handful of her team in the small elevator. She nodded to him and he nodded back, then the doors closed and they were gone. Kett paced from wall to wall, the adrenaline making him restless. Savage was doing the same, a bundle of nervous energy.

"Can't stand not being up there," she said when she saw him looking.

"Me neither," said Porter, flexing his injured arm. "Why do they get all the fun?"

Kett followed the numbers on the lift, seeing it work its way up to sixteen. He winced, realising he was chewing his bottom lip. There was a shout from the stairwell, an angry command from the armed coppers who were positioned there. Then silence again, whole minutes full of it.

Savage's radio crackled, Gorski's voice filtering through.

"Roof exit busted open but there's nobody up there. Heading to sixteenth, we'll use the stairs from now on."

"How many empty flats on the top floor?" Kett asked when the radio had clicked off.

"One," Savage said.

Outside, a fire engine was rolling across the plaza, its blues off. The tension was unbearable and Kett moved to the lift, pushing the button.

"Sir?" said Savage.

"By the time we get up there it'll all be over," he said.

He could tell she wanted to say more, but she didn't. The lift worked its way down, the gears seeming to make the entire building vibrate. There was no other sound inside the block of flats, as if everyone here had gone to sleep. It made Kett think of Sleeping Beauty, of the castle full of unconscious people, trapped inside their own dreams for a hundred years.

It made him think of the notes that the killer had left them.

"The story said, '*This time there will be time to hang*

around,'" he said. "Right? '*Another day, but when midnight falls so will she.*'"

"Yeah," Savage said. "I think he's planning to throw her to her death."

Kett thought so too. The firefighters were setting up an enormous inflatable cushion on the northern part of the plaza, which was all well and good. But there was only one of them, and four sides to the tower block.

"It might be simpler than that," said Porter. "He might just be planning to hang her."

Kett's skin crinkled into goosebumps, his scalp pulling tight.

The lift doors rattled open like a pair of predator's jaws. Kett walked in just as Savage's radio squawked.

"Top floor clear," said Gorski. "Taking the stairs to fifteen."

"Roger," Savage said as she followed Kett into the lift. Porter entered too, the entire car wobbling with his weight.

"Nobody leaves," Kett called to the PC who stood in the doorway.

He pushed the button for the fifteenth floor and the doors creaked shut painfully slowly. The lift moved like it was being pulled up by hand.

"It's going to be bloody midnight by the time we get up there," Kett said, impatience chewing at his nerves.

The lift shuddered upwards, Kett popping his lips all the way to the fifteenth floor.

"You do realise how annoying that is, right, sir?" said Porter.

"What?"

"That noise you make with your lips. *Pop pop pop.*"

"I have no idea what you're talking about," Kett said. "Get your ears checked, Pete."

Porter would have protested but he was out of time. The lift reached its destination, the doors opening into a narrow corridor. There was no sign of the firearms team but Kett could hear them shouting from nearby. He followed the sound of voices, past doors that stayed shut and silent. Rounding the corner he saw an officer of the tactical team standing guard outside a flat, the shouts dying out inside. Savage's radio buzzed.

"You should get up here," came Gorski's voice from inside, followed a fraction of a second later by its echo from the radio.

Kett walked to the door, seeing a short entrance hall with a bathroom straight ahead. The hall angled right and Gorski appeared there, rifle in hand.

"That was quick," she said. "It's clear, but you need to see this."

She pressed herself against the wall so that Kett could squeeze past, then she moved towards the front door.

"We'll keep working our way down but I'll leave Prendergast here."

"Thanks," Kett shouted after her.

The flat was small but it was beautifully decorated, the paint brand new and the carpets recently cleaned—the smell of carpet shampoo almost overpowering. Kett patted his pockets, coming up empty, but when he turned around he saw that Savage was already holding out a pair of shoe covers and some gloves.

"One of these days, sir, you'll remember to bring some."

"That's pretty optimistic of you," he replied as he pulled the baggies over his boots. He snapped the gloves on, too many fingers and not enough holes as always.

Immediately to the right was a bedroom, decorated for a child but completely empty. Another bedroom sat next to it, this one just as bare. There was nothing in the bathroom, the airing cupboard or the toilet, and Kett was fast losing hope as he pushed through the door into the living room.

"Whoa," he said.

He moved to the side to let the others in, and for a moment they all stood there trying to make sense of what they were looking at.

"I'm pretty sure this is our guy," said Savage.

"You *think*?" Porter replied.

The room was empty of everything except for a mattress in the far corner, sheets and a duvet folded neatly on top of it. Somebody had decorated in here too, far more recently and far more crudely than the other parts of the flat. The walls were spray-painted with a crazed mural of pictures and words, angry balloon faces and squat castles and knights on horseback, all wrapped in strand after strand of neon green which trailed on the floor and stretched up to the ceiling like vines. It might have been done by a child, if that child was seven feet tall and had lost their mind.

One wall had no pictures, but there was text here, every letter two-foot-tall.

NOBODY WILL LIVE HAPPILY EVER AFTER.

But even this paled in significance compared to what had been displayed on the floor. It was a serial killer's tool-box, there was no doubt about it. Coils of ropes, handcuffs and chains had been laid out next to a plastic tub full of duct tape. Several large pieces of ironmongery sat there too, reminding Kett of the metal plate that had secured the chain to Fran's coffin. A rack of tools lay on its back, half-empty, a welder's torch propped up next to it. A stained blanket had been rolled out beneath the archway that led into the small kitchen, and on it was an assortment of weapons. Two brand new machetes in plastic sheaths, a long-handled claw hammer that made Kett's skin crawl, a box of nails and screws and, at the very end, two rusty saws and a one-handed axe.

"Fuck me," said Porter.

Kett stepped over the weapons into the kitchen. In the stainless-steel sink was a white chopping board, its surface slick with blood. A carving knife sat on it, equally gruesome. A few more dishes had been left on the counter, waiting to be washed, including a couple of glasses, fingerprints standing proud in the milky light from the window.

"Has anyone called Hay?" Kett said.

"I did, sir," Savage replied. "She'll be here by now, or very close."

"Get her up here."

Savage clicked the radio, walking to the window to get better reception. Porter stepped over the weapons into the kitchen, almost tripping. He grabbed Kett's arm until he found his balance, and even then he seemed reluctant to let go. Kett opened the cupboard doors, finding cereal boxes and open packets of crackers and not much else.

"Check the fridge, Pete," he said.

Porter ducked down, opening the little fridge that sat beneath the counter. He swallowed hard.

"Fingo," he said.

"*What?*"

Porter had paled.

"I'm sorry, sir, I started to say finger and bingo at the same time, my brain got confused."

Kett looked over the big DI's shoulder.

"Shit."

There was a finger in the top shelf of the fridge door, in the compartment where the eggs were supposed to go. It sat in a puddle of congealed blood, surely too shrivelled and bent to be real. The nails were unpainted and chewed to shreds.

"Oh no," said Savage as she entered the kitchen. "Is that...?"

"Yeah, a *fingo*," Kett said.

He stood straight, his back cracking. Pain sloshed between his ribs, that fragment of Keefe's bullet seeming to dance wildly in there.

"Where is she?" Savage said. "Where's the rest of her?"

There was nowhere else in the flat the missing woman could be, no place to hide a hostage.

Or a body.

"We'll find her," Kett said.

"It's too late," Savage replied. "We're too late."

"No, we're winning," Kett said. "Look, he needs this stuff. He wasn't ready for us to get here. This is bad for him."

But his words rang hollow, and all he could think about was his conversation with Clare.

Either he thinks we're all idiots.

Or he wants us here.

And he had the awful feeling that the killer was standing in the dying night right now, watching them, and laughing.

CHAPTER TWENTY-THREE

KETT WALKED INTO THE MAJOR INVESTIGATION TEAM'S bullpen, checking his watch as he held the door open for Savage. The day felt half-done already but it wasn't even nine yet. He was frozen, his clothes still soaking wet and his bones aching from the cold.

"Tea," he said, the only word his numb lips felt capable of forming. It was safe enough to say it, because Porter had stayed at Normandie Tower with Cara Hay and her forensic team. Savage nodded, rubbing her eye with her fist.

"You want me to, sir?" she said through a yawn.

"No. I'll do it. Need to clear my head. Want one?"

"Please," Savage said.

"You, sir?" he asked Superintendent Clare as the boss shuffled through the door. He looked at Kett and harrumphed like an angry Victorian headmaster, then nodded.

"Make it strong," he said as he walked to his office.

"I'll get the new information up on the board, sir," Savage said.

"Thanks, Kate," Kett replied. "I'll see you there in a minute."

He walked to the little kitchen and filled the kettle, closing his eyes while he waited for it to boil. When he opened them again he was surprised to find that he wasn't alone in the small room. Richard Johnson hovered in the doorway looking more like a Narnian fawn than ever in his green velvet jacket and what could only be described as baby-shit brown corduroys.

"Where did you come from?" Kett asked.

"I'm stealthier than I look," said Johnson. "I creep up on you."

"Like mould. What do you want?"

"I wonder if now is a good time to evaluate how your return to work is going? A quick assessment, it won't take longer than an hour or so."

"Richard, you do realise there's a killer out there, right?"

"I believe there's one in here, too," Johnson said, bristling with self-righteousness.

Kett did his best to ignore him but the comment had hit hard. He picked up the kettle and poured water into three mugs. Even the smell of the tea did little to calm him.

"Want one?" he asked, trying to diffuse the tension.

"I only drink Himalayan green tea," Johnson said.

"Of course you do."

"You are already showing signs of the aggression which led to your dismissal," Johnson said. "As far as I'm concerned, you're a ticking time bomb whose anger will ultimately lead to a terrible tragedy. I—"

"Right now, Richard, I'm a ticking time bomb holding a kettle of boiling water. Maybe the interrogation can wait."

Johnson licked his lips, taking a step back. Kett returned the kettle to its cradle and gently stirred the teabags.

"Get the milk, will you?"

"I'll do no such thing," Johnson replied, and Kett glared at him.

"Milk."

The psychologist tutted, but he opened the fridge and handed Kett the bottle. Kett added milk to the teas before passing it back.

"Good boy," he said, and Johnson's jaw dropped.

"Now listen here, Mr Kett," he started.

"That's DCI Kett," Kett growled, the words seeming to push the man back against the fridge, pinning him there. "Detective Chief Inspector, whether you like it or not. We've got one woman dead, one woman in hospital, and three more victims out there, and right now this unit is the only shot we have of bringing them back. You want to evaluate something? You want to help? Then figure out where they are."

He didn't wait for a reaction, scooping up the mugs with such urgency that scolding tea slopped over his hand. He swore his way through the door and all the way down the corridor, pushing into the Incident Room to see Savage standing to attention. When she saw it was him, she turned back to the wall.

"Thought you were the boss," she said. "You sound more and more like him every day."

"Toss off," Kett said, before hearing himself. He put the mugs down, blowing on his burned skin. "Right, where are we? Anything from Fran yet?"

"I've just checked," Savage said. "She's back in surgery, hasn't spoken. Her condition has worsened, they're saying it's fifty-fifty."

"Not good. Have we got anywhere with the Normandie flat?"

"It's privately owned," said a voice from the door as Spalding walked in. "Right now, it belongs to a Greg Smith. He bought it four months ago. Want to guess who owned it before that?"

"No idea," Kett said.

"Melody Quinn. Mother of Fortune, one of our missing women."

"Seriously?" said Savage. "What do we know about Greg?"

"Uniforms spoke to him this morning. He doesn't live in the flat, bought it as an investment. He'd been decorating, he had no idea anyone had even been there, and no idea how they got a key. They're his prints on the glasses we found in the kitchen. But he has no connection to the women other than this one, and his alibi's watertight."

"Why would the killer do that?" Kett asked, picking up his tea then putting it down again with a yelp. "Why use a property that's connected to his victim? That's another message. He's telling us something."

"This is personal," Savage said, nodding. "You think that was Fortune's finger in the fridge?"

She reached back, pulling a photo from the wall—the five women in a pub beer garden—pointing at it.

"They're all wearing nail varnish here, except for Fortune."

"Good spot," said Kett. "So the killer takes Fortune to her old house and—"

"She never lived there either," Spalding said. "It was her grandmother's, her dad's mum's. When she died, it passed to her mother, but they already had a house. That's why they sold it."

"Okay," said Kett. "This is good. It makes it more likely that the women know their attacker. A family friend, a neighbour. We're going door to door in the Normandie, right?"

"Got half the Force on it," said Spalding. "Nothing yet."

Kett swallowed, his throat painfully dry. He tried the tea again but if anything it felt hotter. It was torture.

"Goddamnit," he said. "This personal connection, I can't help feeling it goes back to Martha Hansen-Andrews, to what happened to her that night in September. We've checked Martha's friends and family, haven't we?"

"No leads there at all," said Spalding.

"And we've still got her dad in custody?"

"We do," said Superintendent Clare as he walked into the room. "He's not said much else. There's nothing at all tying him to Normandie Tower. Early days, though."

"Maybe that's why the flat was just left there for us," Kett said. "Something this big would need to be set up in advance. Jenny in her tower, Fran in her coffin. If Joffre Andrews is behind this then he'd have automated some of it, he'd have set it in motion a long time ago. Maybe he couldn't get his stuff out of the flat in time because he was in here, in custody. Maybe if we hadn't arrested him, Fortune would have been there instead of all of his equipment."

"I'm hearing a lot of maybes," said Clare. "This guy doesn't seem to want to leave much to chance. But the theory works. If it's Joffre, we'll find something in the flat that proves it. He's not going anywhere."

"Okay," said Kett. "What about Holden?"

"That malicious little scrote has been charged for what he did to Porter," said Clare. "But he's managed to dredge up a pretty decent alibi for the time when the women went missing—caught on cameras all over Cathedral Close on Friday afternoon and evening. Unless he's working with somebody else, it's not him."

"We'll keep digging," said Kett. "Until then, we work the drug connections. Jenny Eyler dated a dealer called Ryan Snelling, right?"

"Right," said Spalding, pointing to the young man's photograph on the wall. "He was with the Beggar Boys when they first started, although they went by another name back then."

"Okay, good. And Fran was also dating a dealer, Simon Womack. There's a connection, because Womack was a Beggar Boy too. They lived right next door to a cannabis factory that was ripped off by his outfit. Then, the very next day, her gangbanger boyfriend was burned to death inside his own car. Beggar Boy dealers were peddling in the churchyard next to the stairs where Martha died. These links are too big to be ignored."

"I agree," Savage said. "It feels like a drug thing. What if a rival gang thought Simon Womack was turning against them. They decide to take him out, and anyone connected to him who might know too much, including Jenny and Fran. It's worth following up."

"Agreed," said Clare, glancing at his watch. "We've got time before Hay finishes her examination. Spalding has the names we got from the database, and from the moron who tried to shag a holly bush. Kett, Savage, go knock on some doors."

"Soon as I've drunk my tea, sir," Kett said.

"If you're not careful your bloody tea will get tossed in!"

"Oh, sir, *no*," Kett said, grimacing. "It really doesn't mean—"

"The *sink*, Kett! I'll toss it in the sink. Now bugger off, the pair of you."

Kett took one last look at the steaming mug and then

shivered his way towards the door. Clare called out after him before he could leave the room.

"Kett, where's your coat?"

"Caught a little blood from Porter yesterday," he said. "Not to mention rolling around in Holden's shitty binbags. I can't find my other one."

"That doesn't fill me with confidence in your skills as a detective," Clare said. "Can't have you freezing to death on your second day back. Come with me."

Kett followed him from the room, waiting outside Clare's office while the Superintendent rummaged around inside.

"It's not been worn for a while," Clare shouted. "But it's warm."

He appeared in the door holding what looked like the corpse of a Highland Cow. When he held it up—struggling with the weight of it—it turned out to be a suede overcoat with a bright orange fur collar. Kett managed a laugh, but it only lasted until he realised the Super was serious.

"What?" barked Clare. "What's wrong with it?"

"I mean..." Kett shook his head. "What *is* it?"

"A coat, you idiot. I've had it since the 70s."

"The 1670s?" Kett asked, looking at the enormous collar.

"It's the BTJ," the boss went on proudly. "Indestructible, and very warm. Take it."

"I know I'm going to regret asking, sir, but what does BTJ stand for?"

"Big Tossing Jacket," Clare said. "Fiona named it for me. Take it."

"Um, no. Please tell me you never wore this with those skin-tight wedding trousers. You'd have looked like a grizzly bear giving birth to a naked mole rat."

"Take it."

"No, sir, I don't want your tossing jacket."

"Take it, Detective."

"I'll be fine, I don't feel too co—"

"Take the tossing jacket!" Clare roared.

Kett did as he was told, the coat so heavy there might have been somebody else living inside its greasy folds. He slid his arm in like he was performing an anal examination on a sickly cow, and Clare helped him with the other side. It felt like wearing somebody else's skin, the collar a little too much like human hair for his liking, and a shudder ripped through him.

"You look like a slightly younger me," said Clare, patting him on the shoulder.

"A slightly younger Hannibal Lecter," said Kett.

"But you're warm though, right?"

"Like I've crawled up an elephant's arse," Kett muttered. "Can I go?"

"You can," Clare said. "And don't come back without good news."

CHAPTER TWENTY-FOUR

Savage drove, the bulky Mondeo as nimble as a Formula One car in her hands. Kett sat in the passenger seat, wrapped in Clare's Big Tossing Jacket and sweating profusely. The collar was infuriatingly itchy, like it was crawling with bugs. Savage kept glancing at him and he could tell she was trying not to smile.

"Don't," he said.

"I didn't!" she replied. "It's just I've never seen one used like that."

"One what?"

"A merkin."

"A *what?*"

"Pubic wig," she said. "You know, a toupee for your private area. That's what the collar looks like."

Kett would have replied but Savage pumped the accelerator, overtaking a car. He closed his eyes, holding his breath until they were back on the right side of the road. Acid and adrenaline stewed in his empty stomach, every belch like he was breathing fire.

He *really* needed a cup of tea.

"Here we are, sir," Savage said, hauling the big car around one more corner into a *cul-de-sac* on the northeast side of the city, a stone's throw from Jenny's house. She pulled them up to the kerb but kept the engine running.

"Number eighteen," Kett said. He scanned the little bungalows that lined the street, none of which looked like it would be home to a gang of drug dealers. "You're sure?"

"Yeah," Savage said. "They're operating out of streets like this more and more, less likely to be raided and plenty of vulnerable residents they can take advantage of. Spalding said that this place is rented by a family for their son, it wouldn't surprise me if he had some kind of disability. They prey on it."

She glanced in the rearview mirror and Kett turned in his seat to see an IRV pull up behind them. He couldn't see the face of the driver in the cloud-drenched windscreen but the sheer size of him made it clear it was Duke. Kett was glad he was here. This was the kind of meeting that would require brawn as well as brains.

"Phil Spenser, our holly-loving friend, must have sung like one of Sue Hansen's birds," Kett said, reading Spalding's notes. "Spenser was part of a crew that called themselves the Sesame Street Boys." He frowned. "Wait, that can't be right. Sesame Street?"

Savage nodded.

"Yeah, we've picked up a few of them over the years. Minor drug stuff but very little violence. They weren't exactly in the Premier League. Gangs like that are getting snuffed out by the county lines crews from London, and by outfits like the Beggar Boys. These guys play with a whole new set of rules."

Kett sighed.

"I saw a lot of gang activity when I was in the Met. Gets

worse every year. These guys don't have a problem with violence, it's bred into them. Murder too."

"You think that's what happened?" Savage said, drumming the wheel impatiently. "Maybe Fran found out what her boyfriend was doing and tried to stop him, or his crew thought that Fran and Jenny and the other women were getting too close. Either the Beggar Boys decided to take them out before they talked, Simon too. Or another gang targeted them as an attack on the Beggar Boys."

Kett chewed his lip for a moment, biting at the scab that had formed there.

"This seems too theatrical for a gang," he said. "The fairy tales, the brambles and the coffin. The notes, too. It doesn't fit."

Or did it? He'd seen things like this before, hadn't he? Corpses with pencils in their eyes, bodies hung up by their ankles, a bucket to catch the blood from their ruined throats. The real gangs had no problem putting on a show if it helped get their message across.

"I don't know," he continued. "Maybe they're trying to make a point, or cover their tracks, but this still doesn't feel right. Something's missing. I just can't figure out what."

"Well, let's see what we can get from these knuckleheads," said Savage. "You ready?"

Kett stepped out of the car into the November chill. It had stopped raining but the air was heavy with a damp that was far worse. It sat against his skin like a mouldering coffin lining. Duke unfolded himself from the IRV, twisting his head to the left and the right. He looked like a wrestler about to hurl somebody out of the ring. In contrast, the PC who climbed out of the passenger side was the size of a child. Both of them stared at Kett and it took him a moment to remember the coat. He pulled it off, slinging it onto the

Mondeo's seat. It slid slowly into the footwell like it had sprouted legs and was crawling back to whatever cave Clare had found it in.

"Right then," Duke said, actually cracking his knuckles. "Let's do this."

"Calm down, Constable," Kett said. "I don't want anyone else getting thrown down the stairs."

"It was an *accident*," Duke said, his face miserable. "I know everyone says it wasn't, but honestly I tripped on something and accidentally pushed Holden down the stairs. I tried to grab him but it was too late, he was gone."

"Right," Kett said, not sure whether to be disappointed or relieved. "Not a vigilante, then, just a klutz."

He crossed the road, Savage by his side. Number eighteen looked identical to the other bungalows along the street but the closer they got, the more Kett noticed the differences. The gravel drive was overgrown, the curtains drawn and yellow with dust, the garage roof halfway to collapsing. The front door didn't just have one lock, it had five, brand new and heavy-duty.

"Duke, head around the back," he said. "But be sharp, and do not engage unless you have to."

"Yes, sir," said Duke.

"Savage, let them know we're here."

Savage hopped over the low, weed-strewn flowerbed and crunched up the drive. When she knocked on the door it sounded like artillery fire.

"Police," Savage shouted. "Open up."

No reply, but Kett could hear movement from inside. He scanned the street, seeing half a dozen net curtains twitching.

"Last chance," Savage said.

"Hang on," came a muffled voice. "I need more time."

One of the locks clicked back, the others following painfully slowly. It seemed like an eternity later that the door opened, and even then it was halted by the security chain. A wide-eyed, friendly face peered through the crack —a man in his late twenties. Kett couldn't be certain, because of the dark, but he might have had Down's Syndrome.

"How may I help you?" the man asked, stumbling over the words.

"My name's DCI Robbie Kett, Norfolk Constabulary," Kett replied, holding up his warrant card. The man studied it, his brow furrowed. "What's your name, son?"

"Freddie," said the man. "Freddie Wilson."

"You're not in any trouble. I just need to ask you a few questions. Is this your house?"

Freddie nodded.

"You alone here?"

The man hesitated, looking over his shoulder for a moment before turning back. From inside, Kett heard the sound of quiet laughter.

"Yes," he said.

"You're sure about that?"

Freddie shook his head, then nodded.

"I need to go," he said. "I'm sorry."

"Hold on," Kett said. "You're not in any trouble, Freddie, but if you're *having* trouble, we could help."

Freddie's tongue explored his lips, his fingers clamped around the door, his eyes even wider now, full of uncertainty.

"Are you here to take away my cat?"

"No," Kett said. "Did somebody tell you that?"

He shook his head with enough urgency for Kett to know it was a lie.

"We're the police, Freddie," he said. "We're the good guys."

The man nodded, closing the door for long enough to undo the security chain. When he opened it again Kett saw a long hallway, and past that a living room where two more men sat.

"I thought you said you were alone."

"Please don't take my cat," Freddie pleaded.

"We won't," Savage told him. She took his arm, gently leading him outside. "Come on, we can talk in the garden. This weather is rubbish, isn't it?"

Kett made his way down the hallway into a big room that turned out to be both kitchen and living space. There were three men here, not two, and their expressions of ugly contempt couldn't have been more different from Freddie's open, trusting face.

Two of the men sat on the sofa, both in their early twenties and decked in black tracksuits and expensive, spotless white trainers. One had a shaven head, the other boasted an impressive set of dreadlocks. The third guy sat on a chair to the side, a little older but dressed the same. He had a beer bottle in one hand, despite the fact it wasn't even ten yet, and a PlayStation controller in the other. A football game was playing on the small TV, and the table and the floor were littered with bottles and ashtrays and pizza boxes.

"Freddie fucked up," said the man with dreadlocks, his voice abrasively loud. "What a surprise."

"Morning, *Officer*," said the guy with the shaven head. Kett noticed that there was a little black cat on his lap, almost perfectly camouflaged against his trousers apart from its bright yellow eyes. The man's hand, complete with bruised and swollen knuckles, rested on top—far harder than it needed to be. "How can we help?"

"You can start by giving me your names," Kett said.

"I'm Tom, he's Dick, and that one in the chair is Harry," he said, and they all laughed. Their eyes were dead, though. They were eyes of men who'd already experienced great violence, Kett knew, who'd done terrible things. The atmosphere in the room was claustrophobic, not helped by the clouds of cigarette smoke.

"How do you know Freddie?" Kett said.

"Friend, *innit*," said Dick, the man with dreads.

"You mind if I have a look around?"

"Got a warrant?" said Tom. "No, you don't. So maybe just fuck off, yeah? Maybe just send Freddie back in so we can have a word with him about his stupid flappy mouth."

He'd taken hold of the scruff of the cat's neck, hard enough to make it growl. Kett took a step towards him.

"You don't want to do that."

More laughter, but the shaven-headed guy let go of the animal. It sprang off his lap, bolting for the door.

"You're the Beggar Boys, then?" Kett said, his pulse thumping in his tonsils. "Shit name, that."

"Never heard of them," said Tom.

"*Boys* is right, though. Bunch of little kids. I was expecting something a little less pathetic, to be honest."

This seemed to hit a nerve.

"We're not kids," said Tom, running a hand over his shaven head. It was pitted with sores where he'd cut himself with his razor, and so was his face. "You have no fucking idea."

"You look like children to me. What's that? FIFA?"

The man in the chair—the one that Tom had referred to as Harry—looked at his PlayStation controller like it was the first time he'd noticed it.

"I know who you are," Kett said. "I know that if I look

hard enough I'll find the marijuana plants you took from Phil Spenser and his crew. But you're right, I don't have a warrant."

All three men scoffed, grinning at each other.

"What I do have, though, is permission."

The bullet behind his ribs had begun to sting and he scratched it. The lads were starting to notice the way his knuckles were swollen, the scars that peeked out from the collar of his shirt, and the darkness in his eyes. They were starting to see that he was a man who had experienced great violence too.

"Permission to get the fucking truth out of you, no matter what it takes."

"Yeah?" said Tom, fidgeting in his seat.

"Yeah. So let me start by telling you I don't give a shit about the drugs. I'm here because of Simon Womack."

"Who—" Tom started, but Kett cut him off.

"He was killed yesterday. Somebody tied him up in his own car and set fire to it."

The men responded with a silence that felt deafening.

"I'm telling you because I know Simon was one of you. I know he was part of this shitty little crew, and I know that none of those Sesame Street idiots would have the guts to execute him, not like that. So who would?"

Dick, the guy with dreads, leaned forward, his elbows on his knees.

"Nobody would mess with us," he said. "Not like that. Simon was a made man, any attack on him is an attack on all of us. They know we'd retaliate."

"Told you we should have done something about Seb," said Harry from his chair. The others glared at him.

"Who's Seb?" Kett asked.

"Don't," said Tom, but Harry ignored him.

"Friend of ours, got hit a couple of months ago."

"Hit?"

"Killed," said Harry.

"We don't even fucking know that," Dick said. "Pussy probably bailed, fucked off somewhere. Piece of shit."

"Nah," said Harry. "He wouldn't have done that. He's dead, man. I know it."

"This was in September?" Kett asked. Harry shrugged.

"All I'm saying is that we never went after anyone for that, we never retaliated."

"Against *who*?" said Tom, flapping his arms. "We didn't know who did it."

"Against everyone," Harry went on, angry. "We needed to send a message but we didn't, and that made us fair game. Whoever tapped Seb is from the same gang who tapped Simon, guaranteed."

"Right," Kett said. "*If* this was a gang killing. But I don't think it is. I don't think the man who killed Simon Womack has anything to do with the gangs or with the drugs. I think he was killed because of the girls."

He didn't miss the way that the skinhead and the dreadlocked man glanced at each other.

"Simon Womack was Fran Herbert's boyfriend, and Fran is one of five women who were abducted on Friday night. We've found her, and we've found Jenny Eyler. Fortune Quinn, Poppy Butterfield and Beatrice Goodwin are the others. Where are they?"

"Wait," said Tom. He was pushing himself out of his seat and Kett let him get halfway up before planting a hand on his greasy, shaven forehead and pushing him back onto the sofa.

"Sit down," he growled.

"You can't—"

And Kett fixed him a look that stole the air from his lungs. The men moved restlessly, but nobody tried to stand.

"Jenny Eyler is dead," Kett said. "Let that sink in. The others are missing. I think you know where they are. I think you know what happened to them. I think one of you might even be behind it."

"Whoa," said Tom, his head damp with sweat. "I don't even know who the fuck they are."

Kett stared him out, waiting. It only took five seconds for him to throw his hands up.

"Okay, fuck, I know Fran, Jenny too. We all do. But we didn't do nothing to them, I swear."

"When was the last time you saw them? Any of them?"

"Like, weeks ago," Tom said. "Back in the summer. Macky—Simon, I mean—was with Fran, yeah, but they weren't serious or nothing. They just lived together but they were both screwing other people. He was, anyway. Macky wasn't loyal to nobody, not his girl, not his old crew. He was a wanker but he gave us info, you know? He was useful."

"Fran knew about the gangs? The drugs?" Kett asked.

"Yeah, of course, she did some drops for him," Tom said. He held up his hands. "Not that I had anything to do with that, it was all him."

"What about the other women? Jenny, Poppy, Fortune and Beatrice. They knew?"

"They weren't stupid," Tom said. "Jenny was with Ryan for a while, before he was banged up. She weren't a good girl. Come on, this is bullshit. We've not done nothing wrong. We never touched them, not like that."

He seemed to shrink into himself, glancing nervously at the other men.

"Like what, then?" Kett said, towering over him.

"Nothing, man. They just went to the same parties, they hung out."

"You had relations with them?" Kett asked, looking at each of the men in turn.

"No, not like that," said Tom. "Just a bit of fun. It was all consequential."

"Consensual?" Kett corrected, and he nodded.

"That's what I said. I never hurt them."

"What about Martha Hansen-Andrews?" Kett said, and the temperature seemed to plummet. The skinhead put both hands to his face, groaning.

"We had nothing to do with that," he said through his fingers.

"With what?"

"That fucking car accident. Nothing, okay?"

The room grew suddenly dark, and it took Kett a moment to work out why. Duke had walked in, blocking the light from the open front door. In the little bungalow he looked like a giant, his hat scuffing the ceiling, his shoulders almost stretching from wall to wall. All three of the young men looked past Kett with wide, frightened eyes. They might not have been boys when he'd entered the room, but they were now.

"You think I'm fucking around," Kett said. "But I'm really not. The last piece of shit Duke here dealt with is in hospital after he got thrown down the stairs. Isn't that right, Duke?"

"Well, it was an acci—"

"So answer the question," said Kett. "What happened that night?"

"Look, I mean it, we had nothing to do with it." Tom ran a hand over his shaven, pitted scalp. "I said it already, Jenny isn't a good person. She's fucking evil, man. She had it in for that Martha girl."

He seemed to choke on his own words, coughing hard. The other men sat and listened. Their mouths might as well have been stitched shut.

"Keep going," said Kett.

"Jenny fucking hated Martha. She was always calling her a bitch, slag, whore, all those things. And I don't mean like every now and again, I mean all the time. She was obsessed with her. With *hurting* her."

"Why?" Kett asked when the man's words dried up.

"Fuck do I know why bitches do what they do? Jealous. Martha was fucking some guy that Jenny had once dated, something like that. But Jenny wasn't all that and she knew it. Martha was fitter, whatever. She had something about her. Jenny hated that. Her and Fran asked us to do something about it, asked us to scare her, that was all."

"Scare her? This is the night she was hit by the car?"

"Yeah, back in September. They were out for the night and Jenny and Fran were supposed to bring Martha to this alley in the city. We were going to, like, fuck her up, but not really, not seriously. Just give her a once over."

"Wait," said Kett. "You're talking about attacking her?"

"Not properly," said the man with dreadlocks, shrugging his bony shoulders. "Bust her up a bit, bone or two, smash out a tooth, that sort of thing. A warning."

"Jenny wanted her to pay, wanted her to suffer," said Tom. "Most of all, she just wanted her to fuck off and never come back."

"Because she was jealous of her?"

"Yeah, fucking bitch shit, I don't know."

"And you were happy to do it?"

This time it was Tom who shrugged, like hurting some-body was the easiest thing in the world.

"But it never happened," said Tom.

"What do you mean?"

"I mean Jenny and Fran never showed up, not with Martha anyway. That night we waited for near enough an hour then Jenny showed up on her own, fucking crying her eyes out."

"What time was this?"

"After midnight," he said. "She was going on about how Martha was dead or something, how she'd been hit by a car. We bolted."

"Did she say what had happened?" Kett asked.

The skinhead sniffed, considering his words.

"She never said. Not exactly, like. She thought Martha had figured out what she was doing, that she was going to get a beating, and she just legged it. Jenny said she wasn't anywhere near her when she got hit by the car, and believe me if that girl had pushed Martha she would have boasted about it, she'd have told all of us. She said when she caught up to Martha she was already on the road, all mangled up and shit. But—"

The silence felt heavy enough to crush the room, and even Kett couldn't find the strength to break it. Thirty seconds passed before the man started talking again.

"The next time we saw Jenny was weeks later, and I asked her what had gone down that night. She wasn't happy. That's what surprised me, you know? She wanted Martha hurt but she wasn't happy about what happened. Because Martha had got hurt *too* bad. You wouldn't wish that on your worst enemy, right? Fucking vegetable. No point ruining somebody if they don't know it, is there? And Jenny didn't want to talk about it but she did say one thing that stuck with me. She saw Martha that night, on the side of the road after she'd been hit, right? She said she pretended to help her but she was just going in to see the damage. She wanted to see how hurt she was. Brains and blood and shit. Apparently, Martha only said one thing as she was lying there. One word, pretty much."

Kett waited.

"She just said 'Monster.' That's all."

"Monster?"

"Yeah," he said, just a whisper. "Monster."

CHAPTER TWENTY-FIVE

KETT SUCKED IN A LUNGFUL OF DAMP AIR, WISHING with all his might that he had a cigarette between his lips. It had been years since he'd last had one—since Billie had told him she was pregnant with Alice—and the cravings weren't as bad now as they once had been. But at times like this it felt like his blood was on fire, and a cigarette was the only thing that could put it out.

And the nicotine-drenched fumes from the bungalow hadn't helped.

"Good riddance to them," Savage said as Duke herded the three men into the back of a police van, their wrists snapped into handcuffs. The big PC went to close the door but the last guy—the one with dreadlocks—hadn't quite made it all the way in, squealing as the door trapped his foot. Duke swore loud enough to be heard across the street, tripping up the steps as he went to help and almost ending up in the cage himself.

"It's like somebody put a police uniform on a brontosaurus," Kett said.

The other man they'd met in the house, Freddie, was

sitting in the driver's seat of the IRV, the door open. The little black cat was curled up on his lap, and the PC who had ridden over with Duke was standing next to him, showing Freddie which buttons did what. Kett had heard Freddie ask several times if he could take the car for a spin around the block, and he was tempted to let him—some small compensation for what the three gang members had done to him, and done to his house.

"They really are the scum of the earth, men like that," said Savage. "They make out they're your friend, they bring you booze and food and whatever, then they don't leave. Poor Freddie."

"He'll never have to see them again," Kett said. "I'll make sure of it. And at least they gave us something."

"Not much," Savage said. "A monster. What do you think she meant?"

"I don't know. But the more I learn about this, the more I think this whole thing centres on whatever happened to Martha Hansen-Andrews in September. Jenny, Fran, maybe the other women too, they invited Martha out for drinks with the explicit purpose of leading her to an alleyway where these Beggar Boy arsewipes would beat her senseless. But something happened before they got there, something that split the group up and sent Martha running."

"Makes sense that Martha would call Jenny a monster, right?" said Savage. "If she found out what Jenny was planning to do to her. That really is monstrous."

"Yeah," said Kett. "That's what I was thinking. There were five women in that friendship group and it's pretty clear that Jenny was the leader. Martha was an outsider, Jenny hated her with a passion. So Jenny and Fran planned the beating, maybe one of the others tried to stop it. They were drinking, they started to argue, Fortune or Beatrice or Poppy tells Martha that she's going to get hurt and so Martha bolts. She reaches the stairs by St Lawrence's Church, trips at the bottom and falls into the path of the car. It's a narrow pavement, easily done, especially in the dark."

"And she's injured, but when Jenny catches up, Martha tells her what she thinks of her, that she's a monster."

"Maybe," said Kett, frowning. "I think we're getting there, but something's missing. The pieces aren't slotting together."

"Yeah," said Savage. "And I've looked at the CCTV from the night Martha was injured. All six women are walking together, they look happy. Footage from about eleven-thirty on Prince of Wales Road shows them heading down to the river, to the Waterfront. All looks good. Martha was hit by the car thirty minutes later, give or take, across town. At the time of the accident, right after midnight, CCTV shows Jenny and Fran on St Benedict's, about thirty seconds behind Martha. Close enough to be suspicious, but nowhere near close enough to have actually pushed her. There was no way they could have done it. The group had split up by then, the other three weren't anywhere near there."

Kett nodded.

"You know, if it was one of the other women who warned Martha that she was about to be hurt, maybe it's the same woman who's behind all this," he said. "She could be angry enough about what happened to her friend to go after Jenny and Fran. It might be like it was by the coast, with those kids. If we think the finger we found in the flat belongs to Fortune then we're looking at Beatrice or Poppy as potential suspects. Did the background checks bring up anything useful?"

"Nothing that led me to think they could be responsible for this," said Savage. "Fortune's a black belt in Ju-Jitsu, I think, but other than Jenny, none of them have ever been on our radar. We can't rule it out. I know Dunst has compiled a list of everywhere they used to hang out and Uniforms are checking every location. Nothing yet."

"And the driver of the car that hit Martha, that was a dead-end too, right?"

"It was a woman on the way back from seeing her mother. She was distraught. I've watched the footage of her interview, I don't think she has anything to do with this."

Duke was running across the road, his hat in his hands.

"Shall I take the Backstreet Boys to holding?" he asked.

"Yeah, thanks," Kett replied. "Kate, can you check out the rest of the drug leads for me? Take the car and a Uniform, don't take any chances."

"Sure, sir," she said. "Most of the names are known to us, all minor players. Good to cross them off the list, though. Where are you going?"

"I don't know," he said. "For a walk, I think. I need to clear my head."

"Shall I let Clare know about the lads or will you?"

"I'll do it," he said.

He ran a hand through his wet hair, took one last look at the bungalow, then set off.

"What about your coat, sir?" Savage said, a glint of a smile in her eyes.

He thought about leaving it, but the rain was relentless and he hated the cold. He sloped back to the Mondeo and collected the heavy jacket from the footwell, pulling it on. It weighed as much as a big dog—and smelled like one too— but the chill in his bones began to thaw immediately. He caught sight of himself in the car's window, sighing.

"You could be his twin," said Savage, a hand to her mouth to hold in the laughter.

He lifted his middle finger, using his other hand to call Clare as he walked away. The Super answered almost immediately.

"Speak!" he thundered.

"Uh... That's generally what people do on the phone, sir. We've got three men inbound, Beggar Boys. Jenny Eyler asked them to attack Martha Hansen-Andrews back in September. She wanted them to hurt her."

"What?"

"They never got the chance to do it. Martha ran off before they got to the alley where she was supposed to be attacked, and then she was hit by the car. These men have no problem with violence towards women, but they don't seem to have the intelligence to be behind the abductions. I'm not ruling it out, though, and the fact there are three of them working together would explain how they got the coffin into the Samson and Hercules. They might have taken Jenny and the others to cover up what they'd been asked to do to Martha. I don't know. Ask Porter to interview them when he's back, find out where they were on Friday."

"I'll do it," said Clare. "I'm in a foul mood as it is. Where are you now?"

"Following a lead," Kett said.

"You're wearing my coat?"

"I was, but a bunch of angry shepherds bundled me into a trailer to take me back to the farm."

"Kett..."

"And a gorilla tried to make me its bride."

"Kett!"

"I'm bloody wearing it, sir!" he snapped, hanging up.

He didn't know where he was going, exactly, but by the

time he'd reached the main road, his thoughts were settling. Crimes like this were so rarely random, especially when they involved such a close group of friends. Everything pointed to that night in September when Martha had been hit by the car, but with no real hope of finding out exactly what happened then, how was he supposed to work out what was going on now?

It screamed revenge, though. Five women responsible for their friend being injured, and now those same five women were being systematically and brutally murdered. Joffre Andrews, Martha's dad, didn't give off serial killer vibes and his alibi was tight, but it didn't mean that he wasn't behind it.

And anyway, Martha had *two* parents.

He looked up, scanning street signs and realising that it wasn't a long walk to Martha's house. Savage and Porter had reported back after they'd visited Sue Hansen yesterday, and Clare had left a car there to keep an eye on her, but this was something Kett needed to do for himself.

Going to talk to Martha's mum, he texted Savage.

They'd done a background check on her too, of course, but nothing had come up. Sue Hansen had been a teacher for a few years after college but had quit when it had become too stressful. After that, she'd not done much at all until Martha had been born, and then she'd been a full-time mother—*like there was any other kind*, Kett thought. She'd never been in trouble with the law, and nobody they'd spoken to had a bad word to say about her.

Nobody had much to say at all.

Could she be the one who'd taken the five women? Who'd slit Jenny's throat and wrapped her in thorns and dragged her up the steps of Cow Tower? Who'd rigged up a weighted coffin to trap Fran Herbert? The crimes spoke of a mother's fury, for sure, the actions of somebody who wanted not just to kill her victims but to hurt them, and to shame them. They were the actions of somebody who wanted the whole world to know what these women had done, and what their punishment had been.

But murder on this scale was a big ask for anyone, not just emotionally but physically.

Unless she wasn't working alone.

Unless she and her estranged husband were working together.

Kett stopped, realising he'd walked too far. He doubled back and took the next turn into a street lined with flats, trying to remember which number belonged to Sue Hansen. In the end, it was the undercover police car that gave it away, a detective he didn't recognise sitting in the passenger seat reading the paper. Kett rapped on the window.

"Nothing to be had here," said the man as he wound it down. "Piss off."

"I'm police. DCI Kett."

"Oh, shit, sorry sir," said the detective, sitting up in his seat. "I thought you were homeless. The coat and everything."

"Any movement?" Kett asked.

"Got a Sainsbury's delivery about an hour ago," the man said, unable to take his eyes off the jacket's furry collar. "But nobody's left, and nobody else has visited. Why are you wearing that, sir? Working undercover for Vice?"

"Which flat is it?"

"White door, sir."

Kett walked over to it and knocked hard. When nobody answered he made his way to the big front window, cupping a hand to the glass. It was too dark to see much but he could just about make out the hospital bed that sat against the far wall, a lump of shadow lying in it. The room was alive with birds, little finches who gyred in tight circles.

He scanned the rest of the room, his body gripped by an electric jolt as he realised somebody was standing by the bed, watching him. He stood back, offering a wave.

"Mrs Hansen? Have you got a minute?"

It took her a while to move, and when she did it seemed too slow, like time inside the flat had stuttered and stalled. A few seconds later the front door opened and Kett walked into a cool, dark hallway that smelled of damp, dust and something sharper. The living room door was closed but the birds were chirping so loudly they might have been sitting on his shoulders.

"My name's DCI Kett," he said, holding up his warrant card. Sue didn't even glance at it as she shunted the stubborn door closed.

"I know who you are," she said. "Saw you on the news, didn't I?"

"Maybe," he said.

"Yeah, I did."

She leaned against the front door like she was trying to block the way out.

"You want to know something funny?"

He could tell by the way her small teeth were bared— the only part of her face visible in her silhouette—that there was nothing funny about what she was about to say.

"When this happened to my Martha, I prayed it would be you who showed up at my door. I prayed for it, because I heard what you did to that pig man in London and what you did to those creeps who took the newspaper girls. I wanted you to be the one, because I knew you'd find justice for my girl. I knew you'd make them pay."

She shook her head, her face drowning in shadow.

"And now you're here. Not for Martha, not for my beautiful girl, but for those women who did this to her. You've taken their side just like everybody else."

She spoke with such anger that her whole body shook with the force of it, spittle hitting Kett's face. He wiped it away. Even with Clare's coat on he was shivering hard in the damp chill of the hallway.

"I'm sorry," he said. "And you have to believe me, if I'd been on the Force when Martha was injured I'd have done everything I could for your daughter."

"Sure," she said, opening the living room door. Light fell on her face, chasing away the darkness, and Kett saw that there wasn't anger there, just a terrible, hollow expression of loss. When she walked she did so with the staccato movements of somebody who had forgotten how to be human, and she had to rest a bony hand on the bed to stop herself from falling. She was painfully thin, the skin hanging off her bones.

The room was full of birds, a storm of finches that battered past Kett's head as they escaped into the hall. The sound of them was surreal.

"It's not too late to get justice for Martha," Kett said as he watched them fly. "I believe you when you tell me that Jenny wanted to hurt your daughter. I believe it."

She looked at him like he'd spoken another language, like she couldn't understand him.

"If you help us find the missing women, I promise you I'll find out the truth. I can still make them pay for what they did to her."

Sue scoffed, leaning over to brush a hair away from Martha's eyes.

"You'll help me if I help you. There we are. Nothing for nothing, eh?"

Kett walked into the middle of the room so that he could see the young woman in the bed a little more clearly. Martha didn't look like somebody who had been hit by a car. Her cheeks were flushed, her breathing steady, her hair freshly washed and brushed and plaited—just the slightest hint of a long, deep scar beneath the hairline. According to the medical reports, Martha had experienced severe trauma to her brain. She couldn't do anything for herself, other than the very simplest of tasks. But right now, she looked like any other young woman asleep in her bed.

"I don't need you to make them pay," Sue said, chasing a finch away from Martha's arm. "Not anymore. Somebody else is taking care of that."

"Somebody you know?" Kett asked, speaking over the chatter of the birds as they reappeared. The noise and movement of them was almost overwhelming.

"It's her guardian angel," Sue replied, looking at him with a strange, dead-eyed smile. "God knows that Martha was wronged and he has sent his angels to do his bidding, to seek retribution."

"To murder these five women?" Kett said, pulling the collar of the coat around his neck to guard against the chill of the room, the fur tickling his ears. "You know for sure that they were all involved in what happened to Martha? Because I don't."

"We'll find out, won't we?" she said. "If they die, then they were guilty. If they live, then they weren't. Only *He* knows."

"But what if you're wrong?" Kett said. "What if these women are innocent?"

In the bed, Martha moaned, her body shifting beneath the heavy blankets. Sue rested her hand on her daughter's shoulder, hushing gently.

"I won't have you upsetting her," she said. "We're done with you, done with the police. I want you to leave."

A bird landed in Kett's hair, a sharp beak drumming against his scalp. He gasped at the pain, swiping it away. Another landed on his arm, tweeting angrily.

"Leave," Sue said. "Before you do any more harm."

Martha groaned again, one hand leaving the blanket and grasping at the air. Her eyes opened, staring at the ceiling then grinding in their sockets until they found her mother.

"Hush, baby girl," Sue said. "You don't have to worry."

Martha blinked, struggling to lift her head. She found Kett and he saw the way her expression tightened, the tendons in her neck jutting out like steel wires. The hand that had escaped seemed to point at him, a finger extending.

"Hush now," said Sue, more desperate. She shot a look at Kett. "Look what you've done, you horrible man."

The birds were growing agitated, one of them batting against the window behind Kett. Martha looked like she was struggling to get out of the bed, the support rail the only thing stopping her from falling. She was still reaching for Kett, her finger trembling.

"Go," Sue said. "Now!"

Martha opened her mouth and screamed, the sound of it deafening in the confined space. It seemed to go on forever, loud enough to make Kett's skull feel like it would shatter. He retreated to the door, his hands to his ears, that scream still clawing at the walls, at the ceiling. He didn't understand how anyone could have enough air in their lungs to scream for so long.

Then, just like that, she fell silent.

Sue was doing her best to settle her daughter, fighting to keep her in the bed. Kett scrubbed his eyes with shaking hands, making the most of the distraction. He walked down the corridor into a small, dark kitchen, flicking on the light. It was clean in here, everything in its place. On the walls hung dozens of needlepoints, each one a quotation from the Bible, and a half finished one lay on the table. He ducked out, checking the toilet, then each of the two bedrooms, the finches following him and crying out a warning.

There was nothing here.

"Hey!" came a voice from the living room. "Where are you? Don't you dare go in there."

Kett returned to the hallway to see that Martha was sitting upright in the bed. The young woman was calmer now but she was making a series of small, grunting noises deep in her throat.

Sue held her daughter's hand against her chest, her face flushed, strands of hair pulled loose and stuck to the sheen of sweat on her cheeks. She looked like she was unravelling, and Kett felt a wave of immense sadness and grief.

"Can I call anyone for you?" he said, his voice hoarse. "Can I do anything to help?"

"You can go," Sue replied. "Don't ever come back here."

Kett nodded, pausing for a moment before opening the front door. He stepped out quickly before the birds could make a break for it, casting one quick look back as he went. Martha stared at him from the shadows of the living room, fear still swimming in her eyes as she watched him leave.

Fear and something else, he thought. Something he couldn't quite grasp.

Something that seemed almost like recognition.

He wrenched the stiff door shut behind him, escaping into the air, into the light. He hadn't told Sue a lie. If he'd been on the Force in the summer, if he'd been on Martha's case, he would have stopped at nothing to find out what had happened to her.

He'd have stopped at nothing to bring her justice.

Maybe it wasn't too late.

He pulled his phone out of his pocket as he walked back to the street, the echo of Martha's scream still ringing in his skull, in his ears—so loud that he didn't hear the roar of an engine until the IRV was right next to him. The siren blipped and he whirled around to see Savage leaning out of the driver's window.

"Get in, sir," she said. "We've found Fortune."

"What?" he said, breaking for the road. "Alive or dead?"

"Alive, sir," she said as she reached over and opened the door for him. "But not for long."

CHAPTER TWENTY-SIX

SAVAGE HANDED KETT HER PHONE AS SHE ACCELERATED up the street, the siren wailing. There was a video already playing, and it took Kett a moment to make sense of the bundle of squirming rags he saw there. A face peeked out from the darkness, etched with pure terror. It was almost certainly a woman, but the quality of the footage didn't make it easy to see who it was.

"How do you know it's Fortune?"

"Because it's streaming from her Facebook account," she said. "It's live."

"*Live?*"

It said so right there on the bottom of the screen. Savage braked hard then turned left, the engine roaring. Kett had to hold onto his stomach with his free hand to stop it from exploding out through his spine.

"It started about ten minutes ago," she said. "Spalding saw it. That's all there's been so far, just footage of the woman wrapped in tarps. But there's somebody else there because the camera's moving. Somebody's holding it. And sir, look at the caption."

Kett used a thumb to shrink the video, seeing Fortune Quinn's Facebook page. Beneath the thumbnail for the live shoot was a line of text.

Our hero thought he was quick, but he wasn't quick enough. Save her now, fuckers.

"He's angry," Kett said.

"Yeah, he thought he was smarter than us, and he's pretty furious that we found his flat in the Normandie before he could use it. Whoa! Move it, you *flomping wingnut!*"

The cyclist who'd ridden onto the road wobbled back onto the pavement as Savage barrelled past.

"Sorry, sir," she said, flooring it.

"You know where this is?" Kett said.

"No, but the tech team is working on it."

"They'd better be quick. Something's happening."

The camera lurched, revealing a dark ceiling then a stone wall, then Fortune again, from further away this time. She cried out, her words distorted almost past recognition.

"No! Don't! Just let me go, please! I—"

She slid across the floor like somebody was dragging her by her feet, her screams filling the car like cold water. Her head was the last thing to vanish, and something trailed behind her.

A rope.

"Christ," Kett said. "Porter was right. He's going to hang her."

Savage was on the wrong side of the road as she tore across a junction, her face a mask of concentration. Kett studied the screen, seeing big flagstones. Old ones.

"It's a church," he said.

"What's happening?"

"Nothing, he dragged her away. I can't see her."

He could hear her, though, those same awful shrieks. Somebody shouted, a man's voice, full of anger. Then the same voice began to laugh, the sound of it worse than the screams. Kett tried to turn the volume up but it was already as loud as it would go. He put the speaker to his ear, holding his breath. There was more laughter, then a voice he couldn't make out.

"What's happening?" Savage said again.

They were almost in the city, the traffic thicker here as they approached one of the main roads into town. Two more IRVs were speeding down the hill, their blue lights blazing as they cut through the red light. Savage didn't follow them, heading straight ahead. She thumped the wheel in frustration.

"I don't know where I'm supposed to be going. He could be anywhere."

There was still nothing happening on the video, just that same shot of the floor. Even the sounds had died out now.

"He made it too easy for us last time," Kett said. "He's not going to make that mistake again."

Savage pulled over to the side of the road, her teeth clamped together so hard that her jaw was bulging. Kett held the phone out so that she could see it, and both of them stared at that dark, empty room.

The camera moved, everything lurching and blurring. Kett heard footsteps, saw a flash of light before darkness. It was too bright inside the car, the screen obscured. He cupped a hand to it, squinting.

More light, the shot angling up to a large, open window.

Somebody stood there, and as the cameraman walked closer Kett saw that it was Fortune Quinn. The tarps had been unwrapped, her jeans and jumper filthy, her feet bare.

Her hands had been tied behind her back and a coil of rope sat over her shoulder. She looked delirious with terror, staring right at the camera, right at Kett.

"Oh no," Savage said, her hand to her mouth. "Please no."

A voice filtered through the speakers, just a whisper.

"There are no happy endings here," it said.

"Please," said Fortune. "Please don't. Please."

Kett brought the phone closer, trying to make sense of the view behind the woman. There were no landmarks there, no castle, no cathedral. It could be anywhere.

"Rapunzel," said the voice. "Oh Rapunzel."

"Please," begged Fortune.

Please, begged Kett.

But the killer wasn't listening. The camera wobbled as he approached the young woman. She tugged at the binds around her wrists, she kicked out at him, but there was nothing she could do and nowhere she could go. She tilted her head back and screamed to the ceiling.

"There's nothing around her neck," Kett said. "But I can see rope. What the hell is he doing?"

He didn't have to wait for an answer.

"Let down your hair," said the faceless man.

Then he gave Fortune a mighty push.

She fell back through the window, vanishing. The rope snapped taut and she screamed again.

The camera moved after her, looking down.

"It's in her hair," Kett said.

The rope was thrashing as Fortune struggled, noosed around her long hair. The view was clearer now. Kett saw the river, and past that a large, squat building.

"Shit," he said. "That's the old Toys R Us."

Savage nodded, looking up.

"St Benedict's Street," she said, pulling away from the kerb and punching the accelerator. "That's the same church I was at this morning."

"This morning?"

"Yeah, with the dog. St Lawrence's. It's where—"

"Martha was hit by the car," Kett finished for her. "Christ. Go!"

He pulled out his own phone, calling Clare.

"Speak!" said the boss when he answered.

But Kett couldn't.

On Savage's phone the killer was walking up to the window where Fortune was hanging.

And in his hand was a lighter.

"Kett?" Clare said.

The car accelerated down the hill, taking the turn at the bottom so fast that the tyres squealed. Savage almost lost control but she flicked the wheel, bringing them back.

"St Lawrence's Church, sir," Kett said. "On St Benedict's Street. He's hanging her out the window."

Clare didn't reply, but Kett heard the sound of his voice as he relayed the location.

On-screen, the killer reached out and held the lighter to the rope. It must have been primed because it caught immediately, the fire dripping down the rope into Fortune's hair.

"Hurry up, Kate," Kett said.

"Another minute, sir," she replied.

Fortune didn't have another minute. The fire was moving fast and she was fighting hard, all of her bodyweight tugging on the rope.

"Where are you?" asked Clare.

"Nearly there, get the fire service out with the cushion, and get an ambulance, sir."

The camera dropped to the floor, going dark for a

second until it slid over the edge of the window, a perfect downward shot. Fortune was there, her hair pulled back so tight that her forehead looked enormous. The fire hadn't reached her yet but it wouldn't be long.

And Kett was certain the rope would give out first.

Savage took the last corner onto St Benedict's, the car bumping over the kerb and knocking the phone from his hand. He left it in the footwell, leaning forward and looking through the top of the windscreen to see the church ahead.

Fortune was right there, hanging by her hair from the top of the tower, smoke billowing upwards.

The road was mobbed as people started to notice her, crowds spilling from the shops and cafes. Savage was practically out of the window.

"Move!"

Kett opened the door, breaking into a run. Out here, he couldn't see Fortune past the roofs of the buildings, but he could hear her—her screams so loud, so desperate, that they didn't sound human. Ahead, another IRV stopped outside the church, followed by Porter's Mondeo. The DI was out in a heartbeat.

"You see her?" he yelled.

"Get the church door open!" Kett shouted back.

Porter vaulted the railing. Kett tried to follow only for Clare's jacket to catch on something. He shrugged it off and left it, struggling over the barrier. Fortune swung over their heads, kicking so much that she was like a pendulum. The fire had spread to her hair, the smoke so thick that the sky was growing dark. It was pointless calling to her, Kett knew. She'd be lost to the terror, to the agony.

"Get it open!" he said again, pointing down a set of steps.

Porter tried the handle but it didn't budge. He stepped

back and charged the old door with his shoulder, grabbing his injured arm as he rebounded. Kett moved in, ramming his boot into the lock. It trembled, something cracking.

"Together," he said. "Now!"

They ran as one, hitting the door at the same time and forcing it open with an explosion of dust. Porter fell to his hands and knees, up again in a heartbeat. Kett ran into the nave, Savage right behind him. She was holding a small fire extinguisher in one hand.

"There," she said, running to a smaller wooden door. She pulled it open to reveal a set of spiral stairs.

Kett followed her up as fast as he could in the narrow dark. The tower seemed taller than it had any right to be, the stairwell shrinking with every turn. There was no air in here, no air in his lungs—just smoke, the space full of it.

They reached the top and Savage stepped out into the tower, coughing uncontrollably. The rope had been fixed to a metal hook above the stone window and the fire had spread to the wooden ceiling. Below, Fortune still struggled, but her movements were growing slower, weaker. Kett ran to the window, one hand a shield against the heat.

"Hey," he yelled, his lungs contracting and reducing the word to a spluttered cough.

Fortune's hair was alight, there was nothing he could get hold of.

The rope was about to go, cracking like kindling as the threads began to snap.

"Move!" Savage yelled, and there was a hissing roar as she emptied the fire extinguisher.

In the sudden cloud of gas, Kett was blind. He lunged for the window, misjudging it. For a second he thought he was going over, the world yawning open beneath him.

Then he found the stone ledge and rooted himself in

place. He snatched the only thing he could reach—Fortune's hair—not pulling, just holding. Porter grabbed what was left of the rope and hauled the woman upwards, up, up, until Kett could hook his hands beneath her armpits. He fell back and she came with him, sliding into the tower, crushing his chest as she landed on him.

Savage rolled her away, calling her name as she patted the last of the flames from her scalp. Fortune's eyes were open but she wasn't in the room, she was lost somewhere else, delirious. Her body writhed, foam bubbling between her lips.

"You're safe," Savage said. "You're safe, you're safe."

And she kept on saying it, cradling the woman's blackened head on her lap.

"You're safe, Fortune. You're safe."

Kett wasn't sure if he had the strength to stand, then Porter's hand was there. He let the big DI pull him to his feet and he held on to him until the tower stopped spinning.

"Fuck me," he said, hacking up phlegm. "Get the paramedics up here, Pete."

Porter nodded, ducking through the low door. Kett looked at the window, seeing the phone that sat on the ledge. It seemed like a small miracle he hadn't knocked it off when he was pulling Fortune inside.

"You got gloves?" he asked Savage, and she nodded, pulling some free and handing them over.

He put them on and picked up the phone, seeing that it was still recording. His own face filled the screen, pale skin beneath smudges of soot. He looked about a thousand years old.

And people were watching him, he saw. Over a hundred of them. Shocked little emojis floated upwards, the comments appearing too fast for him to read. He didn't know what to do with it so he put it back where he'd found it.

The killer had been here just minutes ago. He couldn't have gone far.

Kett limped to the stairs, the pain in his smoke-blasted chest like he'd been shot all over again.

"Stay with her," he said to Savage, as if she'd do anything else.

"Where are you going, sir?"

"I'm going to find him," he said. "And I'm going to end him."

CHAPTER TWENTY-SEVEN

By the time Kett left the church through its splintered front doors, St Benedict's Street was awash in blue light. Four IRVs blocked the road and two ambulances sat either side of them. Porter was running this way with one paramedic while the other struggled to get over the metal railings, his medical bags on the floor.

"She alive?" the DI asked as he ran past.

"Yeah," said Kett.

The two men entered the building, the second paramedic running in after them—the seat of his trousers ripped. Kett doubled over, coughing so hard he thought he was going to lose a lung. For an awful second, despite the light of the day, despite the crowds who choked the streets, he was right back there in Bingo's house as the Pig Man tried to burn his children alive.

Reality seemed to disintegrate, the way it often did in nightmares, and Kett reached for the railing to ground himself. He missed it, flailing, almost falling. Then a hand grabbed his arm through the fence, firm but gentle, and he blinked his way back to the world to see Superintendent

Clare. The Big Tossing Jacket was draped over his other arm, but he didn't mention it.

"You okay?" the Super asked, genuinely concerned. "You've gone the colour of Porter's tea."

Kett nodded, swallowing bile. Clare let go of him and looked up at the church, at the dwindling plume of smoke.

"You got her?"

"Yeah. I think she'll live. Bastard strung her up by her hair. He must have left minutes before we arrived, we need CCTV from every shop and restaurant along the street. Phones, too. If we're quick, we can catch him."

Kett took an unsteady breath and climbed over the railing, making his way down the street. There were uniformed police everywhere, grilling anyone who'd stopped to watch. The air was full of distress, of shocked voices and sobs. Kett didn't blame them. Even after everything he'd seen in his twenty-year career, after everything that he'd been through since he'd arrived in this city, what had happened to Fortune Quinn defied belief.

He'd see her hanging there, her hair on fire, her face twisted in agony, for the rest of his life.

He moved down the street, scanning the crowds, looking for anything that stood out, anyone who didn't belong. The employees of the comic shop next to the church were clustered outside the front door and he called to them.

"You see anyone leave the church in the last ten minutes? A man, maybe wearing a cloak? A hood?"

They shook their heads but the girl with the pink hair who he'd spoken to yesterday pointed to the steep steps that led down the flank of the church.

"Busy up here. If he'd wanted to hide himself he'd have gone that way. Goes down to the river."

Kett followed the girl's finger, clattering down the

uneven steps, past the café where he'd ordered tea. There were new faces in the window there, more students, and the barista, Bert, stood with them.

"You seen anyone run this way?" Kett shouted through the open door. "Last ten minutes or so?"

They shook their heads.

"Is it true?" asked one of the girls. "Did someone hang themselves up there?"

Kett didn't answer, he just took the stairs as fast as he dared. It was as he was nearing the bottom that his foot slipped on the weathered stone and he clattered onto the narrow pavement, his arms wheeling, his knee twisting.

A car roared past, its wing mirror almost clipping Kett's hip. It didn't stop, but through the window he saw kids in the back seat staring at him like he was a crazy person. Their mother was oblivious behind the wheel as she drove up the hill and swung left at the top. A truck was right behind her and its horn blared, fading into the chatter of the city. The street was full of cars and the killer could have been in any of them.

Or none.

"Fuck," he said, fishing out his warrant card and holding it up to the van. "Stop right there, nobody gets past. Got it?"

The driver nodded. There was nothing else down here, no pedestrians, no sign of life in the shops. A handful of PCs were coming down the stairs and he called to them.

"Stop traffic and start asking questions. Search those buildings, and one of you get down to the river. Whatever it takes."

They scattered, and Kett turned to the steps again. The Church of St Lawrence sat above him on its buttress of flint, looking like a medieval wall, like a fortress. Whatever secrets it was hiding, they could hide there for centuries if they wanted to.

He made his way back up the ancient staircase, his right knee throbbing, his chest on fire. When he passed the little café again he saw Bert standing in the door holding a take-away cup of tea. He was dressed in his big, black coat and his assortment of hats but he was still shivering.

"Hey, this is for you," he said, his face knotted with worry.

"For me?" Kett said. "Really?"

He took the tea, the warmth of the cup making him feel instantly better.

"Least I can do after yesterday," Bert said, his teeth chattering. "I can make some for the rest of your team, if you want? It's no bother. Half the stuff I do these days is for old people's homes, homeless shelters. I don't charge. You have no idea how much of a difference a good cup of tea can make if you're having a shit day."

"You're preaching to the choir, son," Kett said, pulling the plastic lid off the cup and taking a sip. It was far too hot, making his tongue go instantly fuzzy, but he didn't care. The tea hit his belly with an explosion of warmth and comfort. "Thanks."

"What happened?" Bert asked. The three students peeked past his shoulders, their eyes wide. "Did somebody..."

"No, they're alive." Kett looked at the front of the café, at the painted wires secured there. "You don't have CCTV by any chance, do you?"

The man shook his head, his expression dark.

"Had it, but the dealers up the hill just kept spray-painting it. Gave up in the end. The comic shop has it, the place at the top of the steps. Talk to Michelle, pink hair."

Kett nodded, climbing one step before turning back.

"By the way, those dealers won't be bothering you for a little while."

He saw the man's frown lines deepening.

"It won't come back to you, don't worry."

"Thanks, I guess," Bert said, shivering back through the door.

"If you hear anything, or see anything, come and find me."

Kett grabbed the metal rail with his free hand and hauled himself up the steps like he was scaling a mountain. The street had grown busier in the five minutes he'd been off it, the news vans trying to nudge past the police cars and the reporters already buzzing by the church.

Like flies, he thought.

He stayed out of their way, hugging the other side of the street, walking a hundred yards before he realised how futile it was. The killer could have been standing right next to him and he wouldn't have a clue.

He made his way back to the church, doing his best to ignore the barrage of questions from the reporters.

"Is this related to the Sweet Briar Rose killing?" yelled one.

"Can you tell us if there's a serial killer in Norwich?"

"Have you got a name for him yet? How about the Fairy Tale Killer?"

"Move them back," Kett said to the constables who were guarding the front of the church. "And somebody get the bloody gate open."

He climbed the railings again, dropping into the church-yard. The last thing he wanted to do was walk back through that coffin-shaped slice of darkness into the damp and dark of the church, but he pushed through the doors anyway, hearing voices echoing in the nave.

The paramedics had managed to get Fortune down the stairs and she was in better shape than Kett had feared. She was sitting on a pew as the paramedics examined her, shaking so hard that the heavy wooden bench was rattling. One of the paramedics was exploring what was left of her hair. The other was examining her right hand, and the stump of her index finger. Clare stood close by, his angry face like one of the gargoyles who perched on the roof outside.

"Anything?" he said.

Kett shook his head.

"Needle in a haystack, he could be anywhere."

Fortune had her eyes closed, but she was remarkably composed given what she'd been through.

"Fortune?" Kett said.

She didn't open her eyes, but her head twisted towards the sound of his voice.

"I'm DCI Robbie Kett. I know it's going to be hard for you to think about it, but can you tell me anything about who did this to you?"

She shook her head. When she spoke, her voice was like gravel.

"He wears a hood. A cloak. I've never seen him. Are you the one who pulled me up?"

"One of them."

"Can this wait?" the paramedic asked. "She's sustained some very serious injuries."

"It can't wait," Kett told him. "We've still got two women missing, we need to find them."

"Two?" said Fortune, finally opening her eyes. Both

were shot through with burst vessels. "Who? Have you found the others?"

"We found Jenny," said Kett. "And Fran."

"Thank god," Fortune said. "Did he do this to them too? Are they okay?"

Kett looked at Clare, who shook his head.

"We can talk about this later," Kett said. "I don't want you to worry. We're still looking for Poppy and Beatrice. If you know anything about—"

"Is she dead?" Fortune said. "Jenny? Please say she's okay."

Kett sighed.

"I'm sorry to have to tell you this, but Jenny was murdered."

Fortune kicked her legs out in front of her, as if she was fighting for air. Her back arched, everything growing tense, ready to erupt. But she breathed out slowly, retracting her legs beneath the bench. Tears rolled down her cheeks, carving paths in the smoke and the dirt, but other than the occasional sniff she was utterly silent.

"Fran's okay," Kett said. "She was badly hurt, but she's alive."

No reaction, just more quiet tears.

"It's not too late to save the others, but I need your help. I need you to tell me everything you remember. Everything you saw. Everything you heard."

Fortune swallowed, pulling her injured hand away from the paramedic and cradling it against her chest.

"I'll go see where the stretcher is," the man said, heading for the door. Outside, Kett could hear an angle grinder and he hoped it was somebody taking the chain off the gate. He moved to the bench and sat down where the paramedic had been.

"You mind?"

Fortune shook her head, closing her eyes again. Her teeth were chattering, the sound of it like hail. This close, Kett could see that although much of her hair had been burned away, what was left seemed undamaged. The other paramedic saw him looking.

"Surprisingly strong," he said. "I heard somewhere you could hold up a bus with a full head of human hair. Not when it's on fire, mind."

"Fortune, do you know who did this to you?" Kett asked.

The young woman shook her head.

"Did you see his face?"

The shaking continued, harder this time.

"Is he working alone?"

More shaking.

"I don't know," she said. "It was so dark there."

"Where?"

"Where he was keeping us. I don't know what happened. We were going out..."

She frowned, reaching back inside her memories.

"We were going out, like we always do. But..."

She swallowed, licking her chapped lips.

"It was Jenny who said she needed to do something before we went to the pub. She said she needed to talk to somebody. We never thought anything of it."

"What time was this?"

"Six-thirty, maybe. Seven. Early."

"Did she say what it was about?"

"Money," Fortune said. "It was always about money with her. She said she was taking us somewhere to get rich."

"Did she mention the name Kevin Dufrane?" Kett asked.

"No. I mean, maybe. He was one of the losers she was

fleecing, wasn't he? She might have been meeting him later but this was something else."

"Drugs?" barked Clare, loud enough to make the woman flinch.

"She didn't say, and she... she never did them."

It was a lie, as clear as day.

"Jenny's gone, Fortune," said Kett. "She can't get in any trouble. Was she going to collect drug money? Collect it from her friends in the gang? The Beggar Boys?"

"It wasn't that. She was done with all that. After the summer, after what happened..."

"We know about Martha," Kett said when she didn't continue. "Is this about what happened that night in September?"

Fortune swallowed again, wincing.

"We know that Jenny was going to attack her. We know what she and Fran asked the Beggar Boys to do."

The young woman hung her head, shaking it from side to side.

"I didn't know, I swear it. I didn't know until we were nearly there and Poppy said something. She told Martha what was going to happen and Martha... she ran. I didn't know anything about it until she was gone, and then it was too late."

She looked up.

"Is this Martha's dad? Is he doing this?"

"You tell me."

"It's not..." She shook her head, frowning. "No, it wasn't him. Didn't sound like him."

"It can't be him," Clare said. "Joffre Andrews is still in custody."

"Did the man who did this say anything about Martha?"

asked Kett. "Did he mention what happened in the summer? Did he speak about revenge?"

"No," she said. "He didn't say much at all and what he said... It didn't make any sense. He kept telling stories, stupid kids' stories."

"Fairy tales?"

She nodded, her left hand exploring her right, seeking out the missing finger. The wound was neat, but it was infected.

"Do you remember any in particular?" Kett asked.

"I really think we should continue this conversation in the hospital," said the paramedic.

"I'm okay," said Fortune. She leaned forward, almost folding herself double. "I don't remember much because I think he drugged us. Somebody did, because I'd only had a couple of drinks at home and one on the way after I'd met the girls."

"One on the way?" Kett asked.

"A bottle of voddy. I think it was Jenny's."

"You all drank it?"

"Yeah. It was a peace offering from Jenny because she was making us walk across town."

"You remember where you were going?"

Her eyes roved back and forth behind their lids.

"A house," she said. "I wasn't really paying attention."

"Can you describe it for me?"

She was trying, Kett saw.

"It had a blue door. No front garden."

"Bungalow? Two floors?"

"Three, I think. It was down an alley, or a courtyard. Magdalene Street, maybe?" She shrugged. "I wasn't going to go in but it was pissing it down and so me and the girls waited downstairs while Jenny did whatever she was supposed to be doing. And... And there was a man there. I didn't see him, but I heard him."

"He gave you a drink?"

"Jenny brought them down. She was smiling, because she was going to make us all some money. I didn't like it, I never liked the stuff she did. But I didn't think... I had no idea."

Her eyes peeled open, so red that it looked as if she was crying blood.

"We woke up in a different place. Some kind of... of prison. Stank of shit. I was tied up and... and this had happened."

She held up her hand, the stump of her missing finger seeping.

"Fucker took my finger, and I don't even know where it is."

"You were kept in this place with the other women? All five of you?"

"No, not Jenny. The others, yeah, but she was never with us. We weren't allowed to talk. If we talked, he came for us. He never beat me but he beat Poppy pretty hard because she wouldn't shut up. Kept screaming about her boy right until he said he was going to cut out her tongue."

What little heat was left in Kett's body seemed to evaporate.

"She was quiet after that."

"And you never saw him? Never saw his face?"

"Never. It was too dark and the door was locked, and if the lights were on he wore a hood."

She gestured to her own face.

"Like a cowl, or a cloak or something. Like out of a fairy tale."

She sniffed, her body still quaking. There was a

clatter of wheels and the second paramedic struggled through the door with the stretcher. It caught on the wall and Clare helped him, both of them manoeuvring it to the pew.

"You're welcome to ride with us," the paramedic said to Kett. "But she really needs a hospital."

"I can go with," said Porter as he ducked through the low door that led from the stairwell. "Fuck all upstairs."

"There's no note?" Kett asked. "No more of the story?"

"Nothing," said Savage as she followed. "Hay might have more luck."

Both paramedics were helping Fortune to her feet, guiding her to the stretcher.

"Fortune," said Kett. "Do you mind if we check your pockets? The man who took you all likes to leave notes."

"There's nothing in them," she said. "He took everything. Phone, wallet, keys. He took it all."

She let go of the paramedic, touching her left pocket and then her right.

Then she frowned.

"Wait," said Kett. "Let us."

But her fingers were already sliding in—awkwardly, because she was using her left hand like she was cross-drawing a gun. She gasped, then groaned.

"Savage, gloves!" Kett yelled, but she was already running, reaching the woman's side just as her hand slid free of her pocket.

She was holding a finger.

"No!" Fortune screamed.

She dropped it and Savage managed to catch the severed digit in a loose glove before it hit the floor. Fortune staggered into the stretcher, retching out words.

"Is it mine? Is it mine?"

It wasn't, that was clear enough. The nail was painted black. Fortune stared at it, her eyes bulging.

"It's Poppy's," she said, another low groan. "Oh god, it's Poppy's."

"Hang on," said Savage, wrapping the finger in the glove and passing it to Kett. She worked her hand into the woman's pocket and pulled out a scrap of paper. Fortune was slapping at her legs like she expected more body parts to appear there, to crawl out of her pockets like maggots and patter over the flagstones.

"It's okay," Savage said. "It's okay, calm down. That's it, that's all there is."

The paramedics pushed past Savage, helping Fortune onto the stretcher. Both of them threw a filthy look Kett's way as they wheeled the young woman towards the door. He barely noticed. He stood there and held that finger, a finger that seemed too small, too brittle to be real. It was a finger from a hand that had once clung onto a parent's coat-tails, which had waved, which had explored, which had stroked the face of Poppy's own child. The horror of it sat in his stomach.

"What does it say, then?" Clare said.

Savage unfolded the note as carefully as she could, scanning the text and then looking at Kett. He knew from her expression that it was bad.

"Read the tossing note, Kate," Clare ordered.

She didn't need to. She turned the paper around and let them read it for themselves. Just two lines this time, in small, smudged type.

The End.
Fuck you.

CHAPTER TWENTY-EIGHT

"THROUGH HERE! THIS HAS TO BE IT."

Kett ran down the middle of the road, pointing towards a wide brick archway that was sandwiched between a charity shop and a takeaway. Magdalene Street was only a short walk away from the church where Fortune had been hanged but Kett had ridden here with Savage and Porter in an IRV. More had followed, blocking off both ends of the road. The sound of horns rose into the wet air like the cries of some alien zoo.

"Fortune said it was a courtyard, right?" he asked.

"Yeah, or alleyway," Savage replied.

They walked through the archway together, more uniformed police following close behind. The tactical unit was on its way but they weren't going to get here fast enough. By now the killer had to know that Fortune had survived. If he was keeping the two other women here then there was only a very small window in which to find them.

If they were still alive, of course.

The End.

Fuck you.

The killer had been playing a game with them all this time, and he was losing. If he decided to cut his losses and run then he had no need for Poppy and Beatrice anymore. Theirs wouldn't be a storybook ending, it wouldn't be a riddle like the others.

He'd execute them.

"Careful, sir," said Savage.

The alleyway opened into a wide courtyard, a row of imposing, three-storey buildings to the right and smaller houses to the left. Behind a low wall directly opposite was a public car park. The only blue door in sight belonged to the last of the taller houses, nestling in a wide car port and hidden behind a scraggy assortment of bushes.

"Number eight," Kett said quietly, gesturing towards it.

They moved fast and low, the sound of their boots like thunder. The curtains of the ground floor window were pulled tight so Kett moved around the side, the long grass doing its best to trip him. There was no back garden to speak of, and no more windows on the ground floor here. By the time he'd returned to the front, Duke was there, the breaching ram looking like a toy in his giant hands.

"Just give the order, sir," he said.

Kett called Clare, the Super answering immediately.

"They're fifteen minutes away," he said. "It's your call."

Kett hung up, nodding to Duke.

"Do it."

Duke charged the door like a Viking warrior, the ram almost demolishing the flimsy blue uPVC. He stood back and Kett took the lead, his boots crunching glass as he entered a small, dark hallway.

"Police!" he roared.

"Police!" Porter boomed, right in his ear.

There were two rooms down here, both doors locked.

"Get them open, Duke," Kett said, taking the stairs as fast as he could. He reached the first floor, finding two bedrooms and a cupboard.

"Porter, in there," he shouted, pointing to the closest bedroom.

He kept climbing, up to the second floor where a large open-plan kitchen and living room sat in shadow. When he flicked the lights nothing happened, so he stumbled to the huge windows and tugged the curtains open—expecting bodies, blood.

And finding nothing.

It was empty.

He swore beneath his breath, pausing to let his heart settle. Savage ran into the room, followed by another couple of PCs who proceeded to practically rip the doors off the kitchen cupboards.

"Hold up, fellas," Kett said to them. "I don't think he's hiding beneath the sink."

The PCs stood down, returning to the stairs. Savage crossed the room, her gloved hands twitching. She stopped by the sofa and Kett followed her line of sight to see that there were books lying there amongst the cushions.

"Fairy tales," she said. "A whole lot of them."

She was right. There were seven books, all hardbacks. Three were enormous compendiums of original fairy tales, the kind you don't tell children. Two of the covers had illustrations of a woman sleeping in a room made from thorns, her hands crossed over her chest, her face serene. The third showed Rapunzel in her tower, reaching down for her prince—a man who staggered beneath her, blinded by thorns.

The other books were for kids, their covers gentler. One was uncomfortably familiar because they had it at home.

Kett had read from it less than a day ago, the tale of Rumpelstiltskin. He felt a surge of panic at the coincidence until he realised that this copy was new, unlike theirs which had been the victim of a tug of war between Moira and Evie.

Savage was holding out a fresh pair of gloves for him, and he took them.

"What makes you think I didn't bring some this time?" he said as he fought to get them on.

"Did you, sir?"

"No."

He pushed the books away from each other to get a better look at them, then pried one open. Another illustration of a prince greeted him, this one standing proudly next to a stack of mattresses.

"They have to mean something, these stories. You don't go to all this trouble to tell a story if it's not important."

"I think so too," Savage said, picking up one of the bigger books and flicking through the pages. "You have to ask yourself what the original stories were for, right? Why did people tell them?"

"Cautionary tales," Kett suggested. "You told your kids about witches in the woods, about ogres, so they'd learn to watch out for danger. For monsters."

For pig-headed men.

"Yeah, they're instructional," Savage said. "But it's more than that. They're supposed to make children feel like they can do anything, survive anything. I read somewhere that kids who read fairy tales are more resilient, because they've seen these other children winning against impossible odds."

She shrugged.

"And there's the whole virginity angle, of course."

"The *what*?" Kett said.

"Sleeping Beauty pricking her finger on a needle. It's, you know, symbolic."

"Of *virginity*?"

"Yeah," said Savage. "The dangers of it. I don't know. I might have got that wrong, sorry."

"Don't ever apologise," said Kett. "It's good. If you've heard it, our killer might have too. It might be relevant." He looked at the smug prince and his pile of mattresses. "They're always about a prince who saves a princess, right?"

"Most of the time, yeah."

"It's why I hate reading them to the girls. There aren't many princes out there, not really. There are plenty of trolls, but hardly any princes. I hate the thought of them waiting for a man to come along and save them."

"Other than you, of course," Savage said, and he smiled.

"Yeah, but that's different. I want them to know that they can do anything, if they have to. That they can save themselves."

"Some men don't want women to feel like that," Savage said. "Some men make women feel bad just so they can pretend they're saving them. It's the worst kind of abuse because it's disguised as chivalry. You don't even see it."

"Men like Kevin Dufrane," Kett said.

"Exactly," said Savage. "He's still in hospital, right?"

"Discharged but being watched. He's not been out of his mother's house."

He left the books, scanning the rest of the room. There was a large, black suitcase on a table by the window and he walked over to it. The clasps were old and stubborn, but eventually he got them open and lifted the lid.

"Kate, look at this."

It was a typewriter, one that was battered and stiff with age. Several of the letters had jammed against the roller, the keys depressed. There was a sheet of paper in it with a single word.

boo.

More paper had been screwed into balls beneath the table and Kett groaned his way onto his knees to recover them. He peeled the first one open to see a few lines of type-written text.

Once upon a time there was a very special princess who lived in a castle with her mummy and daddy, the queen and the king. On her first birthday, a kind fairy granted the royal parents a wish. Any wish that they could think of. The king wanted to wish for great beauty and wealth for his daughter, but the queen asked instead for eternal life. "I cannot grant this," the fairy said, "but I can give your daughter five lives. Four times she may die and be reborn. But after the fifth death, she will die forever." And the fairyy

After the typo, it stopped. Kett pulled open another one, feeling Savage standing over him. It was exactly the same, only this one stopped after the second line, where *wish* had been misspelled.

"He missed the *h*," said Savage. "He's a perfectionist."

"Can you get Hay on the phone?" Kett said. "Tell her to skip the church, come straight here."

"Will do," she said.

Kett stood up, the pain rising from his lower back into his chest. He checked the rest of the screwed-up notes but they were all versions of the same thing. There were more in a wastepaper basket that was hidden by the hem of the long curtain, but nothing useful. He made his way to the kitchen, the old boards creaking beneath him. A single white cup sat in the sink, full of dirt, the only piece of crockery in the entire room. Every drawer and cupboard was empty. No cutlery, no food, no cleaning products. Plenty of dust, though. It sat everywhere.

"She's nearly here," Savage said. "Anything?"

"Not yet," he said.

"Porter says there are more books downstairs."

Kett made his way out of the room, squeezing past the loft ladder and the Uniforms on the stairs. Porter stood in the smallest bedroom on the first floor and Kett peered past his broad shoulders to see that it was an office. The desk had been cleared but more books sat on an antique mahogany case by the window.

"Books," grunted Porter.

"I can see that, Pete, thank you."

The books were all academic, mostly literature based. Kett couldn't see any here that referenced fairy tales but there were plenty of folk stories and Greek and Roman myths. He opened the only drawer in the desk to see a handful of papers, yellow with age. There was a name on two of them, bills of sale for items of furniture—a bed and a wardrobe. They were dated 2003.

"Harold Fisher," he said. "Ring any bells?"

"Nope," said Porter. "But this has to be our guy, right? The books upstairs, the typewriter, and the fact that this is where Jenny and her friends were attacked and drugged."

"Harold Fisher?" came Savage's voice from the landing. Kett nodded to her.

"You know it?"

"No, but I'll make some calls."

"Start with Clare," Kett said.

There was nothing else in the room so he squeezed past Porter, waiting for another couple of PCs to traipse up the stairs before heading to the ground floor. Duke had got both doors open, the floor covered in splinters. The first room was a utility room packed with boxes, but Duke pointed him towards the second. Kett knew from the smell what he was going to find even before he looked.

Blood.

A lot of it.

It fanned out across the floor and the right-hand wall, great smudges of it over the linoleum, crisscrossed by footsteps. It spoke of a brutal injury, one there was no coming back from.

Like a cut throat.

"Jenny," he said, more to himself than anyone else. He tried not to picture her final moments, but how could he not see them, played out across his imagination?

He turned to the other room and its collection of boxes.

"Had a quick peek, nothing much in there," said Duke, still holding the ram.

Kett opened the flap of the first box, releasing a cloud of dust. More yellow paperwork sat there, invoices and bank statements—thousands of them. The same name appeared there, over and over. Harold Fisher. Kett pulled out one, a payslip from the University of East Anglia. It was dated 1998 and made out to Professor Fisher.

"Savage?"

"Right here, sir," she said. "I Googled him. Harold Fisher's a professor up at the university. *Was*, anyway."

"I was about to tell you the same thing," said Kett.

"Do you need me to tell you what his speciality is?"

"Fairy tales," Kett said.

"Specifically, the original stories. He's an expert on them. Want to know something else interesting?"

Kett motioned for her to hurry up.

"He was in the papers after his wife divorced him back in 2007. She claimed he threatened to kill her."

"Shit," said Kett. "Where is he?"

"Clare's looking into it, sir. But this is him, isn't it? This is the man. It has to be."

Kett nodded.

"Can you start combing through all this? Find out as much as you can about him. If he's got the other two women somewhere then there might be something here that tells us where they are. And—"

"Sir?" came a shout as Porter thundered down the stairs. "Look at this."

He thrust a hardback book at Kett so urgently it almost cracked him on the nose.

"*The Legacy of Perrault*," Kett said, reading the title and seeing the etching of Cinderella on the cover. "By Professor Harold Fisher."

"Look at the back."

He turned the book around to find a photograph of a man in his sixties who was taking himself far too seriously. He was sitting in a grand library dressed in a beige suit with patches on the elbows and a brown bow tie. His arm rested on his knee and his chin rested on his knuckles. One eyebrow sat high on his head, the rest of his expression full of smugness. He was a portly man, his hair pure white, a thick moustache resting on his top lip.

"Doesn't exactly look like a serial killer," said Savage.

"And there's more," Porter said. "That book was published sixteen years ago. He was old then, he's got to be decrepit now."

"Tossing hell," Kett said.

"That's my word, Kett," came a reply from the door as Clare strode in. "Find your own. I've spoken to the university, Fisher's eighty-two and he's been in a home for the last seven years. Dementia."

"Fuck!" said Porter.

"The house is rented out by his son, who lives in Canada," Clare went on. "Last tenant left eighteen months ago and he's had nobody since. Damp problem, apparently."

"He's not our man," Kett said, resisting the urge to hurl the book at the wall.

"He's not our man," Clare echoed.

"But somebody was using his house," said Kett. "Somebody arranged to meet Jenny and the other women here on Friday night, and then drugged them when they arrived. And..."

He cocked his head, something trying to worm its way into his skull.

"And what?" said Clare.

"The fairy tale stuff, all this Sweet Briar Rose bullshit. It's not personal, is it? It's not some obsession that our killer has, some message he's trying to spread, some clue that we can use to find him. He was just squatting here, reading Harold Fisher's books. That's where he got the idea from, of telling a story. If Fisher had been a mathematics professor we'd probably be trying to crack a number code. If he was an expert on turnips we'd be digging in fields. It's coincidence, there's nothing in it."

Silence fell on the entrance hall. Kett looked at the book in his hand again, feeling like he was sinking into a pit. This time he couldn't stop himself. He hurled it into the utility room, watching it spin off the wall and land on one of the boxes with a fanfare of dust.

"We've got nothing," he said.

He thought of Poppy, of Beatrice, knowing that they weren't going to find them in time.

Knowing that it was too late.

"We've got nothing."

CHAPTER TWENTY-NINE

The End.

Fuck you.

Kett paced back and forth across the courtyard, those words ringing in his head. His thoughts were a storm, circling darkly and full of flashes that he couldn't make any sense of in the gyring chaos. Behind him, Cara Hay and her team proceeded to tear Harold Fisher's house apart.

They wouldn't find anything, Kett was sure of it.

Over the low wall, people milled around in the car park. A few of them noticed the police who swarmed nearby but most were oblivious, laughing to each other as they threw their shopping in the boot, as they tended to their children and their dogs. Tinny music blared from an old Fiat that was idling by the exit, a couple of teenage lads in tracksuits standing beside it and looking at something on their phones.

Kett kept walking, gravel crunching beneath his boots. It had started to rain again, cold fingers of wind probing the gaps in his shirt, his collar. He almost wished he still had Clare's coat.

Almost.

He thrust his hands into his trouser pockets instead, trying to ignore the cold, trying to ignore everything other than the case.

The End.

Fuck you.

He'd been certain that the fairy tales meant something, that they were integral to the killer's motives. He'd been *so* sure. But it was a coincidence, nothing more. The killer had been living in Fisher's empty house, he'd been reading his books, and he'd decided to dress up his victims as fairy tale princesses.

No story there. Just random, psychotic madness.

Just chance.

He reached the other side of the courtyard. There were no doors in the buildings here, and very few windows—all belonging to the shops along Magdalene Street. Uniforms were already talking to anyone who might have seen somebody going in and out of Number Eight. All they needed was a lucky break.

He turned and looked back at Fisher's house. From here, the front door was hidden inside the mouth of the car port. After the killer had drugged the women and killed Jenny, he easily could have dragged the others into a van. Nobody would have seen a thing, especially at that time of night when it was already dark.

Kett retraced his steps, feeling the first seeds of panic start to bloom inside his chest, like brambles around his heart. This was his fault. He'd come back to the job too soon. He wasn't ready, he was rusty.

Maybe he shouldn't have come back at all.

He saw Poppy's face, and Beatrice's—all smiles in the

photographs they'd found, full of joy, full of hope. He wondered if they were still alive. And he thought of Poppy's son, Raff, the way his face would fall when he heard that his mummy wasn't coming home, when he learned that he'd lost her forever.

It was like he'd been gut-punched and he had to stop walking, folding his arms around his stomach. He took a deep breath and puffed air out through his lips, seeing the clouds of breath form in front of him like smoke signals.

He thought of his own girls, sitting at home waiting for him. He thought of Evie, the way she'd sometimes stand by the window in the living room, her big eyes watching, her face a knot of worry that would light up when she saw his car.

He thought about Alice, the way she'd pull every emotion inside herself to try to control her chaos of thoughts and feelings, until she was so full she might explode. He thought of the way she ran to him when he walked through the door, her hugs like rugby tackles, the way she seemed to learn to breathe all over again when she held him, the way the anger left her safely—like air being let out of a bicycle tyre.

And he thought about Moira, about those quiet moments when she stopped yelling, the way she'd meet his eye and just look at him and just let him look at her. The awe of it, the pure, voiceless wonder of it.

And he craved them. He needed them.

He found his phone and called Billie, surprised when she picked up almost immediately.

"Thank God," she said. "You're okay? I wanted to call but I didn't, because I knew how bad it was. But the girls saw it, Robbie, they saw you on the TV, they saw that girl in the church. It's all over the news and they saw you but they saw her, too, on the rope. Is she okay?"

She tripped over her own words and fell quiet. He could hear the tears that threatened to fall and knew she was trying not to cry.

"I'm okay," he said. "Fortune is okay. She's actually remarkably okay, all things considered. She would have walked out of the church if they'd let her."

He heard Billie moving through the house, heard a door close behind her, and when she spoke again the hollow sound of her voice let him know she was in the bathroom.

"Who would do that, Robbie? It's... it's..."

There were no words, and he didn't try to fill the silence.

"Can you come home?"

"No," he said, knowing it wasn't a genuine question. "Not yet."

"It sounds bad, Robbie. *You* sound bad."

He looked at Fisher's house again, at the hive of activity that was taking place inside, and felt like he was drowning.

"It is bad," he said. "I think I made a mistake."

"By going back? No, Robbie. You didn't. You didn't. You knew it was going to be like this, because it's never any other way. Not with cases like this, not with people like this. It's a nightmare, a horror show, but they need you. However bad it is, it will be a lot worse if you're not there."

He heard Evie's voice, moaning about something as usual, then the sound of her knocking on the bathroom door.

"I'll be there in a minute, sweetie," Billie said. Evie replied and Billie laughed. "No, I'm not having a big poo."

"She's obsessed," said Kett. He missed them so much he could feel the sting of it in his eyes, the lump growing in his throat. "Can I say hi?"

"I've only just calmed them down after the TV thing," she said.

"It's fine. I'd better—"

"No, sorry. Hang on."

He heard her unlock the door, Evie's whines growing in volume.

"You want a quick word with your dad?"

"Yay!" Evie said, and the world seemed a little bit brighter. There was the sound of the phone being passed between hands, then dropped, then scooped up. "Dad, we saw you on TV! You looked very grumpy."

"Dad!" came a shrill cry that could only belong to Alice. "Is that Dad? Can I talk to him?"

"No!"

"Dad, we saw you on the telly! Let me say it."

"Dad!" came Moira's voice. "Mine, give it!"

It was chaos, the way it always was, but it made him smile. He closed his eyes and listened to them fight, Billie's voice muted in the background. Then Evie won out.

"Are you coming home? Can we have Smarties?"

"Soon," he said. "I'll bring you some, I promise."

"Can we finish the story? Bumbellpumpkin?"

"Rumpelstiltskin," Kett said. "I don't know. I don't think I'm in the mood for fairy tales, sweetie."

"He's not a fairy. He's a baddie. Can we? I want to know if the princess finds his name."

"She does," Kett said. "It's a rubbish end to the story, from what I remember. Some guy stumbles across the monster by accident."

"Dad! I don't want you to tell me! I want you to read it."

He paused, feeling something stretch its wings inside his head.

By accident.

"Story!" Moira shouted. "Pimplestomkin!"

"It's Rumpypumpyman, you idiot," Alice said.

"Rumpelstiltskin," Kett said again. He couldn't recall exactly how the story ended. Something about the young woman's guard travelling across the countryside, seeing a strange, monstrous man dancing by a fire, shouting his own name—conveniently answering the only riddle that would save her.

Just an accident. Just passing by.

Just *chance*.

"Look, sweetie, I've got to go. I'll bring Smarties. Be good."

He hung up, not wanting to lose sight of whatever was trying to take flight from the vortex of his thoughts. He looked at Fisher's house again, feeling the idea slip right out of his skull.

"Rumpelstiltskin," he said to himself. "What are you missing, Robbie?"

Just passing by, just seeing something you shouldn't, something big.

Something monstrous.

"Sir?"

Porter was walking out of Fisher's house, Savage behind him. Both of them looked miserable.

"Anything?" Kett asked.

"Bugger all," Porter said. "Place has been wiped clean. The only thing he left were those half-finished stories, the typewriter—which we think belonged to Fisher anyway—and a cup in the sink. Hay is taking samples of the blood, and we've got his footprints, but there are no fingerprints, no fluids, and the dirt in the cup turned out to be coffee grounds."

"Coffee?" Kett said.

And the thought stretched its wings and hauled itself into the light.

"Oh shit," he said, his hands in his hair. "Shit, shit, shit."

"What?" said Savage.

"Rumpelstiltskin."

Just passing by, just seeing something you shouldn't.

Seeing a monster.

"You're losing me, sir," said Savage.

"I was trying to work out the connection, what all this had to do with Martha Hansen-Andrews. I couldn't figure out if it was revenge, if somebody was punishing Jenny and the other women for what happened that night. But it didn't fit, it wasn't her father, it didn't seem to be her mother. It had to be somebody else. *Something* else."

Savage bounced on the balls of her feet, impatient. But she knew better than to rush him.

"That night in September, Martha found out that Jenny was going to hurt her and she split off from her friends before they could reach the alleyway where she was going to be attacked. She ended up on St Benedict's Street and she took the stairs by the church, heading out of the city. She would have walked right past Bert's coffee shop. What if..."

And he suddenly doubted himself. It seemed too much of a coincidence.

"Trust it, sir," Savage said. "What are you thinking?"

"What if it was like Rumpelstiltskin," he said. "Martha walked past the coffee shop at midnight, at the exact right moment to see something she shouldn't have. Something important."

"That's some assumption," said Porter, frowning. Kett shook his head.

"Think about what those Beggar Boys told us. They said Jenny had run to Martha's side after she was hit by the car, and she'd said one word. *Monster*. What if she wasn't talking about Jenny at all. What if she was talking about what she'd seen? *Who* she'd seen?"

"Who?" Savage said.

"Bert, the guy from the coffee shop."

"Why would she call him a monster?" said Porter. "He's not, is he?"

"No, but what if he was doing something *monstrous*?"

There was something else, something he wasn't getting. He thought back to Martha's house, the look the young woman had given him when he'd visited her, a look of terror.

A look of *recognition*.

He reached up to his collar, remembering that he wasn't wearing Clare's coat anymore. But he *had* been wearing it when he'd gone to visit her, that stupid coat with the fur collar. With the light behind him she wouldn't have been able to see his face. Just that awful, furry coat.

Bert had worn a coat just like it.

Martha had thought Kett was *him*.

"I know it sounds crazy," he said. "I can't really explain it. But I think it's Bert. He was right there next to the church. He had time to push Fortune out of the window and get back to his shop before I got there."

"So were a lot of people," said Porter.

Kett's mind was moving like a machine, everything slotting into place.

"Bert told me himself he made coffee for the old folk in the care homes. What if that's where he met Fisher? It would have been easy enough to find out about this house, find out it was empty."

Savage frowned.

"Those are some big leaps, sir," she said.

"Not big enough. He... *Shit*, he asked me for help. His crossword. When I met him yesterday he asked me for help with a clue."

"Clue?" Porter said.

"Uh..." Kett fought to remember. "Something about a poem. *Starting a poem, willy-nilly*. No, wait, *Continue a poem willy-nilly*. That was it."

Porter thought for a moment, his brow furrowed.

"Willy-nilly is code for an anagram," he said. "I'd need to see it written down."

"Once upon a time?" said Savage. Porter counted the letters on his fingers, his tongue between his lips.

"Oh, shit, yeah," he said. "That works. Once upon a time."

"Seriously?" Kett said. "That piece of shit, he was confessing to it right there and then and I was too stupid to see it."

He broke into a run, heading for the street. Porter and Savage moved with him, their footsteps echoing across the courtyard. Savage was on her phone.

"Boss?" she said. "Kett's following a lead. He thinks he's found our man."

"Hey!" Kett yelled to a PC who was doing her best to keep people back from the line of police tape that had been stretched across the street. "Keys?"

She whistled to another copper and he pulled them from his pocket, tossing them to Kett.

"That one," he said, pointing to an IRV, its blue lights flashing.

Kett passed the keys to Savage and she dropped into the driver's seat.

"Little unfair," Porter muttered, slinking into the back.

"Not really," said Kett, slamming his door. "Need to get there before next week. Go, Kate!"

She revved the engine, the PC lifting the tape to let them out. It took a few seconds for the crowds to part, then she floored it, the big car growling as she drove them into Tombland, past the Samson and Hercules where they'd found Fran Herbert, accelerating up the hill. She took a right into a one-way road. Luckily the traffic was quiet, the few cars happy enough to mount the kerb to let her pass.

"I don't get it," said Porter as they re-joined the main road. "Even if this is our man, why would he go after five women? Why kill them?"

Savage eased them through a red light then accelerated again, hitting forty. From here, Kett could see the fork where St Benedict's Street met Westwick Street, the hill on the right leading steeply down to the bottom of the steps where Martha had been injured.

"Stop the car," he said, bracing a hand on the dash as Savage hit the brakes. "Porter, take the high road. Savage and I will take the low one, meet you in the middle of St Lawrence's Steps, at the coffee shop."

"Yes, sir," Porter said, scrambling out.

"And be careful!" Kett yelled as Savage peeled away from the kerb. She thumped over a speed bump, Kett's head hitting the ceiling, then she stopped because they were on another one-way road and two lines of traffic blocked the way.

Kett got out, jogging down the hill. Savage outpaced him easily, reaching the bottom of the stone staircase and staying close to the wall as she waited for him to catch up.

"How do you want to do this?" she said.

"Fast and hard," Kett replied. "So you should go first."

He wasn't even sure he'd make it up the steps.

Savage grit her teeth as she climbed. Porter appeared at the top, nodding at them as he descended. There must have been some Uniforms left at the church because two of them had his back, their batons drawn.

Savage reached the little path between the two flights of stairs, taking a deep breath. The coffee shop door was open but the lights were off. It was too dark to see anything through the window.

"Police!" she yelled, running inside. Kett heard a scream from behind the dark glass, then Savage shouted again. "Stay where you are. Stay down!"

Porter was in next and Kett followed close behind, breaking right when the big man went left. There was barely enough space for them in the tiny café, and it was small enough for Kett to see that it was almost empty. There was just one young woman on the floor—one of the students who had been here earlier—her chair overturned and her jumper drenched with coffee.

"There's a door behind the bar," Kett said, and Savage opened it.

"Clear, sir," she said. "But you should see this."

Kett tried to swallow his heart back into his chest as he squeezed past Porter and through the door. The room beyond was a storage space, shelves laden with bags of coffee, boxes full of mugs.

And a chain hanging from the ceiling.

"What the..."

There was a drain in the middle of the floor, right beneath the chain. The smell of bleach made Kett's eyes water and he turned to the café again.

Porter offered his hand to the young woman and she

took it hesitantly, immediately pushing herself back into the window to get away from him. She looked terrified.

"Where's Bert?" Kett asked her.

"He's gone out," she said. "He left after what happened in the church, said he needed some alone time. Told me to lock up when I went, although I don't think he left me any keys."

Kett rubbed his eyes, seeing starbursts against the dark.

"Was he here with you all day?" he asked. "When the woman was attacked?"

"The woman in the church?" she said. "I thought she did it to herself? That's what Bert said. No, he was out then too, making his deliveries. He got back just before you turned up, made you that cup of tea."

"And do you know where he is now? Do you know where he's delivering?"

She shook her head.

"This is really, really important," Kett said. "It might make the difference between somebody dying or somebody surviving. *Think*."

"I don't know," she said. "I just come here to do coursework, that's all."

"And do you know anything about that?" Kett said, pointing through the door to the storeroom. She followed his finger, shaking her head.

"I've never seen the door open. I swear, I don't know anything."

"How well do you know him?"

"Bert? Hardly at all, I've only been coming here since I started at college. He's a nice guy, isn't he? He gives me free drinks sometimes. Oh, and he left you something, Bert did."

"He left *me* something?" Kett said.

"Yeah." She pointed past him to the door behind the

bar. "He said it's in there. DCI Kett, right? He said it was for the policeman with the kind face who he made tea for. That's you, isn't it? He said you probably wouldn't come for it, but that if you did it was ready."

Savage disappeared through the door again, snapping on another pair of gloves.

"It's a red box, I think," the woman said. "He didn't say what it was."

"Got it."

Savage reappeared, dropping the box on the counter. It was the size of a deck of playing cards, and as light as a feather.

Kett already knew what he'd find when he opened it.

"He told me I should make you a cup of tea, too, if you want one?" the girl said. "I don't really know how it all works, I just come here to use the Wi-Fi, sorry. But I can try. How hard can it be? I do it at home but we've got a different kettle and—"

"Can you do me a favour and wait outside?" he said to her.

She was more than happy to do that, snatching her laptop and practically running out of the door. She had her phone to her ear almost immediately, sobbing into it. Kett looked at Porter.

"Keep an eye on her."

Porter followed her out. Kett wiggled the lid of the box until it came free. Inside was a cushion of crimson tissue paper.

And sitting on the paper was a severed finger.

Kett met Savage's eye, saw his own expression of hopelessness mirrored there. And for a second he was drowning in it again, in the dark, in the cold.

Only for a second, though.

Then the anger burned through, impossibly bright.

"What are you thinking, sir?" Savage asked.

"Bert's playing a game," he said, closing the box. "He's laughing at us. But I'm not laughing, and I'm not playing."

He walked to the door, pulling out his phone.

"This fucker is going down."

CHAPTER THIRTY

"So, what do we know about this fur-coat-wearing, crossword-playing, coffee-drinking tosspot?"

Superintendent Clare held court inside the cavernous nave of St Lawrence's Church, the sound of his brogues echoing as he paced back and forth. The rain had started again, harder now, and this was the nearest place that the team could take shelter. There wasn't time to head back to HQ, not if they wanted to find Poppy and Beatrice alive.

Not that there's much hope of that, Kett thought.

He sat shivering with Porter and Savage on the front row of pews, Spalding leaning against the wall and Dunst sitting right at the back sucking on a cigarette that Clare hadn't let him light up.

"We know that Bert isn't his real name," said Spalding, squinting at her phone. "The café *is* owned and run by a man called Bert—Robert Haig—but he's abroad. We're trying to trace him."

"Everyone thinks he's Bert, though," said Dunst from the back, the church dwarfing his voice. "The people who work in the shops, the girls who were drinking there every day, they assumed he was Bert, the owner. He just showed up one day and started making coffee. The door didn't open and close properly because he'd broken in, but nobody seemed to notice."

"When?" said Clare.

"Early summer," Dunst said. "The place was closed for a few weeks when the real Bert left, then it opened again and our killer was working there."

"Find a connection between the two men," Clare said. "There has to be one. What else?"

He doesn't match anyone on the database," said Spalding. "We're still checking, but his face and his prints haven't set off any red flags."

"I don't believe that," Kett said, earning a scowl from the angry DS. "If he's the man who's behind this, he's a professional. He's done this before. There's no way he hasn't messed up somewhere, left a trace of himself."

"But he's clever," said Savage. "Clever and cold and calculating."

"You haven't even given me a good reason why he'd do it," Clare said, glowering at Kett. "Why on earth would he take five women hostage and kill them one by one? It's too risky. Even the men who took the newspaper girls only managed three. You abduct them one at a time, you take them when the time is right."

"Unless there's a deadline," Kett said. "Unless he knew he had to take them all or lose everything."

He stood up, the brutal cold of the church making his bones ache. When he put his hands to his face he could still smell smoke from Fortune's burning hair and it was all he could do to stop the acid from clawing up his throat.

"Think about it," he said. "That night in September. Martha's just left her friends after finding out they're planning to hurt her. She's walking home, devastated, scared. It's almost midnight. She reaches the stairs and passes the coffee shop. There's a light, there's somebody there, and she looks through the window at the exact right moment."

"The exact *wrong* moment," said Savage.

"She sees our killer?" Clare said. "That's some leap, Kett."

"And he's doing something bad. He's doing something monstrous. I don't know what, but you saw the chain in that little room behind the bar. The drain on the floor. Those aren't good things. Martha interrupted him, she was a witness. Either she panicked and started running, or he flat out hurled her down the stairs. She falls into the road and the car hits her, an innocent woman does our killer's job for him. He goes back inside and turns off the lights before Jenny runs past. Martha's bleeding out on the street but she manages to tell Jenny what she saw."

"A monster," said Clare. "But it still—"

"Hang on," Kett interrupted. "There's more. Martha's mum told me that Jenny went to speak with Martha after the accident. To say sorry, maybe. I don't know. What if Martha said something to her?"

"I thought she couldn't speak?" said Spalding.

"She's still in there somewhere," Savage said. "Part of her, anyway."

"There's enough of her left to think that I was Bert," said Kett. "She saw the coat, that furry collar, and thought I was him. If there's enough of her mind left to make that connection then maybe there was enough for her to communicate something to Jenny."

Spalding conceded the point with a nod. Kett continued.

"So Martha somehow tells Jenny about the coffee shop,

about the killer. Or she says just enough for Jenny to figure it out. Jenny doesn't go to the police. I don't know why, but—"

"Because of her boyfriend," Savage said, leaning forward. "Because of the gang. She doesn't trust us, and she certainly would have got in trouble for talking to us."

"Right," said Kett. "But it's more than that with her, I think. Fortune said that Jenny claimed she was going to make them all rich. She wasn't talking about the money she was getting from men like Kevin Dufrane. This was something else."

"She was going to blackmail Bert," said Savage.

Clare's mouth fell open.

"Tossing hell, it fits," he said.

"It does," said Kett. "And wait, didn't those Beggar Boys tell us one of them had gone missing in the summer?"

"Seb Wilkes," Savage said. "You think our killer was behind that, too?"

"I don't know," Kett said. "But it makes sense. The Beggar Boys were active round there, asking for money. Maybe Bert got tired of them and decided to take one out. Jenny works out that Bert killed Seb, or somebody else. She knows that *Bert* knows Martha saw him. So she does what any self-respecting arsehole does in this situation, she blackmails him. She tells him she'll stay quiet if he pays up. So Bert asks her to come to the house off Magdalene Street to collect the money, and she does. But she's not alone, she brings her friends with her so that he won't try anything."

"And he assumes that they know too," Savage said. "You're right, sir, there was a deadline. If he didn't kill them all, any one of them could talk."

"So why *didn't* he kill them all?" Clare said, running a hand down his face hard enough to pull the skin away from his bloodshot eyes. He looked like a man who had forgotten how to sleep. "If he was worried, why not just kill them in the house? They were drugged, right? Out cold. It would have been easy. All this tossing fairy tale nonsense, all the brambles, the coffin, hanging a woman by her bloody hair. None of it makes sense because he must have known there was a chance they'd be saved. A chance they'd talk."

"Unless he realised they *didn't* know," Kett said. "Unless he made Jenny talk before he cut her throat. She tells him the others have no idea why she was there, they have no idea he's a killer. And he believes her."

"I don't think Jenny had time to wake up before he killed her," said Savage.

"Right," Kett said. "So he gets it out of the others somehow, after he's taken them to wherever he was keeping them. He finds out they don't know anything. But what the hell, he's got four more victims to play with. He's not going to pass on that."

"But *why*?" Clare said.

"Because at the end of the day, he's a killer," Kett said. "He *is* a monster."

"That's extreme," Porter said.

"It is," Kett replied. "It's why I'm certain he's done it before. We're looking into similar crimes, right? Not fairy tales, because that was a red herring. But murders that seem to have been staged in some way. Something theatrical."

"DCI Pearson and her unit is on it back at HQ," Clare said. "Have we seriously not got anything else on this guy? Somebody must know something about him."

"Other than the fact he works in the coffee shop, no," said Dunst. "He's a mystery man."

"Wait," Kett said. "He mentioned deliveries, taking teas and coffees to care homes. I think he was telling the truth because that's where he met Fisher, the professor who owns the house. He must have got talking to him, worked out his house was empty. Do we know which care home Fisher was living in?"

"A place out in Taverham. Hang on," said Savage, opening her notebook and flicking back through the pages. "Four Acres."

"We've spoken to them?"

"I'm on it," Savage said, pushing herself out of the pew, her phone to her ear.

"Porter, the coffee shop must have had deliveries, bills, utilities. Somebody must know something."

The big DI fished out his phone, nodding.

"We'll find him, sir," Kett said to Clare, as much to convince himself as the Superintendent.

He closed his eyes for a moment, rubbing his temples to try to stem the pain that was crawling into his head. For a minute or so, nobody spoke, the team taking a collective breath to settle themselves.

"The care home is checking now, sir," said Savage, the phone still held to her ear. "They recognised Bert's description, say he comes by a couple of times a week with teas and coffees. He drives, but they say there's no registration number on the visitor's log."

Come on, Kett thought. *Give us a break.*

"Hello?" Savage said into the phone. "That's fine... Yeah? You're sure? Hang on." She looked up. "Pen."

Clare already had one in his hand.

"AW11 KGS, thank you." She hung up. "That was from the security feed. Green Ford Transit."

"I'll run it," said Spalding.

"Good work," said Clare. "I've got the tactical team on standby. We're ready to go as soon as we find him."

"I've found him," Spalding said. "Car's registered to a Stanley Frost, lives just outside the city. New Road, out in Bowthorpe."

The team moved as one, breaking for the doors.

"Do not engage," Clare said as they ran into the rain. "Gorski has the lead on this. Is that clear? You *do not* Kett this one up."

"Can we not find another word for that?" Kett said.

There was the sound of a horn blaring and he looked across the street to see PC Duke leaning out of the window of an IRV.

"Wanna ride?" he yelled.

"Only if you let her drive," Kett replied, nodding to Savage.

"That's not fair," said Duke. "I'm—"

"Even slower than Porter," Savage said. "Budge up."

Duke slid over the gear stick into the passenger seat, only for Kett to open the door.

"In the back."

"But—"

"Now, Duke!"

Duke practically fell out of the car, running to the back door only to be beaten by Porter. He ran to the other side and climbed in so fast his helmet fell onto the road. He'd only just managed to grab it when Savage took off, the door swinging shut by itself as she accelerated.

"Oh shoot," Duke said, fighting to get his seatbelt in.

Savage bullied her way through traffic, the windscreen wipers going full pelt as the rain grew heavier. It was only just noon but the heavy clouds had turned the day into evening, headlights kaleidoscoping on the wet windshield. Behind them the road blazed blue, a convoy of police.

Only when they hit the dual carriageway did Savage

slow down to let the tactical unit roar past, the van kicking up spray. She slotted in behind it, navigating off the main road and into the flat, open countryside.

From there it was a straight shot, another eight minutes and change before the van's lights blazed red and Savage pumped the brakes. The IRV slipped and shuddered into the driveway of an old, white farmhouse, almost hitting the back of a bright green Ford Transit.

"It's him," she said.

Kett's door was open before they'd come to a halt. Gorski was already out, her face hidden behind her visor. The sight of the rifle in her hands made Kett's ribs cry out in memory of the pain of being shot.

"Stay back," she said.

He nodded, trying to rub the agony from his chest with the heel of his hand. Even if he had been allowed to run in, he doubted he'd have been able to. He felt like his batteries had been drained.

"They'll get him, sir," Savage said as she walked to his side.

The house was wide and low, sitting beneath a picturesque, thatched roof. The gardens on all sides were as wild as jungles, a towering hedge masking whatever lay beyond. There was no sign of life through the dark windows, no noise at all other than the muted call of the birds and a distant tractor.

Gorski ushered her unit forward, the officers fanning out with silent precision. One approached the low front door with a ram, waiting for some unspoken command before beginning the breach. The door was strong, only opening after the third attempt—just seconds, but more seconds than they had to spare.

"Armed police!" Gorski yelled.

"Armed police!" shouted the other officers, a battle cry that echoed back from the house, that seemed to fill the entire street. In a few seconds the driveway had emptied, the building full of shouts and crashes.

Then, loud enough to scatter the birds from the trees, loud enough to stop Kett's heart, a gunshot.

CHAPTER THIRTY-ONE

A SECOND GUNSHOT, THIS ONE LOUDER.

"Fuck," said Porter, climbing out of the car.

"That's not a rifle," said Savage. "That's a shotgun."

A third shot. Somebody screamed and Kett was moving before he could stop himself—only for Savage to hook him back.

"Don't, sir," she said, her fingers like steel rods in his arm. "It's not worth it."

And he heard Billie say it too, heard her ask him to promise.

Think of our girls. Before you do anything, think about them.

He clamped his hands in his hair in frustration, that little shard of bullet seeming to worm its way deeper inside, still trying to kill him after all these months.

The house had fallen silent.

Come on, Kett thought. *Come on.*

He heard the roar of an engine, the honk of a horn, then Clare's Mercedes appeared—riding the verge almost diagonally as it fought to get past an IRV. The Super left it there, tumbling out of the door and running over.

"What did I miss?"

"Shots fired," Kett said. "We're waiting."

Waiting, waiting, the seconds impossibly slow as they grew into minutes. It was an eternity later that an armed officer appeared from the overgrown hedge to the left of the house, his rifle secure. He pulled up his visor.

"We got him."

Thank God.

"Is he dead?" Kett asked.

"He wishes he was."

The man stood to one side, pulling back a section of hedge as best he could to let Kett and the others through. There was an old wall hidden behind the thick foliage, and a large gate that opened onto a back garden that was drowning in brambles.

"Watch your feet," the officer said. "They're lethal."

"What happened?" Clare asked.

"We breached through the main house, sir. It was clear, but when we moved out here we found the suspect in the barn."

He nodded to the other side of the walled garden to a wide, low wooden outbuilding. Another structure stretched out from the back of it, this one made of stone. A stable, maybe.

"He had a loaded shotgun. Managed to get both rounds off but he didn't make contact. Gorski took him out with a shot to the leg. That's him you can hear now."

A high-pitched, agonised cry rose up from the direction of the barn, followed by a desperate shout. Even from here Kett recognised Bert's voice.

"Help me, please!"

"What about the women?" Kett asked, picking up his pace.

"You mean wo*man*?" said the officer. "We've got one. Locked up. But we're still searching. It's a big place."

Kett walked through another gate to see the entrance to the barn. Both of the wide doors were open and several members of the tactical team stood there, sheltering from the rain. Gorski was down on her knees with another officer, both of them tending to the man who lay there in a puddle of his own blood.

It was Bert.

Kett remembered to breathe, his lungs aching. *Everything* aching.

"This your man?" the tactical officer asked.

"Yeah," said Kett. "That's him."

Bert must have known he was being talked about because he lifted his head from a pillow of hay, glaring at Kett. There was blood on his face, running from his nose and staining his teeth. Without his hats, Kett saw that his hair was short and dark, no sign of grey anywhere.

His hands had been cuffed behind his back, although there was no way he was going anywhere. Gorski had cut off his left trouser leg right beneath his crotch and there was an ugly wound in his thigh, perfectly circular and bleeding hard. The officer who knelt by Gorski's side was trying to tie a tourniquet but the man's endless gyrations weren't making it easy.

"Tighter," said Gorski. "And you, stop moving."

She tried again and Bert thumped his head back, screaming wetly at the ceiling.

Kett circled past them into the shadows at the back of the barn where two more armed officers stood next to a studded wooden door. Kett could hear sobbing from the other side of it.

"Her name's Poppy Butterfield," said one of the men. "Says she's alone. Reeve's gone back for some kit to get the door open."

"Poppy?" Kett said, putting his fingers to the door.

A sob answered him, so powerful that it descended into a series of hacking coughs.

"My name's DCI Robert Kett. I'm police. You're safe."

Another sob, even louder than the last.

"Are you alone in there?"

He heard something hit the other side of the door, the sobs closer now.

"Please," Poppy said. "Please get me out. I need to get home, I need to see my son."

"He's safe," Kett said. "Rafferty is safe, he's well. He can't wait to see you, Poppy. But I need you to answer the question. Are you on your own in there?"

"Yes," Poppy said, sniffing. "I don't know where the others are."

"They're with us," Kett said. "But not Beatrice. Do you know where she is?"

"No," Poppy said. "She's not here. Is he dead? Did you kill him?"

"Bert? No, he's still alive. But he's never going to hurt you again, Poppy. I can promise you that."

"Watch out, sir," came a voice, and Kett moved to one side as a couple of uniformed police approached the door. One was holding a crowbar and the other held a motorised saw. "I'm going to need you to stand back, miss. Right back, against the far wall. It's gonna be loud."

"Hang on," Kett said. "Poppy, can you see anything that

looks like a trap. Chains, ropes, weights? Anything that might happen if the door is opened?"

"What are you talking about?" she shouted back. "No, nothing. Just get me out of here, *please*."

"Take it slow," Kett said to the men. "This guy likes to set traps."

"Yes, sir," the man with the saw said.

There was nothing Kett could do to help so he made his way back across the barn. Now that he was taking the time to look he saw that the building was an arsenal. Workbenches had been set up along the two longest walls and each one was littered with weapons and tools. Some looked like they'd been here when the barn had been built, caked with dirt and stiff with rust. Others were brand new—a block of kitchen knives that was still inside its plastic wrapper.

Pieces of machinery sat in piles on the benches and beneath them. They seemed random until Kett looked closer. One was a suit made from welded sheet metal, holes for the arms and legs and a bigger one for the head, all lined with barbed wire. Another was a homemade bear trap, its hinged jaws rigged with knives. Kett wouldn't have believed it if he hadn't seen it, and seeing it made him more nauseous than ever. He had to stop for a moment, swallowing bile.

Ahead, Gorski and the other officer had managed to secure the tourniquet. Clare, Savage and Porter stood in a circle around Bert, and behind them was a sea of uniformed police. Something in the way they were standing, almost perfectly still, framed in the barn door in the sickly light of the day, made them look like a Renaissance painting.

All except for Bert, who writhed and grunted in a nest of bloody straw. He was trying to sit up, and Kett put the notion out of his head by planting a boot on his shoulder and pinning him to the floor.

"Kett," said Clare, a low, growled warning.

"No, it's good," Gorski said, pushing a bandage against the wound. "If he wants to live, he needs to lie down and *stop fucking moving.*"

Across the barn the motorised saw came to life, screaming as it cut through the studded door. Sparks lit up the dark like hellfire.

"Where's Beatrice?" Kett said.

Bert laughed.

"You're too late," he said, his voice hoarse. "Just like with Jenny, just like Fran. You're too late. That babe is lost, forever gone. The end."

"Fran's alive," Kett said. "Your coffin didn't work."

"Bullshit," said Bert, flashing those crimson teeth. "I know she's dead."

"What's your name?"

"Bert," he answered, grinning.

"It's not Stanley Frost, then?"

The grin grew wider.

"Maybe it is. Maybe you'll never know. There's so much you'll never know, you stupid fucks."

"Like how Martha Hansen-Andrews saw you kill a man that night in September? Like how Jenny Eyler found out and tried to blackmail you?"

This, at least, wiped the smile from his face.

"So I'm going to ask you again, Bert. Where is Beatrice Goodwin?"

The man stopped struggling, resting his head on the ground and staring at the ceiling. He looked ashen, his teeth chattering. Beneath the bandage the wound in his leg was leaking rather than spraying, but he'd lost a lot of blood. He needed a hospital.

"I made it too easy," he said slowly. "But it's always so hard with you lot because you're usually so fucking stupid. I've left you clues before, you know. Not here but in other parts of the country, other dead girls. I've left clues and nobody's ever come close. You know how infuriating that is? To go to these lengths to kill somebody and for it to be dismissed as an accident, or chalked up as an unknown. So this time I thought I'd make it easier, give you some help. But I made it too fucking easy. How did you figure out it was me? It was the crossword clue, wasn't it?"

"Believe it or not, it was the coat," Kett said. "The Big Tossing Jacket."

"*What?*" Bert asked, frowning.

"And Rumpypumpyman," he added, earning confused looks from everyone else.

Across the room, the saw cut out. The other officer was jamming the crowbar into the broken lock, both of them straining.

"Who was it?" Kett asked. "That night. Who were you with when Martha saw you? What were you doing?"

Bert laughed, still lost in the darkness between the rafters.

"Some horrible little cunt," he said eventually. "I told you, didn't I? Those Beggar Boys who kept asking me for money. It wasn't even my café, I just broke in one night because it was shut, and when people turned up the next day I started making them drinks. It was good cover. I couldn't have given less of a shit what those pricks did to the place. But they kept pushing, and there's only so far you can push a man like me."

"Seb Wilkes," Kett said, and Bert's bloodshot eyes rolled in their sockets to find him.

"Was that his name? I have no idea. I had him strung up in the storeroom, had half his arm off. The fucker kicked the door open. I still don't know how he did it. I look through the window and who do I see looking back? That girl. Talk about wrong place, wrong time."

"You pushed her down the stairs?"

"I was going to bring her inside," Bert said, grinning. "Have some fun. But the silly bitch tripped over her own feet and tried to headbutt a car."

He laughed, a chuckle of genuine joy that turned Kett's stomach, that robbed the words from his head. Nobody knew what to say, the barn impossibly quiet once Bert's giggles had died away.

Once upon a time, Kett thought, this would have been the end of the man. He'd have been torn to pieces where he lay and the world would have been a better place because of it.

"Jenny Eyler was blackmailing you, wasn't she?" he asked.

"She was trying. She had no idea. No fucking idea what she was getting herself into. None of them did."

"The others knew?"

"Fran did. The others didn't have a clue. But I didn't want to waste them. Good meat is good meat."

Kett's stomach was tying itself in knots.

"What about Simon Womack?"

"The one with the gold car? Oh, that was his girlfriend's fault. Fran. She told him everything. Couldn't leave that little loose end now, could I?"

"So you burned him alive?"

"Wasn't alive for long," Bert said with another high-pitched laugh. "You want to know why, don't you? That's all you ever ask. All *they* ever ask, when they're sitting in their own shit, screaming at you to stop, when they're wriggling in lighter fluid begging for mercy. '*Why? Why are you doing this to me? Why why why?*'"

He shrugged.

"And I could tell you, Robert Kett, but you'd never believe it."

"Try me."

"You'll find out, soon enough," he said, baring those teeth again in a Halloween smile. "Soon enough you'll learn why I'm here in this shitty little city."

There was a crunch as the door at the back of the barn finally opened. Kett braced himself, waiting for the rattle of an anchor falling, for the sound of a triggered trap. But there was just a sob as Poppy stumbled out of her cell and fell into the arms of the tactical officer. He had to drop his crowbar in order to stop her from sliding to the floor, hooking his arms under hers and calling for help. Savage ran over to them.

"It's a stable block," said the other man, peering inside. "I'll check it out."

"You'll never find the other poor little babe," Bert said. "It'll be like she vanished off the face of the earth."

There was a shout from outside and a uniformed constable appeared in the doors.

"We've got a body," he said. "Man. ID in his wallet says he's Stanley Frost."

"Oh dear," said Bert. "Poor Stanley."

"Nobody else in the stable," said the tactical officer as he stumbled out of the door, speaking through the hand he held over his mouth and nose. "There is a *lot* of shit in there, though."

"Everybody's gotta go," said Bert with another giggle.

"Last chance," Kett said to him.

"Yeah, and then what?" Bert replied. "What can you possibly do to me? By the end of the day that little babe will be dead. I'll be tucked up in a nice warm bed somewhere, full belly, full heart, waiting to be let out. And it will happen, because it always does when you know the right people."

He grinned at Kett again, and the fuse of Kett's patience burned to its quick. He met Clare's eye, asking a question that he knew he couldn't put words to. Clare clenched his jaw, swallowed noisily, then offered the slightest of nods in response.

Kett planted his boot on Bert again—not on his shoulder this time, but on the wound in his thigh. The man responded with what would have been a scream if he hadn't choked on his own spit. He broke into a round of breathless coughs, arching his back in agony.

Kett pushed harder into the wet, into the heat.

"Where is she?" he said, his voice a growl.

"Sir," said Gorski, looking at Clare. He didn't answer, and she stood up. "Superintendent!"

"I can make this a lot worse," Kett said, grinding his foot. It felt wrong. It felt *awful*, vomit hammering at the back of his throat. He forced himself to see Beatrice's face, the young woman's smile, and drove the toe of his boot into the man's thigh.

This time, Bert found his voice, his scream filling the barn from the floor to the rafters.

"That's enough!" Gorski shouted. "Kett, back the fuck away."

"Stand down, Gorski," Clare said.

"Get off me!" Bert groaned. "Stop, I'll tell you. I'll fucking tell you."

Kett stepped back, the barn spinning wildly. When he glanced at Clare the Super wouldn't meet his eye, his skin waxy and lifeless. Only Gorski was looking at him, her face warped with disgust.

"What the fuck?" she said.

Savage was making her way across the barn, her arm around Poppy's shoulders, her hand shielding the young woman's eyes from the killer on the floor.

"We need to get her warm and dry," Savage said, and Kett nodded. He wiped his mouth with the back of his hand and turned his attention back to Bert.

"Tell me where she is."

The killer pushed himself up as best he could with his hands secured behind his back. He seemed like he was about to throw up, spit hanging from his bottom lip, snot dripping from his nose. He made a noise that might have been a growl, the whites of his eyes the brightest thing in the room. He looked like an animal, Kett thought. Like a rabid dog.

"She's alive," he said in a low groan. "But not for long. She's in a box, but—"

"You bastard!"

Kett looked up to see Savage falling back like she'd been pushed, hitting the wall. Poppy was screaming as she ran right for Bert.

"Knife!" Savage shouted.

Poppy was half a dozen yards away, nothing but air between her and the man on the floor.

She gripped a rusted blade in both hands.

Kett launched himself over Bert to intercept her but she dived beneath his arms and slammed the blade into Bert's throat with every ounce of her bodyweight, practically pinning him to the floor.

"No!" Kett said.

She pulled the knife out with a gout of blood, but before she could stab him again Kett hauled her back by the scruff of her neck, spinning her across the floor. Savage did the rest, pulling her close with one arm and pulling the knife away with the other. She threw it across the floor and wrapped Poppy tight as the young woman sobbed and spat and screamed.

"You bastard! How do you fucking like it?"

Kett dropped to his knees, pushing his hands to Bert's throat. The man was spasming, bucking wildly. There was too much blood for Kett to see the wound.

"We need an ambulance!" Kett shouted.

They didn't need an ambulance. They needed a morgue.

Or a miracle.

"Bert," Kett said. "Where is she? Where's Beatrice Goodwin? It's not too late."

Bert opened his mouth, spraying blood. Bubbles burst from his ruptured throat as he fought for his last breath.

And then, when he couldn't find it, he stuttered into stillness.

"Bert?" Kett said. He thumped a fist on the man's chest, again, and again, and again until he felt a hand on his shoulder. Porter was there, shaking his head.

"He's gone," the big DI said.

"Fuck!" roared Kett, staggering to his feet.

Everyone was looking at him now, and he knew why. He could feel the heat of Bert's blood on his face, on his hands, he could feel the tightness of his jaw as he bared his teeth.

He looked like a monster.

"He's gone," Porter said again.

"And he's not the only one," Kett croaked.

Poppy had buried her head in Savage's chest, grasping at her clothes with her mutilated hand, losing herself to her grief. Kett would have cried too, if he could remember how.

"Beatrice is gone," he said. "We've just lost any hope of finding her alive."

CHAPTER THIRTY-TWO

"Take it apart," said Kett. "All of it. Every inch of it. Don't dismiss anything, however small."

He watched the tide of Detectives and Uniforms scatter from the barn, following his order. Only Clare and Porter remained standing. Savage still sat on the rotting timbers of the floor, Poppy cradled in her arms. She was stroking the young woman's hair and whispering to her, doing her best to hold back her own tears.

Bert lay on his deathbed of blood and straw, his glassy, doll-like eyes staring at the ceiling. Kett thought about closing them then decided he didn't deserve it. Some people gave up the right to eternal rest.

"Well that was a tossing disaster," said Clare. His voice was weaker than Kett had ever heard it, weaker even than it had been when the Super had been shot and stabbed. "An absolute, unmitigated, tossing disaster. Savage, what were you thinking?"

"I'm so sorry, sir," she said. "I didn't... I had no idea she was going to do that."

"And you, Kett. Don't even get me started. We cannot, we *will* not, ever condone torture."

Kett stared at the floor, the horror of what he'd done holding him coffin-tight in coldness and darkness. He started to reply but Clare waved him down.

"Don't. I've only got myself to blame."

"We can find her," Kett said, clearing his throat. "Bert wasn't expecting us. He wouldn't have had time to hide the evidence. But we have to be quick."

Clare nodded.

"You got Poppy back," the Super said, finally looking up. "Get Beatrice back alive and maybe—*maybe*—we can get through this with our jobs intact, and without criminal charges. I'll go check on the ambulance. But Kett, do me a favour first."

"Sir?"

"Clean your face."

Clare walked out of the barn, standing for a moment in the rain before heading for the road.

"Fuck me," Porter said when he'd gone.

"I had no idea," Savage said again.

"This isn't your fault," Kett told her.

"She must have picked up the knife when she fell out of the cell," Savage said. "Or had it in there. I didn't see it."

"None of us did. This isn't on you. It isn't on her. It's on *him*."

He pointed a crimson finger at Bert.

"Every molecule of blame is on that piece of shit."

"Hello?" came a shout from outside. A paramedic stepped into view—the same one from the church that morning. He looked at Bert with eyes that were as wide as pickled eggs. "Holy shit. I'm not sure I can do much with him."

"Her," Kett said, nodding at Poppy. "Kate, can you stay with her? See if you can get her to talk."

"Will do," Savage said.

Kett walked out of the barn, grateful for the heavy rain on his face. His skin was itchy, crawling beneath the touch of the dead man's blood. He scrubbed at it, standing to one side to let the second paramedic wheel the stretcher through the door.

"Holy shit," the man said.

Kett left them to it, heading for the open back door of the farmhouse. It led into a small kitchen, all exposed oak and flagstones. Three uniformed constables were ransacking the drawers and cupboards, raining cutlery and crockery onto the floor. They all stopped when Kett entered, standing back and watching him the way somebody watches a wild animal.

A *dangerous* animal.

He kept his head down as he walked across the kitchen and through a door, finding a bathroom in the hallway beyond. It was spotless, and given the fact that Bert was dead, it felt safe enough to use without worrying too much about forensics.

"Give me a second," he told Porter as the DI appeared behind him.

"Sure," Porter said. "All the time you need."

Kett closed the door and took a moment to breathe, then he pulled off his blood-stained jacket and rolled up the sleeves of his shirt. There was a mirror in here, but he couldn't bring himself to look in it.

He was too afraid of what he would see looking back at him.

He ran the hot tap, a combination boiler booming to life in the kitchen. The water was scalding, the little room filling with steam almost immediately. But he didn't care. The hotter the better. He washed his hands first, ignoring the pain as he scrubbed the blood away. Then he pushed his face into the sink, the water running black, then red, then finally clear. Even then he didn't stop—not until it was too much to bear.

He turned off the water and used his fist to smudge the steam from the mirror. His skin was red and angry, but it was *him* that he saw looking back, not a monster. He looked exhausted. He looked like a man about to fall off the edge of a cliff into the yawning abyss of death.

All he wanted to do was go home, see Billie, see the girls. But he couldn't.

It wasn't over yet.

"Come on, Robbie," he said to his reflection. "Finish this."

There was no towel, so he dumped his ruined jacket in the sink and opened the door. More Uniforms explored the hallway and the living room but Porter's voice cut through the chatter.

"Sir. Up here."

Kett took the wide stairs two at a time, seeing Porter leaning out of one of the five doors on the long landing.

"There's that," he said, pointing to the door opposite. Kett glanced inside to see what might have been a theatre dressing room. Clothes were suspended from the picture rail on hangers, dozens of outfits that didn't seem to match each other at all. More worrying still was the collection of wigs that sat neatly on stands by the window. One of them was dark and shot through with grey. It looked profession-ally made.

Hanging above it was a robe, complete with a large hood.

"What the hell?" Kett said.

"And there's *this*," Porter said, waving him on.

Kett followed the DI into another large bedroom that was being used as a study. There were bookcases and papers everywhere, the walls covered in sketches and photographs and documents. Superintendent Clare was already there, his arms braced on an antique desk that seemed to bow beneath the weight of the books that had been stacked on it.

"It'll take weeks to go through all this," the Super said.

"We haven't got weeks," Kett replied, walking to another desk that sat against the far wall. This one was littered with illustrations that had been photocopied from various sources, and others that looked as if they'd been freshly drawn. He didn't bother with gloves, picking up a notebook and trying to make sense of the scrawled handwriting and the complex patterns of lines and squiggles. "Bert said she would be dead before the end of the day. He said she was in a box. See anything like that?"

"Plenty," said Clare. "Half of this stuff seems to be plans. Blueprints. He was making some evil contraptions."

"Yeah, there were some in the barn," said Kett.

"These look like the plans for the coffin that Fran was crushed in," said Porter, studying a large sheet of draftsman's paper that had been pinned to the wall. Kett walked to his side, scanning the drawings, the measurements, seeing blueprints of the Samson and Hercules and its hidden swimming pool. In the illustrations it was a man in the coffin, not a woman, his expression of agony drawn with cruel precision.

"This must have taken days to plan," Kett said. "He must have known for a while that Jenny was trying to blackmail him."

"Unless they weren't originally for Jenny," said Porter.

"He might have been planning these for years. Jenny and her friends were just unlucky enough to attract his attention."

"Good point."

There were more papers tacked to the walls. Kett recognised a sketch of Cow Tower, and pinned next to that was a photocopy of an illustration—Sweet Briar Rose in her chamber of thorns, fast asleep. There were more sketches, more notes, but Clare was right, it would take weeks to go through them.

He went back to the desk, sifting through the mountain of documents, finding nothing. Porter had opened the drawers and was pulling things out, throwing them to the floor—more books of fairy tales, local legends, mythology. He pulled out a couple of packets of developed photographs, opening them up.

"Here," he said, laying them on the desk one by one. Kett saw shots of the Samson and Hercules, the alleyway behind it, more of the church where Fortune had almost died, Cow Tower and the river.

Then something new.

"Where is that?" Kett said.

The photo showed a river. A family stood by the water's edge throwing bread to the swans who drifted there. A warehouse sat in the background, its face covered with graffiti, its windows shuttered.

"Riverside, maybe?" said Porter. "Down by the swimming pool. Loads of empty warehouses there at the moment."

"It is," Clare said, peering over Kett's shoulder. "I know it. Are there more?"

There were. Porter slapped them down on the desk—another two shots of the front of the warehouse, then one from the back, taken on the other side of the river. The next four or five must have been shot inside, the bare walls and debris-covered floor lit up by the flash. He turned over the final photo like he was playing a card in a game of poker.

"Fuck me," he said, echoing the words that had entered Kett's head.

In the middle of the photo was what could only be described as a casket, a coffin of metal and glass, or maybe clear plastic. It was open, resting against—or maybe secured to—an old piece of machinery. The photograph wasn't great, but it was clear that the inside of the device was lined with broken glass.

Kett felt what little warmth was left in him disappear.

"That's a box," Clare said. "That's where Beatrice is."

The Super pushed himself away from the desk, running for the door. Porter followed, stopping only when he saw that Kett wasn't following.

"Sir?"

"Go," Kett told him.

"You're not coming?"

Kett hesitated, looking at the photo again, then at the wall. Something didn't feel right.

"He kept calling her a babe," he said. "Beatrice. Did you hear that?"

"Bert?" Porter said, shrugging. "I think so. I thought he was just being a creep."

"Maybe," said Kett. "Go with Clare. Beatrice is almost certainly there. I'll stay here. We're missing something, I'm sure of it."

Porter nodded, disappearing. Kett heard him clomp down the stairs, heard the sound of shouts and the stampede of the police as they ran for their cars.

Please find her, he thought. *And please be alive.*

It was a big ask. If Bert really had locked Beatrice inside that glass casket then she'd be close to bleeding out now.

Or long dead.

He scanned the documents on the wall, seeing more of the same but nothing useful. The rest of the drawers were mostly empty so he went back to the papers and the books on the desk. He almost howled with relief when he lifted an A3 sketchpad to find a map underneath. It was a tourist guide to Norfolk, big enough to cover the entire desk when he unfolded it. The majority of the map was taken up by the rump of the county, but an inset box showed the inner city.

His heart sank.

Somebody had covered the map in little crosses—over thirty of them.

"Sir?"

Kett glanced back to see Savage at the door.

"How's Poppy?" he asked.

"They had to sedate her," she said, weaving around the mess on the floor. "Clare told me to come up here. He said they've found Beatrice?"

"I don't know," said Kett. "Bert has some kind of casket set up in a warehouse by the river. Broken glass. It's nasty."

"But you don't think she's there?"

Kett sighed.

"I don't know. Something's bothering me and I can't put my finger on it. Look at this."

He stood to the side to let her in, and both of them studied the map.

"That cross is right on Cow Tower," Savage said, moving her finger over the inset box. "There's another in Tombland, give or take. And there's St Lawrence's Church. Did you say a warehouse by the river? That could be it. What are the others?"

"That's what I'm worried about," said Kett. "They're everywhere. Up by the coast, the woods, the middle of nowhere. There's too many of them. Anything look familiar to you?"

"Some of these are where we found the boys on the stones," she said, pointing to the western section of the county. "Dereham. That cross looks like it's bang on the Stone of Hoe."

"And that's Elsham," said Kett, pointing to the coast. "Where the kids went missing. That's some coincidence, Kate."

"Or not," she said. "Did you notice how he called you by your name back then, right before he died?"

"Yeah," said Kett.

"Maybe he's been reading up on you."

Kett snatched a pencil from the floor, drawing a circle around the crosses in Elsham and Dereham, then around the one in Thetford which sat right where they'd investigated the Black Shuck case. Savage took the pencil from him and marked off a few more.

"That wasn't the only thing that bothered me," Kett said as he watched her. "He kept calling Beatrice 'babe'. It seemed weird."

"Yeah, I thought so too," Savage said. "Not just pervy, but odd. It was like he was trying to tell us something. Another clue."

"Making it too easy," said Kett. "Why babe?"

Savage shrugged, lifting the map to see the papers underneath.

"The fairy tale stuff was just a whim, right?" she said. "He didn't believe in it. It wasn't symbolic."

"Right," said Kett. "He just got the idea from Fisher's house."

"But he stuck to it. He was committed. You said a glass casket?"

Kett nodded, fishing out the photo from beneath the map.

"There's one in *Snow White*. She lies in it when people think she's dead."

"That's good," Kett said. "She's probably there, isn't she?"

"I think we've got to remember that Bert had two women left. He built that glass casket for one of them, but it might not have been Beatrice. Maybe he hadn't got around to putting Poppy in it yet."

"That's it," said Kett, snapping his fingers. "That's what felt wrong. The note we found at Poppy's house, didn't it talk about, uh, something about a butterfly in a glass cage?"

"A butterfly in a glass cage whose beauty would never fade," Savage said. "There was even a photo of Snow White. He was going to put *Poppy* in the coffin."

"So where's Beatrice?"

They studied the map together—just three crosses that hadn't been circled. One sat in Yarmouth, the other near Watton, the third right on the western border of the county.

"Babe," Savage said.

She turned to the floor, to the piles of books that sat there. She used her boot to separate them before picking one up. Kett had to duck down to see the title: *Folklore of East Anglia*.

"Babe, or *babes*?" she said.

"Huh?"

She flicked through the pages and the book's broken spine made it easy for her, flopping open. She held it up.

"*Babes in the Wood*," she said before Kett had a chance

to read the title. "A Norfolk fairy tale. You've heard of it, right?"

"Yeah, it's like Hansel and Gretel."

"Kind of, but without the witch, and without the happy ending. The brother and sister in this story get left in the woods by their uncle, and they die."

"Left where?" Kett said.

"Well, it's a fairy tale, so it's not exactly real, but..."

She skimmed the book then returned to the map, frowning. She pointed to an X.

"Right there. Wayland Woods. Half an hour away."

CHAPTER THIRTY-THREE

Half of the police had left with Superintendent Clare, taking almost all of the IRVs as they stormed back into the city to find Beatrice. The tactical unit had gone too. By the time Kett had managed to source the keys for one of the remaining cars nearly twenty minutes had passed. He threw them to Savage as he walked out of the front door onto the driveway, his other hand holding his phone to his ear. Clare must have been busy because it went straight to his voicemail.

"It's me, sir," Kett said after the beep. "We found another possible location for Beatrice. Hopefully we won't need it but Savage and I are heading there, just in case the glass coffin was for Poppy. Wayland Woods, out near Watton."

He thought about asking for backup but decided not to. Bert was dead, and the evidence so far pointed to the fact that he was working alone.

It wouldn't be the first time he'd been wrong about tag-teaming killers, though.

He made one more call to request that an ambulance

meet them there, then he clambered into the passenger seat, shivering so hard he almost dropped the phone. His shirt was wet through with rain and it felt like he'd been filled from his head to his toes with iced water. Savage cranked up the heat as soon as she'd started the engine.

"It'll warm up in a bit," she said. "I can get you a blanket from the house?"

"A *blanket?*" he said when he realised she was being completely serious. "I'm not an old man, Kate."

She checked the road then pulled out, only for a shape to hurl itself onto the front of the car. Savage slammed on the brakes, both of them staring in shock at the face that peered in through the swishing wipers.

"Duke?" Kett said. "What the hell are you doing?"

The big PC lumbered to the back door and climbed in, the car's suspension sinking with his weight. He took off his helmet, shaking the water from his jacket like a wet dog.

"I missed the last convoy, sir. I was investigating the other side of the farm. Didn't want to miss this one."

"It's hardly a convoy," Kett said. "Close the door, Duke, it's bloody freezing."

He did as he was told, clipping himself in.

"Where are we going?"

"For a walk in the woods," Kett said.

Savage hit the accelerator hard, the tyres spraying gravel. Duke groaned as they took the corners, one hand grabbing the strap above the door, the other planted firmly on the cage between the front seats and the back. They were already on the right side of town, and five minutes later Savage had got them over the bypass and onto the Watton Road. With the sirens on they cut through traffic easily, hitting seventy on the straight stretches.

"Easy, Savage," Kett said, more than once. "We can't help anyone if we're roadkill."

And every time he said it she hit the brakes, only to attempt to break the sound barrier again five minutes later.

"Sorry, sir," she said as they hurtled through the bleak and barren countryside. "I just want to find her. I want her to be okay. That... that *arsehole*. We can't let him win. We can't let her die."

After that, Kett stopped telling her to slow down.

"Any chance we could turn the heat off?" Duke asked, fidgeting in his jacket. "I'm roasting back here."

"No," said Savage. The big PC reached for the window instead and Kett glared at him.

"Touch that and you're walking home."

Savage kept the speed up, overtaking cars and vans and buses as she cut through the town of Watton. She was out again two minutes later, speeding south until the open fields gave way to a dense woodland.

"I'm not a hundred percent sure where to go," she said. "But this is where the x was on the map."

It was confirmed a moment later when they reached a car park, a brown sign declaring it to be Wayland Wood. Savage pulled in, the car bumping through a gauntlet of giant puddles until she brought them to a halt. She was the first out, practically bouncing, her eyes bright as she searched the car park.

Kett braced himself as he left the warmth of the car and stepped into the brutal cold. Duke followed them out, tripping on the seatbelt and doing a strange routine of foot shuffles and star jumps to stop himself falling over.

The place was deserted. Even the birds sounded muted, as if they were frightened to call attention to themselves.

"Any ideas?" Kett said.

"No," said Savage. "But it's not massive. If we split up, we could cover it quickly."

Kett nodded, wishing he'd made the call for backup. He pointed to a path on the right.

"Duke, that way. Look out for anything that might be a box. In the trees, underground, it could be anywhere."

"On my own?" he said.

"That's generally what splitting up means," Kett told him, and he grudgingly broke into a run.

There was only one other path and Savage was halfway to it.

"Beatrice?" she shouted. Her voice chased pigeons from the canopy, their wings clapping. "Beatrice Goodwin? It's the police. If you can hear me, call out."

Silence. Savage vanished into the trees, Kett right behind her. The woods closed in around their heads, making the unfriendly day even darker. Rain pattered onto swathes of bracken, but other than that the whole world seemed to have fallen silent.

Until Savage called out again.

"Beatrice Goodwin, this is the police."

He heard the shrill call of her police whistle, three short bursts.

"Beatrice," Kett joined in, his voice hoarse. "This is the police."

They walked in silence then tried again, the trees doing their best to mute their voices, as if they wanted to keep their treasure for themselves.

Savage had reached a junction and was heading left, blowing the whistle again. Kett took the right-hand path, losing sight of her immediately. He heard her call, though, and every now and again Duke's ghostly voice would echo through the thick foliage—sounding too far away. It was as if the woods were expanding, unhinging their jaws ready to swallow them whole. It seemed to be growing darker with every step, the ground a minefield of giant tree roots and thick coils of bramble. He felt as if he was walking into a fairy tale, into a place where monstrous things had happened.

Where they could happen again.

"Kett!" came Duke's voice. "Savage! Over here!"

His voice was broken into whispering parts, it was impossible to know where it was coming from.

"Duke?" Kett called back. "Where are you?"

"In the woods!"

Kett rolled his eyes, fighting through the thickening vegetation. The thorns left weeping welts along his bare arms, his neck, his face, going for his eyes too. He thought of the cover of the book he'd found in Fisher's house, the blinded prince from Rapunzel, and wondered if that would be his fate.

"Sir?" said Savage, closer now.

"Kate? Where are you?"

"Here," she said. "Look to your left."

He turned, seeing a flash of movement through the branches.

"There's a path here, sort of," she said.

Kett pushed between two trees that seemed to contract in the wind like forceps, pincering him. Then he staggered onto the path, Savage's hands on his arms to steady him. He shook her loose.

"I'm not an old man, Kate," he said, and she looked at him doubtfully.

"So you keep telling me."

"I'm only forty-*bloody*-three!"

Duke called out again, closer now. Savage led the way,

the path winding in random shapes around trees and bushes before leading them to the edge of a huge pond. It was a good job Duke was standing on the edge of it, Kett thought, because he wouldn't have seen it otherwise. The surface was green, covered in an algae so thick that it looked solid enough to walk on.

Trees surrounded the pond, sickly branches reaching over it almost protectively. Vines plunged into the water in various places, lost amongst the logs that floated there, something almost artificial about the angle of them.

"What?" Kett said, and even as Duke answered him he saw it.

Not vines, but *ropes*.

"They meet in the middle," Duke said. "They're attached to something there."

There was a wide, flat object in the pond, maybe four foot long and four foot wide, protruding no more than an inch or two from the water. It was covered in pieces of wood and decomposing leaves, but the rough shape of it was still painfully obvious.

"It's a box," said Savage.

The ropes all led to it, seven of them, the other ends secured to the trees. Some were tight, others were slack. Kett couldn't make any sense of it. The box seemed to be slowly sinking, tiny bubbles of air erupting on the surface of the pond like a punctured beach ball.

"We need to cut her free," said Duke, pulling a pocketknife out of his trousers.

"Wait," said Kett. "Don't touch anything."

He walked to the edge of the pond, the stagnant stench of it overpowering.

"Beatrice? Beatrice Goodwin? Can you hear me? It's the police."

They all held their breath as they waited for a reply. Only the silence of the woods answered, impossibly heavy. Kett looked at Savage.

"We all saw what happened with the coffin," she said. "This could be rigged. I'm going in."

"In *there*?" said Duke.

Savage was already wading into the water, her face creased with misery. She stumbled on something, almost falling.

"Be careful," Kett said to her. She didn't answer, up to her waist now and still sinking. The box was twenty yards away and Savage was up to her armpits before she was halfway there.

"Dammit," she said. "It's too deep. I'll swim."

"Kate, we don't know what's in there," Kett said.

She was already splashing through the water, her legs kicking, her hands trying to push the carpet of logs and leaves out of her way. If she went under, they'd never find her.

"The hell with this," Kett said.

The nearest rope was to his left and he stumbled towards it, his foot plunging into the water up to the ankle as he slipped. He grabbed a branch to stop the rest of him following, the rotting bark as cold as a corpse's skin. He pulled himself along, finding solid ground again.

The rope had been expertly tied, looped over and over like a Gordian knot. Duke was right, they'd have to be cut.

But then what? They'd have to cut all but one of the ropes in order to pull the box to shore, and if they did that, it could sink.

"Duke," Kett said. When there was no answer, he looked back to see that the PC had gone. "Duke?"

Savage was almost at the box and she was struggling.

She reached for the nearest rope, missed it, and for a second she vanished beneath the pool-table-green surface.

"Kate!" Kett roared.

She pushed up again, eyes closed, grabbing the rope. The box bobbed in the water, the other ropes flexing and the trees groaning. More leaves rained down on the pond, doing their best to bury it. Savage gagged, using her free hand to wipe the algae from her face.

"You're okay," Kett called to her. "You're okay, just breathe."

She did, taking a deep breath that became a low, retching groan.

"I'm... okay..." she managed, spitting.

Something was pounding through the trees, grunting. Kett actually did a double take when he saw Duke crash out of the bushes holding a huge, rotting tree trunk. The PC was gurning, his arms bulging and a vein in his forehead the size of a pencil. It was no wonder, the trunk had to have been twenty-foot long and two-foot thick. He staggered into the pond and hurled it like he was tossing a caber.

"What the fuck are you doing?" Kett said.

The trunk hit the surface, sinking for a second before bobbing back up. Duke shunted the rest of it into the pond, where it floated. He waded in after it, holding one end and pushing it towards Savage and the box.

"Grab it," he said.

Savage let go of the rope and took hold of the floating tree trunk. It was big enough to hold her, allowing her to pound on the lid of the box with her free hand.

"Beatrice?" she shouted, breathless.

They all listened, waiting.

A hollow knock.

"Beatrice? Is that you? It's the police. Knock again if you can hear me."

Knock knock.

Savage looked back, a thin smile on her face.

"It's her," she said. "Beatrice, are you safe?"

No answer.

"We're going to get you out. Can you breathe okay?"

Silence.

"Beatrice," Savage said, louder now. "Is there water inside the box?"

Knock knock knock.

"Is it filling up?"

Knock knock knock.

"Fast?"

And the knocks kept coming, urgent now.

"Christ," said Kett.

He pulled out his phone, calling Clare. When the Super answered he sounded like a charging bull.

"You'd better have good news for me, Kett. There's nobody here, nobody in the casket. We've searched the whole bloody place."

"We've found her, sir," Kett said. "But she's rigged in some kind of trap beneath the water. We need fire and rescue, but I don't think there's time. There's no access here, it's right in the middle of the woods. Can you get us a helicopter?"

"I can try," Clare said. "Where are you?"

"Wayland Woods, just outside of Watton."

"I know you, Kett," Clare said. "I know you're not going to let that woman die. Figure it out, we're on our way."

CHAPTER THIRTY-FOUR

You're not going to let that woman die.

Figure it out.

It was easier said than done.

Kett threw his phone to the ground, holding onto the rope as he waded into the pond. Duke was already halfway there, easing himself along using the floating tree trunk.

"Just hang on," Savage shouted to the woman in the box. "Don't panic. Slow breaths, Beatrice, okay? Nice and slow."

She looked at Kett, her expression full of panic. Even in the time they'd been here the box had sunk further, the top of it practically invisible now beneath the scum. Savage fumbled her free hand in the water.

"There's something here," she said. "I think it's a... I think it's a float of some kind, but it's deflated."

Kett pushed on, hand over hand along the rope. The bottom of the pond dropped fast, the water up to his chest. The smell of it was unlike anything else, fetid and dead and stripped of oxygen. The wet ground sucked at his boots like cement. Duke had reached the end of the tree trunk, the water up to his beard.

"Can you stand here?" Savage asked him.

"Just," he said. "On my tiptoes."

"Check the other side."

The big PC waded to the far end of the box, ducking his head into the water in order to get beneath the ropes. He came up gagging each time, his eyes wild.

"There's a..." he started, retching out a burp. "Another thing here. Another float, I think. Slow puncture."

"Can you feel a lock? An opening?" Kett called out, practically hanging on the rope now. His movements were making the box jerk, waves pushing out from the middle of the pond.

"There's something here," Savage said. "Sir, you're going to need to let go. You're pulling it down."

He did as she said, sinking to his chin, the treacherous ground almost pulling him under. Bugs crawled over the surface of the pond, hundreds of them, exploring his face, his ears, his mouth. He pushed through them, grabbing Duke's floating tree trunk and clawing for air.

"It's a padlock," Savage said. "But I can't get to it beneath the water. I can't see what I'm doing. Duke, give me the knife."

Duke fumbled in his pocket, holding it out. Then he lost his footing and it slipped out of his fingers, disappearing.

"Oh, shit!" he said. "I'm sorry."

Savage pounded on the box.

"Beatrice, can you hear me?"

Nothing.

"Beatrice?"

She looked at Kett, desperate.

"We need to get the box out of the water."

"It's impossible," said Kett. "We'd have to cut the ropes,

all of them, and it would sink. I don't think we could push it to shore."

"No," said Savage. "We just need to get it above the surface so I can break the lock."

"Can we use the ropes?" Duke said. "Pull it up?"

It would be too hard, Kett knew.

But there was another way.

"Duke, we need to get underneath it," he said.

"You *what?*" Duke replied. "Under the box?"

"If we push it up, Savage might be able to bust the lock. You've got your baton?"

The PC nodded, reaching for his belt beneath the water.

"Do *not* drop it," said Kett.

Duke took his time, pulling the baton free and passing it over the top of the box like it was an explosive. Savage took it, extending it gently. She nodded to Kett and he nodded back.

"Do it fast," he said.

Kett looked at Duke.

"Ready?"

"No," said the PC. "I hate swimming."

"You don't need to swim. Just sink. On three. One."

He took a flurry of shallow breaths to prime his lungs.

"Two."

Then a deep one.

Three.

He nodded to Duke and they dived together. Kett was instantly blind and deaf, a rush of panic making his ears roar. Terror almost drove him right back to the surface but he forced himself deeper, reaching out and finding the bottom of the box. He hooked his fingers under it and pulled himself down, managing to wiggle his body beneath the bulk of it. Something heavy thumped into him and past another crippling bolt of adrenaline he realised it was Duke.

He planted his boots in the filth of the bottom of the pond, wedged his shoulder beneath the box.

And pushed.

It was heavy, but he felt it lift. He straightened his legs, feeling his boots sink into the mud, feeling his back and his chest scream with agony. Duke was right next to him, a reassuring presence. Kett doubled down, his teeth gritted so tight they might have shattered.

The box rose. He felt the impact of the baton as Savage struck the padlock, and again, and again.

He was running out of air, his lungs like clenched fists. The panic was back. What if he couldn't get out in time? What if the ropes snapped and the box pinned him to the bottom of the pond?

He thought of Billie. He thought of his girls.

He thought of Beatrice, drowning just inches above him.

And he held on, every muscle shaking, every fibre of his body burning.

The box rattled and he felt something snap.

Savage's voice, so quiet it might have come from another world.

He felt Duke move away, the water rippling as the big man propelled himself to the surface. The box dropped, pushing him down, the ground sucking at his boots, refusing to let go. He kicked free, screaming now, the box so much bigger than it had felt before—big enough that it seemed to fill the space above him, like he had fallen beneath the ice. The last of the air left his lungs, his body spasming as it tried to force him to breathe.

A hand in his hair, pulling hard.

Kett broke free of the pond, breathing algae, breathing rot, his chest juddering like a piece of broken machinery. He flailed but Duke was there, holding him up, letting him suck in wet air, saying something that Kett couldn't hear past the jet engine roar in his skull.

Without them holding it up, the box had dropped back beneath the surface—full of water.

But the lid was open.

Beatrice was halfway out of it, as desperate for breath as Kett had been.

"Easy," Savage said as she tried to guide Beatrice onto the floating tree trunk. "Easy, don't rush it. You're safe. You're safe."

Beatrice climbed over Savage, almost dunking her before she managed to grab the log. She held herself there, her sobs the loudest sound in the world, her wide, terror-filled eyes moving from Savage to Kett to Duke then back again.

"You're safe," Savage said again. "You're okay, Beatrice."

"You're okay, sir," said Duke with complete sincerity, the giant PC still holding Kett up in the water. "Shhh now, you're safe."

"I know I bloody am," Kett said, pushing himself away. He grabbed the nearest rope, hauling himself back to dry land with muscles that felt tissue thin. He almost couldn't scrabble up the muddy bank, but somehow he managed it, resting on his elbows and his knees for a moment, his head pressed to the dirt, while he filled his lungs over and over and over. Everything felt too bright, the woods as sharp as crystal, the sound of the rain deafening.

Duke pulled himself up beside him, standing there dripping pond water.

"That was—" he started, then he ejected a spray of green vomit into the bushes.

Kett clambered to his feet, clapping the PC on the back as he retched and dribbled.

"Thank you, Aaron," he said. "But next time, don't pull me up by my bloody hair."

"Sorry, boss," Duke groaned.

Beatrice was edging along the tree trunk, Savage right behind her. Kett waded back in, meeting them halfway and offering the young woman his hand.

"Easy now," he said. "You're almost there."

Her entire body was trembling, her teeth chattering so much that Kett could barely understand her when she spoke.

"He's... he's... He might... might still be here."

"He's dead," said Kett as they reached the side of the pond. He stepped up first then carefully pulled Beatrice onto dry land. "He's dead. You don't ever have to worry about him again."

Beatrice collapsed to her knees, then slumped onto her side, her head resting on a pillow of marsh flowers. She curled her legs up to her chest, wrapped her hands around her waist, and just cried.

Bert might have been dead, but she'd be worrying about him for the rest of her life. She'd see his face every time she closed her eyes, and every time she woke up.

Kett held out his hand and Savage took it, hauling herself out of the pond. She looked like she, too, was about to collapse. Instead, she wrapped her arms around Kett and held him. He hugged her back, both of them standing there in silence as the rain hammered down.

Then Duke was there, stinking of vomit as he wrapped his big, wet arms around them both.

"Nope," said Kett, pulling free.

He searched the ground, finding his phone and seeing three missed calls from Clare. He dialled him back, watching Savage as she knelt down next to Beatrice and pulled the young woman close. He thought he could hear a helicopter, but his ears were so full of water he couldn't be sure.

"Speak!" barked the Superintendent when he answered. Kett could hear the growl of an engine, the muted cry of a siren.

"She's alive," Kett said. "We got her."

Clare's sigh of relief filled the line like a hurricane.

"Thank toss for that. She's definitely alive?"

Beatrice had her head on Savage's lap now, her sobs growing quieter.

"Definitely, sir."

The throbbing pulse of the helicopter was getting louder.

"Ahmed, slow down, we're good," Clare said, his voice faint. "Control says there's an ambulance in the car park. Get her there."

"Will do," Kett said. "You can call off the chopper."

"Thanks," Clare said with a heavy dose of sarcasm. "I'm going to look like a right tit sending it back."

Kett laughed, the sound of it surprising him. The phone felt too heavy.

The entire *world* felt too heavy.

"I'm going to go now, sir," he said.

"Then go," Clare replied. "And Kett."

"Sir?"

"Good work, son."

CHAPTER THIRTY-FIVE

"So, HERE WE ARE AGAIN, SIR."

Savage sat on the tailgate of the second of three ambulances that were parked in a line across the car park of Wayland Woods. She was wearing somebody's yellow jacket and wrapped tight in a foil blanket, but she was still shivering hard.

Kett stood next to her, a blanket wrapped around his shoulders too. It wasn't doing much good. The cold was locked deep inside him. He couldn't imagine ever being warm again.

Still, it helped that in the ambulance next door Beatrice Goodwin was alive and well. Kett could see her sitting up in the stretcher while paramedics checked her blood pressure. She saw him looking and waved, and he waved back. She was missing the index finger of her right hand, but the smile she gave him was as bright as the sun.

Savage was smiling too.

"What?" he said.

"I said here we are again, sir, back in an ambulance.

How many times is that now? The ambulance service is going to start charging us an admission fee soon."

Kett laughed, even though it hurt his chest. He wasn't sure if it was all the water he'd swallowed, or that little shard of bullet working its way deeper, but his lungs felt like they were on fire. *Everything* ached.

But he was used to it. He was used to the pain.

"Well done, Kate," he said. "You got her out."

"Team effort, sir. I'd never have been able to get the padlock open if the box wasn't out of the water. I'd never have done it without you and Aaron."

There was no way he'd have been able to lift the box by himself, either. If Duke hadn't been there, Beatrice would have died.

"Where is the big lunk, anyway?" Kett asked.

"In the woods," Savage said. "Told me he had business to attend to. I think it was *toilet* business."

"Right," said Kett.

He was suddenly aware of the sound of sirens, the growl of a distant engine. The smile fell away from Savage's face.

"You okay?" said Kett.

"No," she replied, staring at the ground. "I'll never forgive myself for what happened with Poppy."

Kett started to reply but she lifted a hand that asked for patience.

"It's not just that Bert died. I mean, that's bad enough. Now he doesn't have to answer for what he's done. He doesn't have to suffer. But Poppy, that poor woman. She'll have to live with that forever."

"She will," Kett said. He turned to the woods, losing himself in the swaying branches. "But she'll be okay. She'll learn how to mute it, how to *not* see it. We all do."

He heard the crack of the hammer as it sunk into the

back of the Pig Man's head, felt the vibration of Schofield's shattering skull travel up his arm.

Then he pushed it away, he pushed it into the darkest part of his mind, because he could.

"We all do," he said again, and when he turned back to Savage he saw the understanding there. The sadness, too.

"We lose a little bit of ourselves," she said. "Every time. But it's worth it. It has to be worth it. Right?"

"It's worth it," Kett said, looking at Beatrice again. They were closing the doors of her ambulance, ready to go, and she waved at Kett once more before he lost sight of her. A few minutes later the ambulance lumbered away, rocking on the uneven ground before pulling onto the road. An IRV appeared seconds later, Superintendent Clare actually hanging out of the passenger window like an angry dog.

"Kett!" he barked.

Clare disappeared, yelling something at the driver. The car skidded to a halt and the Super unfolded his lanky frame from inside. More cars were arriving, the car park shimmering in a haze of blue light. It was almost like they were underwater again, and Kett had to remind himself that he could breathe so that the panic wouldn't take hold of him.

"Tossing hell, look at the state of you!" Clare said. "I've got my BTJ somewhere, I'll find it for you, keep you warm."

"I think I'd rather have hypothermia, sir," Kett said.

"Rubbish. Was that Beatrice on her way out?"

"Yeah. She's doing okay. She'll live."

The Super walked around the back of the ambulance to see Savage. He looked for a second like he might be about to give her a bollocking, but when he saw the expression on her face he seemed to relax.

As much as he *ever* relaxed.

"You did good, Kate," he said. "You got her. I don't want you worrying about the other thing, okay? We got four of those women back alive, and their killer is dead. There will be more paperwork coming out of my tosshole than ever, but that's my job. You did your part, all of you. Let me take care of the rest."

"Thank you, sir," said Savage through chattering teeth. Clare looked around.

"Where's PC Duke?"

"PC *Puke*, you mean?" Kett said. "Toilet problems, apparently."

Clare pulled a face.

"Robbie!"

Kett looked past the Super to see Porter running across the car park. The big DI skidded around the back of the ambulance.

"Bloody hell, sir, I heard what happened. I should have been here. I'm sorry."

"It's okay," said Kett. "We had Duke."

"Where is he?"

"Taking a shit in the woods," Clare growled. "Like a bloody animal."

"Oh, right," Porter said. "Beatrice okay?"

Both Savage and Kett nodded.

"Poppy's doing well," Porter said. "Fortune too. And Fran's recovering. Four out of five is more than we could have ever hoped for. And you two both look okay, mostly. A little green. I'd call this a win."

He glanced at the ambulance.

"We've got to stop making a habit of this."

Savage laughed.

"That's what I said!"

And Kett laughed too, feeling warmer for it.

The sound of wet feet rose up and they all turned to see Duke limping out of the woods.

"Un-tossing-believable," Clare muttered. "It's Bigfoot."

The big PC looked like a Yeti, his uniform torn, his beard matted with vegetation and pond slime. One of his shoes was missing, and Kett wondered if he'd lost it at the bottom of the pond. He was trying to do up his trousers but he was shivering so much he couldn't manage. He looked up at them and grunted. Kett heard the sound of a camera shutter. Porter was taking a photo on his phone.

"What?" the DI said, grinning. "Can't let him forget about this."

"Go easy," Kett said. "It would have been a very different story if he hadn't been here."

"Get in the ambulance," Clare said when Duke had reached them. "I want you in the hospital for a check-up, you bloody great Neanderthal."

Duke was happy enough to oblige, Savage hopping off the tailgate so that he could climb in.

"You too, Savage," Clare said.

"I'm fine, sir, honestly," she said. "Just need a change of clothes."

"And a cup of tea," said Kett.

"Definitely a cup of tea," she said.

Porter cracked his knuckles.

"Leave it to me."

Then he was gone.

"Where the hell is he going to find a cup of tea around here?" Savage asked. "We're in the middle of the woods."

"Probably from *de caf*," said Kett. "But I'm off before he comes back. I'll head to the hospital, see if I can get some information out of the women while it's still fresh. We—"

"Stop that noise coming out of your face, Kett," Clare

said. "You're soaking wet, you're probably a nose hair away from catching cholera, you're almost certainly in some kind of shock and, to be brutally honest, you smell like a hippo's arsehole. I'm getting a Uniform to take you home."

"I—"

"Home!" Clare roared, making Kett jump. "Now!"

"Yes, sir," Kett said.

He walked to the nearest IRV, Savage by his side. Incredibly, the reporters were already arriving, a news van trying to bully its way past the line of police cars. Savage opened the door of the car for him and Kett did his best to scowl at her.

"What do I keep telling you, Kate?" he said as he fell inside. "I'm not an old man!"

She smiled, patting him on the shoulder.

"You keep telling yourself that, sir."

SAVAGE WAS RIGHT. It was hard to deny that he felt like an old man as he stood outside his house thirty minutes later and watched the IRV pull away. He felt like Methuselah, older than time, barely able to shuffle up the path to the front door.

He heard the kids first, of course, Evie and Moira shouting at each other in the living room. He couldn't work out if they were having an argument or playing a game, but either way the sound of them called to him, made him so desperate to get inside that he could have kicked the door down.

His numb fingers couldn't fish the keys out of his wet pocket, but Billie must have sensed him because the door opened and there she was. She hitched in a breath, the fingers of one hand resting on her lips as she looked at him—seeing past the dirt, past the scratches and cuts on his face, past the agony in his chest to the place where he *really* ached.

She didn't speak, she just motioned for him to come to her and he did. She pulled him close and hugged him tight, and he thought he might cry with the relief of it except the cold had made him too numb. He just stood there and let her hold him until the living room door opened and Evie fell out.

"Dad!" she screamed.

"Daaad!" Moira joined in, grabbing her sister around the waist like she was about to suplex her. They danced around the hallway like drunkards, laughing their heads off.

Billie let go of him and he missed her touch instantly.

"Can we have a story, Dad?" Evie said, pushing her sister away. "I want to know what happens to Stumblerumblebum."

"Pimplefartypants," said Moira, giggling at her own joke.

Kett didn't find it quite as funny. He never wanted to hear the name Rumpelstiltskin again.

"Daddy needs to rest," said Billie to a round of groans. "And I mean this in the nicest possible way, but he needs to wash. Immediately."

Kett nodded, looking at the stairs like they were as tall as Everest. His shoulders ached so much from holding up the box it was like he had broken glass in the joints, his back too.

"I'll get the kettle on," Billie said.

This gave him the strength he needed, and he climbed slowly to the landing, unbuttoning his shirt as he went. Alice was in her room, the chinchilla on her lap, and she called to him as he passed.

"Daddy! I found you on my iPad!"

She held it up and he saw the news, the photo of the five young women that Savage had taken from Jenny Eyler's house, then rolling footage of the woods he'd left half an hour ago.

"You shouldn't be watching that, sweetie," he said. "It's scary."

"It's cool," she said. "Everyone says you're a hero."

I'm not, he thought, seeing Bert on the floor, screaming; seeing himself driving his foot into the wound in his leg. *I'm the very opposite of that.*

I'm a monster.

HE WASN'T sure how long he spent in the shower. It might have been hours, because by the time he turned off the water the bathroom was lost behind a wall of steam and darkness had fallen. He dried himself then wrapped the towel around his waist, heading for the bedroom. He wasn't planning on staying in there for long, but once he'd pulled on some jogging bottoms and a T-shirt the only thing he found himself capable of was collapsing into the bed. He pulled the duvet up to his chin, still shivering.

Billie walked in a few minutes later, a steaming mug of tea in her hand. He wasn't sure which of them he was more excited to see.

"The last one went cold," she said. "Just brewed another."

She sat next to him, her expression full of sadness, as if she saw the weight he carried on his bruised shoulders.

"You got them back," she said. "I saw it on the news. You got them home."

"Not just me," he said.

She took a shuddering breath and he reached a hand out of the quilts, resting it on hers.

"You're freezing," she said.

"Went for a swim."

"That's what this is?" she asked, looking at him. "That's all that happened?"

"I was never in any danger, not really. It was just cold. And I did what you asked me to do, Billie. I thought about you, I thought about the girls. I never put myself in danger, I promise."

She nodded, staring at the floor. Kett rested his head on the pillow. He didn't know if there was anything he could do to make it better.

"It's..." he started. "It's something I did."

And he couldn't bring himself to say any more than that, because the shame of it felt big enough to swallow him whole. Billie took his hand in both of hers, her touch impossibly warm.

"Did it help get them back?" she asked. "Whatever it was, did it help save those women?"

Kett nodded.

"Then you don't need to feel bad. Not ever."

He didn't know what to say, so he didn't say anything at all.

"Are happy endings always like this?" Billie asked after a moment. "All that fairy tale stuff. I mean, is this even a happy ending? I don't know."

"It is," he said. "And yeah, I think they are. I don't think happy endings are about being happy. Stories, fairy tales— the old ones, anyway—they're bloody and brutal and awful and lonely. And nothing goes back to how it was before."

He breathed a laugh through his nose.

"Maybe that's just it. Everything changes. *We* change. But we survive, you know? And that's what we're celebrating, that's what a happy ending is. It's knowing that we got through it. Even if things change, even if nothing's ever the same. We made it."

Billie nodded. She looked as if she was about to say something else but then Moira staggered into the room, holding a pile of books that was so tall she couldn't see over the top. She bounced off the bed and dropped them all a little too theatrically for it to be an accident. She was beaming.

"Story," she said.

"I don't think so, Moomoo," Kett told her. "Not today."

"I'll read you one," said Billie as she helped Moira climb onto the bed. The little girl pulled back the covers and bundled in next to Kett, radiating heat like a hot water bottle. There was a patter of footsteps and Evie ran into the room.

"Where's Moira?"

"Here!" Moira shouted.

"No fair!" Evie said, throwing herself onto the bed and burrowing beneath the duvet like a rabbit. She wrapped her arms around her dad, squeezing tight, and Kett felt a little of the cold start to flow out of him.

A little of the pain, too.

"Actually, I've got a better idea," Billie said. "Why don't we tell Daddy a story?"

"Yeah!" said Evie. "Once upon—"

"Not a fairy tale," Kett said. "Anything but that."

"Are we having a story?" Alice said, peeking into the room. "Can I listen?"

"You can tell it," said Billie. "Just don't bring your iPad."

Kett heard it clatter to the floor then his oldest daughter

was up on the bed, everyone screaming as she trampled over their legs. She pulled back the covers and squeezed in next to Moira, leaning over to give Kett a kiss on his cheek.

And just like that, he was warm again.

"I want it to be a space story," said Evie. "There's a king in space and his name is—"

"Farty Butt Cheese," said Moira.

"No! His name is Daddy, and he lives in a spaceship that he parks on the moon. And he's married to Mummy, and they spend the day—"

"Farting," said Alice. Evie glared at her, her fists bunched.

"No! They solve mysteries, like why the Moon is made from cheese."

"Made from farts!" Moira said.

"Stop it!" screamed Evie. "There are no farts in this story. Daddy, tell them."

And he would have, of course, if he wasn't already fast asleep.

CHAPTER THIRTY-SIX

Monday

"CHEERS MATE, KEEP THE CHANGE."

Kett climbed gingerly out of the taxi, making his way towards the ugly bulk of Norfolk Constabulary HQ. It was already midmorning, the world bathed in a reluctant but welcome blanket of cold sunshine. He could barely remember falling asleep last night, and the next thing he'd known was that it was after nine on Monday morning and the house was empty. Billie and the girls had written him a note before they'd left for school.

You are the best man we know.

He had it in his pocket, as comforting as a talisman.

He'd reached the main doors before he heard the sound of a car horn behind him. Squinting across the car park, he saw a familiar boat-sized Rover sitting in a visitor's space, and an equally familiar round face peering over the wheel. The window wound down as Kett walked over, Norman

Balls waving to him. The odd little conspiracy theorist was wrapped in a brown parka that was so big it could have doubled as a sleeping bag.

"Balls," Kett said. "What on earth are you doing here?"

"I've cracked it," Balls said, jittering. He tapped the passenger seat and Kett ducked down to see that it was covered in paper files. The footwell was a lake of Red Bull cans, which probably explained why the little man seemed so wired.

"Cracked what?"

"The Sweet Briar Rose case," he said.

"We—"

"Hear me out, Robbie. Fairy tales. I spent the whole night asking myself why a serial murderer would model their kills on old stories. The answer is easy. It reflects a time in their life when they were free and happy. They're looking to recreate that innocence of childhood. So I did some digging, and after some serious detective work I've figured out who the killer is."

Kett almost told him not to bother, but Balls seemed so excited it was almost cruel to stop him. He leaned towards Kett, speaking in a whisper.

"It's Superintendent Colin Clare," he said, his eyes wild. "You've seen how angry he gets. The job is too much for him, he's killing people and posing them like fairy tales in order to recapture his—"

"Killer's dead, Balls," Kett said. "Died yesterday, it just hasn't hit the news yet. It wasn't Clare."

Balls pouted, raising a finger.

"You're not a detective," said Kett, cutting him off. "Sorry."

He tapped the roof of the car then made his way through the doors, keeping his head down as he walked to the Major Investigation Team's bullpen. There was no need to worry about drawing attention, though, as the room was almost empty. Porter sat at his desk, rocking his chair back on two legs as he chewed on a pencil. Clare was perched next to him, both of them studying something so intently that Kett had walked right up to them before they noticed he was there.

"Wasn't expecting to see you today, Kett," said the Super.

"Plenty of loose ends to tie up," Kett said. "Not to mention the paperwork. How are Beatrice and the others?"

"Good," said Porter once he'd pulled the pencil out of his mouth. "Amazing, really, when you think about it. They've reinforced Fran's ribs and they think—tentatively, mind—that she might make a full recovery. I mean, she won't be running any marathons, but she's not going to need any help breathing."

"Poppy, Fortune and Beatrice are all up at the NNUH," said Clare. "But they'll be out in a day or two. Remarkably resilient, those women."

"You sound surprised," said Savage as she walked through the door from the kitchen. "Takes a lot to beat a strong woman down."

"Indeed it does," said Clare. "The contraption our killer used to try to drown Beatrice was incredibly cruel. Forensics fished it out of the pond and they're still working on it as we speak. The box was being held by four floats but all had slow punctures, and the box itself was perforated by very small holes. Even with the ropes, it was designed to drop beneath the surface. She was trapped there for hours, slowly sinking."

"Who does that?" Savage said. "I'm glad he's…"

And she stopped herself, putting her hand to her

mouth. She closed her eyes and Kett knew she was seeing Bert bleeding out on the barn floor. Clare must have noticed too.

"I've spoken to the CPS and Poppy won't be charged with anything. That was our error."

"Sir—"

"*Ours*, Kate," he said. "Not yours. It was a cock-up for sure, and one we'll be suffering in countless panels and reviews and training sessions for decades to come. But I honestly don't think there was anything you could have done in that moment to stop Poppy from doing what she did —not without putting yourself in danger. At the end of the day, the suspect reaped what he sowed. The official report will call it an accident, I call it a toss-up, but I guess most people will be happy enough to call it justice."

"Thank you, sir," Savage said quietly. Clare nodded.

"Just don't let it happen again. And as for you."

He glared at Kett, his teeth grinding so hard that Kett could actually hear it.

"Never," he said. "You understand me? You just can't go there."

Kett nodded, hearing Bert's scream try to shatter its way through the barn roof, feeling the heat of his wound through the sole of his boot.

"Never," he said, nodding.

"Good," said Clare. "We're almost certain that, other than Fran, none of the women knew about Jenny's plan to blackmail Bert. And Fortune, Poppy and Beatrice weren't involved in what happened to Martha Hansen-Andrews back in September. It was Jenny and Fran who arranged for her to be attacked by the Beggar Boys. The others are good to go as soon as they're better. Fran, on the other hand, will have to face up to what she's done."

"So Sue Hansen will get her shot at justice," said Kett. Clare nodded.

"In time. Now, since you're here, our number one priority today is finding out who Bert actually was. Hang on, where's my pencil?"

"Oh, this pencil?" Porter said, holding out the one he'd been chewing. "Sorry, sir."

"I don't want it now it's been in your mouth, Pete," Clare said, disgusted. "I need it to scratch my nose, it's full of scabs and they itch like a bastard."

Porter's face fell and he dropped the pencil like it had tried to bite him, scrubbing his hand over his mouth.

"We know he wasn't Coffee Shop Bert," Clare went on, using a finger instead. "And we know he wasn't the owner of the house, Stanley Frost, because we found what was left of him in a shed. Emily thinks he died two months ago, but nobody reported it because apparently he was an arsehole with no family and no friends. So far, we've got nothing on this killer. His photo hasn't pinged any of our databases and there was no ID to be found anywhere in the house. More worryingly than that, he doesn't have any fingerprints."

"What?" said Kett. "None?"

Something was creeping up Kett's spine, a cold finger of fear.

"Burned off," Clare said. "The ones we found in Fisher's house and in the farmhouse don't belong to him. Does that remind you of anyone?"

"The ghosts," Kett said. "The ones who came after me, the ones sent by…"

He stopped, because he couldn't bear to say the name.

"By Hollenbeck, yes," Clare said.

And Kett was right back there in the dark, Keefe's rifle aimed at his heart.

They won't stop coming.

They'll never let you go.

"No," Kett said. "That doesn't make any sense. This guy did what he did because Martha saw him murdering somebody, and because Jenny tried to blackmail him. This doesn't have anything to do with *them*."

"But why was he here in the first place?" Clare said. "Ask yourself that, Kett. Why would a killer like him be lurking in this city? He told you, didn't he?"

You'll find out, soon enough. Soon enough you'll learn why I'm here in this shitty little city.

Kett couldn't answer, he didn't have the words. Clare sighed, staring at the floor.

"Show him, Pete."

"Show me what?"

Porter slid a sheet of paper over the desk. On it was a printout, a list of phone numbers and text messages. There weren't many, and two had been highlighted in yellow. Porter tapped them with his finger.

"We found Bert's phone. This is a readout of everything on it."

Kett had to bend down to see the text, and even then he struggled.

"Need to borrow some glasses, sir?" Porter asked.

Kett ignored him, squinting until it came into focus.

The Kite is on the case. Springtime or winter?

"Fuck," he said.

"Kite, Kett," said Clare. "That bit doesn't take a genius to figure out. But what about the rest?"

"Springtime or winter," Kett said. "I don't know."

Until he read the next text, a reply, and it all became clear.

Spring, for now. But the Kite needs to cool down very soon. Prepare for your test. Be ready.

"It's a hit," he said. "He was here to take me out."

"That's what we think," said Porter. "Assassinating you was his, I don't know, his way of getting in. What else would he be testing for?"

"No," Kett said. He wouldn't believe it, *couldn't* believe it. Because if it was true, if the killer had been sent here by Hollenbeck, then all of this violence—Martha, Jenny and the other women—it had all happened because of him.

It was *all his fault.*

"It's a possibility," Clare added, seeing his distress. "But admittedly a slim one. We may be reading into it too much. The other number is a dead end. We're still sifting through the material we found at Bert's house, but this guy was a monster, no doubt about it. If he was here because of Hollenbeck then it's fair to assume he was planning to do to you the same things he did to those women. We all said it, that he'd been working on those devices for too long for it to be purely related to Jenny Eyler's blackmail attempt. The coffin we found Fran in was designed for somebody with a broader chest. It was designed for a man. It's the only reason she survived it. If..."

The Super couldn't bring himself to finish. He looked at Kett. They *all* looked at him, Porter rocking back in his chair, the pencil back between his teeth, Savage standing across from him, her arms wrapped around her chest.

"If this is Hollenbeck, we have to be very, very careful," Clare said. "If this really is them, then we have to consider shutting down the unit to keep you safe."

"No," said Kett. "No, we don't."

He balled his hands into fists and planted them on the desk.

"If Bert was one of theirs, we took him out. That's three of their ghosts out of the picture. One dead, two in prison. We're winning."

They won't stop coming.

"Don't forget who these people are, sir, and what they've done. The lives they've ruined, the crimes they've committed. They're counting on us being afraid, they want us to give up."

They'll never let you go.

"But we're police. We're not going anywhere."

Kett looked at them all in turn, thinking of his wife and the pig-headed man who'd taken her, thinking of his daughters inside the fire of Bingo's apartment.

Thinking of the world he would be leaving his girls if he didn't do what was right.

"If this is Hollenbeck, let them come," he said, managing a grim smile. "I'm ready."

Visit
alexsmithbooks.com
for previews, exclusives, giveaways
and much more!

THE GOOD TIMES NEVER LAST
JAW
BREAKER
A DCI ROBERT KETT NOVEL
ALEX SMITH
THE INTERNATIONALLY BESTSELLING SERIES

JAW BREAKER

THE NINTH DCI ROBERT KETT NOVEL

After the horrors of their last case, DCI Kett and the rest of Norfolk Constabulary's Extreme Crime Task Force are in need of a break.

And that's just what they think they're getting when Superintendent Clare takes them on a team building exercise in the middle of a quiet Norfolk town.

But what was supposed to be a week of recovery and fun soon becomes something much more sinister, when two local men turn up dead—poisoned by a horrific new designer drug nicknamed Jaw Breaker.

As more people fall victim to this invisible killer, Kett and the team find themselves dragged into the middle of a bloody civil war between gangs, cultists, coppers and some very angry locals.

And they learn that R&R doesn't always stand for Rest and

Relaxation—sometimes it's all about Revenge and Retribution.

Relentless action, compulsive mystery and dark humour abound in the internationally bestselling series that Thrilling Fiction calls "Heart-stoppingly gripping!" from the million-selling author that James Patterson describes as "fresh and ferocious!"

ABOUT THE AUTHOR

Alex Smith wrote his first book when he was six. It wasn't particularly good, but it did have some supernatural monsters in it. His latest books, the DCI Robert Kett thrillers, have monsters in them too, although these monsters are very human, and all the more terrifying for it. In between, he has published thirteen novels for children and teenagers under his full name, Alexander Gordon Smith—including the number one bestselling series Escape From Furnace, which is loved by millions of readers worldwide and which is soon to become a motion picture. He lives in Norwich with his wife and three young daughters.

Find out more at alexsmithbooks.com